Jersey turned the key in the ignition. And then, he heard the *click*.

One frozen instant in time. His eyes widening, his bewilderment honest. But, but, the double-blind policy. Nobody knew his name. He never knew theirs. How could, how could . . .

And then his eyes went to the red visitor's parking pass hanging from his rental-car mirror, the lone visitor's pass in a minuscule city parking lot of only twenty vehicles.

His client's thoughtfulness . . .

Calm and controlled, Jersey thought helplessly. Easy does it. Nothing here he hadn't done before. Nothing here he couldn't handle . . .

The current from the car's starter box hit the electrical ignition switch of the custom-made bomb, and Jersey's rental car exploded into the bright morning sky.

Lisa Gardner sold her first novel when she was twenty years old and has since been published in over a dozen countries. In 1993 she graduated *magna cum laude* from the University of Pennsylvania with a degree in international relations. Now living in the New England area with her husband, she spends her time writing, travelling and hiking. Visit her website at www.LisaGardner.com.

By Lisa Gardner

The Perfect Husband
The Other Daughter
The Third Victim
The Next Accident
The Survivors Club

THE SURVIVORS CLUB

Lisa Gardner

ORION

An Orion paperback

First published in Great Britain in 2002
by Orion
This paperback edition published in 2003
by Orion Books Ltd,
Orion House, 5 Upper St Martin's Lane,
London WC2H 9EA

A CIP catalogue record for this book is
available from the British Library.

ISBN 0 75284 963 8

Printed and bound in Great Britain by
Clays Ltd St Ives plc

ACKNOWLEDGMENTS

As a general rule, I enjoy researching all of my novels. Murder, mayhem, investigative procedures, it's all good stuff. This time around, however, I had a particularly wonderful experience, and for that I'm deeply indebted to the Rhode Island State Police. Not only are they one of the best law enforcement agencies in the country, but they are also helpful, generous and patient people. From explaining the proper protocol for rendering a salute to demonstrating the new AFIS technology, the officers went out of their way to answer my questions and impress upon me the pride they have in their organization. It worked. I'm very impressed by the RI State Police, and I have even started following the speed limit. Well, okay, so the latter half only lasted for a bit. I tried and that says something about their powers of persuasion right there.

Of course, as with all novels, I promptly warped most of the information they graciously provided. In this novel you'll find police procedure and forensics testing happening at approximately the speed of light. Also, my police detectives are perhaps a tad rougher around the edges and a bit more familiar with murder suspects than their real-life counterparts. Remember, the RI State Police detectives have real jobs. I, on the other hand, am a fiction writer who makes things up.

I would like to thank the following members of the RI State Police for their assistance: former Superintendent Colonel Edmond S. Culhane, Jr. (ret.); Superintendent Colonel Steven M. Pare; Major Michael Quinn; Inspector John J. Leyden, Jr.; Lieutenant John Virgilio; Lieutenant Mark Bilodeau; Corporal Eric L. Croce; and Detective James Dougherty.

From the Providence Police Department I would like to thank Lieutenant Paul Kennedy and Sergeant Napoleon Brito. They also gave me the warmest reception, as well as a wonderful collection of gory anecdotes. Let's just say I never fully appreciated the history of dismemberment in the Ocean State before visiting the PPD.

Finally, I owe the following people my deepest gratitude for assisting me in the development of this novel:

Dr. Gregory K. Moffatt, Ph.D., Professor of Psychology, Atlanta Christian College, a wonderful friend and a very wise man.

Albert A. Bucci, Assistant to the Director, State of Rhode Island Department of Corrections, who provided a highly enthusiastic overview of prison life.

Margaret Charpentier, pharmacist and general shoulder to cry on, as well as her fellow pharmacist/partner in crime, Kate Strong.

Monique Lemoine, speech language pathologist and very kind soul.

Kathy Hammond, phlebotomist, Rhode Island Blood Center, and my bloodsucker of choice.

Jim Martin, Public Information Officer, Department of the Attorney General, Rhode Island.

The Providence Preservation Society.

Kathleen Walsh, executive assistant and overall savior of my sanity.

And finally, my very tolerant husband, Anthony. This time around, it was his Ghirardelli double-chocolate brownies that saved the day.

Once again, all mistakes in the novel are mine. Anything you think is particularly brilliant I'll take responsibility for as well.

Happy reading!
Lisa Gardner

THE SURVIVORS CLUB

Eddie

It started as a conversation:

"The scientists are the problem – not the cops. Cops are just cops. Some got a nose for jelly doughnuts; others got a nose for pensions. The scientists, though . . . I read about this case where they nailed a guy by matching the inside seam of his blue jeans with a bloody print left at the murder scene. I'm not kidding. Some expert testified that the wear pattern of denim is so individual there's something like a one-in-a-billion chance that another pair of jeans would leave the same print, yada, yada, yada. Fuckin' unreal."

"Don't wear blue jeans," the second man said.

The first man, a kid really, rolled his eyes. "That's fuckin' brilliant."

The second man shrugged. "Before you lecture me about Calvin's sending someone to the big house, perhaps we should start with the basics. Fingerprints."

"Gloves," the kid said immediately.

"Gloves?" The man frowned. "And here I expected something much more innovative coming from you."

"Hey, gloves are a pain in the ass, but then again, so is serving time. What else are you gonna do?"

"I don't know. But I don't want to wear gloves if I don't have to. Let's think about it."

"You could wipe down everything," the kid said shortly. "Ammonia dissolves fingerprint oil, you know. You could prepare a solution, ammonia and water. Afterwards, you could spray it on, wipe stuff down. You know, includ- ing . . ." The kid's voice trailed off. He didn't seem quite able to say the word, which the man thought was pretty funny, given everything this "kid" had done.

The man nodded. "Yes. Including. With ammonia, of course. Otherwise they might be able to print the woman's skin using Alternate Light Source or fumigation. Instead of spritzing, the other option is to put the woman in a tub. To ensure that you're being thorough."

"Yeah." The kid nodded his head, contemplating. "Still might miss a spot. And it involves a lot of maneuvering. Remember what the textbook said: 'The more contact with the victim, the more evidence left behind.' "

"True. Other ideas?"

"You could leave fake prints. I once met this guy from New York. His gang liked to cut off the hands of their rivals, and use them to leave false prints at their own crime scenes."

"Did it work?"

"Well, half the gang was in Rikers at the time . . ."

"So it didn't work."

"Probably not."

The man pursed his lips. "It's an interesting thought, though. Creative. The police hate creativity. We should find out where those people went wrong."

"I'll ask around."

"A fingerprint is nothing but a ridge pattern," the man thought out loud. "Fill in the valleys between the ridges and there's no more print. Seems like there's gotta be a way of doing that. Maybe smearing the fingertips with superglue? I've heard of it, but I don't know if it works."

"Wouldn't that interfere with feel, though? I mean, if you're going to lose sensation, you might as well return to gloves which you know will do the trick."

"There's scarring. Repeated cutting of the fingertips with a razor to obscure the print."

"No thank you!"

"No pain, no gain," the man said mildly.

"Yeah, and no pleasure, no point. What do you think scar tissue is gonna do to the nerve endings of your finger-tips? Might as well hack 'em off and be done with it. Keep it simple, remember? Another thing the textbook pointed out – simple is good."

The man shrugged. "Fine, then it's gloves. Thinnest latex possible. That resolves the matter of fingerprints. Next issue: DNA."

"Shit," the kid said.

"DNA is the kicker," the man agreed. "With fingerprints you can watch what you touch. But with DNA . . . Now you have to consider your hair, your blood, your semen, your spit. Oh, and bite marks. Let's not forget about the power of dental matches."

"Jesus, you are a sick son of a bitch." The kid rolled his eyes again. "Look, don't bite anything or anyone. It's too risky. They've nailed thieves by matching their teeth to indentations left in a hunk of cheddar in the fridge. After that, God knows what they can do with a human breast."

"Fair enough. Now back to DNA."

"Pull an O.J.," the kid said grumpily. "Let the lawyers deal with it."

"You really think lawyers are that good, all things considered . . ." The man's tone was droll.

The kid got hostile. "Hey, what the fuck is a guy supposed to do? Wear a goddamn condom? Hell, man, might as well fuck a garden hose."

"Then we need a better idea. Blaming the cops is no kind of defense. They don't handle the DNA anyway. The hospital sends it straight to the Department of Health via a courier. Or don't you read the paper?"

"I read – "

"And a bath won't help there either," the man continued relentlessly. "Just look at Motyka. He stuck the woman in a tub and that worked so well he's now facing life in prison. The semen goes up into the body. You need something more, some kind of flush action, I don't know. Plus there's the hair. Hair can also yield DNA, if they get a root, or they can simply match hair at the scene to hair on your head. Bathtub won't help with hair, either. Some anal-retentive crime tech will retrieve your hair from the drainpipes – they can retrieve blood samples from there too, you know. You can't approach this half-assed."

"Shave."

"Everywhere?"

"Yes." The kid's tone was grudging. "Yeah, shit. Everywhere. Tell people you're into swimming. What the fuck."

"Shaving is good," the man conceded. "That resolves the hair. What else? They'll swab the woman's mouth. Remember that."

"Yeah, yeah, yeah, I read the same book you did."

"No touching anything with your bare hands – not even an eyeball."

"I read about that case, too."

"No blue jeans, I guess."

"Wear dust covers over your shoes to limit soil and fiber," the kid added. "And, whenever possible, resort to social engineering. Breaking and entering leaves behind tool marks, and tool marks can also be matched."

The man nodded: "That covers most of the trace evidence except for DNA then. We still need to figure out DNA. They get one little sample of semen, send it to the DNA database . . ."

"I know, I know." The kid closed his eyes. He appeared to be thinking. Hard. He finally opened them again. "You could try confusing the issue. There was that guy who was arrested as a serial rapist based on DNA, then while he was in prison, another rape was reported with the same kind of DNA found on the girl's panties."

"What happened?"

The kid sighed. "They busted the guy in prison for that, too. Perpetrating fraud, something like that."

"He raped the other girl while he was behind bars?"

"No, man, he jacked off into a ketchup packet while he was behind bars, then mailed it to a friend who paid a girl fifty bucks to smear the stuff on her underwear and cry rape. You know, so it would appear like there was another guy running around with the same DNA, who was actually the rapist."

4

"There is no such thing as two guys with the same DNA. Not even identical twins have the same DNA."

"Yeah, and that would be the problem with the plan. The scientists knew that and the prosecution knew that, so they pressured the girl until she confessed what really happened."

"Is there a moral to this story?"

"Pay the girl more than fifty bucks!"

The man sighed. "That is not a good plan."

"Hey, you wanted an idea, I gave you an idea."

"I wanted a good idea."

"Ah, fuck you, too."

The second man didn't say anything. The kid lapsed into silence as well.

"Gotta beat the DNA," the kid muttered after a bit.

"Gotta beat the DNA," the man agreed.

"The Raincoat on your John Thomas," the kid mocked from Monty Python. "Ah, who needs it?"

"Wouldn't necessarily help anyway. Condoms leak, condoms break. Police are also getting better at tracing the lubricants and spermicide. That gives them a brand, then they start checking stores and next thing you know some pharmacy worker just happened to notice some guy buying some box . . ."

"You're screwed."

"Yeah. Those scientists. Any little thing you introduce into the scene . . ."

The kid suddenly perked up. "Hey," he said. "I have an idea."

I
Jersey

The blonde caught in the sights of the Leupold Vari-X III
1.5–5 x 20mm Matte Duplex Illuminated Reticle scope
didn't seem to fear for her life. At the moment, in fact, she
was doing her hair. Now she had out a black compact and
was checking her lipstick, a light, pearly pink. Jersey
adjusted the Leupold scope as the reporter pursed her lips
for her own reflection and practiced an alluring pout. Next
to her, her cameraman let his heavy video equipment fall
from his shoulder to the ground and rolled his eyes. Apparently, he recognized this drill and knew it would be a while.

Ten feet away from the blonde, another reporter, this one
male – WNAC-TV, home of the Fox *Futurecast*, because
heaven forbid anyone call it a *forecast* anymore – was
meticulously picking pieces of lint off of his mud-brown
suit. His cameraman sat in the grass, sipping Dunkin'
Donuts coffee and blinking sleepily. On the other side of the
stone pillar that dominated the sprawling World War
Memorial Park, a dozen other reporters were scattered
about, double-checking their copy, double-checking their
appearance, yawning tiredly, then double-checking the
street.

Eight-oh-one A.M., Monday morning. At least twenty-
nine minutes until the blue van from Adult Correctional
Institutions (ACI) was due to arrive at the Licht Judicial
Complex in downtown Providence and everyone was
bored. Hell, Jersey was bored. He'd been camped out on the
roof of the sprawling brick courthouse since midnight last
night. And damn, it got *cold* at night this early in May.

Three Army blankets, a black coverall, and black leather Bob Allen shooting gloves and he still shivered until the sun came up. That was a little before six, meaning he'd had two and a half more hours to kill and not even the chance to stand up and stretch without giving his position away.

Jersey had spent the night – and now the morning – hunkered behind a two-foot-high decorative-brick trim piece that lined this section of the courthouse's roof. The faux railing afforded him just enough cover to remain invisible to people in the courtyard below, and more importantly, to the reporters camped in the grassy memorial park across the street. The railing also offered the perfect rifle stand, for when the moment came.

Sometime between 8:30 and 9:00 A.M., the blue ACI van would pull up. The eight-foot-high wrought-iron gate that surrounded the inner courtyard of the judicial complex would open up. The van would pull in. The gate would swing shut. The van doors would open. And then . . .

Jersey's finger twitched on the trigger of the heavy barrel AR15. He caught himself, then eased his grip on the assault rifle, slightly surprised by his antsiness. It wasn't like him to rush. Calm and controlled, he told himself. Easy does it. Nothing here he hadn't done before. Nothing here he couldn't handle.

Jersey had been hunting since the time he could walk, the scent of gunpowder as reassuring to him as talcum. Following in his father's footsteps, he'd joined the Army at the age of eighteen, then spent eight years honing his abilities with an M16. Not to brag, but Jersey could take out targets at five hundred yards most guys couldn't hit at one hundred. He was also a member of the Quarter Inch Club – at two hundred yards, he could cluster three shots within a quarter-inch triangulation of one another. His father had been an American sniper in 'Nam, so Jersey figured that shooting was in his genes.

Five years ago, seeking a better lifestyle than the Army could afford him, he'd opened shop. He used a double-blind policy. The clients never knew his name, he never knew theirs. A first middleman contacted a second middleman who contacted Jersey. Money was wired to appropriate accounts. Dossiers bearing pertinent information were sent to temporary P.O. boxes opened at various MAIL BOXES ETC. stores under various aliases. Jersey had a rule about not hitting women or children. Some days he thought that made him a good person. Other days he thought that made him worse, because he used that policy to try to prove to himself that he did have a conscience when the bottom line was, well, you know – he killed people for money.

If his father knew, he definitely wouldn't approve.

This gig had come along five months ago. Jersey had been instantly intrigued. For one thing, the target was a genuine, bona fide rapist, so Jersey didn't have to worry about his conscience. For another thing, the job was in Providence, and Jersey had always wanted to visit the Ocean State. He'd made four separate trips to the city to scope out the job, and thus far, he liked what he saw.

Providence was a small city, bisected by the Providence River, where, no kidding, they ran gondola rides on select Friday and Saturday nights. The slick black boats looked straight out of Venice, and the mayor even had a bunch of good ol' Italian boys manning the vessels in black-striped shirts and red-banded strawhats. Then there was this thing called WaterFire, where they lit bonfires in the middle of the river. You could sit out at your favorite restaurant and watch the river burn while tourists bounced around the flames in gondolas. Jersey had been secretly hoping someone would catch on fire, but hey, that was just him.

The city was pretty. This courthouse, on the east side of the river, was an impressive red-brick structure with a soaring white clock tower that dominated an entire city block. Old world colonial meets new world grandeur. The front of the courthouse sat on Benefit Street, which seemed to be a mile-long advertisement for old money – huge historical homes featuring everything from Victorian turrets to Gothic stone, interspersed with green lawns and neatly constructed brick walls. The back of the courthouse, where Jersey was, overlooked the sprawling memorial park, the grassy expanse littered with dignified bronze sculptures of soldiers and significantly less dignified pieces of modern art. The modern art carried over to the Rhode Island School of Design (RISD), with its urban campus stretching alongside the courthouse.

Rhode Island didn't have much in the way of violent crime. Thirty homicides a year, something like that. Of course, that would change today. The state was better known for its long history of financial crimes, Mafia connections and political corruption. As the locals liked to say, in Rhode Island it isn't what you know, but who you know. And in all honesty, everyone did seem to know one another in this state. Frankly, it freaked Jersey out.

Jersey started to yawn again, caught it this time and forced himself to snap to attention. Eight twenty-one A.M. now. Not much longer. On the grass across the street, the various news teams were beginning to stir.

Last night, before coming to the courthouse, Jersey had sat in his hotel room and flipped back and forth between all the local news shows, trying to learn the various media personalities. He didn't recognize the pretty blonde down below, though her cameraman's shirt indicated that they were with WJAR, News Team 10, the local NBC affiliate. Network news. That was respectable. Jersey was happy for her.

Then he wondered if the woman had any idea just how big her morning was about to become. His target, Eddie Como, aka the College Hill Rapist, was major news in the Ocean State. Everyone was here to cover the start of the trial. Everyone was here to capture shots of slightly built, hunch-shouldered Eddie, or maybe get a glimpse of one of his three beautiful victims.

These reporters didn't know anything yet. About Jersey. About his client. About what was really going to happen this sunny Monday morning in May. It made Jersey feel benevolent toward all the bored, overhyped, overgroomed individuals gathered on the grass below. He had a treat for them. He was about to make one of them, some of them, very special.

Take this pretty little blonde with the pearly pink lips. She was up first thing this morning, armed with canned copy and thinking that at best, she'd get a shot of the blue ACI van for the morning news at her station. Of course, the other twenty reporters would shoot the same visual with pretty much same copy, nobody being any better than anyone else, and nobody being any worse. Just another day on the job, covering what needed to be covered for all the enquiring minds that wanted to know.

Except that someone down in that park, sitting on the grass, surrounded by war memorials and freakish exhibits of modern art, was going to get a scoop this morning. Someone, maybe that pretty little blonde, was going to show up to get a routine clip of a blue ACI van, and come away with a picture of a hired gun instead.

There was no way around it. The only time Jersey would have access to Eddie Como was when the alleged rapist was moved from the ACI to the Licht Judicial Complex on the opening day of his trial. And the only time Jersey would have access at the Licht Judicial Complex was when Eddie was unloaded from the ACI van within a fenced-off drop-off roughly the size of a two-car garage. And the only way Jersey could shoot into a drop-off zone enclosed by an eight-foot-high fence was to shoot down at the target.

The massive red-brick courthouse took up an entire city block. Soaring up to sixteen stories high with swooping red-brick wings, it towered above its fellow buildings and zealously protected its back courtyard and the all-important drop-off zone. So Jersey's options had been clear from the beginning. He would have to access the courthouse itself, easily done in the cover of night once he learned the routine of the Capital Security guards.

He would have to take up position on the sixth-story roofline immediately overlooking the drop-off point to have a clean shot down into the fenced-off area. He would have to line up the shot in the cover of darkness. And then, when the van finally arrived sometime between 8:30 and 9:00 A.M., he would have five seconds to stand, blow off the top of Eddie Como's head and start running.

Because while the state marshals who escorted the inmates probably wouldn't be able to see him – the angle would be too steep – and while the prisoners themselves wouldn't be able to see him – they would probably be too busy screaming at all the brains now sprayed in their hair – the reporters, every single greedy, desperate-for-a-scoop reporter camped across the street – they would have a clear view of Jersey standing six stories up. Jersey firing a rifle six stories up. Jersey running across the vast roofline six stories up.

The shot itself was going to be easy. A mere seventy feet. Straight down. Hell, Jersey should forget the assault rifle and drop an anvil on the guy's head. Yeah, the shot itself was downright boring. But the moments afterward . . . The moments afterward were going to be really entertaining.

A disturbance down the street. Jersey flicked back to the pretty blonde in time to see her drop her lipstick and scramble forward. Show time.

He glanced at his watch. Eight thirty-five A.M. Apparently, the state marshals didn't want to keep the reporters waiting.

Jersey brought his rifle back down against him. He adjusted the scope to 1.5, all he would need for a seventy-foot head shot. He checked the twenty-cartridge magazine, then chambered the first round. He was using Winchester's .223 Remington, a 55-grain soft-point bullet, which according to the box was best for shooting prairie dogs, coyotes and woodchucks.

And now, the College Hill Rapist.

Jersey got on his knees. He positioned the rifle along the top of the rail, then placed his eye against the scope. He could just make out the street through the stone archways lining the outer courtyard. He heard, more than saw, the black wrought-iron fence of the inner courtyard swing open. Calm and controlled. Easy does it. Nothing here he hadn't done before. Nothing here he couldn't handle.

He flexed his fingers. He listened to the reassuring crinkle of his black leather shooting gloves . . .

The prisoners would be shackled together like a chain gang. Most would be in khaki or blue prison overalls. But Eddie Como would be different. Facing the first day of trial, Eddie Como would arrive in a suit.

Jersey waited for the barking sound of a state marshal ordering the unloading of the van. He felt the first prick of sweat. But he didn't pop up. He still didn't squeeze the trigger.

Twenty reporters and cameramen across the street. Twenty journalists just waiting for their big break . . .

"Courtyard secure! Door open!"

Jersey heard the rasp of metal as the van door slid back. He heard the slap of the first rubber-soled shoe hitting the flagstone patio . . .

One, two, three, four, five . . .

Jersey rocketed up from his knees and angled the AR15 twenty-two degrees from vertical. Searching, searching . . .

The dark head of Eddie Como emerged from the van. He was gazing forward, looking at the door of the courthouse. His shoulders were down. He took three shuffling steps forward –

And Jersey blew off the top of his head. One moment Eddie Como was standing shackled between two guys. The next he was folding up silently and plummeting to the hard, slate-covered ground.

Jersey let the black-market rifle fall to the roof. Then he began to run.

He was aware of so many things at once. The feel of the sun on his face. The smell of cordite in the air. The noise of a city about to start a busy workweek, cars roaring, cars screeching. And then, almost as an afterthought, people beginning to scream.

"Gun, gun, gun!"

"Get down, get down!"

"Look! Up there. On the roof!"

Jersey was smiling. Jersey was feeling good. He clambered across the courthouse roof, the gummy soles of his rock-climbing shoes finding perfect traction. He turned the corner and rounded the center clock tower, which rose another several stories. *Now you see me. Now you don't.*

Shots fired. Some overpumped state marshals shooting their wad at an enemy they couldn't see.

Jersey's smile grew. He hummed now as he stripped off his gloves and cast them behind him. Almost at the rooftop door. He grabbed the front of his black coveralls with his left hand and popped open the snaps. Three seconds later, the black coveralls joined his discarded rifle and gloves on the rooftop. Five seconds after that, Jersey had replaced his rock climber's shoes with highly polished Italian loafers. Then it was a simple matter of reclaiming the black leather briefcase he'd left by the rooftop door. Last night, the briefcase had contained the dismantled parts of an AR15. This morning, it held only business papers.

From world-class sniper to just one more guy in a suit in five minutes or less.

Jersey pulled open the rooftop door. He'd jammed the lock with wire last night so it would be ready for him. Moments later, he was down the stairs and joining the main traffic flow, just another harried lawyer too busy to look anyone in the eye.

Capital Security guards and state marshals rushed by. People inside the courthouse were looking around, becoming increasingly aware that something had happened but not sure what. Jersey, following their example, pasted a slightly puzzled expression on his face as he journeyed forth.

Another gray-clad marshal sprinted by him, voices screaming from the radio at the man's waist. He hit Jersey's shoulder, knocking him back. Jersey spluttered, "Excuse me!" The state marshal kept running for the stairs leading to the roof.

"What happened?" a lady walking next to Jersey asked.

"I'm not sure," he said. "Must be something bad."

They exchanged vigorous nods. And thirty-two seconds later, Jersey was out the front door, taking a left and heading back down steeply pitched College Street toward the memorial park. He resumed humming now, in the homestretch. Even if some police officer stopped him, what would the officer find? Jersey had no weapons, no trace of gunpowder on his hands or clothes. He was just a businessman, and he always carried valid ID.

The screech of sirens abruptly split the air. The city wasn't big and the Providence Police had their headquarters downtown. Cops would be streaming in from all over, roadblocks just a matter of time. Jersey picked up his step but remained calm. His thoughtful client, no doubt familiar with the parking crunch in downtown Providence, had sent Jersey a RISD visitor's pass for the parking lot just across the street. The cops would be here in two minutes. Jersey would be gone in one.

The sirens roared closer. Jersey arrived at the tiny college parking lot at the base of College Street and South Main. Found his key for the blue rental car. Unlocked the doors, threw in his briefcase, slid into the seat.

Calm and controlled. Easy does it. Nothing here he hadn't done before. Nothing here he couldn't handle.

Jersey turned the key in the ignition. And then, he heard the *click*.

One frozen instant in time. His eyes widening, his bewilderment honest. But, but, the double-blind policy. Nobody knew his name. He never knew theirs. How could, how could . . .

And then his eyes went to the red visitor's parking pass hanging from his rental-car mirror, the lone visitor's pass in a minuscule city parking lot of only twenty vehicles.

His client's thoughtfulness . . .

Calm and controlled, Jersey thought helplessly. Easy does it. Nothing here he hadn't done before. Nothing here he couldn't handle . . .

The current from the car's starter box hit the electrical ignition switch of the custom-made bomb, and Jersey's rental car exploded into the bright morning sky.

A dozen city blocks away, on Hope Street, the well-groomed patrons of the trendy restaurant rue de l'espoir — made even trendier by its all-lowercase name — looked up from their decadent business breakfasts of eggs Benedict and inch-thick slices of French toast. Sitting in comfy booths, they now gazed around the rich, earthy interior where the walls were the same color as aged copper pots and the booths were decorated in hues of red, green, brown and eggplant. The tremor, though slight, had been unmistakable. Even the waitresses had stopped in their tracks.

"Did you feel that?" one of the servers asked.

The people in the chic little restaurant looked at each other. They had just started to shrug away the minor disturbance when the harsh sound of screaming sirens cut the air. Two cop cars went flying down the street. An ambulance roared by in their wake.

"Something must have happened," someone said.

"Something big," another patron echoed.

Sitting at a small table tucked alone in the far corner, three women finally looked up from their oversized mugs of spiced chai. Two were older, one was younger. All three had caused a minor stir when they had walked through the door. Now the women looked at one another. Then, simultaneously, they looked away.

"I wonder," said one.

"Don't," said another.

And that was all they said.

Until the cops came.

2
Griffin

At 8:31 A.M. Monday morning, Rhode Island State Police Detective Sergeant Roan Griffin was already late for his 8:30 briefing. This was not a good thing. It was his first day back on the job in eighteen months. He should probably be on time. Hell, he should probably be early. Show up at headquarters at 8:15 A.M., pumped up, sharply pressed, crisply saluting. Here I am, I am ready.

And then . . . ?

"Welcome back," they would greet him. (Hopefully.)

"Thanks," he would say. (Probably.)

"How are you feeling?" they'd ask. (Suspiciously.)

"Good," he'd reply. (Too easily.)

Ah, shit. Good *was* a stupid answer. Too often said to be often believed. He'd say good, and they'd stare at him harder, trying to read between the lines. Good like you're ready to crack open a case file, or good like we can trust you with a loaded firearm? It was an interesting question.

He drummed his fingers on the steering wheel and tried again.

"Welcome back," they'd say.

"It's good to be back," he'd say.

"How are you doing?" they'd ask.

"My anxiety is operating within normal parameters," he'd reply.

No. Absolutely not. That kind of psychobabble made even him want to whoop his ass. Forget it. He should've gone with his father's recommendation and walked in wearing a T-shirt that read "You're only Jealous Because the Voices are Talking to *Me*."

At least they all could've had a good laugh.

Griffin had joined the Rhode Island State Police force sixteen years ago. He'd started with four months in a rigorous boot camp, learning everything from evasive driving maneuvers to engaging in hand-to-hand combat after being stung with pepper spray. (You want to know pain? Having pepper spray in your eyes is pain. You want to know self-control? Standing there willingly to be sprayed for the *second* time, that is self-control.) Following boot camp, Griffin had spent eight years in uniform. He'd boosted the state coffers writing his share of speeding tickets. He'd helped motorists change tires. He'd attended dozens of motor vehicle accidents, including way too many involving children. Then he'd joined the Detective Bureau, starting in Intelligence, where he'd earned a stellar reputation for his efforts on a major FBI case. Following that, he worked some money laundering, gunrunning, art forgery, homicide. Rhode Island may not have a large quantity of crime, but as the detectives liked to say, they got quality crime.

Griffin had been a good detective. Bright. Hardheaded. Stubborn. Ferocious at times. Funny at others. This stuff was in his blood. His grandfather had been a beat cop in New York. His father had served as sheriff in North Kingstown. Two of his brothers were now state marshals. Years ago, when Griffin had first met Cindy on a hiking trip in New Hampshire, first looked into her eyes and felt her smile like a thunderbolt in his chest, he'd blurted out, before his name, before even hello, "I'm a cop." Fortunately for him, Cindy had understood.

Griffin had been a good detective. Guys liked working with him. The brass liked giving him cases. The media liked following his career. He went on the Dave Letterman show when the Rhode Island State Police won a nationwide award for best uniform. He led Operation Pinto, which shut down a major auto-theft ring in a blaze of front-page *Providence Journal* headlines. He even got appointed to the governor's task force on community policing, probably because the little old ladies had been asking for him since he'd strutted across Letterman's sound stage. (Officer Blue Eyes, the *ProJo* had dubbed him. Oh yeah, his fellow detectives had definitely had that made into a T-shirt.)

Two and a half years ago, when the third kid vanished from Wakefield and the pattern of a locally operating child predator became clear, there had never been any doubt that Griffin would head the investigation. He remembered being excited when he'd walked out of that briefing. He remembered the thrum of adrenaline in his veins, the flex of his muscles, the heady sense that he had once again begun a chase.

Two days before Cindy went for a routine checkup. Six months before everything went from bad to worse. Eleven months before he learned the true nature of the black abyss.

For the record, he'd nailed that son of a bitch. For the record.

Griffin made the left-hand fork on Route 6, headed into North Scituate. Five minutes from headquarters now. He drove by the giant reservoir as the landscape opened up to reveal a vast expanse of water on his right and rolling green hills on his left. Soon he'd see joggers, guys grabbing a morning run. Then would come the state police compound. First, the flat, ugly 1960s brown building that housed Investigative Support Services. Then, the huge old gray barn in the back, a remnant of what the property used to be. Finally, the beautiful old white semimansion that now served as state police headquarters, complete with a gracefully curving staircase and bay windows overlooking more rolling green hills. The White House, the rookies called it. Where the big boys lived.

Damn, he'd missed this place. Damn.

"Welcome back, Griffin," they'd say.

"Thanks," he'd say.

"How are you feeling?" they'd ask.

And he'd answer –

In the left-hand lane, a blue Ford Taurus roared past, red lights flashing behind the grille. Then came two more unmarked police cars, sirens also screaming. What the hell?

Griffin turned into the parking lot of state police head-quarters just in time to see detectives pour out of ISSB and race for their state steels. He recognized two guys from the Criminal Identification Unit (CIU), Jack Cappelli and Jack Needham, aka Jack-n-Jack, climbing into the big gray crime-scene-investigation van. Then they had flipped on the lights and were peeling out of the lot.

Griffin swung in front of the ISS building. He hadn't even cut the motor before Lieutenant Marcey Morelli of Major Crimes was banging on his window.

"Lieutenant." He started to salute. Morelli cut him off.

"Providence just called in reports of rifle fire and a major explosion at the Licht Judicial Complex. ATF and the state fire marshal get the explosion. We get the shooting. All units respond."

"A shooting at the *courthouse?*" His eyebrows shot up. No friggin' way.

"You been following the Como case? Sounds like somebody got tired of waiting for the trial. Better yet, the media's already there, catching the before and the after. Can you say 'Film at eleven'?"

"Somebody up there hates you, Lieutenant."

"No kidding. Look, whatever just happened, we know it's going to be big. I've already asked the detective commander for additional resources, plus I want all of Major Crimes down there ASAP. The uniforms can handle the canvassing, but I want you guys on initial interviews. Find out when, where, why, how, radio it to every uniform in the area so they can be on the lookout for the shooter, and hey, catch this guy yesterday. You know the drill." Morelli paused long enough to take a breath, then narrowed her eyes as, for the first time, she truly saw his seated form. "Jesus Christ, Griffin, I thought you'd spent the time fishing or something like that."

"Well yeah. And some weights." He shrugged modestly.

"Uh huh."

"And some running."

"Uh huh."

"Okay, boxing, too."

The lieutenant rolled her eyes. Griffin had spent the last year of his eighteen-month medical leave mastering the art of sublimation – funneling nonproductive tension into a productive outlet. He'd gotten pretty good at it. He could sustain a five-minute mile for nearly ten miles. He could box sixteen rounds. He could bench-press a Volvo.

His body was good. His face was still a little too harsh – a man not sleeping well at night. But physically . . . Griffin was a lean, mean machine.

The lieutenant straightened. "Well," she said briskly, "The Boss is on his way. So get moving, Sergeant. And remember, there are only a hundred cameras about to document every step we take."

Lieutenant Morelli resumed running. Griffin sat there for one more moment, honestly a little dazed. *My anxiety is operating within normal parameters,* he thought stupidly. Ah fuck it. Back is back. He flipped on his lights and joined his fellow officers, roaring toward Providence.

3
Jillian

She is driving to her sister's apartment. Work has held her up, she is running an hour late. Traffic is miserable, of course. Another accident on 195, when isn't there an accident? She is thinking about all the things she still has to get done. Cash-flow analysis of the first six months. Cash-flow projection of the next six months. Storyboards for Roger. Copy proofs for Claire.

Toppi called her at work to say that Libby was having a bad day. Please don't stay out too late.

She is driving to her sister's apartment, but she is not thinking about her sister. She is not looking forward to dinner with Trish. It has become one more thing to do on a long list of things to do, and part of her suspects that this is bad. She has lost perspective. She has let her life get away from her. The rest of her is too busy to care.

She has her responsibilities. She is the responsible one.

Trisha is off to college. Trisha has her first apartment, tiny, cramped, but beautiful because it is all hers. Trisha has new friends, new life, new goals. She wants to be a playwright, she told Jillian excitedly last week. Before that she had wanted to study communications. Before that it had been English. Trish is young, beautiful, bright. The world is her oyster, and Jillian does not doubt that Trish will become exactly who she wants to become, doing exactly what she wants to do.

And this pains her in a way she doesn't understand. Lifts her up, pushes her down. She is the surrogate mother, proud of her child's accomplishments. She is the tired older sister,

21

feeling a nagging twinge of jealousy when she has nothing to be jealous of. Yes, her path was harder. No, she was never nineteen and carefree. No, she has never gotten to live on her own, not even now. But she went to college, earned a business degree. At thirty-six she runs a successful ad agency, calling all the shots. She didn't sacrifice everything for her mother and sister. She carved out her own life, too.

And yet . . .

Visiting Trish is hard for her these days. She does not do it nearly as often as she should.

Now, she drives around Thayer Street, looking for a place to park. The third week in May, the sun is just starting to set and the sidewalks are crowded with Brown University summer students, milling outside of Starbucks, the Gap store, Abercrombie & Fitch. Jillian still gets a twinge of unease over Trisha living in the city. Especially after the recent reports of two rapes, the second of which was only two weeks ago. One was over at Providence College, however, and the other was some woman in her home.

Trisha knows about the attacks. They even talked about it last week. Some of the girls have started carrying pepper spray. Trish bought a canister as well. Plus she inspected the locks on her apartment. Her apartment is really very secure. A little basement studio, with only tiny windows set high in the wall and not big enough for a grown man to crawl through. Trisha had also installed a bolt lock when she signed her lease last spring. It's a key in, key out kind of lock; supposedly one of the best money can buy.

"I'll be fine," Trish told Jillian in that exasperated way only a teenager can manage. "For heaven's sake, I've taken two courses in self-defense!"

Jillian finally finds a parking spot deep down on Angell Street. She has a bit of a hike now to Trisha's apartment, but that's not unusual given the state of Providence's parking. Plus, it's a balmy, dusky evening and she could use the exercise.

Jillian doesn't have pepper spray. She contemplates this as she locks the door of her gold Lexus. She does what she's seen on TV – she carries her car keys in her fist, with the biggest key sticking out between two fingers like a weapon. She also keeps her head up and her footsteps brisk. Of course, this comes naturally to her. She has never been the shrinking violet type. She likes to think that Trish got her independent spirit from her.

Trisha lives at the edge of the Brown campus. Generally, they meet at her apartment, then walk to Thayer Street with its host of ethnic restaurants and upscale coffee shops. Jillian could go for some Pad Thai. Or maybe grilled lamb.

For the first time, her footsteps pick up. Thayer Street has such great restaurants; it's nice to be out and about on College Hill, with its youth and vitality. And the night is lovely, not too hot, not too cold. After dinner they can go for some ice cream. Trisha can tell her all about her summer internship at Trinity Theater, whether the set guy – Joe, Josh, Jon – has asked her out yet. There would be fresh gossip on her group of friends, of course, The Girls. Tales of adventure from their recent trip to Providence Place Mall, ladies' night out in Newport, etc., etc.

Jillian could relax, sit back, and let Trisha go. Tell me about *every* hour, minute, day. Tell me *everything*.

For this is where the proud surrogate mother and tired older sister come together: they both love to listen to Trish. They love her enthusiasm. They cherish her excitement. They marvel at her wonder, a nineteen-year-old woman-girl, still learning about the world, still convinced she can make it a better place.

Jillian arrives at Trisha's apartment complex. Once, it was a grand old home. Now, the building is subdivided into eight units for the college crowd. As the basement renter, Trisha has her own entrance around back.

Jillian rounds the house as the sun sinks lower on the horizon and casts the narrow alleyway into gloom. Trisha has a powerful outdoor spotlight above the back door. Jillian is slightly surprised, given the rapidly falling night, that Trish has not turned it on. She'll mention it to her.

At the door, Jillian raises her hand, she lets her knuckles

23

fall. And then she catches her breath as the door soundlessly swings in to reveal the darkened stairs.

"Trisha? Trish?"

Jillian moves cautiously down the steps, having to use the handrail to guide her way. Had Trisha grown tired of waiting for her? Maybe she'd decided to start her laundry and had run down the street to the Laundromat. That had happened once before.

At the bottom of the stairs is another door, this one wooden, simple. An inside bedroom door. Jillian puts her hand on the shiny brass-colored knob. She turns. The door sweeps open and Jillian is face-to-face with a deep-shadowed room.

"Trisha?"

She takes three steps in. She glances at the tiny kitchenette. She turns toward the bed, and –

A force slams into her from behind. She cries out, her hands popping open, her car keys flying across the room, as she goes down hard. She catches herself with her left palm and promptly hears something crack.

"Trish?" Her voice high-pitched, reedy, not at all like herself. The bed, the bed, that poor woman on the bed.

"Goddamn bitch!"

A weight is pressing against her back. Rough hands tangle in her hair. Her head is jerked back. She gasps for air. Then her head is slammed against the floor.

Stars. She sees stars, and her scattered senses try to understand what is happening. It's not a cartoon. There is no Coyote or Road Runner. This is her, in her sister's apartment, and oh my God, she is under attack. That is not a store mannequin tied naked and spread-eagled to the bed. Trish, Trish, Trish!

All of a sudden, Jillian is pissed off.

"No!" she cries.

"Fucking, fucking, fucking," the man says. He has her hair again. Her head goes up. Her head goes down. Her nose explodes and blood and tears pour down her face. She whimpers, but then her rage grows even hotter. She must get this man! She must hurt this man! Because even in pain, even in shock, she has a deeper, instinctive understanding of what has just happened here. Of what this man just did to her sister.

Her hands come out from beneath her, flailing wildly, trying to whack at the weight on her back. But her arms don't bend that way, and he's still beating her face and the world is now starting to spin. Her head goes back, her head goes forward. Her head goes back, her head goes forward . . .

He is sliding down her back. He is rubbing against her and there is no mistaking his arousal. "I'm going to fuck you good," the man says. He laughs and laughs and laughs.

Jillian finally twists beneath his body. She beats at his thighs. She knits together the fingers on her right hand and tries to jab them into his ribs. And he whips her head from side to side to side until she can no longer feel the sting. She is in a dark, black place with a weight crushing her body and a voice stuck in her head and he is going to fuck her good.

His left hand curls around her throat. It starts to squeeze. She tries to claw at his wrist, but encounters only latex.

Oh no. Trish. Oh no.

She must get him off. She can't get him off. Her lungs are burning. She wants to fight. She wants to save her sister. Oh please stop, please.

Somebody. Help us.

The lights grow brighter behind her eyes. Her body slowly, surely, goes limp. The man finally loosens the grip his legs have on her ribs. His weight comes up off her body slightly.

And she jabs her hand forward as hard as she can and nails him between the legs.

The man howls. Rolls to the side. Clutches his balls. Jillian twists her shoulders, grabs at the floor, and tries to find something to pull herself free.

And then the weight is completely gone. The man is gone. He is curled up on the floor and she's gotta move.

Phone, phone, phone. The kitchen counter. It's on the kitchen counter. If she can just get to the phone, dial 911.

Jillian pulls herself across the hardwood floor. *Gotta move, gotta move. Trisha needs her. She needs her.*

Come on, Jillian.

And then, before she even feels him, she hears him coming again.

"No," she whimpers, but she's already too late.

"Goddamn, fucking bitch! I'm gonna KILL you! I'm gonna SNAP your goddamn neck, I'm gonna pop out your fucking eyes. Goddamn . . ."

He slams down upon her back and grabs her throat with his steely hands. *Squeeze, squeeze, squeeze. Can't swallow. Can't breathe.*

Her chest, growing so tight. Her hands, plucking at his gloved hands. *No, no, no.*

Come on, Jillian. Come on, Jillian.

But he is too strong. She realizes this as the world begins to spin and her lungs start to burst. *She is proud. She is smart. She is a woman who believes she controls her own life.*

But he is brute strength. And she is no match for him.

She is sinking down. She wants to say something. She wants to reach out to her sister. *She is so sorry. Oh Trish, oh Trish, oh Trish.*

And then, all of a sudden, the hands are gone.

"Fuck!" Fast footsteps run across the room. Footsteps pounding up the stairs. A distant boom as the external door bursts open.

Jillian draws a ragged, gasping breath of air. Like a drowning victim bursting free from water, she bolts upright, desperately dragging more oxygen into her lungs.

He's gone. He just . . . gone.

The room is empty. It is over. *She's alive, she's alive. She is not stronger. She is not more capable. But she is lucky.*

Jillian pulls herself unsteadily to her feet. She staggers across the room. She falls onto the bed next to her sister's form.

26

"Trish!" she cries out.

And then, in the unending silence of the room, she realizes that she is not lucky at all.

Seven A.M. Monday morning, Jillian Hayes remained prostrate on her bed. She stared up at the ceiling. She listened to the sound of her mother's muffled snoring down the hall, then the faint *beep, beep, beep* of Toppi's alarm clock going off for the first time. The adult-care specialist hit snooze right away. It would take three or four more alarms before Toppi actually got out of bed.

Jillian finally turned her head. She looked out the window of her East Greenwich home, where the sun was shining bright. Then she looked at her dresser, where the manila envelope still lay in plain sight.

Seven A.M. Monday morning. The Monday morning.

The phone next to her bed bleated shrilly. Jillian immediately froze. It might be another reporter demanding a quote. Worse, it might be *him*. He probably hadn't even started the ride to the courthouse yet. What did he wake up thinking about on a day like today?

The phone rang again, loud and demanding. Jillian had no choice but to snatch it up; she didn't want it to disturb her mother.

"Did I wake you?" Carol asked in her ear.

Jillian started breathing again. Of course it was Carol. Good ol' Dan was probably up and out already. Heaven forbid that even on a day as important as this day, he stay at home with his wife. Jillian said, "No."

"I couldn't sleep," Carol said.

"I now know every pattern on my ceiling."

"It's funny. I feel so nervous. My stomach is tied in knots, my hands are shaking. I haven't felt like this since, well" – Carol's laugh was brittle – "I haven't felt like this since my wedding day."

"It will be over soon," Jillian said quietly. "Do you think we should call Meg?"

"She knows about breakfast."

27

"All right."

"What are you going to wear?"

"A camel-colored pantsuit with a white linen vest. I laid it out last night."

"I went shopping. Nothing in my closet felt right. Then again, what do you wear for this sort of thing? I don't know. I found this butter-yellow Chanel suit at Nordstrom. It was nine hundred dollars. I'm going to burn it when the day is done."

Jillian thought about her camel suit, then the coming day. "I'll join you," she said.

Carol's voice grew soft. "What did you do with the clothes you were wearing that day?"

"When the police finally gave them back, I took them to the dry cleaners. And I've never . . . I've never picked them up."

"We'll be thinking about Trisha today."

Jillian's throat grew a little tight. "Carol . . . Thank you."

And then, of course, the most important question, the question the whole phone call had been about.

"Do you know . . . Do you know what will happen?" Carol asked.

Jillian's gaze went back to the manila envelope on top of her dresser. Then she glanced at the clock. Seven-ten A.M. At least one hour to go.

"No," she said honestly. "But I guess we're about to find out."

4
Waters

Nine-oh-five A.M. Downtown, the scene was pretty much what Griffin had expected. Lots and lots of flashing lights. Very little organization. Even with an official vehicle and blaring horn, it took Griffin thirteen minutes to fight his way through the last three blocks around the courthouse. Almost immediately, he saw the problem. The media wasn't just there. They were *there*.

White media vans choked off the main artery of South Main Street. Choppers flooded the air. He'd already figured that most of the local news stations had sent reporters to cover the opening day of Eddie Como's trial. Apparently, at the first sound of rifle fire, the reporters had yelled a collective yippee and called in every station resource they could muster. Now if only the police could manage such great coverage of the scene.

Griffin drove his car up onto the curb, parking on cobblestones that technically formed a courtyard around one of the RISD buildings. Three students hastily scrambled out of his way, cursing. About four dozen more remained rooted in place, staring awestruck at the unfolding drama.

Climbing out of his Taurus, Griffin was immediately assaulted by the acrid stench of burning gas and scorched metal. Thick black smoke poured out of the parking lot just across the street, where men were frantically shouting orders and shooting four streams of water onto a mangled heap of flame-covered autos. The state fire marshal was already there, along with a collection of rescue vehicles and illegally parked police cars. A slew of Providence detectives stood alongside the fire marshal, waiting for the firemen to squelch the flames so they could move in to secure the scene.

"Jesus," Griffin muttered, coughing twice, then wishing he hadn't because it sucked more of the smoke into his lungs. Plus, this close, he caught another, richer smell underlying the odor of gasoline.

Griffin turned toward the courthouse on his right and found more chaos. Reporters, hastily contained on the grassy lawn of the memorial park, strained against blue police barricades and shouted questions in the ears of the poor Providence cops assigned to stand guard. Across from them, an ambulance was perched on the courthouse curb, along with the ME's van and more police cars than Griffin could count. Providence, state, marked, unmarked, even one belonging to Brown University's campus police. Apparently if you wore a badge, you were now part of this party.

Griffin shook his head. He pushed his way through the swelling crowd of city gawkers as a young officer in a Providence uniform and slicked-back black hair spotted him from across the street and jogged over to meet him.

"Sergeant!"

"Hey, Bentley. Imagine meeting you here." Bentley played softball with Griffin's younger brother, Jon. For the record, the state's team had creamed their corn three years in a row.

Bentley pulled up in front of Griffin, looking a little jazzed. Griffin didn't blame him. In all his years, he hadn't seen anything like this. He kept thinking he'd stepped out of his car into LA. All they needed now was a movie producer hawking film rights on the nearest street corner.

"I'm first responder," Bentley said in a rush. "I was across the river on patrol. Heard the rifle crack myself and stepped on the gas. My God, you shoulda seen the press. I thought they were gonna scale the courtyard fence to get more photos. We spent the first five minutes just getting them under control, never mind looking for the shooter."

"No kidding?" First responder. Griffin was suitably impressed. "You'll be the stuff of legends," he assured the young Providence cop as he headed across the street with Bentley in tow. "So what do we got?"

"One down, Eddie Como, DOA at the scene. Shot was fired shortly after eight-thirty A.M. as he was unloaded from the ACI van. According to initial reports, it was a rifle shot from the roof. Five, ten minutes later, an explosion came from the RISD parking lot."

"Car bomb?"

"Fire marshal isn't saying anything yet, but between you and me, five cars are wrecked, so I'm guessing that's a safe bet."

"Fatalities?"

"Don't know. Scene's too hot. I saw what looked like an arm, though, so there's at least one victim. Plus there's the, well . . ."

"Smell," Griffin filled in for him.

"Yeah." Bentley swallowed heavily.

"Uniforms searching the area?"

"Yes, sir."

"Stopping anyone with an overcoat?"

"Yes, sir."

"Any luck?"

"No, sir."

Griffin nodded. "Yeah, your arm probably belongs to a guy who used to be good with a rifle. Didn't anyone ever tell him there's no honor among thieves?"

"Sounds like the Mafia," Bentley volunteered.

Griffin shrugged. "What does the Mafia care about the College Hill Rapist? Dunno. One thing at a time. I gotta go here. Keep us posted on the search, okay?"

Griffin had arrived at the yellow crime-scene tape. Across the street, several of the reporters spotted him and a fresh shout went up.

"Sergeant, Sergeant – "

"Hey, Griffin!"

Griffin ignored them, focusing instead on the state uniform posted outside the yellow tape. Griffin didn't recognize the female officer, who was now asking his name, rank and badge number for the crime-scene logbook. Of course, in eighteen months, some things were bound to change. He told himself that was all right, though the thought left him feeling uncomfortable. Work was work. Just like riding a bike. He ducked beneath the tape.

Inside the enclosed courtyard, he saw several things at once. The blue ACI van pulled over to the left, doors still open and the interior emptied out. Three gray-clad state marshals standing to the right, talking to another Major Crimes detective. A strung-out row of blue- and khaki-suited prisoners still shackled together and now seated on the ground. In the middle was a really big pool of blood, topped by what was left of Eddie Como's body. The guy shackled to the left of Como's body was covered in blood and brains and sat in stunned silence. The guy to the right was also covered in blood and brains, but he wouldn't shut up.

"No way. No fuckin' way. Not happening. Really, really not happening. Why are we still tied up, man? I mean, like we're really going to run off right now. Because of course this isn't happening. Really not happening. *Get these fucking things off me!*"

The state marshals ignored him. So did Jack-n-Jack, the crime techs from CIU. Both were already moving around the flagstone courtyard with a digital camera, capturing the scene. Deeper in, the two death investigators from the ME's office were also diligently recording their findings. At the moment, they were standing over what might have been a man's jaw.

"Hey, Griffin," Jack Cappelli said, finally looking up.

"Look at you," Jack Needham said, also looking up. "Ooooh, that's gotta be Italian."

Griffin obligingly ran a hand down the silk-wool blend of his blue-gray sports coat. Cindy had picked it out for him. It had been one of her favorites. "Of course. Nothing but the best for this job. Now tell me the truth. Did you miss me?"

"Absolutely," they said in unison.

"Jack killed your plant, Griffin," the first Jack piped up.

"Can't prove it," the second Jack said.

"Bet I can. I shot a round of black-and-whites documenting the scene."

"In other words," Griffin deduced, "it's been a little slow lately."

They both nodded glumly. Then the first Jack perked up again. "But not anymore. Hey, do us a favor. Kill those choppers, Griff."

"Yeah, they're messing with our scene, Griff."

Griffin obligingly looked up at the swarm of media helicopters buzzing the sky, then grimaced. Media choppers were such a pain in the ass. If it wasn't bad enough to have to worry about an overly aggressive photographer capturing some sensational image of the victim, the wash from the rotor blades ruined half the evidence. He picked up his radio to contact the State Aeronautics Department just as the guy shackled to the left of Como's body raised his hand to his blood-spattered face.

"Stop!" Jack-n-Jack ordered as a single unit. "No touching! Remember, you are part of the crime scene. We need your face to analyze spray."

"Ahhhhhhh," the guy said.

Jack-n-Jack looked at him and snapped a fresh photo.

Griffin suppressed a grin. Yeah, just like old times. You know, other than the fact that they'd never had an assassination at the state courthouse before. He finished securing the airspace above the judicial complex, then returned his attention to Jack-n-Jack.

"What do we got?"

"Single head shot. Entrance wound top of the skull. Exit wound beneath the chin. No sign of powder burns. We're guessing a rifle with a soft-point slug, which would provide enough force to penetrate the skull and enough spread to do . . . well, to do *that*."

Jack-n-Jack pointed to the body. It was a good thing Griffin had seen Eddie Como's face on TV, because he definitely couldn't see it now. Soft-point bullets expanded on impact, creating a wonderful mushrooming effect.

"So a steeply vertical rifle shot." Griffin looked up. A rooftop sniper would be consistent with initial reports. Unfortunately, from this angle inside the courtyard, he couldn't see anything tucked back from the roofline six stories up. That didn't bode well for witnesses. On the other hand, that's why they paid him the big bucks. He pulled out his Norelco mini-recorder and focused on the five shackled prisoners.

"Anybody," he said. "I'm pretty sure all of you could use the brownie points."

None of the guys looked particularly impressed. Finally, the first guy shook his head.

"Man, we don't know nothin'. We were just climbing out of the van and then boom! We hear this crack like fuckin' lightning overhead and the next instant, we all get yanked off our feet. Look back and Eddie's on the ground, state marshals are yelling gun, gun, and Jazz here" – the first guy gave the kid shackled to the right of Eddie's body a derisive glance – "is already screaming, 'I've been hit, I've been hit.' 'Course he ain't been hit. He's just wearing most of Eddie's brains."

Griffin looked down the inmate line. They all nodded. This seemed to be the official summary of events. He glanced back up at the roofline, trying to figure out if he should separate them all and push the issue. Not worth it, he decided. Even knowing there were two crime-scene techs on the roof, he couldn't see a damn thing from this angle. Across the street, on the other hand . . .

A voice came over the radios secured to Jack-n-Jack's waists.

"We got a gun," a crime-scene tech reported from the roof. *"AR15 assault rifle with a Leupold scope, two-twenty-three Remingtons in the magazine. Also have three Army blankets, black coveralls, a pair of shooting gloves, and a pair of shoes. Oh, and three empty wrappers from snack-sized packages of Fig Newtons. Apparently our guy didn't just want ordinary cookies, but fruit and cake."*

"Cigarette butts?" one Jack asked hopefully.

"*No cigarette butts,*" the tech reported back. "*Sorry, Jack.*"

"Bummer." The first Jack looked at the second Jack morosely. Cigarette butts contained such a wealth of information, from brand specifics to DNA-yielding saliva.

"Cheer up," Griffin said supportively. "You have shoes. Think of everything you can get from shoes."

The Jacks brightened again. "We like shoes," they agreed. "We can do things with shoes."

Griffin gave the pair another encouraging nod, then walked over to the state marshals. Detective Mike Waters had the three men huddled around his Norelco Pocket Memo, making official statements.

"Griffin!" the first marshal said. He pulled back from the recorder long enough to vigorously pump Griffin's hand.

"Hey, Jerry. How are you?" Heavyset with thinning gray hair, Jerry was an old-timer with the state marshals. He'd helped train Griffin's older brother, Frank. Then again, Jerry had helped train just about everyone in the gray uniform.

"Fine, fine," Jerry was saying. "Well, okay, could be better. Jesus, I heard you were coming back but I didn't realize it would be today of all days. You always could pick 'em, Griff. Hey, you actin' as ringleader of this circus?"

"Nah, just another working stiff. Hey, George. Hey, Tom." Griffin shook the other two men's hands as well. Beside him, Detective Waters cleared his throat. Griffin belatedly turned toward his fellow officer. Mike Waters was five years Griffin's junior. He was tall and lanky, with a penchant for navy blue suits that made him look like an aspiring FBI agent. He was smart though, deceptively strong and thoughtfully quiet. A lot of suspects underestimated him. They never got a chance to make that same mistake twice.

There had been a time when Griffin would have greeted Mike with a hearty "Cousin Stinky!" And there had been a time when Waters would have responded with a booming

"Cousin Ugly!" That time was gone now. One of the open questions in Griffin's life was would that time come again.

"Sergeant," Waters said, nodding in greeting.

"Detective," Griffin replied. The three state marshals perked up, gaze going from officer to officer. They had probably heard the story. For that matter, they had probably helped spread the story. Griffin tried but couldn't quite keep his gaze from going to Waters's nose. That was okay. Waters's gaze had gone to Griffin's fist.

Both men jerked their eyes back to the marshals. The silence had gone on too long, grown awkward. Griffin thought, *Shit*.

Waters cleared his throat again. "So as you guys were saying . . ."

"Oh yeah." Jerry picked up the story. "We secured the courtyard."

"We opened the van doors," George supplied.

"We took up position," Tom filled in. "Started the unloading – "

"Boom!"

"Ka-boom!" George amended.

"Definitely a high-powered rifle. Nice sharp crack. I honestly thought for a second that someone was shooting deer."

"Then I saw red. Literally. Stuff sprayed everywhere."

"Kid dropped straight down. Dead before he hit the ground. You hear about this stuff, but I've never seen anything like it."

"I yelled 'gun.' "

"He did. Jerry yelled 'gun,' we all dropped into a crouch. You know, with the sun coming up behind the roof like that, you just can't see a damn thing. Scariest goddamn moment of my life."

"I thought I saw movement. Maybe somebody running. That's it, though."

"Then we could hear all the reporters yelling across the street. 'On the roof,' they were shouting. 'There he goes, there he goes.' "

"Distinguishing features?" Waters prodded. "Height, weight?"

"Couldn't even make out if it was a man or woman," Jerry said bluntly. "I'm telling you, it was more like catching the flash of a silhouette. Moved fast though. Definitely one well-conditioned sniper."

Waters gave the marshal a look. " 'One well-conditioned sniper,' huh? Well, let me run straight to my lieutenant with that. I mean, by God, Jerry, let's get out the APB."

The three marshals squirmed. "Sorry, guys," Jerry finally said with a shrug, "but from here . . . Look up yourself. You can't see a damn thing."

"Try the reporters, though," George spoke up. "They had a much better vantage point. Hey, they might have even gotten the guy on film."

The three marshals, not above getting a little revenge after they'd been put in the hot seat, smiled at them. While they'd been talking, the roar from the reporters had grown even louder outside the courthouse. Now they sounded kind of like King Kong – right before he burst his chains.

Waters sighed. Looked miserable. Then morosely hung his head. He hated the press. Last time he and Griffin had worked together, he'd let a statement slip within a reporter's earshot and paid for that mistake for weeks. Besides, as he'd later confided to Griffin, his butt looked even bonier on camera. Two fine citizens had written letters to the editor requesting that somebody in the Rhode Island police department start feeding him.

"Are you sure you didn't see anything?" he prodded the state marshals one last time.

The state marshals shook their heads, this time a bit glee-fully. But then, Jerry, kind-hearted bastard that he was, took pity on him.

"If you don't want to mess with the press, you can always go straight to the women," Jerry said.

"The women?" Griffin spoke up.

"Yeah, the three women Eddie attacked. Haven't you seen them on the news?"

"Oh, those women," Griffin said, though in fact he hadn't watched the news in months and knew very little about the College Hill rape case.

"Let's face it," Jerry was saying. "If anyone has reason to turn Eddie into liver pâté, it's the three ladies. My money's on the last one, the business one, what's her name? Jillian Hayes. Yeah, she's a cool one, could kill a man with her eyes alone. Plus, after what Eddie did to her sister . . ."

"No, no, no," George interrupted. "The Hayes woman wasn't even raped. You want to know who did it, it was the second one, Carol Rosen, the high-society wife from the East Side. My brother's wife works in the ER at Women & Infants and she was there the night they brought in Mrs. Rosen. Man, the things Eddie had done to her. It's a miracle she didn't need plastic surgery to repair her face. Twenty to one, the shooter wore pearls."

"You're both wrong," Tom spoke up. "One, no way some woman made this shot. Like an ad executive or rich socialite is going to go climbing all over the courthouse roof with an assault rifle. Key to this shooting is the first victim. The pretty young coed, Pesaturo – "

"Oh, leave the girl alone." Jerry looked stern. "Meg Pesaturo doesn't even remember anything. 'Sides, she's just a kid."

"She *says* she doesn't remember anything. But that always sounded pretty fishy to me. Maybe she just wanted to keep it private. A family matter. And you know who her family is." Tom gave them all an expectant look. They obligingly leaned forward, even Griffin. Law enforcement officers were never above a bit of juicy gossip.

"Vinnie Pesaturo," Tom said, in the waiting hush. "Yeah, the Carlone family's favorite bookie. If Vinnie wanted something done, you can be sure it got done. So maybe pretty little Meg doesn't remember anything. Or maybe she's adopting the party line, while Vinnie sets everything in motion. A rooftop sniper, a nearby explosion. Oh yeah, this has got the Carlone family written all over it. Mark my words, Meg Pesaturo is the one."

5
Meg

She is laughing. She doesn't know why. The police are here. Some girl, her roommate, she is told, is crying. But Meg is standing outside. She is looking up at the dark night sky, where the stars gleam like tiny pinpricks of light, where the breeze is cool against her cheeks, and she is hugging herself and laughing giddily.

The police want to take her to the hospital. They are looking at her strangely.

"It's a beautiful night," she tells them. "Look, it's a gorgeous night!"

The concerned officers put her in the back of a police cruiser. She hums to herself. She touches her cheek, and she has a first glimmer of memory.

A touch, whisper light, impossibly gentle. Eyes, rich chocolate, peering into her own. The beginning of a slow, sweet smile.

"Who am I?" she asks the officers up front.

"Why don't you wait until we get to the hospital."

So she waits until they get to the hospital. It's all right with her. She's singing some tune she can't get out of her head. She is daydreaming of whisper-light touches. She is shivering in anticipation of a lover's kiss.

At the hospital, she is whisked through the emergency room doors, led to a tiny exam room where a special nurse, a sexual assault examiner, comes bustling in. She seems to know the officers, which is fine by Meg, because she doesn't know anyone at all.

"How bad?" the nurse asks briskly.

"You tell us. The roommate came home and found her tied to the bed. She claims she doesn't remember a thing, including her name – "

"What's my name?" Meg speaks up.

They ignore her. "She claims she doesn't remember her roommate either," the police officer says, "not anyone, not anything. The roommate gave us contact information, so the parents are on the way."

The nurse jerks her head toward Meg. "Original clothes?"

"No, the roommate released her from the bindings and dressed her before calling us." The police officer sounds disgusted. "Someone's gotta teach these people to know better. We found a ripped T-shirt on the floor, plus a pair of panties. They're already on their way to the lab."

"I'll bag these clothes as well, just in case any hair or fiber has rubbed off inside them. I'll mark them as second-set clothing. That work for you?"

The officers shrug. "We're just the limo drivers; what the hell do we care?"

"Hey," Meg says again. "Isn't it a beautiful night?"

The officers roll their eyes. The nurse dismisses them and comes over to Meg. The nurse has blue eyes. The eyes look at her kindly, but they are also sharp.

"What is your name?" she asks as she snaps on a pair of gloves.

"I don't know. That's what I was asking them. That girl called me Meg. Maybe I'm Meg."

"I see. And how old are you, Meg?"

Meg has to think about it. A number pops into her mind. "Nineteen?"

The nurse nods as if this is an acceptable answer. "And what day is today?"

This is easier. "Wednesday," Meg says immediately. "April eleventh."

"All right. I just need to check a few things, Meg. I know this may feel uncomfortable, but I'm not going to hurt you. Please understand we're all here to help you. Even if it seems that we're asking too much, we have your best interests at heart."

The nurse reaches out. She takes Meg's wrist with her gloved fingers. Immediately, Meg recoils. She yanks back her hand.

"No," Meg says, though she doesn't know why. She is shaking her head. The night is not so beautiful anymore. "No," she says again. "No, no."

"Your wrist is bleeding," the nurse says patiently. "I just need to look at it, see if it needs treatment." She reaches out again with her gloved hand and takes Meg's wrist.

"No!" This time Meg flies off the table. She clutches her bleeding wrist against her chest, feeling her heart pound as she searches frantically for some means of escape. The door is closed. She is trapped in the tiny exam room with this woman and those gloves. The gloves smell. Can't the woman smell them? They have a horrible, horrible smell.

Meg turns around and around. No place to go. No way to escape. She shrinks down onto the cold, white floor. She cradles her bleeding wrists against her, and for reasons she can't explain, she whimpers.

The nurse is looking at her. Her face has not changed. Her expression is set, unreadable, but at least she doesn't come any closer.

"Does your wrist hurt?" the nurse asks quietly.

Meg has not thought about it. But now that the woman mentions it . . . Meg looks down at her wrists. Big, huge welts circle the tiny forms. She can see fresh blood and dark purple bruises marring her skin.

"They . . . they sting," Meg says. Her voice holds a trace of wonder.

The nurse squats down until she is eye level.

"Meg, I'm here to help you. If you let me, I will treat your wrists and help them feel better. I also want to help you another way, Meg. My job is to assist in catching the person who did this to you, who made your wrists sting. To do that, I need to take some pictures. And I need to examine the rest of you as well. I know this isn't easy right now. But *if you will trust me, I promise I won't hurt you."*

Slowly, Meg nods her head. She isn't afraid of this woman. In fact, she has come to like her stern face and unwavering gaze. This woman seems strong, in control. Meg rises back up. She holds out her raw, torn wrists.

But the moment the woman touches her again, places those latex-covered fingers against her skin . . .

"I'm going to be sick," Meg says, and just barely makes it to the stainless steel sink.

The door opens, then closes as the nurse leaves the room. Meg runs the water for a bit. She rinses off her face, which she had already done twice before the police came, another thing that made them growl in disapproval.

Meg's mouth hurts. She finds a mirror and studies her face for a long time. The corners of her mouth are bleeding slightly. The flesh there is torn.

Meg is honestly confused. She searches her memory for some kind of hint, but all she can recall is a faraway sensation of whisper-light touches against her skin. Soft, teasing caresses. And she is holding her breath, hoping he will come closer, closer.

Please, kiss me.

She shivers. And a moment later, she realizes that for the first time all night, she is afraid.

From outside comes the sound of voices. The nurse and the police officers are once more talking about her.

"Latex? She was tied up with strips of latex? For God's sake, gentlemen, that's the kind of detail you might want to mention to me. I just approached her all gloved up and she about climbed the walls. No wonder she was scared out of her mind."

"So you think she was raped?"

"Of course she was raped. Have you looked at her mouth? Consensual lovers don't generally gag their partners."

"Yeah, yeah, but . . . listen to her. 'Isn't it a beautiful night.' And she's humming all the time and smiling to herself. What's that about?"

"It's called euphoria, Officer. Because even if Miss

42

Pesaturo doesn't consciously remember being raped yet, her subconscious knows damn well what happened and it's telling her she's grateful to be alive."

The officers don't say anything more. A moment later, the door bursts open and the nurse comes bustling back in. Meg stares at the woman's hands, but they are bare now. The woman opens a cabinet, pulls out a separate box. She hands the box to Meg.

"Are these okay with you?"

Meg looks into the box. It also contains gloves, but these are different. She takes one out, holds it in her hand. It is thin and smells of rubber. The box says it is a vinyl glove. She sniffs again. She has an instant memory of dish soap and sudsy water. That's all.

She hands the box back to the nurse. "Okay," she says and her voice is now equally grave.

The nurse spreads a white drop cloth on the floor. Meg stands on the drop cloth and takes off her clothes, including her bra and panties. The nurse puts each item in a separately marked bag. Meg holds out her arms. The nurse shoots Polaroids of her naked body, including her mouth, wrists and ankles. The nurse runs a comb through her pubic hair. The results go into another bag.

Then Meg must lie back on the table. Her feet go into stirrups. Her heart is pounding again. She tries not to think about it. She tries to remember she must trust this woman, because something horrible has happened even if Meg can only recall rich chocolate eyes and a gentle lover's kiss.

Meg shivers. The room is too cold. She is frightened by the swabs the nurse is taking. Frightened by the things they might know that she doesn't. She is overexposed, and even when the nurse hands her a pink hospital gown, it is not enough.

There is evidence of vaginal penetration, the nurse tells her. Traces of fluid in the cervix. Is Meg on birth-control pills?

This sounds right to Meg. She nods. It is only the beginning, however. She doesn't have to take the morning-after

43

pill unless she really wants to, but there is still the risk of sexually transmitted disease. Herpes. Gonorrhea. AIDS. She will give blood samples today, and more in the coming weeks as they continue to look for signs of infection. For example, it can take up to six months to detect the first sign of AIDS after initial exposure.

Meg nods again. Her euphoria is gone. She is tired. More tired than she has ever felt. Her mouth hurts. Her ankles, her wrists. She sits with her legs tightly crossed and she hopes, somewhere way down deep, that no one will ever touch her again.

A knock on the door. An officer sticks in his head. Meg's parents are here. A Providence detective is here. They need to ask her some more questions . . .

"You're going to be all right," the nurse tells Meg.

Meg just looks at the woman. She finally understands that this kind, stern woman is paid to lie. Meg has been raped. Meg has lost her mind. Meg does not recognize the man and woman now rushing into the room sobbing her name.

Meg will be many things in the days, weeks, months to come. But she will not be all right. That will be a much longer-term project. It will take years. Most likely, it will take the rest of her life.

Monday morning, 7:10 A.M., Meg finally crawled out of bed. She hadn't slept well last night, though she wasn't sure why. Today might be the big day, but it would be a bigger day for everyone other than her. The prosecutor, Ned D'Amato, wasn't even going to call her to testify. As D'Amato so bluntly put it, what could she contribute? She still didn't know anything about that night. During cross-examination, the defense would eat her alive.

Kind, gentle Meg. Sweet, lucky Meg, who still didn't remember a thing.

From downstairs came the distant clang and clatter of pans. Her mother must already be in the kitchen, whipping up breakfast. Then came a high-pitched giggle, followed by a shrill demand for "Pancakes, pancakes, pancakes!" Meg's little sister, Molly, liked to get up at six.

Meg's lack of memory didn't bother her so much anymore. About four months ago, she realized she possessed a deeper, instinctive knowledge of things if she was just willing to listen to her inner voice. For example, she couldn't remember her mother's name, age or general description. But the minute her mother had burst into the hospital exam room and wrapped her arms around Meg's trembling shoulders, Meg had known that this woman loved her. She felt the same way about her father and Molly. And when they brought her back here she'd definitely had a sense of coming home, even if she couldn't have given a street address.

Sometimes, little things got her going. A song on the radio would shake the cobwebs in her mind. She would feel a memory stirring, rising up, like a word stuck on the tip of her tongue. If she tried too hard, however, strained her mind, the thought would disappear almost immediately. She'd have to wait for the song to air once more, or the scent to ride the wind, or the déjà vu to return.

Lately, she'd been working on not working so hard. She focused on her inner voice more. She let the moments of semiclarity linger like a fog in front of her eyes. She spent long periods of time thinking of nothing and everything. Post-traumatic amnesia was the mind's way of coping, the doctors had told her. Forcing the issue only created more trauma. Instead she should rest, eat healthily, and get plenty of exercise. In other words, take good care of herself.

Meg took good care of herself. These days, she didn't have anything else to do.

Now she heard the sound of voices, closer, down the hall. Hushed voices, the way people spoke when they were fighting and didn't want others to hear. Her parents, again. She'd gone to sleep listening to the same sound.

Her Uncle Vinnie kept coming by. Yesterday he'd been here until almost ten at night, speaking low and furiously with her father. Her mom didn't approve of Uncle Vinnie. Her mom didn't like him coming over so much, and obviously didn't like whatever he and her father had been talking about.

Meg herself didn't get it. Uncle Vinnie had a loud, booming laugh. He smelled of whiskey and stale cigars. His head was nearly bald, his stomach bursting huge. He looked to her like Kojak crossed with Santa Claus. How could you not like Kojak crossed with Santa Claus?

Meg waited on the other side of her door until her parents' voices finally faded away. Molly was still downstairs. Probably now decorating the floor with bits of pancakes. Her mother had probably returned to her. Her father had to get ready for work. Meg crossed the hall unnoticed and crept into the upstairs bathroom, where she took a long, steaming shower.

She needed to get moving if she was going to be at the rue de l'espoir by eight.

Twenty minutes later, clad in jeans and a T-shirt, her long, damp brown hair pulled back in a ponytail, her face freshly scrubbed, she went galloping downstairs. By now her father had probably left for work, which made it easier for her, easier for him. One year later, he couldn't look at her without seeing a rape victim. And Meg couldn't look at him without seeing him look at her as someone who had been raped.

Her mother was easier. She had cried, she had raged and she had been so damn happy the day the police had arrested Eddie Como. But she was also happy to have Meg home again, plus she had her hands full with Molly, and there were so many things to be done. Life was busy. Life went on. She also probably understood better than Meg's father that women were stronger than they looked.

Now, Meg threw her arms around her mother's trim, efficient form and squeezed her good.

"I gotta meet Carol and Jillian downtown," she said, kissing her mom on the cheek. This was the kind of thing she could tell her mother. Her father didn't approve of the Survivors Club meetings. Why should his little girl sit around with two older women talking about rape? For

46

God's sake, what was the world coming to?

Meg didn't mind the discussions. Frankly, she had been a little surprised and a little pleased that Jillian had invited her to join. After all, Meg didn't know anything. She hadn't turned militant like Jillian. She hadn't gone half-crazed like Carol. Meg was still Meg. She talked about her family, about the people she was learning to love all over again, while Jillian coolly discussed topics such as victims' rights and Carol railed against the injustices of a world created by men.

"Pancakes?" her mom asked hopefully.

"Meg!" Molly screamed. "Good morning, Meg!" Molly was a morning person.

Meg let go of her mother and crossed the kitchen to plant four wet kisses on Molly's syrup-smeared face. "Molly! Good morning, Molly!" Meg wailed back.

Her five-year-old sister, her parents' little midlife oops, but a happy oops, giggled at her. "Are you going to eat pancakes?"

"Nah, I'm going to drink chai."

"No chai. Eat pancakes with me."

"Can't, got a hot date. But I'll see you this afternoon."

She kissed Molly's syrupy cheek again, then tickled the little girl until she squealed and squirmed in her chair.

"You're leaving already?" her mother asked from the stove.

"Sorry, I'm running late. I'm supposed to be at rue de l'espoir by eight."

"You'll call." Meaning if Meg heard anything from the courthouse, from Ned D'Amato.

"I'll call."

Her mom finally stepped away from the stove in the tiny kitchen. She held the flipper in one hand, wore an oven mitt on the other. She looked at Meg for a long time.

"I love you," her mother said abruptly.

"I love you, too."

"You'll call me?"

"I'll call you."

"All right then." Meg's mother nodded, returned to the stove and dished out a fresh plate of pancakes in a kitchen where there was no one left to feed.

Meg headed out the door. The sun was bright, the morning cool but already warming with the promise of heat. A beautiful day, but that didn't mean anything. After all, one year ago, it had been a beautiful night.

Meg climbed into her little brown Nissan, parked on the street. She tried not to notice the expired parking sticker for Providence College still stuck on her window. Her father no longer felt college was safe enough for his little girl. If he had his way, she would never go back.

And Meg? What did Meg want? She was the lucky one. Everyone told her that. Detective Fitzpatrick, Ned D'Amato, Carol, even Jillian. Sure she had been raped, but that had been it. No broken bones, no scars, no burial plots. She had been the College Hill Rapist's first victim and after her, he'd definitely done worse.

Meg started the engine of her car. Meg drove down the street. Meg felt once more the eyes that followed her so often these days. Meg did not turn around.

But she shivered.

It had been four months now. She didn't know what was going on. But one thing was clear. Somehow, someway, sweet lucky Meg was no longer alone.

6

Maureen

In downtown Providence, Griffin and Waters walked together out of the courtyard. Griffin thought he should say something.

"Tell me about the Eddie Como case." Okay, he probably should have said something more personal than that.

Waters shrugged. "I don't know much. Providence handled the case."

"Give me the headlines."

"Four women were attacked, one was killed. The first was a student at Providence College, Meg Pesaturo. Guess her family is connected, though that's news to me. The next victim, the Rosen woman, lives in one of those big, historical homes near Brown, which you can believe got the whole East Side screaming for better police protection. The third attack was at Brown, another college student, except the woman's sister walked in during the rape. He beat up the older sister pretty badly, and the younger wound up dead. Anaphylactic reaction to latex, something like that."

"The guy was wearing gloves?"

"Yeah, plus he tied them up with latex tourniquets. You know, the kind they use in the hospital when they're drawing blood. That's how the Providence police caught him in the end. Turns out the victims had donated blood at a campus blood drive prior to the attack. Police did a little digging ... Eddie Como was a phlebotomist with the Rhode Island Blood Center. Theory is he used the blood drives to identify potential targets, then looked up their home addresses in the blood donor database."

Griffin waved his head from side to side, working out a kink in his neck. "Circumstantial case?"

"No, they had DNA. Perfect match, all three victims. Como's the guy."

"Going to get buried at trial?"

Waters nodded vigorously. "Going to get *buried* at trial."

"Interesting. So on the one hand, Eddie's probably going away for life. On the other hand, according to the state marshals, three women still wanted him dead."

"You haven't seen the crime-scene photos," Waters said. And then they arrived in front of the press.

"Sergeant, Sergeant, Sergeant!" The roar went up, followed by an immediate hail of questions.

"Is Eddie Como dead?"

"What about the state marshals?"

"Are there other fatalities?"

"What about the explosion? Was that a car bomb?"

"Who's going to be leading the case? Providence? State? When will we get a briefing, when will we get a briefing?"

Griffin held up his hand. Bulbs immediately flashed. He grimaced, suffered a spasm of bad memory, then got it under control.

"Okay. This is the deal. We're not answering any of your questions."

Collective groan.

"We're here to ask you our questions."

A fresh pique of interest.

"I know, I know," Griffin said dryly, "we're excited about it, too. In case any of you haven't noticed, you're all witnesses to a shooting."

"It's Eddie Como, isn't it? Someone killed the College Hill Rapist!"

The rest of the reporters started in again, kids turned loose in the candy store. "When do we get a briefing? When do we get a briefing?"

"Who's going to handle the case?"

"What can you tell us about the explosion?"

"Has anyone interviewed the women yet? What do the victims have to say?"

Griffin sighed. Reasoning with the press was such a waste of breath. But in this job, you had to do what you had to do. He and Waters squared their shoulders, shoved aside two of the blue police barricades and waded bravely into the fray. Four microphones promptly appeared in front of Griffin's face. He pushed them back, homed in on one reporter in particular, and stabbed at the man with his finger.

"You. You and your cameraman can start. Over here."

He and Waters pulled the two away from the group. The pair weren't very happy, but then Waters and Griffin didn't much care. Griffin made the reporter review his notes, while Waters had the cameraman play back his tape. At the last minute, they were rewarded with a grainy image of the back of a man running across the courthouse roof. The focus was all wrong, though. The cameraman had been zoomed in on a close-up shot of his reporter talking in front of the court-yard. When he yanked up the camera after hearing the gun-fire, the shooter was too far away to yield a good image.

"He was wearing all black," the reporter provided. "With something on his head. Maybe a stocking. You know, like bank robbers do in the movies."

Griffin grunted. Waters noted the names and news affili-ate for the twosome, then they moved on. Their second sub-jects were even better. This cameraman liked gunshots so well, he dropped his five-thousand-dollar piece of hardware onto the lawn.

"I don't do well with loud noises," he said sheepishly.

"For God's sake, Gus," his reporter snapped, "what hap-pens if they send us to Afghanistan?"

"We work for the UPN affiliate in the smallest state in the nation, Sally. When the fuck are we going to be sent to Afghanistan?"

"Did you at least look up?" Griffin intervened in this lovefest.

"Yeah," Gus said. "Saw a person, running across the roof."

"Person?" Waters pressed.

Gus shrugged. "All I could see was the back. Could be a man, could be a woman. In this day and age, who the hell knows?"

"Real observant, Gus, real observant."

Griffin turned toward Sally. "And you?"

The hard-faced brunette gave Griffin an appraising stare. "I thought it was a man. Broad shoulders. Short, dark hair. Dressed in black coveralls, like the kind mechanics wear. Now then. You're looking good after your little vacation, Griffin. A sergeant of Major Crimes, light caseload from being gone so long. Twenty to one they're going to put you in charge of this baby. So why don't you give me an interview? Five minutes on the record. My boss will clear it with your boss. What do you say?"

Waters was looking at him strangely. He probably hadn't given any thought to who would be assigned as the primary case officer yet. The decision generally wasn't made right away. Sally was correct, however. Griffin was a sergeant, he had lead case experience and at the moment he had a remarkably light caseload.

"I'm sure the detective commander will be giving a statement to all of the reporters shortly," Griffin told Sally. Then he walked back to the crowd. "Next!"

It took him and Waters two hours to make it through the nest of reporters. In the end, they had a description of a white male who was between five and six feet tall, who might have brown hair, blond hair or black hair, who was either heavyset or rail-thin, who was wearing a ski mask, a Zorro-like mask, a stocking mask or nothing at all, and who may or may not bear a striking resemblance to James Gandolfini's character on *The Sopranos*.

"That's it, I think we can arrange for a lineup right now," Waters said.

"Absolutely. And here I thought it would take all day to learn that nobody saw nothing. Instead it's been what, two and a half hours?"

"The Boss will be pleased," Waters agreed.

They both sighed heavily. They wandered away from the reporters, who had spotted the major arriving at the courtyard across the street, and were now resuming their manic cries for a briefing.

"What do you think?" Waters asked quietly, looking around to make sure no gung-ho reporter had spotted their break from the crowd. Acrid smoke from the car explosion still wafted through the air. It gave their voices a raspy edge.

"We're pissing in the wind," Griffin said. "Single head shot, so most likely the guy was a pro. Left everything on the rooftop, so most likely he knew the assault rifle, etc., was untraceable. I'm betting the minute he finished shooting, he stripped down to civilian threads and headed into the courthouse where he blended into the rest of the pedestrian traffic."

"He simply strolled down the street to his getaway vehicle," Waters filled in.

"Where he made an even bigger exit than he planned."

"A description's not going to help much, except down at the morgue," Waters agreed.

"We're still going to have to know who he is to confirm his occupation, then figure out who hired him."

"I don't know. Based on what we've heard, Uncle Vinnie's looking better all the time. Has a grudge, has the connections to hire a gun. Seems to me that Tom was onto something. Or" – Waters's voice grew more thoughtful – "the East Side wife obviously has money. Maybe she arranged for the hit. Or maybe all the women conspired together – I heard that they formed some kind of support group. Of course, I'm not sure why they'd kill the hired gun. Then again, once you've decided to kill one felon, what's one more?"

Griffin merely grunted. He didn't like to rush to conclusions when working a case. He flipped through his spiral notebook. "Hey, Mike, what happened to NBC?"

"I don't know. *Seinfeld* ended, *ER* lost Clooney?"

"No, no, I mean, we haven't interviewed anyone from WJAR. You really believe Channel Ten didn't send a news team?"

Waters frowned. He looked around the memorial park. And then his eyes widened. "There, at the end of the block. Doesn't that white van say News Team Ten?"

"Well, what do you know. Two reporters have actually left the herd and are holed up on their own. Now, why would two reporters run away from the pack?"

"They have something."

"No, no, Mike, *we* have something. Let's get 'em."

Sixty seconds later, Griffin rapped on the van's sliding metal door. It didn't magically open. He knocked louder. Immediately, the voices inside shut up.

"Come on, guys," he called out. "This is Sergeant Griffin of the state police. Now open up, or I'll huff and I'll puff and I'll blow your van down."

Another long pause. Finally, a click, then the door slid meekly back. Perched inside, Maureen Haverill gave both detectives her best reporter's smile.

"Griffin!" she said warmly. "I heard you were returning to the fold."

Maureen Haverill had been working at the local NBC affiliate for five years. A petite blonde, she was perky enough for one of those national morning news shows and probably figured it was only a matter of time. At the moment, her blue eyes were particularly bright. She looked like an addict who'd just gotten a fix. Or a reporter who'd just landed a scoop. Her cameraman was out of sight. Probably frantically dubbing the tape. Damn.

"Both of you, out, now." Griffin's voice was harsh.

"Griffin – "

"Out!"

Maureen scowled. She made a big show of carefully maneuvering out of the van, the helpless blonde in a too-short, too-tight pale green skirt. She probably bought her cameraman another thirty seconds.

"So help me God, Maureen," Griffin informed her, "you dub that tape and I will nail you for tampering with evidence."

"I don't know what you're talking about."

"Jimmy," he called out. "You, too. *Now.*"

A big head of rumpled red hair reluctantly appeared. "We were just making some notes," Jimmy said sulkily. "Can't two reporters get a little work done?" The hulking redhead climbed out onto the sidewalk. He kept his eyes carefully averted. There was a fresh sheen of sweat glistening across his forehead.

"I want the tape," Griffin said.

"What tape?" Maureen tried again.

"The tape you're frantically copying for your lead story, which will probably be airing at any moment. It would be a shame, Maureen, if some junior reporter had to provide the vocals for the piece because you were detained behind bars."

"You can't arrest me! On what grounds?"

"Obstruction of justice."

"Oh please. That's horseshit and you know it."

"It's been eighteen months. My grasp of the law is a little rusty. I'll arrest you first, then let the courts sort it out."

Maureen started to look pissed. "Dammit, I have Fourth Amendment protection against illegal search and seizure!"

"Then it's a good thing we're standing next to a courthouse. I'll stay with you. Detective Waters can run across the street and get a subpoena. Thirty minutes later not only will we still seize the tape, but I promise you that when we're done, we'll provide copies of the visual to every single news organization in this state. You understand? Every single one."

"No way. That's my scoop!"

"Yes way. That's our evidence and once we seize it, we can do whatever we see fit."

"Goddammit, Griffin! I liked you so much better before – " Maureen's protest ended abruptly. She seemed to realize what she was about to say, then even she had the good grace to blush.

Griffin said nothing. He just stared at her. He'd gotten good at this stare over the last year. Sometimes, especially in the first few months after the Big Boom, he'd find himself standing in front of a mirror just staring like this. Like he

55

was trying to look into his own eyes and get some sense of the man living there.

"I want the tape," he repeated. "It's evidence. And anything you do to it, including developing it or copying it, would be considered tampering with evidence. We got sixty state detectives crawling all over this one city block, Maureen, not to mention well over a hundred uniforms. Do you really think the attorney general is going to take kindly to hearing how some local reporter tampered with a potentially critical piece of evidence?"

Maureen gnawed her lower lip, looked a great deal less certain. "I want a deal," she said abruptly.

"Why, Maureen, are you confessing to a crime?"

"We cooperate, hand over the tape – "

"You mean we seize it."

"We *hand* it over. In return for some kind of consideration. An exclusive interview with the colonel."

Griffin laughed.

"The major," she amended.

Griffin laughed harder.

"The detective commander. Come on, Griffin. This is *exclusive* footage you're taking from me. Best damn visual of my career. We deserve at least an interview. Plus, exclusive rights to the copy of the tape. No releasing it to the general population. If they didn't look up, it's their own fucking problem."

"Your compassion touches me."

"Yeah, yeah, yeah. What do you say? Five minutes with the detective commander, exclusive tape rights."

"Thirty seconds, primary case officer, exclusive tape rights."

"Three minutes."

"One, with approval in advance of the questions. Otherwise, you're only going to get no comment."

Maureen scowled. She shot him a sideways glance. "Are you going to be the lead investigator, Griffin?"

"A lead investigator will be assigned when a lead investigator is assigned."

"Because that would be a good story, you know. Rhode Island's golden boy returning to the war. A lot of people didn't think you'd come back after the Candy Man case. A lot of people weren't sure you'd have the interest, and others weren't sure you'd have the guts. Do you love the job that much, Griffin, or is it one of those things that simply gets under the skin?" She changed tactics. "I understand that he still sends you letters."

"One minute with the primary case officer. Yes or no, Maureen. The deal is off the table in five, four, three, two – "

"Okay," she said hastily. "Okay. One minute with the primary case officer. We'll take it." She sighed, devoted another moment to looking forlorn as she saw her dream of a lead five o'clock news piece go up in smoke, then got over it. "That'll teach us not to shoot live," she muttered. "Well, you might as well come inside. You're going to want to see this."

In the back of the van, Jimmy had his huge camera hooked up to an external monitor. He and Maureen hadn't developed the tape yet, but had been running it over and over again, looking for the best cut. Now Jimmy hit play one last time. The visual lasted seventy-five seconds, and it showed everything. Absolutely everything.

"How the hell did you get this?" Griffin demanded immediately, angrily. He took two steps forward before Waters could stop him, and had Maureen pressed against the control panel running along the side of the van. "Are you toying with us?"

"No, no, I swear – "

"Did you get an anonymous tip? A Deep Throat telling you something big was going down, but you just didn't feel like sharing it with us?"

"Griffin, Griffin, you have it all wrong – "

"You never taped the ACI van! That entire footage is of the *rooftop!* There are eleven other news teams out on that lawn, Maureen. All of them were looking at the van, all of them were shooting the van. So why were you looking up? What the hell did you know that they didn't?"

"I don't know!" she cried. Her chin came up, her shoulder squared against the control panel. "I just . . . The whole morning I kept thinking someone was watching me. I'm not kidding. I had shivers down my spine, hairs going up on the nape of my neck. No matter where I went, what I did, I could just feel . . . something. Then, I heard a shout that the van was coming, so I started to adjust my mike and I . . . I looked up. One last time. At the roof. I swore I saw a movement. So I hit Jimmy on the arm and told him to shoot the roof. Now."

"I thought she was nuts," Jimmy spoke up from the rear. "But hey, it's not like a shot of the outside of a blue van is anything special. So I focused on the roof of the courthouse and well, what do you know? This guy pops up and opens fire. Really damn freaky. I figure we could get national coverage out of this."

"Awards," Maureen spoke up. "Definitely awards." The light in her eyes had gone full glow again. Pressed against the side of the van, she shivered.

Very slowly, Griffin stepped back. His hands were still fisted at his sides. He worked now on letting his fingers go, forcing his shoulders to come down and his breathing to relax. He felt suddenly disgusted. And he was aware for the first time that Waters was watching him nervously. Maureen and Jimmy, too. Everyone was probably thinking about that damn basement. Maybe they should.

He took another deep breath, focused on his racing pulse and slowly counted to ten.

"Tape," he prodded once he trusted himself to speak. Reluctantly, Jimmy opened his camera and popped out the digital cassette. Waters provided the evidence bag. Jimmy gave the tape one last, lingering look, then dropped it in.

"You'll remember our deal," Maureen said.

"Yeah, yeah, yeah."

"If we can get a copy before four," she said seriously, "we can still make the five o'clock news."

"I'll be sure to tell CIU." Copy before four. She'd be lucky to get a copy in six months.

Maureen leaned against the side of the van. She'd lost this round, but he could tell she was already plotting her next battle. "Hey, Griffin, be honest. That guy's dead now, isn't he? Blown up in that parking lot after assassinating Eddie Como?"

"No comment."

"That's what I thought. You'll be talking to the vics now? The three women?"

"No comment."

"Maybe they'll hold a press conference. That would be nice. Over the last year we've certainly scored some serious ratings off those three and their little club." Maureen bit her lower lip. "I wonder if there's a way I could get them to do an exclusive this time . . ."

"The rape vics like to hold press conferences?" Griffin looked at Waters in confusion.

Maureen, however, did the honors. "Jesus Christ, Griffin, where have you been? Right after the death of Trisha Hayes those women practically owned the five o'clock news. The sister, Jillian, got them united in some sort of group. The Survivors Club, they call it. Then they started sending out the press releases. Worked like a charm. Before they went public, people knew about the attacks, but weren't losing a lot of sleep over it. You know how people are – violent crimes happen to someone else. Especially rape. That definitely happens to other women – you know, poor women, minority women, women living in high-risk areas or leading high-risk lives. Except one day, the general public turned on the TV and there were the three victims – beautiful, white, well-educated and well-to-do. Two aren't even sweet young things but respectable, middle-aged women, leading respectable, middle-class lives.

"People went nuts," Maureen said bluntly. " 'Look at these poor women, so tragically victimized in their own homes. Arrest someone, arrest anyone, but by God, get us justice before that becomes my daughter, my sister, my mother, my wife. What the hell have the police been doing anyway?' I understand after their first appearance, the AG's phone didn't stop ringing for a week."

"They gave the crimes a face," Griffin filled in.

"The Survivors Club gave the crimes three extremely attractive faces. Ever take Psych 101? People really do judge a book by its cover. Ugly people get what they deserve. Pretty people, on the other hand . . ."

Griffin nodded. He understood. "They hold a lot of press conferences?" he asked curiously.

"I don't know. Five or six."

"Always all three women?"

"*Always* all three women. No individual interviews, they made that clear in the beginning."

"What about their families?"

Maureen shrugged. "Sometimes you saw Carol Rosen's husband or Meg Pesaturo's mother in the background, but the press conferences were very clearly the women's show. After all, they were the ones viciously attacked while the Providence cops sat on their asses for six weeks."

"They're bitter?"

"My words, not theirs."

"Emotional?"

"Sometimes. Not often. More like . . . focused. For each venue, the Survivors Club had clear demands. For example, when they held a press conference in front of the PPD, they were asking for more foot patrols in College Hill. When they were in front of the mayor's office, they launched an appeal for community policing. In front of the AG's office, they wanted a more aggressive investigation, get a suspect and get him off the streets, now, now, now. We're talking a serial rapist, after all, and we all know serial rapists don't magically stop on their own."

"In other words, they whipped the public into a frenzy," Griffin mused. Oh yeah, he could see that. The Providence detectives had to love those afternoons. Nothing like a public flogging by the very people you were trying to help, to make you feel good about the job. Of course, if it had been the state's case, they would've nailed the guy day one. That went without saying.

"Eddie Como attacked four women in six weeks," Maureen said firmly. "He killed one of them. How do you think it must feel to be Jillian Hayes right now, knowing that if the Providence detectives had been paying more attention after the second attack, maybe the third attack never would've happened? Maybe her sister would still be alive."

"She say that?"

"She never had to. Just by standing up there, she reminded the public of what happened to her sister and in turn, what could happen to one of their sisters as long as the rapist remained at large. The public responded to that. Hell, the public ate it up. I'll bet you the women could hold a press conference this afternoon announcing that they'd shot Eddie Como, and no one would bat an eye."

"They're that attractive?" Griffin asked dryly.

"No!" Maureen rolled her eyes. "They're that . . . compelling. Think about it. You got Jillian Hayes, the hardworking older sister who runs her own business while taking care of her invalid mother. She's polished, she's poised, plus she's always holding a bright, smiling photo of her younger sister, who was only nineteen when Eddie Como killed her. Then, you have Meg Pesaturo, looking like Bambi, with her big brown eyes and trembling shoulders. Trust me, there's not a man in this city who can look at her and not want to kill Eddie Como himself. And finally, we have Carol Rosen, a blue-eyed blonde, the socialite wife who on the one hand lives in a mansion, but on the other hand spends her time doing work for local charities. You couldn't cast a better group if you tried."

"A business woman, a college coed and an upper-crust wife. In other words, a little something for everyone."

"Exactly."

"Each taking turns on the mike," Griffin murmured.

"Oh no. Jillian Hayes serves as the spokesperson for the group. She does all the talking."

"All the time?"

"All the time. I'm guessing they have an agreement. Plus, she has a marketing background, and the other two never

61

appeared very comfortable on camera."

"So *they* never made demands," Griffin said slowly. "Jillian Hayes made demands."

"She was speaking for all of them. For God's sake, Carol and Meg were standing right there."

"But Jillian's the ringleader of this so-called Survivors Club?"

"Why, Griffin, you make it sound like she's plotting something."

"Just thinking out loud."

Maureen was quiet for a moment. Her blue eyes had taken on that feral look again. "We have some footage you might like to see."

Griffin and Waters exchanged glances. "Sounds like everyone has footage," Griffin said neutrally. "That's the nature of a press conference."

"We have better footage."

"More gazing up at rooftops, Maureen?"

"Something like that."

"Come on." Griffin was growing tired of this conversation. He made a waggling motion with his fingertips. "Spill it, Maureen. You've already aired whatever you got, that makes it public property. So let's just cut to the chase and your cooperation will be duly noted."

"How duly noted?"

"Next time we meet, I promise not to growl at you as much as I'm going to growl at you now."

"Funny, I would've thought that vacation would have improved your temper, Sergeant Griffin."

"And I would've thought that covering three women who had been brutally attacked would've taught you some compassion. Guess we're both wrong."

Maureen thinned her lips. Behind her, Jimmy turned away before she could glimpse his smile.

"We have this footage of Carol Rosen," Maureen said abruptly.

"The socialite wife."

"Yeah, it's the third or fourth press conference. I don't

even remember for what. But Jillian's talking away at the mike, and Carol and Meg are doing what they do best, standing beside her, when Carol's husband appears. He walks up behind his wife, and I guess she never heard him coming, because the next moment he puts his hand on her shoulder and she about jumps out of her skin. Jimmy happened to have the camera on her when it happened, and the look on her face . . . You could just tell – even in broad daylight, even surrounded by a roomful of people, that woman was terrified. She didn't feel safe. And *that's* what it means to be a rape survivor. It's a powerful TV moment. And, for the record, we're the only ones who got it on tape."

Maureen sounded so proud about that, Griffin could only stare at her. Waters must've been doing the same, because after a second, Maureen snorted and waved her hand at both of them. "Oh, come on. You're big boys, you've been around the block. You know how this game is played."

"You're telling us," Griffin said slowly, "that you think Carol Rosen killed Eddie Como. And you believe this, because you happened to catch a moment on camera, when she was experiencing abject terror?"

Maureen narrowed her eyes. "Do you know what he did to her, Griffin? Have you read the police report from that attack? My God, when Eddie Como was done, Carol Rosen couldn't walk for five days. Jillian Hayes may have lost her sister. Meg Pesaturo may have lost her memory. But from what I've seen, Carol Rosen's pretty much lost her *mind*. I'd kill someone for doing that to me. Wouldn't you?"

It was a loaded question and they all knew it. Griffin didn't say anything. After another moment, Maureen impatiently shook her head.

"Look, we both know what you're going to do next. You're going to find the three victims. You're going to ask which one pulled the trigger. And the minute one of them so much as blinks, you're going to haul her ass to jail. So don't lecture me about compassion, Sergeant. This is a game. And you wouldn't have come back if you hadn't missed playing it."

"Poor me," Griffin murmured.

Maureen shook her head again. "No. Poor Carol Rosen."

7
Carol

She is watching The Ten O'Clock News *on Fox. Her eyes keep drifting shut. An early riser, she has been up since five, and ten o'clock is pushing things a bit. She should turn off the TV. She should go to bed.*

The house is big and silent. The grandfather clock has finished tolling in the foyer, but she can still feel the deep vibrations working their way through the nooks and crannies of her hundred-fifty-year-old Victorian home. There had been a time when she had found that sound comforting. When she had run her hand up the gleaming cherry banister of the central staircase with pride. When she had sought out each tiny room in the attic, in the old wood-shingled tower, like a hunter in search of treasure.

Those days are gone now. More and more she looks at this house she has so painstakingly refurbished and sees her own prison.

"Must you always work so late?" she has asked her husband, Dan.

"Jesus Christ, Carol, someone has to pay for all this. New plumbing isn't exactly cheap, you know."

She doesn't remember him being like this in the beginning. He's the one who actually found the house, who came running through the door of their rental one afternoon and announced excitedly that he'd just seen their future home. An East Side address is a big step up. This is where the great families of Providence once lived. The bankers, the shipping magnates, the jewelry manufacturers. Dan used to talk about one day having a Benefit Street address, but there is no way they could afford those huge, well-pedigreed homes.

This house, however – old, neglected, tragically subdivided into rental units – was different. The purchase price was cheap. The long-term obligation, on the other hand . . .

To be honest, Carol had fallen in love with the home, too. The three-story turret, the wraparound porch, the exquisite gingerbread trim. Yes, it needed a new roof, new wiring, new plumbing. It needed new walls torn down and old walls built back up. It needed carpentry work, it needed masonry work. It needed power washing, it needed sanding, it needed painting.

It needed them. That's what she had thought in the beginning. It needed a nice, young, upwardly mobile couple, with growing financial resources, and lots of tender loving care. They would slowly but surely restore this home to its former glory. And they would fill its five bedrooms with a new generation of happy, bouncing children. That's what old homes need, you know. Not just new wiring, but a fresh injection of life.

They had been so hopeful in those days. Dan's law practice was growing and while she was currently working as his legal secretary, they were certain it was only a matter of time before she'd be a stay-at-home mom with two-point-two children, and what the hell, an extremely well-mannered small dog.

Carol rises off the sofa now. She turns off the TV. She listens to the silence, the absolute, total silence of a four-thousand-square-foot home that remains too empty. And she thinks about how much she hates this sound.

"Jesus Christ, Carol, someone has to pay for all this . . ."

Upstairs, the air is hot and stuffy. The temperature hit almost ninety today, freakish for this early in May but that's New England for you. If you don't like the weather, just wait a minute. Unfortunately, the house has no air-conditioning and the bedroom is unbearably warm. Carol opens a window to cool the room. She can still arm the security system with a window open, but that involves lining up the window connector with the second set higher on the windowsill to complete the circuit. The security company is proud of this innovation. Carol, however, thinks it's stupid. If she lines up the connectors, she can only open the window three inches, which doesn't give her much of a breeze. She needs cooler air to sleep; she opens the window all the way.

It's 10:08, after all. Dan will be home soon.

She strips off her clothes without turning on the light. Outside she can hear cars going by, plus the distant murmur of voices. Lots of college students live in this area, and it seems to Carol that they never sleep.

Carol pulls the down comforter to the foot of the bed. Clad in a silky pink nightgown, she finally slides between the sheets. She sighs, the three-hundred-forty-thread-count cotton cool against her skin.

In a minute, she is asleep.

A sound wakes her. She doesn't know what. She blinks her eyes, disoriented, then sees a figure at the foot of her bed.

"Dan?" she murmurs sleepily. "What time is it, honey?"

The figure doesn't say anything.

"Dan?" she asks again.

And then, suddenly, she knows.

Carol scrambles out of bed. She makes it two feet, then the man grabs her by the hair. Her neck snaps back. She cries out, but the sound is muffled, choked, not at all like her. Scream, she thinks. Scream!

But she can't. Her throat won't work. There is not enough spit in her mouth. All that comes out is a gasp.

As the man pulls her by her hair, back to the bed.

Dan, she is thinking. DAN!

The man throws her down on the bed. She tries kicking out her feet, but somehow he has her ankles in his hand. Frantically, she beats at his head, but her futile efforts don't seem to bother him at all. Then he draws back his other hand. He smacks it across her face.

Her head whips to the side. Her cheekbone explodes, her eye wells up. Before she can recover, he smacks her again.

Her lip splits. She tastes the salt of her own blood as tears roll down her face.

He has something looped around her wrist. She tries to yank her arm back, but the sudden motion only snaps the tourniquet into her flesh. Then he is straddling her body, and though she is sure she is struggling, she must be struggling, he has her hands, then her feet, tied to her wrought-iron bedposts.

She is crying openly now, horrible, heaving sobs. Her body strains against the ties. She twists, she heaves. But she can't do anything. She is caught, her shoulders aching, her legs spread wide, revealing . . . everything.

She is vulnerable. She is helpless. And even as she begs, she knows what he will do next.

Abruptly, he unrolls a strip of material and forces it into her mouth as a gag. Latex, her shocked brain registers. He has bound her with strips of latex, the tough, rubbery substance pinching her skin.

A fresh strip over her eyes. She can't see what will happen next, and that makes it even worse.

Her nightgown yanked from her body. The clink of metal in the silent room as he unfastens his belt. The rasp of metal as he undoes his zipper. Then the soft thud of his pants hitting the floor, his heavy breathing as he comes closer and closer . . .

The bed sagging, his weight descending . . .

Dan, please Dan . . .

And then the man's hand, suddenly, brutally snapping around her neck.

She does not clearly recall the things that come next.

She retreats somewhere inside herself. The room is a black void, a place where someone else, a mannequin, a Barbie doll, an unfeeling woman, exists. She is a tiny, tiny girl, curled up in her head, where her arms are wrapped tight around her bent knees and she is whispering over and over again, "Dan, Dan, Dan."

Then the weight is gone. It takes her a moment to notice. She feels his hands at her ankles. The right noose goes. Then the left. The blood flow has been cut off. She can no longer feel her feet.

He moves up the bed. Her left hand sags free. Then her right.

Her body is beaten and tired and sore. She can't think. She can't move. But it's over, she tells herself, and feels the beginning of hysteria. It's over and she is still alive!

Then the man flips her over. Then the man climbs back on the bed. Then the man does stuff she has only ever read about, and this time she is sure she is screaming. She is screaming, screaming, screaming.

But the gag is in her mouth. The mattress absorbs the sound.

She is screaming and nobody hears a sound.

Time is gone. Reality has suspended. Her eyes glaze over. Saliva pools around the gag and drips onto her lovely Egyptian cotton sheets.

When he is finally done, she is beyond noticing, beyond caring. The man comes back. Sticks something in her unmoving body. Cold liquid gushes everywhere.

He rolls her back over, renews the ties at her hands and feet, then stares down at her face. Finally, almost tenderly, he reaches down and pulls the gag from her mouth.

"It's over," he whispers. "Go ahead and scream. Call your neighbors. Call the police."

The man disappears out her open window. At last, she is alone.

Carol does not scream. She is tied naked and spread-eagle to her own bed. She will not call out for her neighbors. She will not call out for the police. The man knew that, and now so does she.

She lies there instead, feeling the moisture run down her thighs. She lies there, with another man's semen running down her legs and she waits . . .

She waits for her husband to finally come home.

Six A.M. Monday morning, Carol Rosen prepared for her day. The day. Dan was already gone. He claimed that he

69

wanted to get to work early so he could take the afternoon off if she was called to testify. They both knew that he lied. The state prosecutor, Ned D'Amato, has assured them that nothing happens the opening day of trial. The defense uses up the morning with last-minute motions to dismiss, then jury selection takes up the afternoon.

But Dan had insisted. You never know, he said. You never know.

Dan now came home by seven most nights. But even when he was here, he was gone, and it seemed to Carol that he got up earlier all the time. As if by five in the morning, he could no longer stand being alone with her in this house.

Carol hated him for that. But maybe she hated the house even more.

She went upstairs, showered forever with the curtain open, the bathroom door open. She needed lots of space these days. Had to see what was coming. Had to know where she'd been. The security system was always on. She had not turned off the TV in ten months. More often than not, she slept on the sofa in front of its babbling voices and multicolored screen.

After showering, she took out her new butter-cream suit. Dan didn't know about the suit yet. Lately, he'd been obsessed with money. Last month, she'd overheard him liquidating their brokerage account. She hadn't said anything; neither had he.

It was odd. In some ways he was more attentive than ever. Coming home for dinner, asking her what she needed. Right after that night, when she'd still been in the hospital, he had stayed glued to her side. Four days, four nights, probably the most time they'd spent together since their honeymoon ten years before.

When she had finally returned home, he'd already moved them into a different bedroom, one of the round turret rooms far from the scene of the attack. He had bought a new bed, new mattress, new sheets. He'd had elaborate, wrought-iron bars placed over each window.

She had taken one look at the round, shuttered room and

collapsed in a fresh wave of tears. He had held her awkwardly, patting her back, though it was difficult for him to touch her and difficult for her to be touched. He didn't understand her despair, and she couldn't explain it.

For a week, he brought her a fresh bouquet of flowers each night and takeout from her favorite restaurants. Guilt, she decided, smelled like red roses and veal piccata.

The house held a deeper silence now. Dan didn't hear it, but she did.

Carol put on her suit. She stood in front of the mirror and gazed at the woman reflected there.

Most days, she still did not feel like she belonged to herself. That woman with the high cheekbones and stubborn chin could not be her. That woman with the pearl drop earrings and Chanel suit looked like she should be at a garden party, or a museum opening. Or perhaps another social sponsored by the Providence Preservation Society. In other words, the things that Carol used to do.

That woman in the mirror looked too normal to be her.

She took off the suit. When the hour was more civilized, say 7:00 A.M., she would call Jillian and ask her what she was going to wear. Jillian was the expert on these things. She always looked cool, calm, composed. Even at her sister's funeral, she had seemed to know exactly what to say and do.

Now, Carol put on a pair of gray sweatpants and a baggy T-shirt. Then she went downstairs to the gourmet kitchen, where at six-thirty in the morning, she got out a pint of Ben & Jerry's Chunky Monkey ice cream. The morning news anchor babbled away in the family room. The grandfather clock sounded the half-hour gong in the foyer.

Six-thirty Monday morning. The Monday morning.

Carol Rosen looked down at her wrists, pale, delicate and still marred by faint white scars. She looked around her kitchen, with its cherry cabinets and marble countertops, still so goddamn empty. And she thought about her body, her supposedly beautiful, supposedly attractive body that now hadn't been touched in nearly a year. And then she was

71

glad for today. She was extremely happy for today. She couldn't fucking wait for today!

"It's still too good for you, you son of a bitch!" she exclaimed hoarsely in the silent room.

Then Carol put her head in her hands and wept.

8

Fitz

Griffin and Waters exited the World War Memorial Park in time to spot Lieutenant Morelli, Captain Dodge and Major Walsh huddled together in the middle of the crowd of illegally parked police cars. Lieutenant Morelli looked up, caught their eye and hastily waved them over.

"Oh boy," Waters said. Lieutenant Morelli's appearance was hardly unusual. The lieutenant of the Major Crimes Unit in the Detective Bureau, she generally attended a new crime scene if it involved a homicide. The detective commander, Captain Dodge, also wasn't too unexpected. He generally appeared if the case was considered high profile. The arrival of the Major of Field Operations, Major Walsh, the number-two man in the organization, aka the Boss, on the other hand, signified big-guns time. Headline case. High-pressure stakes. The kind of investigation that makes careers or breaks careers. The last time Waters and Griffin had seen this much brass at a crime scene . . .

Waters went back to studiously avoiding Griffin's fist. Griffin went back to pointedly not looking at Waters's nose.

"Major," Griffin said, clicking his heels together and rendering the proper salute. "Captain. Lieutenant." He saluted them, too, then waited as Waters did the same. Waters only saluted the major and captain, however, as he'd already officially greeted Lieutenant Morelli earlier in the day.

"Do we have a description of the shooter yet?" the major asked immediately. He was looking photo-op ready, decked out in a sharply pressed Rhode Island trooper's uniform. The dark gray fabric was edged with deep red piping, and a buff-colored Stetson was pulled low to the ridge of his brow, while dark brown boots were laced up to his knees. Best damn uniform in the nation. Just ask Letterman.

Waters did the honors of holding up the evidence bag. "Better. We have video footage of the sniper, courtesy of News Team Ten. Shows everything down to the nervous tic on the shooter's face."

"Outstanding. Let's deliver this to the crime lab ASAP. Get the tape developed, and print out a visual of the shooter's face to be distributed to all uniforms, Detective." The major looked at Waters expectantly.

"Yes, sir," Waters said crisply, already turning away. Waters was no dummy. A uniform could just as easily serve as evidence courier to the crime lab. The powers-that-be obviously wanted to speak with Griffin alone.

The minute Waters was out of earshot, the major, captain and lieutenant turned their attention to Griffin.

"Sergeant," the major said.

"Yes, sir," Griffin said. In spite of himself, he could feel his stomach tense, as if steeling for a blow.

"You look good," the major said.

"Thank you, sir."

"Assessment?"

"What?" For a moment, he was confused. *My anxiety is operating within normal parameters. No. Wait. Ah, shit.*

"The situation, Sergeant. Tell me what you think."

Griffin's shoulders came down. His stomach unclenched. Talking about the job, he could finally relax. "Professional hit. Shooter camps out on the courthouse roof. Nails his target, Eddie Como, aka the College Hill Rapist, as he exits the ACI van shortly after 8.30 this morning. Shooter then returns to his car to make a quick getaway, except his client left him one last payment in the form of a bomb."

"Confirmation from the state fire marshal?"

"No, sir. My understanding is that the scene is too hot to approach. It will probably be another hour or so."

"But you're sure the shooter is DOA?"

Griffin shrugged. "We know we have one DOA in the

RISD parking lot. Given that the parking lot explosion happened within ten minutes of the shooting, I think it's a safe bet that the two incidents are related. Now, one possibility is that our shooter actually performed two hits – the first being Eddie Como, the second being some unidentified person in the parking lot. But in my opinion, that's a low probability scenario. For one thing, it's uncommon to change MO's – going from sniper to explosives expert. For another, we know the shooter left his assault rifle and a full magazine of two-twenty-threes up on the roof. Why leave the gun if he still had work to do? No, I think it's more probable that the sniper felt he'd completed his task, abandoned his tools in order to make a clean getaway, then ran into an unexpected complication when he got into his car. Ergo, the shooter is now one extracrispy DOA."

The major grunted. Lieutenant Morelli suppressed a smile.

"Next steps?" Captain Dodge spoke up. Griffin turned his attention toward him, forcing himself to remain patient even though he was being grilled like an FNG, a fucking new guy.

"Assuming it's a professional," Griffin said briskly, "we need to identify the shooter, establish that he did kill Eddie Como – which will be pretty easy thanks to the videotape – then find a connection between the shooter and his client. Identifying the shooter shouldn't be too hard. We have a visual of his face. The state fire marshal will retrieve the VIN of his car. The ME will get prints. Bada-bing, bada-boom."

"But that could take days," the captain said pointedly. His gaze swept toward the park, where the media churned up the grass and strained against the police barricades.

"Well then, consider this. The RISD parking lot. It's permit only, right? And we know the shooter must have been parked there for a while, because he was camped out on the roof. Assuming he didn't want to call attention to himself by getting a parking ticket, or worse, lose his getaway by being towed, that means he probably had a parking pass. We contact RISD, obtain a list of names, run the names through the system and get a big head start on names to go with the face."

"Not bad," the captain said.

"Cross-reference the names of people with RISD parking passes, with the rape victims and families," Griffin added.

"Even better," the major concurred.

Griffin, however, had started to frown.

"Uh-oh," Lieutenant Morelli said. "I know that look."

"Ah, I don't know . . ."

"Humor us, Sergeant. At the rate things are going, we could use a good laugh today."

Griffin had to think it through. "We're getting a long list of assumptions here. Assumption one is that we have a sniper hired to kill alleged College Hill Rapist, Eddie Como. Assumption two is that the obvious motive for hiring the shooter is revenge, meaning the obvious suspects are the rape vics and/or their families. The only good rapist is a dead rapist, etc., etc. But how many vengeance cases do you know that involve a hired gun? Your typical distraught father, irate husband, shattered victim, they show up at the courthouse, pull out the family pistol and take care of business up close and personal. They're not concerned with getting caught or covering their tracks. They're obsessed with revenge. They're angry, mad, sad. It's an emotional act. A hired assassin on the other hand . . . That's pretty cold."

"It's been a while," the lieutenant said. "Maybe the person's had time to calm down."

"Which would be my second problem," Griffin said immediately. "It's been what, a year since the attacks? Sounds to me like the vics have been doing pretty well. They formed some sort of survivors club, took their mission to the press, became activists. By all accounts, Eddie Como's arrest was a victory for them. And now they're in the homestretch. The actual trial's about to start. Two weeks from now it would end, and most likely Como would be sentenced to life behind bars once and for all. The women, their Survivors Club, whatever, would have justice. Now, it would be one thing if there was doubt about the outcome of the trial, but from what I've heard they had Como dead to rights – DNA evidence."

"They had DNA on O.J., too," the captain spoke up dryly.

"But Como isn't packing the legal dream team. We're talking public defender. In other words, this kid was toast and we're a mere two weeks from his public toasting. So why shoot him now? If you're really angry, and you want to spare yourself or your loved one the agony of the criminal justice system, shouldn't you have shot Eddie Como when he was collared one year ago?"

"Better late than never?"

"Yeah, I suppose." Griffin was still frowning. "I don't know. A rooftop sniper is cold. Calculated. It feels wrong."

"How much do you know about the Como case?" the major asked.

"Not much," Griffin answered honestly. He looked the major in the eye. "I took a break from watching TV."

"And now?"

"I can watch a little telly. I doubt I'll have the time in the foreseeable future, but I can watch."

"Good," the major said brusquely. He cleared his throat. "So, Providence wants in on the case."

"No kidding."

"Como's their catch. They know him, the rape case, and the victims the best."

"Yeah, well, if they know everyone so well, how did 'their catch' just wind up dead?"

Lieutenant Morelli was biting back another smile. She stopped looking at Griffin, and made a big show of examining her shoes.

"We're going to need their cooperation," the major was saying, "to get information on the explosion. Specifically, Providence would like the lead investigator of the College Hill Rapist case to join our case team looking into the shooting."

"Who was the lead investigator on the rape case?" Griffin narrowed his eyes suspiciously.

"Detective Joseph Fitzpatrick from Sex Crimes."

"Ah, nuts." Griffin only knew Detective "Fitz" Fitzpatrick by reputation, but by reputation, Fitz was a third-generation Providence cop who didn't care much for Rhode Island's Detective Bureau. According to him (as well as some other members of the PPD), the state should stick to doing what it did best – patrolling the highways – while the city cops did what they did best – investigating real crimes.

"Can't we just copy them on our reports?" Griffin asked, already feeling cranky.

"No. Besides, you're going to need to interview the victims next, and Detective Fitzpatrick has a relationship with them that could be quite useful. Plus, he's been in on the Como case since the first attack. He can bring you up to speed."

"Shouldn't he be bringing the primary case officer up to speed?"

The major smiled at him. "Exactly."

"We assume that's all right with you," Lieutenant Morelli spoke up. She gazed at him intently now. The major and the captain did the same. This was it. The closest anyone would come to asking the real question. Griffin understood. Last week, he had passed the fitness-for-duty diagnostic. According to rules and regs, he was back in. That was the system and everyone would honor it. If he was wrong, however, if he wasn't ready, if he couldn't do this job with the full attention and diligence it deserved, it was on Griffin to bring it up. Speak now or forever hold your peace, as the saying went.

"Where do I find Providence's best and brightest?" Griffin asked Morelli.

"Over at the parking lot, mopping up smoke."

"Anything else I should know?"

"The AG doesn't like having a homicide in his backyard. Oh, and the mayor feels major explosions are bad for tourism."

"In other words, no pressure?"

Morelli, the captain and the major all smiled at him. "You got it."

Griffin raised a dubious brow. He nodded his good-bye, then walked down the block toward the smoking parking lot, passing in front of the press again and inspiring a fresh round of screaming questions. For a moment, he got to feel like a rock star, and the adrenaline went straight to his brain. Lead investigator. The thrill of the hunt, the excitement of the chase. Oh, yeah. He did a little two-step, caught the motion, decided maybe he was crazy and felt the best he had all year.

Hot damn, whoever would've thought a high-profile assassination would be just what Sergeant Psycho needed?

Arriving at the smoldering parking lot, he immediately spotted Detective Fitzpatrick in one corner. The heavyset Providence cop wore an ill-fitting gray suit over a pale blue shirt and 1980s navy blue tie. He looked like he was taking fashion direction from *NYPD Blue*, down to his palette of thinning brown hair. Judging by what Griffin had heard, Fitz was a detective from the "old school." Ate doughnuts for breakfast and informants for lunch. Spent his after-hours down at the seedy FOP club in Olneyville, drinking Killians. Not a lot of guys like that around anymore. The new breed of cop was too health-conscious for doughnuts, and too fitness-oriented to go anyplace after work other than the gym. Times were changing, even in law enforcement. Griffin doubted Fitz liked those changes much.

And then suddenly, out of the blue, Griffin missed his wife. He shook his head, wishing he could control his own emotions better and even more frightened that someday he would. Cindy had been fascinated by police work. An engineer herself, she had a wonderfully analytic mind. She'd go over tough cases with him, fretting over pieces of the puzzle, helping him hammer out riddles. She'd love a case like this one. She'd want to know all about Eddie Como, his victims, the hired gun. Frankly, the thought of a female victim turning on her attacker probably would've thrilled her to death. Why settle for simple castration if you could kill the man instead?

Cindy hadn't exactly been a damsel-in-distress kind of girl.

Then, as still happened too often these days, Griffin's thoughts turned. He stopped thinking about Cindy. He started thinking about David. And his fists clenched reflexively while a muscle leapt in his jaw. The tension was there again. Would be for a long time. It was his job now to manage it, to learn better coping skills. Like going running. Like finding a punching bag. Like seeing how many rounds he could go before he finally took the edge off his rage.

A week after the Big Boom, before he understood it was the Big Boom, his brother had come looking for him and found him out in his garage still working the heavy bag. His hands were bleeding. Giant blisters had welled up and burst on his feet. He was still going at it, four fingers broken and the buzzing worse than ever in his head. Frank had had to wrestle him to the ground. It cost him two black eyes and a swollen lip.

Griffin had collapsed shortly thereafter. He had not eaten or slept in over five days. He had a last impression of Frank standing over him. Frank looking at Griffin's bloody hands. Frank with tears on his cheeks.

He had made his older brother cry. He remembered being stunned, being appalled, being ashamed. And then he'd sunk, down, down, down into the great black abyss. He'd sunk down, down, down, whispering his dead wife's name.

Griffin turned away from the parking lot. He didn't want to approach Fitz in this kind of mood, so he practiced his even-breathing techniques while locating the state fire marshal. An ATF agent was standing next to the marshal, a two-for-one sale in information shopping.

"Marshal." Griffin shook the man's hand, then waited a moment as Marshal Grayson introduced him to Special Agent Neilson from ATF. More handshaking and head bobbing. Both the fire marshal and the ATF agent had faces smeared with black soot and sweat. The men looked at once tired and angry, so Bentley had been right about the DOA.

"I heard you were back," Grayson commented.

"Can't fish forever," Griffin said.

Grayson smiled thinly. "On a day like this, I wouldn't mind trying. No, on a day like this I wouldn't mind trying at all."

All three men turned toward the smoking ruins. "What can you tell me?" Griffin asked.

"Not much yet. We're just now getting into the scene."

"One dead?"

"One dead."

"Cause of the explosion?"

The marshal nodded his head toward the pile of five vehicles. "See how the one to the left is almost entirely burnt out? Upholstery's gone, all six windows are blown? That would be the primary scene of the explosion. The other cars bear peripheral damage."

"But that car is off to one side."

"The force of the explosion lifted the vehicle up and carried it through the air. Whoever did this wasn't fooling around."

"So we're talking a car bomb."

"The scene is consistent with some sort of incendiary device. More than that, I don't know yet. The thing about an explosion of this size and nature is that it sets off secondary explosions as well. Several gas tanks went, so we have burn patterns consistent with the use of an accelerant. The seat on the driver's side bears shrapnel, which could either be from a packed pipe bomb, or be fragments from the site of the main explosion, gas tanks, etc. Until I have a chance to take it all apart and put it back together, I won't know what's what."

"I'm going to need to know what kind of bomb," Griffin said. "Are we talking a sophisticated device, something that uses unusual parts, or is it a homemade concoction even a Boy Scout could whip up out in the garage? Oh, and is there a timer, etc.?"

Grayson gave him a look. "When I'm done, Sergeant, you'll know exactly what kind of wires were used to build this baby and if those wires came from a spool used in wiring any other bombs in the United States. But you're not going to know that until I'm done, and I'm not going to be done with this for at least a week or ten days."

"I'm told that the AG doesn't like a homicide in his back-yard and that the mayor feels explosions are bad for tourism," Griffin said. "Just so you know."

The state fire marshal sighed. "I gotta get a new job," he muttered. "Or a new pacemaker. All right. Give me five days. I'll try to have something for you then."

Detective Fitzpatrick chose that opportunity to walk over. "Sergeant Griffin?"

"Detective." Griffin held out his hand. Fitz accepted the handshake, and for the next few seconds they both amused themselves by squeezing too hard. Neither one of them blinked. Having set the tone, they excused themselves from the state fire marshal and walked off to one corner where they could eye each other for weakness in peace.

"Any news on the shooter?" Fitz asked.

"He liked Fig Newtons. Any news on the identity of the owner of the vehicle?"

"It's a rental."

"Ran the VIN?"

"Looked at the plate. Do you have a description?"

"We have several. Where's the body?"

"At the morgue. You got the weapon?"

"We got a rifle. Can the ME get prints?"

"Ask the ME. Got a name?"

"No. But we're guessing he had a RISD parking permit."

Fitz grunted. His breathing had accelerated. So had Griffin's. "These free flows of information are very help-ful," Fitz said. He ran a hand through his thinning hair, then chewed on a toothpick dangling from the corner of his mouth.

"That's what I always think."

"You got a body," Fitz said after another moment. "I got a body. Now what we both need is a link."

"That sums it up."

"You're thinking the women or their families."

"I would like to talk to the women and their families."

"I know these women," Fitz said seriously.

"Okay."

"I've spent a year interviewing them, reassuring them, preparing them for today. You know what that's like."

"I still get some Christmas cards."

"Then you understand why I want to take the lead in questioning them."

"You can start," Griffin said, a phrase that didn't fool either of them.

Fitz narrowed his eyes. He opened his mouth, started to say something harsh, then seemed to think better of it. He shut his trap. He regarded Griffin stonily.

Rhode Island law enforcement was a small, incestuous community, much like the rest of the state. Everyone knew everyone, promoted each other's brother, gave other family members a break. Fitz had probably heard about Griffin, the basement, the Big Boom. He was probably now wondering how much of those stories was true. And he was probably wondering, looking at Griffin's thickly muscled chest and hard-planed face, if pushing Sergeant Psycho was really very safe.

At this stage of the game, Griffin didn't feel a need to comment either way.

Abruptly, Fitz shrugged. "All right. Let's go speak to the women."

"They're all together?"

"Yep."

"A Survivors Club meeting?" Griffin guessed.

"So you've heard."

"I understand they have a penchant for press conferences."

"They take a hands-on approach," Fitz said. Far from sounding bitter, however, the older detective merely shrugged. "Last year, they're the ones who identified the key break in the case. In all honesty, without the Survivors Club, I'm not sure we ever would've nailed Eddie Como."

9

The Survivors Club

"Jillian Hayes is the de facto leader of the group," Fitz explained as he drove through the maze of narrow one-way streets that comprised East Side Providence. "Her sister was the third rape victim, a nineteen-year-old sophomore at Brown. She died during the attack of an anaphylactic reaction to latex."

"I thought the victims were blood donors."

Fitz slid him a sideways glance, obviously surprised Griffin knew that much. "One link discovered in the course of the investigation was that both the first victim, Meg Pesaturo, and the third victim, Trisha Hayes, had donated at campus blood drives in the weeks prior to the attacks."

"So Trisha Hayes gave blood, even though she was allergic to latex?"

"Sure. According to Kathy Hammond, the phlebotomist who assisted Miss Hayes, Trisha informed her that she was latex-sensitive and Mrs. Hammond switched to vinyl gloves, following the Rhode Island Blood Center's policy and procedures. Latex allergies are becoming more common, you know. Most hospitals, blood-donor centers, visiting nurse associations, etc., stock other kinds of gloves as well."

"Do they note latex-sensitivity on the blood-donor card?"

Fitz understood where Griffin was going with this and regretfully shook his head. "No. Too bad, too. If we could've proven that Como had prior knowledge of Miss Hayes's allergy, we could've gone after him for murder.

Instead, we had to settle for manslaughter."

"Too bad," Griffin agreed. He glanced idly at the side-view mirror, caught a glimpse of white and narrowed his eyes for closer scrutiny just as Fitz lurched the car forward.

"So," Fitz was saying. "Jillian Hayes was supposed to meet her younger sister at seven for dinner, but was running late. She showed up around eight, entered the basement apartment and was promptly jumped from behind. Eddie beat the living shit out of her. Choked her with his bare hands. God knows how far he would've gone, except an upstairs neighbor was alerted by the noise and called the police. Eddie took off at the sound of sirens. Jillian dragged herself over to the bed, where she found her sister's body tied up with latex tourniquets."

"That was his signature?"

"Yep, latex tourniquets, all three victims. He used ten ties, one for a gag, one for a blindfold, then two each for the wrists and ankles, forming a double noose that actually grew tighter when the victim struggled. If they relaxed, on the other hand . . . Let's just say Eddie had a keen sense of irony."

"I assume after the neighbor's call, uniforms responded from all over and immediately canvassed the neighborhood. They never stumbled across a guy running from the scene?"

"Nope. But to be fair to the uniforms, we had no description. The only victim who caught a glimpse of the attacker was number two, Carol Rosen, and she says her room was too dark to get a good look. The first girl, Meg Pesaturo, doesn't even remember the attack, so she couldn't help. Trisha Hayes may have seen Eddie, but she never regained consciousness to give a statement. And her sister, Jillian, was attacked in a gloomy basement apartment, so she couldn't provide any details either. In other words, sure, we poured all sorts of manpower into the streets that night, but Eddie either holed up, or played it cool. No one ever stopped him."

"Eddie Como sounds either very lucky or very smart," Griffin muttered. He turned to Fitz. "Hey, see that white van four vehicles back? You know, the one with the satellite dish up top."

Fitz glanced in the rearview mirror. "Yep."

"I'm thinking that's the Channel Ten News van."

Fitz studied it for a moment. "Oooooh," he drawled. "I think you're right. Bringing your admirers with you, Sergeant Griffin?"

"Oh, I don't think it's me they're admiring. You were the one who led the College Hill Rapist case. Ergo, you're the one most likely to know where to find the women."

"Ah shit. Little bloodsucking leeches. You'd think two corpses would be enough to keep them occupied. But no, you're probably right. They want to find one of the victims. Then they can stick a mike beneath her nose and say, 'Hey, Victim Number Two, your rapist was just splattered all over the sidewalk. What are you going to do now? Fly to Disneyland?' Fuck."

Without warning, Fitz flung the vehicle right. The Ford Taurus, technically the same vehicle Griffin drove but in Fitz's case considerably more abused, groaned in protest. Fitz ignored the creaking steering, shuddering shocks and his entire suspension system, gunning the engine as he shot up onto the curb, cut across the corner and landed hard on the cross street.

Griffin grabbed the dash for support, then glanced in the mirror. "Still got 'em."

"That's what you think." Fitz came to a narrow alleyway, jerked left, came to a parking lot, jerked right, then came back to a side street and shot left again. Impressive, Griffin thought. But then, like a great white shark, the van appeared again.

"Maureen, Maureen, Maureen," Griffin murmured. "Feeling a little vindictive over the loss of your videotape?"

"I'm not leading any fuckin' reporter to my women," Fitz growled. "No way, not on my watch."

Griffin took that as a hint to grab the handle protruding from the roof. Good thing. Fitz hit the sirens, shot through a red light without the customary tap on the brake and about plowed into a garbage truck. Apparently not one to sweat near misses, he merely accelerated faster, rocketed through another red light, hung a left, sped four blocks, then hung a right before finally ducking into a parking space between two cars.

"That's gotta do it," he said, breathing hard and fast. Both hands still gripped the wheel. He had a savage gleam in his eye.

For no reason at all, Griffin decided *not* to let go of the safety handle. "I don't see them anymore," he commented.

"Keep looking."

"Aye, aye, Kimosabe."

"I *hate* reporters," Fitz growled.

"Hey, isn't this *People* magazine?"

The magazine had slid out from underneath Griffin's seat. Fitz reached over, snatched it off the floor and flung it into the back.

"I know, I know," Griffin filled in for him. "You only buy it for the pictures."

"Not the pictures," Fitz said grumpily. "The cross-word."

They waited a few more minutes. When the news van still hadn't appeared, Fitz slowly pulled back into the street. Traffic was light here, the neighborhood quiet. In the good news department, they had left most of the madness of the downtown scene behind. In the bad news department, it would take them that much longer to get to their destination. Ah well. Quality time for bonding, Griffin was sure. He flexed his biceps, then rolled his neck.

"Now, where were we?" Fitz asked, finally relaxing at the wheel and picking up the threads of their earlier conversation.

"One amnesic victim, two others who couldn't see the rapist in the dark," Griffin cued up. He turned toward Fitz curiously. "If you never had a physical description, how did you determine it was Como?"

"We didn't right away. You have to understand, this wasn't your typical investigation of a serial crime. Our first victim, Meg, was no help at all thanks to trauma-induced amnesia. She doesn't recall the attack, the day of the attack, or for that matter most of her life leading up to the attack – "

"Most of her life?" Griffin interrupted, baffled. "I thought trauma-induced amnesia was forgetting the trauma. How did she leap from blanking one bad night to blanking her whole entire life?"

Fitz shrugged. "How the hell do I know? Maybe Meg didn't like her whole life and this provided a good opportunity. Maybe her brain doesn't like to differentiate. Beats me. But her doctor swears her amnesia is legit, her parents say her amnesia is legit and she seems to think her amnesia is legit. God knows I've interviewed Meg about two dozen times over the last year and she hasn't slipped up yet. So if she's faking it, she's a damn good actress."

"Huh," Griffin said.

"Huh," Fitz agreed. "Either way, Meg's condition made investigating the initial rape complaint difficult. We tried her roommate, Vickie, but all she knew was that when she came home at two A.M., Meg was mysteriously bound to her bed. Then we turned to trace evidence, which was equally unenlightening – no tool marks, no hair, no fiber, no fingerprints. In fact, at the end of attack number one, all we had was one confused college coed, one traumatized roommate, ten strips of latex and one DNA sample that yielded no hits in the sex-offenders database."

"You follow up on the latex?"

"Of course I followed up on the latex. Only damn lead I had. I made the lab analyze chemical compositions, do brand comparisons, batch comparisons, look at the amount of latex powder used on each strip. Frankly, I learned way too fucking much about latex. And none of it did us any good. The way it's manufactured, there is no way to narrow down a batch or shipment number based on a handful of strips. Three weeks after the first attack, we had hit the wall. Case was dead, dead, and deader."

"Oh yeah? What did Meg's Uncle Vinnie have to say about that?"

Fitz promptly laughed. "So you've heard about him. Uncle Vinnie's a funny guy. He came to my office one day. Wanted to know if I was holding back any information from the family. For example, I might already have a name in mind. And for instance, if I already had a name in mind, then he might have a name in mind, and his name might be able to take care of my name, without any taxpayer expense."

"In his own way, Vinnie's a helpful guy."

"Yeah," Fitz agreed, then promptly sighed. "We probably need to pay Uncle Vinnie a visit. In all honesty, I didn't think of him as an advocate of sharpshooting. Rooftop snipers and courthouse assassinations attract a lot of attention, and I don't think Uncle Vinnie likes to attract attention. Personally, I was betting that someday, Eddie would enter the prison showers and suffer a little incident. You know, one involving someone else's prison shank and Eddie's liver. But hey, live and learn."

"Live and learn," Griffin agreed. He returned to the initial string of rapes, still trying to get a sense of that investigation and how they'd gone from one victim with amnesia to an arrest two months later. "Okay," he said. "So after the first rape, you didn't have Eddie Como in mind. You didn't have anyone in mind."

"After the first rape, we were chasing our tails. We went through the drill. Looked at past boyfriends, rattled the sex-offender tree – who had been recently released from the ACI, who might live in the area, etc., etc. Frankly, Meg didn't date much, and all the known perverts were doing other perversions at the time. Probably watching *Sex and the City* on HBO. None of them go out as much now that they have cable."

"But then came the attack on the East Side."

"Right. Four weeks after the Pesaturo rape came the attack on the East Side."

"Quite a different neighborhood," Griffin observed.

"It's also a college area," Fitz said, but then shook his head. "Yeah, attack number two had some key differences.

89

Carol Rosen's a forty-two-year-old housewife, not a college coed. She lives with her husband in an old Victorian house, which isn't exactly the same as a college apartment. Finally, and this is probably the most significant difference, the level of violence was way up. According to the sexual assault nurse, Meg Pesaturo suffered only vaginal penetration, with minor lacerations on her wrists, ankles and mouth from the tourniquets. No sign of beating, and more importantly, no bruising around her throat. With Meg, Eddie apparently got in, got it done and got out.

"Carol Rosen, on the other hand, suffered vaginal and anal penetration. She had bruises on her breasts and buttocks, multiple contusions on her face, multiple lacerations on the inside of her thighs, plus he started flirting with asphyxiation, squeezing her throat so hard he left bruises from his fingertips. He also tied her up so tightly that she still has scars on her wrists and ankles. On a relative scale of things, Meg was lucky. Carol was not."

"But you're sure it's the same guy?"

"Ten latex strips," Fitz said. "One DNA sample. Oh yeah, it was Eddie again."

"And where was the husband through all this?"

"Dan Rosen works as an attorney, corporate stuff. He just opened his own practice a few years ago and keeps long hours. He didn't get home until after midnight, which was when he discovered his wife tied to their bed. We called in uniforms, we tried a canvass, but once again we had no description and once again we had no luck."

Griffin frowned. "Wait a minute. The first victim has a roommate who just happens to work that night, second victim has a husband who also happens to work late. Does this mean what I think it means?"

"We think he watched the victims beforehand," Fitz agreed. "He targeted them at the blood drives, then he spent some time doing his homework, hence the lapse of time between when he first saw them and when he attacked. Now, this theory works well when we look at Meg and Trish, who were blood donors. We get in trouble with Carol

Rosen, however, because she didn't actually participate in any blood drives. In her case, we think she was a last-minute substitute. A pretty brunette college student who fits Eddie's 'type' lived just one block away. She'd donated blood during the campus drive, and she remembers someone ringing the buzzer of her apartment that night. She wasn't expecting anyone, though, so she refused to open the door. Good news for her. Not so good for Carol."

"That doesn't explain the husband being gone," Griffin pressed.

"Hey, you think I have all the answers to life? Maybe in the course of watching the brunette, Eddie also noticed that Carol Rosen pretty much lived alone. Maybe he simply saw Carol's open bedroom window, conveniently located above the wraparound porch, and decided to go for it. He was hungry. He'd psyched himself up for a big meal and then lo and behold, he'd been denied service. Besides, Eddie was capable of lifting two hundred pounds. Climbing onto a porch overhang was probably nothing to him. And if the woman's husband was also at home . . . Eddie probably figured he could handle it. After all, it's late at night, and he's got a little bit of adrenaline firing through his veins . . ."

"Which he then took out on Mrs. Rosen. So maybe Como was very unhappy at having to change plans. Or maybe he was building to something more."

"Maybe." Fitz slanted Griffin a look. "Jillian Hayes was also beaten very badly. Not her sister, but then again, Jillian interrupted that party. I don't know. It seemed to me after Carol Rosen's attack that we had a sexual predator with a rapidly escalating penchant for violence. And I thought . . . I thought if we didn't catch the guy soon, we'd end up with someone dead. Unfortunately, that day came before even I expected. Eddie Como attacked Trisha Hayes just two weeks later. The guy took hardly any time off at all."

Griffin nodded grimly. "Too bad."

"Yeah," the Providence detective said gruffly. "Too bad."

"So how did you finally determine the perpetrator was Eddie Como?"

"Process of elimination. Once we homed in on the blood-donor angle, we got a list of names from the Rhode Island Blood Center of who worked the relevant blood drives. Lucky for us, the majority of phlebotomists are female. So once we focused on the males we were looking at only ten suspects. Then we started pushing." Fitz rattled off on his fingers. "One, Eddie had access to two of the victims' home addresses, plus plenty of latex tourniquets. Two, while Eddie's not the biggest guy you'll ever meet, he's shockingly strong. Used to be a champion wrestler in high school and still likes to work out with weights. Eddie is . . . was . . . five eight and one hundred fifty pounds, but he could bench-press over two hundred. Let's face it, that's someone with some muscle. Of course, once we got a DNA sample from him, that cinched it."

"How'd you get the sample?"

"We asked."

Griffin stared at him. "You asked, and he just gave it to you? No lawyering up? No pleading the fifth? No claiming illegal search and seizure?"

From behind the steering wheel, Fitz smiled. It was a predator's smile. "Let me tell you something else about the rapes that very few people know. Eddie thought he was smart. In fact, Eddie thought he was so smart that in fact he was dumb, but now I'm getting ahead of myself. See, Eddie had a book on forensics. Apparently, he'd bought it on-line and thought it made him a bit of an expert. He was pretty good at a lot of it. Three rapes later, we had no hair, no fiber, no fingerprints. Not even tool marks. We think he used social engineering, because in none of the attacks did we find any evidence of breaking and entering. So okay, the kid did all right. But he made one mistake."

"No condom?"

"No condom. He thought he had a better idea. Berkely and Johnson's Disposable Douche with Country Flowers."

"What?"

"Yeah, exactly. See, Eddie had been following the Motyka case – we found newspaper articles of that trial in his apartment. Do you remember the Motyka case?"

Griffin had to think about it. "Tiverton, right? Some handyman who had been doing work on a woman's house broke back in, raped her, murdered her, then put her body in a bathtub."

"Yeah. During the trial, the prosecutor argued that Motyka thought immersing the body in water would wash away the semen. Of course it didn't, they matched the sample to him, and now he's spending the rest of his life behind bars. Because semen goes *up* in the body. Because you need more than simple bathwater to wash it out."

"Something like a douche," Griffin filled in.

"That's what Eddie believed. But he wasn't thinking straight. Sure, a douche can wash out a lot of the semen, but it's just rinsing it onto the sheet. And when we process a rape case, we don't just collect samples from the victim, we also collect samples from the sheet. A couple of lab tests later . . ."

"So Como thinks he's come up with the perfect way of beating DNA, hence he's not worried about providing a sample, but oops, he's not so good after all."

Fitz nodded. "There you have it."

"That's not a bad plan," Griffin said honestly. "He have any priors?"

"Nope."

"History of violence with girlfriends?"

"Nope. In fact, his girlfriend was going to be the primary witness for the defense. She claims Eddie's really a kind-hearted, sensitive guy who wouldn't hurt a flea, plus she was with him the nights there were attacks."

"He had an alibi?" Griffin asked with surprise.

Fitz rolled his eyes. "No, he had a pregnant girlfriend who wasn't interested in the father of her child ending up behind bars. Trust me, we looked into it. We never found another witness who could corroborate seeing Eddie at home those nights. Plus, we still had the DNA. If Eddie was really watching *Who Wants to Be a Millionaire?*, then how did his DNA end up at not one, or two, but three crime scenes?"

Griffin bobbed his head from side to side. Fitz had a point. "So the big break came when you made the connection with the blood drives?"

"Yeah, pretty much."

Griffin narrowed his eyes. Okay, now he had it. "And this club, the Survivors Club, they helped you with that."

"Jillian Hayes knew her sister had donated two weeks before the attack. She mentioned it because of the latex strips. We went back to check, and sure enough, good ol' amnesiac Meg had also donated one month prior to being raped. That was the first link we had between the victims. And yeah, everything finally fell into place after that."

Fitz pulled the car over and parked next to the curb. "We're here," he said.

Griffin looked out the window. They had arrived at the rue de l'espoir, a chic little café on Hope Street. Cindy had liked rue de l'espoir. Griffin, on the other hand, preferred its next-door neighbor, Big Alice's, which served the city's best ice cream.

Fitz cut the engine. Now that they were here, he was back to looking uptight, a territorial detective claiming his turf. "Here are the ground rules," he announced. "As the youngest and quietest, Meg's the weakest member of the group. She also knows the least, so pressuring her doesn't do any good. Carol's the most prone to outbursts. I don't think she's dealing so well with the attack, and I get the impression it hasn't done wonders for her marriage. If we play our cards right, we might get something out of her. But here's the kicker. Jillian runs this show. She organized the group, she dictates the agenda. And she – if you'll pardon the phrase – has balls of steel. Piss her off, and the interview's done. She'll clam up, they'll clam up and we'll all end up wasting our time. So the name of the game is prodding just enough to make Carol say something before Jillian gets fed up and sends us packing."

"You're anticipating an antagonistic interview." Which was interesting, because Fitz supposedly had a rapport with these women. After a year of working their cases, he was their police guardian, protector, friend.

"I think these women won't be losing any sleep over Eddie Como's murder," Fitz said carefully. "And I think, even if they are *completely* innocent, they won't care for any investigation into the events surrounding his death. Eddie Como . . . he was scum. Now he's dead scum. How much are any of us supposed to care?"

"Do you think one of them hired the shooter?" Griffin asked bluntly.

Fitz sighed. "None of them are proficient with firearms," he said finally. "If they wanted Eddie dead, they would require outside help."

"But do you think they are *capable* of ordering a hit?"

Fitz hesitated again. "I think they're rape survivors. And as rape survivors, they are capable of many things they never thought of before."

"Even killing a man?"

"Wouldn't you? Come on." Fitz popped open his door. "Let's get moving while we're still one step ahead of the press."

10

The Survivors Club, contd

Inside the restaurant, it was easy to spot the women. They sat alone in a corner, huddled over gigantic red mugs, trying to ignore other people's curious stares. Taking in the three, Griffin had several impressions at once. First, Como had good taste in women. They were a startlingly attractive group: two older, one younger, as if two former models were having lunch with the next generation of talent. Second, all three women were clutching their oversized mugs much harder than necessary. Third, and most interesting, none of the women seemed surprised that Fitz was there.

Fitz walked over to the table. The other patrons had started to whisper. He didn't pay them any attention.

"Jillian. Carol. Meg." He nodded at each of the women in turn. Much more slowly, they nodded back. Fitz didn't say anything more. Neither did the women, and the silence immediately stretched long. Griffin had to admit he was impressed by everyone's composure. He let them engage in their staring contest while he did his own sizing up.

Meg Pesaturo looked almost exactly as he'd pictured her. Pesaturo was an old Italian name, and she looked it, with her golden skin, long brown hair and dark gleaming eyes. She was dressed casually this morning, jeans and a brown T-shirt. Definitely the youngster of the group. She was also the first to break eye contact.

In contrast, victim number two, Carol Rosen, looked like middle-aged money. Upswept blond hair, heavily painted blue eyes, pale designer suit. She sat stiffly, back straight, shoulders square. She'd probably gone to some kind of finishing school where girls learned how to drink tea with their pinkies in the air and never let their husbands see them cry. She returned Fitz's stare with overbright eyes, her lips pressed into a bloodless line and her body quivering with tension.

Griffin had to suppress the urge to take her jogging with him. Or throw her into the boxing ring. He was probably oversensitive, given his own state, but Fitz had been right about this one. She wasn't coping well. Maybe she thought she was, but take it from an expert. Carol Rosen was heading for a Big Boom of her own, and when it came, she was going down hard.

He wondered if her husband could read the signs. And if he could, had he been willing to trade Eddie Como's life for his wife's peace of mind?

He turned his gaze to the last member of the group. Jillian Hayes. Never actually raped, but beaten and otherwise victimized. Ad hoc leader. Grieving sister. And at the moment, as cool as a crisp fall day.

She was much older than he'd anticipated, given the young age of her sister. He'd thought she would be mid-twenties, but she looked closer to mid-thirties, a mature woman comfortable in her own skin. She sat loosely, wearing a tan pants suit with a white linen vest. Her thick brown hair was pulled back in a clip at the nape of her neck. She wore simple gold hoops in her ears, and a chain bearing some kind of medallion around her neck. No rings on her fingers. Short, manicured nails.

Stupid thought for the day – he found himself thinking that Cindy would like that suit.

Man, he wanted to go running now. And then he realized that Jillian Hayes was no longer looking at Fitz. Instead, her brown/gold/green eyes were staring straight at him.

"You're from the state," she said. A statement, not a question.

"Detective Sergeant Roan Griffin," he supplied. Fitz shot him a dark look. Maybe he'd wanted the pleasure of making the introductions. Fuck him. It was now out of their hands.

"Tell us what happened," she said. An order, not a statement.

"We have a few questions," Fitz began.

"Tell us what happened."

"What makes you think something happened?" Griffin spoke up, earning another scowl from Fitz.

"Why else would you be here?"

Good point. Griffin glanced at Fitz, understanding now that this really was going to be fun, so hey, here you go, Fitz. Run the show. Fitz did not look amused.

"We need to know where you were around eight-thirty this morning," Fitz said.

Jillian shrugged. Actually, she raised one shoulder in a cool gesture that was as dismissive as it was submissive. Fitz was right – she was clearly the spokesperson of this group. The other two women didn't even open their mouths but simply waited for her to address the question.

"We were here," she said. "Together. The three of us. As most of this restaurant can attest. Now, Detective, please tell us what has happened."

"There was an incident," Fitz said carefully. "Eddie Como is dead."

Griffin and Fitz simultaneously tensed, waiting for the coming reactions. Griffin homed in on Meg: she'd be the most likely to give something away. But if she was a co-conspirator, she was a damn good one. Because at the moment she appeared mostly confused. She cocked her head to the side, as if listening to something inside her brain.

Carol, on the other hand, released her pent-up breath as a sharp hiss. She leaned forward and grabbed the edge of the table in a white-knuckled grip.

"Are you sure?" she demanded.

"What do you mean?" Fitz asked.

"Have you seen his body?"

"Yeah," Griffin replied. "I've seen the body."

She turned on him fiercely. "Tell me. I want every detail. How he looked. How long it took. Was he in pain? Was it horrible? Was it bloody? I want every detail."

"We're not at liberty to discuss the case – " Fitz began.

"*I want every detail!*"

The other patrons turned to stare again. Griffin didn't blame them. Carol was definitely wound a wee bit tight. Not enough blood in the world to satiate her lust. And probably not enough justice to right her wrong.

"It was quick," Griffin said.

"Fuck!" Carol cried.

Okay, maybe Maureen had a point about her. Griffin amused himself by waiting to see who would do what next. Jillian Hayes simply raised her mug and took a sip of chai, her expression carefully blank. Meg Pesaturo still had her head cocked, listening to something only she could hear. Only Carol appeared agitated. She remained breathing too hard, her hands gripping the edge of the table while she waited for something, anything, to make her feel better about things. Maybe Griffin should've lied and told her that Eddie Como had been shot to pieces one limb at a time. She would probably sleep better at night.

And maybe pay the shooter a bonus? Oh wait, he'd already received one.

Jillian or Meg must have kicked Carol under the table, because she finally sat back and seemed to work on regaining some measure of control.

Fitz cleared his throat. "We think it would be best if you all came with us," he told them.

"Why should we go with you?" Jillian set down her mug. She gestured with her hand to include her fellow Survivors Club members. "We've been here all morning. If Eddie Como's dead, we obviously didn't do it."

"There are a few things we'd like to discuss with you – " Fitz tried again.

"I don't understand," Carol interrupted. "He's dead. It's over. We don't need to talk to you anymore. The case, the trial, everything, it's done."

"The detective is fishing," Jillian told her calmly. "While we didn't shoot Eddie Como, he's thinking we might have arranged for whoever did."

"How did you know he was shot?" Fitz asked sharply. "I didn't say he was shot."

"Detective, haven't you seen the morning news?" Jillian paraphrased softly: " 'Shortly after eight-thirty this morning, shots broke out at the Providence County Courthouse. According to initial reports, it is believed that the alleged College Hill Rapist, Eddie Como, was gunned down as he was being unloaded from the prison van. Sources close to the investigation believe an unidentified man fired the fatal shot from the rooftop of the courthouse. Also, an explosion in a nearby parking lot has left one dead.' Isn't that about right? I think that's about right."

She smiled, cool and undaunted, while Fitz muttered something harsh under his breath. Griffin could only shrug. Of course the press had gone ahead with the story even without confirmation of Eddie Como's identity. The College Hill Rapist was big news. Real big news. And why act responsibly when you could further fuck up a murder investigation?

Maureen, Maureen, Maureen, he thought again, and suddenly had a bad feeling about that tape.

"All right," Fitz said grudgingly. "Eddie Como was shot. He's dead. But I don't think this is the place to have a discussion about that. I think it would be best if all of you accompanied us down to the station."

"No," Jillian said firmly. "But thanks for asking."

"Now, ladies – "

"We don't have to go with them," Jillian cut in. She turned her gaze to Meg and Carol, and once more Griffin was impressed by her composure. "We don't have to answer any questions. Without probable cause, Detective Fitzpatrick and Sergeant Griffin can't make us do or say anything. I would keep this in mind, because Detective Fitzpatrick didn't come here to pay us a friendly visit. This is a big day for us, ladies. Eddie Como was shot, and we've just graduated from rape victims to murder suspects."

"She's right, you know," Griffin spoke up.

"What?" Jillian Hayes zoomed in on him with narrow eyes. Fitz was scowling at him.

"Well, aren't you going to tell them the rest of it?" he asked innocently.

"The rest of it?"

"Absolutely. The rest of it. These women are your friends, right? Surely you want them to understand everything. For example, if you ladies don't want to speak with us, then we'll just have to move on down the list. Contact your friends, your family. Husbands, fathers, uncles, mothers, sisters, aunts. Coworkers. Subject them all to police scrutiny. Oh, and we'll subpoena your financial records, of course." All three women sat up straighter. Griffin shrugged. "You have motive and opportunity, that gives us probable cause. We'll pull your bank records, the bank records of every member of your family. Maybe even your uncle's business." He gazed serenely at Meg. "Or maybe a husband's law practice." He gazed at Carol. "Any recent payments that can't be accounted for . . ." He gave another helpless shrug. "A murder is a murder, ladies. Cooperate now, and maybe we can work out a deal where you don't serve life."

Meg and Carol didn't look as certain anymore. Jillian, on the other hand . . . Jillian was looking at him as if she'd just noticed an unpleasantly buzzing fly in the room, and was now about to squash the bug with her bare hand.

"Diminished capacity," she challenged.

"Not for a hired gun. Requires premeditation. If you were going for a plea, you should've showed up in the courthouse and shot Como yourself."

"Not necessarily. Diminished capacity simply means outside influences made you commit an act you otherwise wouldn't have done – that you were not operating in your proper mind, so to speak. You could argue the trauma of being raped, the fear of being attacked again, drove you to employ a hired gun."

"Sounds like you've been thinking this over."

"You never know what you'll need to know until you need to know it."

"Do you have a legal background, Mrs. Hayes?"

"Ms. Hayes. I have a marketing background. But I know how to read."

"Defense statutes?"

"You're not asking the right question yet, Sergeant."

"And what question is that?"

Jillian Hayes leaned forward. "Did we have reason to be afraid? Did we have probable cause to fear for our lives?"

"I don't know. Did you?"

"He called us, Sergeant. Did Detective Fitzpatrick tell you about that? For the last year, Eddie Como has been phoning and mailing us constantly. Do you know what it's like to get a shiver down your spine every time the phone rings?"

"I've suffered through my fair share of telemarketers," Griffin said. But he was looking at Fitz questioningly.

"He shouldn't have been able to call them," Fitz supplied. "In theory, inmates have to enter a pin number into the pay phones to get a dial tone, and each pin number has only so many numbers approved for calling. Trust me, none of the women were ever approved, but then again, this is prison. For every rule the officials impose, the inmates find a way around the rule. Probably with outside help."

"You can ask to censor outgoing mail," Griffin said with a frown. "Impose a no-contact order."

"If an inmate is threatening. Eddie never threatened them, so we couldn't deny access. Basically, they changed their phone numbers, he went to mail. They put a hold on prison mail, he got someone to mail his letters from a different location. Eddie was persistent, I'll give him that."

"And what was he so persistently trying to say?"

"That he was innocent," Jillian said dryly. "That we had made a huge mistake. He never meant to hurt anyone. This was all some big misunderstanding. And then, toward the end, of course, he was demanding to know why we were ruining his life, why we were taking him away from his child. He murdered my sister, Sergeant, and then he's asking *me* how come I'm denying him access to a child?"

"He wouldn't leave us alone," Carol interjected vehemently. "For God's sake, he even contacted my husband at work! He asked him for a list of recommended attorneys! My rapist, consulting my husband for a good legal defense! And when that didn't yield results, he started mailing us countless letters with all the free stamps available to inmates. Think about that. My rapist, harassing me, with stamps I provide as a taxpayer. The man was a fucking monster!"

Griffin looked at Meg. She merely shrugged. "My parents don't let me answer the phone or get the mail."

"The point is," Jillian spoke up, pulling attention back to her, "you're barking up the wrong tree, Sergeant. So someone blew away Eddie Como. We don't care who did it. And we don't need to know who did it. Frankly, we are damn grateful that he's dead."

II

Jillian

Detective Fitzpatrick and Sergeant Griffin stuck around the restaurant for another five minutes. They thrust, Jillian parried. They punched, she counterpunched. The two cops grew frustrated. Jillian didn't much care. She'd been telling Meg and Carol the truth. They didn't have to say anything or go anywhere. As of this moment, they were still merely Eddie Como's victims. They might as well enjoy that advantage while it lasted.

One year ago, when Jillian had first thought up the Survivors Club, she'd had no illusions about the road ahead. She'd woken up that morning with the crushing realization that Trisha was dead and she was still not. She'd lain there, terrified of each noise in her own home, painfully aware of just how physically weak and inadequate she was, and then she'd gotten mad again. No – she'd gotten furious. She didn't want more police questions. She didn't want DA's walking through her hospital room, cops grilling her about what she had done and said the night her little sister was viciously raped and murdered. She didn't want to get out of bed knowing that the man was still out there. He had killed Trish. He had attacked two other women. And the police hadn't done a damn thing about it.

Jillian had gotten out of bed then. And she had picked up the phone.

Perhaps Meg and Carol had joined the group looking for comfort. Maybe, these days, it even was a source of comfort. But Jillian wasn't ready for soft things yet. First and foremost, she had needed action for Trish, for herself, for all of them. She had formed this group, then honed this group to be their sword.

"We are not the Victims Club," she had told them at their inaugural meeting. "We are the Survivors Club, and while we may have lost control once, we aren't ever going to lose control again. These attacks are our attacks. That rapist is our rapist. And we're going after him. The three of us are going to use the press, we're going to use the attorney general's office, we're going to use the police and we're going to find the man who did this to us. And then we're going to teach him what it means to have messed with us. I promise you that. From the bottom of my heart, I promise you we will get this man and we will make him pay."

And in a matter of three short weeks, they watched the police lead Eddie Como away. What Providence detectives hadn't been able to do for nearly two months, the Survivors Club had accomplished in half that time.

Detective Fitzpatrick and Sergeant Griffin left. A waitress came by. Her look was both curious and sympathetic.

"More chai?"

They shook their heads.

"Stay as long as you'd like, girls. Oh, and don't fret the bill. After everything you've been through, this is on the house."

The waitress bustled away. Jillian looked at Carol and Meg. No one seemed to know what to do next.

"Free breakfast," Carol murmured at last. "Who said being raped didn't have its advantages?"

"We didn't get free breakfast for being raped," Jillian countered. "We received free breakfast for killing Eddie Como. Quick, let's run to Federal Hill. There's no telling how much free food we can get there."

Federal Hill was Providence's Italian section, famous for its restaurants, pastry shops and Mafia connections. Maybe they could get toasted by various mob bosses or receive free cannolis from made men. It was a thought.

Meg spun her now empty mug between her hands. She looked up at Carol, then Jillian. Then she shocked them both, probably even herself, by speaking of serious matters first.

"Maybe you should've told them," she said to Jillian. "You know, about the disk."

"Why? Eddie has contacted us before without the police doing anything about it."

"But this time was different."

" 'Sticks and stones may break my bones,' " Jillian quoted, " 'but words will never hurt me.' "

"He sent the tape to your *house*." Carol now, clearly agreeing with Meg. Carol hated the fact that Eddie Como could access their private residences. As she had told Detective Fitzpatrick six months ago, when the first phone call had come, it was like letting a murderer return to the scene of the crime. Eddie had been charged with three counts of first-degree sexual assault, one count of manslaughter and one count of assault with the intent to commit first-degree sexual assault. After all that, how was it that he still had the freedom to make phone calls and send mail? Eddie Como might have been the one behind bars, but most of the time, they agreed, they were the ones who felt as if they were in prison.

"He's contacted all of us at our homes," Jillian said. "Face it – he likes to play games. He likes trying to mess with our minds. This was just his latest effort."

"But he threatened to kill you," Meg argued. "Detective Fitzpatrick told us he could do something if Eddie became threatening. And that video file" – Meg shuddered delicately – "that was definitely threatening."

The computer disk had been sent to Jillian's house on Friday. The return address had been Jillian's business – yes, Eddie was very smart in his own way. So she'd opened the manila envelope, thoughtlessly popped in the disk, figuring it was from Roger or Claire, and then . . . Then Eddie Como's face had been staring back at her from her own computer screen. And as she fumbled for the eject button or the mouse, or the escape button, or for God's sake, some kind of button, he had begun to speak.

"You fucking bitch," Eddie Como told her as she sat in her own home, ten feet away from her ailing mother, fifteen feet away from her mother's live-in assistant, two feet away from a photo of Trisha, smiling and happy and still so full of life. "You fucking bitch, you've ruined my life. You've ruined my kid's life, my mother's life and my girlfriend's life. Why? Because I'm a spic? Or just because I'm a man? It doesn't matter anymore. I'm gonna get you, even if it takes me the rest of my life. I'm gonna get you even if it's from beyond the grave."

Jillian had gotten the disk out then. She had flung it back into the manila envelope and quickly resealed it, as if it were a poisonous spider that might try to escape. Then she'd sat there a long time, breathing too hard, shaking like a leaf, and in all honesty, very near tears.

Jillian hated being near tears. Crying never helped. Crying never changed the world. Crying certainly didn't fend off the likes of Eddie Como.

"If I was going to contact Detective Fitzpatrick, I would have done it Friday night," she told the group now. "I didn't. So there you go."

"You should've told him," Carol said, voice still disapproving. Carol was very good at disapproving. "Maybe he could've done something."

Jillian rolled her eyes. "It was after eight by the time I opened the envelope. Detective Fitzpatrick was already gone for the day. And . . . and it seemed juvenile at the time. A last-minute scare tactic by Eddie with the trial about to start on Monday. Besides, he's sent this thing out, he's probably already waiting for the police to come or the prison guards to come, or someone to come and give him a bad time. Then he could sit back and amuse himself with how much he rattled my cage. But if I say nothing . . . Then he spends all weekend waiting. Wondering. Not knowing. I liked that."

"Punishing him with silence," Meg said softly. "It's not half bad."

Jillian shrugged modestly. "But it doesn't matter anymore,

does it? Whatever Eddie has done, whatever he's threatened to do . . . It doesn't matter anymore. He's dead."

A strange silence descended over the group. For the first time, alone with confirmation that Eddie Como had indeed been fatally shot, the words began to penetrate, grow real, become the new state of the universe. They looked at each other. No one knew what to say. No more Eddie Como. It defied the imagination. For the last year he had been the center of their world. Everything they hated, despised, feared. Weekly they met simply to talk about how mad he had made them, or how determined, how confused, how heartbroken, defenseless, shattered. Was there a thought that went through any of their heads that did not connect back to Eddie Como? A resolution that did not start with him? A good day, a bad day, a good episode, a bad episode that wasn't directly attributed to him? Meg could not remember her life. Carol couldn't turn off her TV. Jillian couldn't relax, and one way or another it all had to do with Eddie Como. Except now he was gone and the world kept turning and the other patrons kept eating and . . .

"I don't think we can talk about it," Jillian said shortly.

"We need to talk about it," Meg said quietly.

"We have to talk about it!" Carol seconded more vehemently. "We'd better talk about it! I for one – "

"We can't," Jillian interrupted forcefully. "We're suspects. If we talk about the shooting, or the fact that he's dead, later someone – hell, maybe Ned D'Amato – could construe that as conspiracy."

"Oh for the love of God!" Carol cried. "The College Hill Rapist is dead and you're still making up rules and setting agendas. Give it a rest, Jillian! We have spent the last twelve months gearing up for a trial that will suddenly never happen. Oh my God, I don't know where to begin."

"We can't – "

"Let's vote." Carol was emphatic. "All in favor of dancing around Eddie Como's grave, raise their hands."

Carol raised her hand. After a second, Meg's hand also went into the air. She gazed at Jillian apologetically. "When the news report came on, I was so sure they were wrong," she said quietly. "How could someone as evil as Eddie actually die? Did the shooter use a silver bullet? But then the cops came, so I guess this is all really happening, and well . . . I think I'm a little confused. He's dead, but in my mind, he can't be dead. Everything's different, but everything's the same. It's . . . surreal."

Jillian frowned. She still smarted from Carol's agenda comment. But then . . .

Her skin felt funny, too tight for her bones. The air felt strange, too cool upon her cheeks. Meg was right. Everything was different, yet everything was the same, and had there been a night in the last twelve months when Jillian had not gone to bed wishing for Eddie Como's death, praying for Eddie Como's death, *willing* Eddie Como's death with every fiber of her being?

She had won. The Survivors Club had won. And then she finally understood what was wrong. Eddie Como was dead. But she didn't feel victorious.

"Perhaps . . . perhaps we can talk about how we feel," Jillian said slowly. "But no getting into specifics of the shooting. Agreed?"

Meg nodded. More reluctantly, Carol followed suit.

"Well, I for one am happy!" Carol stated immediately. "I'm bursting! Hell, yes. This is a great day in America. The bastard finally got what he deserved! You know what we need? We need champagne. We need to celebrate this properly, that will put it in perspective. Where is that waitress? We're going to get ourselves some champagne, and why not, that piece of chocolate cake."

The waitress magically materialized. Carol ordered a bottle of Dom Pérignon, then the entire chocolate cake.

"Don't worry, we'll pay for it," she told the waitress. "We're not trying to abuse anyone's generosity, we just need a good toast. Do you have any strawberries, honey? Put a strawberry in each glass. That'll be perfect. And then the cake. Don't forget the cake. My God, that looks luscious."

Carol was waving her hands about enthusiastically. Her blue eyes were overbright again, her expression at once glowing and brittle. Meg and Jillian exchanged looks across the table.

"Now then," Carol said in her overloud voice. "Bubbly is on the way. In the meantime, let's tick off all the ways our lives will be better. I'll start. One, we no longer have to worry about testifying at trial. No horrible recaps, no vicious cross-examination, no showing crime-scene photos of our own bodies to complete strangers. Survey says, no trial is a good trial. Thank you, Dead Eddie. Oh look, here's the champagne."

The waitress was back. She had the Dom Pérignon and yes, glasses with fresh strawberries. She popped the cork, poured the three glasses and began dishing out the cake.

Jillian accepted her glass, already picturing the headline. *Eddie Como Is Shot, The Women Eat Cake.* But then, in the next instant, Carol's mood infected her as well. What the hell were they supposed to do? Cry in their coffee? Wring their hands? Maybe this wasn't sane and maybe it wasn't socially acceptable, but they'd had lots of moments less sane than this one. And they had endured plenty of things that should not be socially acceptable.

Trisha tied up, stripped naked, then viciously assaulted as her throat swelled shut, as her lungs gasped for air. Trisha struggling furiously. Trisha trying to scream. Trisha, dying, with her last conscious moments being a strange man looming over her body . . .

"Okay," Jillian said. She held up her champagne flute. "My turn. Here's to no more phone calls in the middle of the day, no more notes in the mail, no more twisted video displays. Thank you, Dead Eddie."

"Here's to no halting our lives every ten years for parole hearings," Meg said. "No worrying that if we don't halt our lives and relive our rapes for some parole board, he will end up back on the streets. Thank you, Dead Eddie."

"No more fear that somehow he'll get out and attack someone else," Carol continued.

"No more fear that somehow he'll get out and attack one of *us*," Jillian amended.

"No more fear!" Meg said.

They drank. The champagne tasted startlingly good. Brought color to their cheeks. What the hell. Jillian poured another round while Carol dug into her cake.

"Good thing the cops left," Meg said somewhere around the third glass. She had barely eaten a bite for breakfast, and the champagne was going straight to her head.

"Oh they'll be back," Carol said. She'd stopped drinking champagne after the first glass and instead gone after the cake. Her lips were chocolate stained. She had a smear of frosting on her cheek, two more smudges on her hands.

"The new one is cute," Meg declared. "Those deep blue eyes. And that chest! Did you see his chest? Now there is a man who looks like he knows how to serve and protect."

"You said that about Fitz, and Fitz is not cute. You just like uniforms." Carol finished off her piece of cake, and immediately dished up another.

"I thought he looked familiar," Jillian mused.

"In this state, everyone looks familiar," Carol said.

"Not to me!" Meg cried gaily and held out her empty glass for more champagne.

"Maybe you should slow down a little," Jillian cautioned her.

"Sensible Jillian. Always in control. You know what this group needs? We need a party. With a male stripper!"

"I don't think a rape survivors group should hire a stripper."

"Why not? Man as an object. It might do us some good. Come on, Jillian, you've had us read all the traditional books and discuss the traditional methods. Why not go off the beaten path for a bit? It's been a year. Let's go wild!"

Meg looked at Carol for support. This was the problem with a three-member support group, Jillian had realized in the beginning. Two people could always gang up against one. In the beginning, it had been Jillian and Carol determining things for Meg. But lately . . .

Now, however, Carol merely shrugged. Apparently, she

was more interested in chocolate cake than some male beef-cake. Of course, Carol had little use for men these days. Not that any of them were doing great, but Carol, in particular, loathed any thought of sex.

"I'm serious about Sergeant Griffin," Jillian said, trying to regain focus. "I know him from somewhere. I'd swear I could picture his face on TV. Maybe I'll look him up."

"No wedding ring." Meg waggled a brow.

"For heaven's sake, Meg. He's an investigating officer, not a contestant on *The Dating Game*."

"Why not? You're very pretty, Jillian. And you can't punish yourself forever."

That ground the conversation to a halt. Even Carol paused with her fork suspended in midair.

"I don't think we should talk about this now," Jillian said quietly.

"I'm just saying – "

"And I don't want to talk about it now. It's been a big morning. Let's just drink our champagne and let it go at that."

Carol resumed eating her chocolate cake. Meg, however, had gotten a faraway look in her eye. She was definitely drunk. Of course, even sober, she generally said more than Jillian or Carol dared. They were older, more wedded to their privacy and carefully erected walls. Not Meg. Never Meg.

Now she said suddenly, "I'm angry. Eddie Como's dead, but I'm still angry. Why is that?"

Jillian picked up her empty champagne flute, twirled it between her fingers. "It's too new," she said softly. "You're going to need time to absorb, we're all going to need time to absorb, that he's truly gone."

Meg shook her head. "No. I don't think that's it. I think that maybe it doesn't matter. No, I'm *afraid* that it doesn't matter. Eddie Como is dead. *And so what?* Are you going to magically move on with your life, Jillian? Will I magically remember my past? Will Carol finally turn off her TV? I don't think so." Her voice picked up a notch. "Oh my God, it's the thing we've wanted most, *and nothing's different!*"

"Meg . . ."

Jillian tried reaching out a hand. Meg, however, pulled away, hitting the nearly empty champagne bottle, knocking it over. Jillian grabbed the bottle. Carol grabbed a napkin. Meg kept talking.

"Think about it. We hated him. All of us. Even me. And he gave our anger a focus. Why did you form this group, Jillian? To catch Eddie Como. And why did we stay together? To fight Eddie Como. Everything, for the last twelve months, has been about him. And it's *easier* that way. When we wake up mad or disoriented or afraid, we know why: Eddie Como. When the police are invading our privacy by asking more questions, or our friends or family are looking at us funny, we know why: Eddie Como. But . . . but now . . ."

Her voice trailed off. Jillian and Carol didn't say anything. Couldn't say anything.

"I'm so angry," Meg whispered. "I don't know who I am. I still have to take AIDS tests and sometimes late at night . . . I just lie there wondering. This man knows more about my body than I do. He did things, he invaded places. He took me away from me. And even if he's dead, I'm still *mad* about that."

"I doubt I'll sleep tonight," Carol said abruptly. "Meg's right. It's not really him. I mean, yes, I'm afraid of Eddie. But I'm also afraid of . . . everything. I'm afraid of the dark, I'm afraid of the quiet, I'm afraid of my house, I'm afraid of my bedroom window. I'm afraid of my husband, you know. We never talk about it, but he knows sometimes I wake up in the middle of the night, look at him and see only Eddie. I like the couch. Bedrooms aren't safe anymore. It's best to sleep on the sofa. Even, even now. It's better to be on the sofa."

They both looked at Jillian. Her turn. That's the way the group worked. One shared, they all shared.

"At least we have some sense of closure now," she tried.

Carol nodded immediately. "Closure. That's good."

Meg, however, shook her head. "You're avoiding again."

"I'm not avoiding," Jillian protested, as she always protested. "I don't have an answer yet."

Carol and Meg simply looked at her. Waited. Lately, they had grown tough.

"My loss is different," Jillian said finally. "My sister is dead. No matter what happened to Eddie . . . nothing is going to bring Trisha back. I've always known that."

"It's easier for you." A trace of bitterness crept into Carol's voice. "You fended him off. You won."

"I didn't win."

"You did."

"I got *lucky*, all right? You think I don't know that? I got lucky!"

"Well, I'm not picky, I would've taken luck!"

"And I would've preferred my sister's life!" Jillian's voice had risen sharply, catching other patrons' attention once more. She caught herself, pressing her lips into a thin line in an effort at control, although her breathing was harsh now, her face red, her nerves shockingly raw. She sat back. She picked up her flute of champagne. Set it down. Picked it up again.

"That was good," Meg said, nodding. "Honest. I think you're making real progress."

Jillian just barely repressed the urge to throttle the girl. Meg's intentions were good, of course. She should appreciate that. But Jillian was *not* an amnesic twenty-year-old. She was thirty-six, she had responsibilities and she remembered everything. Absolutely everything. Goddammit . . .

She picked up the flute, set it back down, picked it back up and fought the desire to send it smashing to the floor. One year later . . . Oh God, look at them.

Carol finally broke the silence. "It's still better, right? Life has been unbearable with Eddie Como alive. Surely it must be better with him dead."

"Closure," Jillian said crisply.

"Closure," Meg repeated.

"Closure," Carol echoed.

"Life will get better," Jillian insisted.

Meg finally smiled. "Think of it this way. It can't get any worse."

12

Tawnya

"Well, they certainly have their act together."

"Jillian, Carol and Meg?" Fitz was once more navigating his battered Ford Taurus through narrow city streets. He glanced over at Griffin from behind the steering wheel. "Don't let them fool you. It's been a rough year. I've seen them all break down a time or two."

"Even Jillian Hayes?"

"Well" – Fitz had to think about it – "maybe not Jillian."

"The sister was quite a bit younger than her. Fifteen, sixteen years? Seems like they might have had less of a sibling relationship and more of a parent-child."

"Possibly. The mother, Olivia, isn't well. Had a stroke several years back and has been wheelchair-bound ever since. Jillian takes care of her with the help of a live-in aide."

"So Jillian's been the head of the family?"

Fitz shrugged. "She's thirty-six, you know. It's not that tragic."

"No. I'm just thinking . . . It's hard enough to lose a sibling. But thanks to Eddie, Jillian lost both her sister and her surrogate child. That's gotta be hard." Griffin thought about Cindy. "That's gotta make you mad," he added gruffly. "Truly, royally pissed off."

Fitz was looking at him strangely. "Guess I hadn't thought about that."

"She was dressed nicely," Griffin said, more neutrally. "What does she do?"

"She owns a small marketing firm. It's fairly successful,

but she also has some other assets. You follow blues music at all? Her mom, Olivia Hayes, was a fairly well known singer in her day. She banked hundreds of thousands, and Jillian has turned it into millions."

Griffin's eyes widened. "That would certainly buy an assassin or two."

"It would."

"She's cool enough." Griffin's tone was goading. He knew Fitz hated this topic.

Fitz didn't say anything.

"In her own words, she's grateful," Griffin pressed.

Fitz flexed his hands on the steering wheel, remained quiet.

"She's also got the most powerful motive, and apparently she's been studying her best defense."

"She doesn't outsource," Fitz said abruptly. "All right? I've spent a year with the woman. Hell, she didn't even trust *us* to catch her sister's killer without her. Ask D'Amato how many phone calls he received from her each day. Ask my lieutenant how often she personally stopped by. Why do you think she formed the Survivors Club? Why do you think she spent so much time in front of the press? What Jillian wants, Jillian goes out and gets."

"Why, Fitz, it almost sounds like you like her."

Fitz growled behind the steering wheel. "Don't make me kill you, Griffin."

Griffin had to smile at that. Even if Fitz managed to land a blow, he'd probably just break his hand. "So personally, you're not betting on Jillian Hayes?"

"If Jillian really wanted Eddie Como dead, she would've pulled the trigger herself."

"Even if she wasn't proficient in firearms?"

"She'd hire a teacher and learn. First day she came into my office, she was carrying a crime-scene textbook, and Robert Ressler's book on sex offenders. After we learned of the DNA match on Eddie Como, she asked our BCI sergeant for a recommended reading list on DNA testing. I'm pretty sure she now knows more than most of our crime-scene techs. The woman can be annoying, but she's never dumb."

"So who do you like for the shooting?"

Fitz thinned his lips. He definitely didn't want to have this conversation. Griffin understood. After the last year, suspecting one of the women was, for Fitz, like suspecting a fellow cop.

"Uncle Vinnie," Fitz said grudgingly.

"An enraged uncle with Mafia ties. I can see that. Though personally, I'm still interested in Meg. That amnesia thing. Something about that bugs me."

"A girl can't forget?"

"Her entire life?"

"Rape is a powerful trauma."

"Yeah, but it also happened a year ago, and trauma-induced amnesia is supposed to get better with time."

"Whose idea of time? I know vets still suffering from post-traumatic stress syndrome and it's been thirty years since the Vietnam War. You need as long as you need, simple as that." Fitz was looking at him sideways again. Griffin wasn't an idiot.

"Personally," he said lightly, "I don't think anyone should need more than eighteen months."

Fitz rolled his eyes, but apparently decided not to pursue the subject. "Dan Rosen," he said abruptly.

"Carol's husband?"

"Yeah. I've interviewed the guy half a dozen times and I don't know . . . There's something about him I don't like. He thinks too much before he speaks. You can practically see the wheels turning in his head as he picks each word, weighs each syllable. For God's sake, I know the man's a lawyer, but his wife was raped in their bedroom. It's bad enough he didn't come home to help her. The least he could do now is stop mincing words."

"They have money?"

"Nah, they got a house that bleeds them dry. At least that's how it looked a year ago when we pulled financials. Back then the practice was pretty new and the house freshly renovated. In other words, they had plenty of assets and not a dime to spare. Maybe his practice is doing better by now, maybe not."

"And assets can always be turned to cash," Griffin pointed out.

"True."

"What about Jillian Hayes's family?"

"What family?" Fitz shrugged. "She's got an ailing mother and a live-in adult-care aide. That's it."

"That's it? No father?"

"Nope. I get the impression that her mom only rented men, never bought."

"She and Trisha were half sisters then?"

"Yep."

"And what about the men in Jillian's life? Was she seeing anyone seriously at the time of the attack?"

"Not that she mentioned."

"And now?"

Fitz slid him another look. "Getting awfully personal, aren't you, Griff?"

"Just making conversation." Griffin drummed his fingertips on the dash. "Hey, Fitz, where are we going?"

"As long as I have backup, we're paying a visit to Eddie's mom."

Ten minutes later Fitz and Griffin arrived at the Como residence. This time, they hadn't beaten the press. Two oversized news vans were already clogging the tiny street of the rundown residential neighborhood. A bank of microphones dominated the postage-stamp-sized yard. Fitz and Griffin didn't see any members of Eddie Como's family outside yet, but that didn't mean anything. Either they'd just finished giving a statement or they were about to speak to the press. Either way, it didn't bode well for Griffin or Fitz.

"Eddie's mother hates me," Fitz announced, parking his Taurus up on the crumbling curb. "Eddie's father died when he was a kid, or he would probably hate me, too. Now, however, it's just his mom, his girlfriend and his baby. Oh, and the girlfriend, Tawnya, she bites."

Griffin, who was about to pop open the car door, stopped and stared at Fitz.

"Bites?"

"Yeah. And sometimes she scratches, too. She's got these nails. They're about three inches long. She likes to paint them with little palm trees and flamingos. Then she sharpens them into points, so that you're thinking about Key West right before she goes for your eyes."

"Is there a back door?"

"A kitchen door."

"Good, because we absolutely, positively, can't have that kind of reunion scene in front of the press."

Fitz looked down the street at the news vans. "Good point. No wonder they pay you state boys the big bucks."

Griffin opened his door. "We also get better cars."

He and Fitz had no sooner headed down the quiet street than the doors of the news vans slid back and two reporters, armed with cameramen, poured out. Griffin and Fitz said no comment a dozen times each before they finally reached shelter behind the tiny white house. There they paused, exchanged grimaces, then knocked on the back door. After a moment, a faded yellow curtain covering the window on the top half was drawn back. They found themselves face-to-face with a small Hispanic woman who regarded them somberly with deep black eyes.

"Mrs. Como." Fitz gave a little wave, a nervous smile. "I'm sorry, ma'am, but I'm afraid we need to speak with you."

Mrs. Como made no move to open the door. "I know what happened," she said from behind the glass. "Tawnya, she was there. At the courthouse. She told me."

"We are very sorry for your loss," Fitz said.

Mrs. Como snorted.

"We're here now to investigate what happened to Eddie," Fitz continued bravely. "I know we've had our differences in the past, but . . . I'm here about your son, Mrs.

Como. Surely you could give us just a moment of your time – "

"My Eddie is dead. Go away, Mr. Detective. You have hurt my family and I don't have to talk to you anymore."

Right about then, a strikingly beautiful girl rounded the back corner of the house. Griffin had one moment to think, *Whoa – she looks just like Meg Pesaturo,* before the young lady was hurling herself at Fitz with neon pink nails unsheathed and white teeth flashing.

"*Hijo de puta!*" Tawnya cried.

"Ahhhhhh!" Fitz said.

He threw his arm up to defend his face just as Griffin snaked out one hand and caught the girl around the waist. He hefted her into air, where she kicked out her legs and beat at his forearm with her puny fists.

"What do you weigh, about ninety-five pounds?" Griffin asked conversationally.

"Son of a bitch! Miserable shit-eating pig – "

"I got a good hundred and ten pounds on you," Griffin continued. "That means I can pretty much hold you like this all day. So if you want to get down anytime soon, maybe you should take a deep breath. Cool the language. We're just here to talk."

Tawnya whacked his arm again. Then she lashed out with her leg. When he still didn't flinch, she finally eased her struggling, though her dark eyes remained locked on Fitz, who was now huddled against the house with his hand cupped protectively around his cheek. Mrs. Como stood behind the closed door, watching it all with an impassive face.

"Ready to play nice?" Griffin asked when a full minute elapsed without Tawnya trying to kill anyone.

She nodded grudgingly.

He released his hold.

She bolted for Fitz, who managed to grab one of her attacking arms this time, twist it behind her back and slap on a pair of handcuffs.

"That's it!" Fitz exclaimed, breathing heavily. "You're in

bracelets until I leave. Just be happy that I don't charge you with assaulting a police officer."

"It's not a crime to kill a swine," Tawnya spat at him.

"Jesus, girl, the father of your child just died. Haven't you had enough violence for one day?"

The bruising words did the trick. Tawnya's shoulders sagged. Her chin came down. For just one moment, it looked to Griffin like Eddie's little spitfire was going to cry. She didn't, though. She pulled it together, then nodded at Mrs. Como, who finally opened the door.

Inside, the house was pretty much as Griffin had expected. Cramped kitchen with a ripped-up vinyl floor and stacked-up flats of baby food. A living room with threadbare gold carpet and a sagging brown sofa. The most expensive item in the room was easily the powder-blue playpen, positioned in front of the window. Tawnya headed for it immediately, then turned and glared at Fitz when she realized she couldn't pick up her son. She rattled the handcuffs.

"Hey, next time think before you scratch," Fitz called back from the kitchen.

Griffin, who had a soft spot for babies – he really loved their smell – crossed over to inspect the playpen himself. Tawnya's son – and Eddie's too, he presumed – was sleeping soundly on his stomach, his diapered butt stuck up in the air as little bubbles blew contentedly out of his mouth.

"Name?" he asked Tawnya.

"Eddie, Jr.," she said grudgingly.

"How old?"

"Nine months."

"He's a cutie. Sergeant Griffin, by the way. State police." Griffin flashed a smile.

"Have you arrested those bitches for killing my Eddie?"

Griffin took bitches to mean Meg Pesaturo, Carol Rosen and Jillian Hayes. "No."

"Then fuck you." Tawnya turned and stormed down the hall. So much for playing good cop. Griffin returned to the kitchen, where Mrs. Como was banging around pans, probably to have something to do. Now sitting at the worn kitchen table and obviously not sure how to proceed, Fitz was chewing on his lower lip.

"Hey, state boy." Tawnya again, yelling from the other end of the house. "Come here. There's something I want to show you."

"Watch the nails," Fitz muttered. "And the teeth."

Griffin walked warily down the narrow hallway. But it seemed that Tawnya no longer had death and destruction on her mind. Instead, she was gesturing awkwardly with her cuffed hands at a brown-and-gold photo album sticking out from a sagging bookshelf.

"Get that. There's something I want you to see."

Griffin inspected the rickety bookshelf. Seeing no sign of booby traps, he gingerly removed the album. When Tawnya still didn't bite him, he followed her back to the kitchen, where she informed him where to place the album, how to open the album and what photos to look at. Griffin was beginning to wonder if Eddie hadn't gone to prison in order to escape.

"Look!" Tawnya told him when he'd finally turned to the desired page. "See that. That's Eddie and me. Look at that face. That the face of a rapist?"

"They don't come with stamps on their forehead," Griffin said mildly, though he got her point. Eddie was a good-looking guy. Small, but trim, neatly dressed in tan khakis and a dark-blue shirt. Clean-cut features, tidy black hair. If you passed him on the street, you wouldn't think twice.

"Now look at me," Tawnya ordered, jerking her chin toward the photo, where she posed in a skimpy black dress, draped luxuriously over Eddie's arm. "I'm hot. Plain and simple. Been beating away the boys since I was twelve. And I *know* how to make my man happy. A guy has a girl like me, you can be sure he comes home for his meals."

"How much cooking were you doing six months pregnant?" Fitz spoke up.

Tawnya shot him a look of pure venom. "I made Eddie happy. I made Eddie *fucking* delirious." She glanced at the stove. "No offense, Mrs. C."

Mrs. Como didn't say anything. Her expression had scarcely changed the entire time they'd been here. No grief, no rage, no denial, no fear. Now she stirred something in a giant metal pot. It smelled to Griffin like bleach. Then he got it. She was preparing to wash diapers by boiling them on the stove. He looked around the kitchen, the cramped quarters filled with baby food, baby clothes, baby toys. And he got the rest of it. For Mrs. Como, Eddie had already been gone for nearly a year. Now her life was about her grandson.

Two Como males gone, one left to go. Did she wonder about that late at night? Did she cry when no one was looking? Or was it simply a fact of life for a woman like her, in a place like this? Seemed like too much of Griffin's job was spent dealing with these kinds of scenes. He felt suddenly, unexpectedly, sad, and that bothered him even more. You needed walls for this kind of business. You needed to compartmentalize if you were going to be a cop and maintain your peace of mind.

He should go for a run soon. Find a punching bag. Beat at the heavy leather until all the tension was drained from him and he had no emotions left. Then he could pretend that sad old ladies didn't twist his conscience and that two years later he didn't desperately miss his wife.

"You were with Eddie the nights the women were attacked?" Griffin asked Tawnya.

"Yeah. I was. Not that Detective Dickwad believed me." She gave Fitz another dark look. Fitz smiled sweetly. "We had an apartment then," Tawnya went on. "A decent place, over in Warwick. Eddie, he made good money with the Blood Center. That's not easy, you know. He had to get special training, take some courses. Eddie was smart. He had plans. And he really liked what he did. Helping people and all that. We were doing all right."

"No one saw you two together those nights."

"*Mierde!* You sound just like him." Chin angled toward Fitz. "Come on, Eddie had a tough job. He was on his feet six, eight hours a shift. He got home, he was tired. He wanted to relax. You know what Eddie liked to do best? He liked to stretch out on the sofa, watch a rented movie and place his hand on my belly so he could feel his baby kick. Yeah, that's your College Hill Rapist. Hanging out with his pregnant girlfriend and telling stories to his baby. And now . . . now. Ah, fuck you all."

Tawnya turned away. In front of the stove, Mrs. Como picked up a pile of cloth diapers and threw them into the pot. Round and round she went with a big metal spoon. The kitchen filled with the smell of bleach and baby powder and urine.

"You know he called the women," Griffin said quietly.

Tawnya whirled back around. "Of course he called them! They fucking ruined his life. Railroaded the police into his arrest. Worked the public into a frenzy talking on the news about this horrible, horrible rapist, gonna kill your daughter next. You know we got death threats, thanks to those women? Even Mrs. C. here, and what'd she do? One day, some guy called a radio station saying that if there was any justice in this world, Eddie, Jr.'s, little penis would fall off before he could turn into his father. Jesus Christ! Someone should lock that man up, threatening a baby like that. I couldn't bring Eddie, Jr., to the courthouse 'cause I was too afraid of what people might do. What the fuck is up with that?"

"You don't think Eddie did it."

"I *know* Eddie didn't do it. He was just a poor dumb spic working in the wrong place at the wrong time. That's the way the world works. White girls get hurt, some yellow or black man loses his ass."

"The state found Eddie's DNA at the crime scenes."

"Bah! Cops fake DNA all the time. Everyone knows that."

"Cops fake DNA?" Griffin glanced over at Fitz as if to ask if such a thing could be true. Fitz shrugged.

"Cops don't handle the DNA," Fitz said. "And in this case, we had two different nurses and one medical examiner handing evidence over to three different couriers to be sent

to the Department of Health. That's a lot of people for conspiracy, but hey, I'm just the poor dumb cop who gets
accused of corruption anytime I do my job. You know –
that's the way the world works." He looked at Tawnya, his
voice dripping sarcasm.

"Why would the cops tamper with evidence?" Griffin
asked Tawnya more reasonably.

"The pressure, of course! Come on – three white women,
attacked in their homes. One in a big fancy house on the
East Side. Cops can't ignore that kind of thing. Then one
dies and the whole state goes apeshit. Cops gotta arrest
someone then. Next thing you know, cops are looking at
blood drives and there you go. Young Hispanic male. Can't
even afford an attorney. Eddie was guilty before they ever
asked him a question. Cops got their arrest, mayor got his
headline, and hey, who gives a fuck about the rest of us?"

"Eddie was victimized by the state?"

"Damn right."

"Because he was a minority?"

"Damn right."

"So if the state already had him on the rapes, who do you
think shot him this morning?"

Tawnya finally drew up short. She inhaled deeply, held the
breath in her lungs, then blew it out all at once. "Everybody
thinks Eddie's a rapist. Everybody wants a rapist dead."

"The threats on the radio station?"

"Yeah. And in the newspaper. And in prison." She added
hotly, "Tell me the truth, you really gonna do something
about this?"

Griffin thought of the bank of microphones outside. He
said honestly, "As of this morning, we had every state detective working this case."

Tawnya narrowed her eyes. She wasn't dumb. "It's
'cause he was shot at the courthouse, isn't it? If they'd got
him in prison, you wouldn't even be here right now. But
they shot him in public. In front of cameras. That makes
you guys look bad."

"Murder is murder. We're on the case. I'm on the case."

Tawnya snorted again, unimpressed. She did know how the world worked.

"Do you have any specific names?" Griffin asked. "People you know of who threatened Eddie? People you heard say they wanted him dead?"

"Nah. Check the papers. Talk to the prison guards. They should know. If they can be bothered to tell you."

"Anyone else we should consider?"

"The fucking women, of course."

"The three victims?"

"Victims, my ass. Those bitches are the ones who picked Eddie. They pushed for his arrest, harassed the cops all the time. Maybe they wanted to make sure it was done all the way. Eddie can't defend himself now. And hey, they don't have to worry about anything unpleasant coming out at trial."

"Was something unpleasant going to come out at trial?" Griffin asked sharply.

"You never know."

"Tawnya," Fitz began warningly. He leaned forward, elbows on his knees, but Tawnya shook her mass of dark hair.

"I'm not doing your job for you, Dickwad. You wanna know what was gonna happen, you figure out what was gonna happen. Now come on. I gotta feed my kid." She turned around, gesturing at the handcuffs with her fingers. When Fitz still hesitated, she shot out, "I'll call the ACLU!"

Fitz grudgingly undid the bracelets, though Griffin noticed the Providence detective now leaned farther away, mindful of his face. Tawnya flashed her teeth at him, then smiled when he flinched.

"I don't care what you guys think," Tawnya said right before she left the room. "I was with Eddie those nights. I *know* he didn't hurt those women. And you wanna hear something else? You guys are screwed. 'Cause that dude's still out there. And now Eddie's gone. No one to blame anymore. No one to hide behind. It's a full moon tonight. Perfect weather for when the College Hill Rapist rides again."

*

Fitz and Griffin didn't speak until they were back on the street, climbing into Fitz's beat-up detective's car.

"Is it just me," Griffin said, "or is Tawnya the spitting image of Meg Pesaturo?"

"Wait 'til you see a photo of Trisha Hayes. Oh yeah, Eddie definitely had a type."

"She would've made a good witness for the defense," Griffin commented.

"Yes and no. Eddie's phone calls to the women . . . One way it could've been done was if someone on his approved calling list, say his girlfriend, had a phone feature, say call forwarding, and, ignoring the recorded warning which specifically says do not forward this call, did it anyway."

"Ah, so pretty little Tawnya takes her girlfriend duties seriously."

"ACI has tapes of the calls if you want to listen."

"Anything good?"

"Only if you buy into conspiracy theories. Eddie seemed convinced that the women were out to get him. Of course, the inmates know their calls are taped, so it might have merely been window dressing for the trial."

"That was going to be his defense? That three strange women were picking on poor little innocent him?"

"The perpetrator as victim. It's a classic."

"And unfortunately, it seems there's always someone in the jury box who buys it."

"Damn juries," Fitz muttered.

"Yeah, whatever happened to good old-fashioned mob justice? String 'em up, cut 'em down. Saves a ton of money on appeal."

Fitz eyed Griffin suspiciously, probably trying to figure out if he was toying with him or not. Griffin kind of was, kind of wasn't. The jury system was a royal pain in the ass.

Fitz glanced at his watch. "It's three o'clock now. Somehow, I don't think we're going to have this wrapped up in time for the five o'clock news."

"Doesn't look it."

"In fact, given that nobody seems to want to magically

confess, I'm guessing this might take a bit."

"It might."

"That gonna be a problem?" Fitz's gaze went to Griffin's overpumped chest and hard-lined face. Griffin understood what he was asking.

"Not for me," he said.

"I was just wondering – "

"I'm back. When you're back on the job, you're back on the job. You can't do policing halfway."

"I never thought so." Fitz's eyes were still narrowed, appraising. "Look, I'm just going to lay it on the table. If we're going to work together on this, I think I have the right to know a few things."

"Such as?"

"I heard about that Candy Man case, that it went on a little too long, then got a little too personal. Did you really beat up two detectives in the kid's house? Nearly put one of them in the hospital?"

Griffin was silent for a moment. "That's what I'm told," he said at last.

"You don't remember?"

"It's a bit of a blur. I wasn't aiming for Detective Waters or O'Reilly anyway. They were simply doing the honorable thing and throwing themselves in the way."

"You were going after Price."

"Something like that."

"And if you'd gotten to him?"

"We'll never know, will we?"

Fitz grunted at that. "You on Prozac?"

"I don't take any meds."

"Why not?"

Griffin smiled. "Not that kind of crazy."

"Just wear my hockey mask?"

Griffin's smile grew. "You could try, Detective, but I don't make any promises."

"Hey now – "

"Look," Griffin said, his tone serious because they weren't going to get this wrapped up by five so they might as well clear the air. "I'm not going to attack you. Two years ago, when my wife died . . . I let too many things go. Personally. Professionally. Life, this job . . . You gotta take care of things. We all learn, one way or the other. Last year was my lesson. I got it. I'm on top of things now."

Fitz remained silent, so maybe he had his own opinions on that subject.

"I'm sorry about your wife," Fitz said at last.

"I'm sorry, too."

"I know a lot of the guys who went to the service. She sounded like a really neat lady."

"She was the best," Griffin said honestly, and then, because two years wasn't nearly long enough, he had to look away. He fidgeted with the door handle. Fitz put the car in gear. They both cleared their throats.

"So what are you going to do now?" Fitz asked as he pulled away from the curb. "About the case."

"Return to headquarters and set up command central. Then, I'll probably go for a run."

"I'll follow up with the crispy corpse. With any luck, we got enough skin to print."

"Hey, Detective, as long as you're returning home, get me a copy of the College Hill Rapist file."

Fitz stopped immediately, his foot hitting the brake and stalling the car in the middle of the street. Griffin kind of thought that might happen.

"Come on!" Fitz exclaimed. "Don't let Tawnya get to you. The College Hill case was a good investigation. We had MO, we had opportunity, we had DNA. Took us six months to put it all together, and I'm telling you now, we did just fine. Eddie Como raped those women. End of story."

"Didn't say he didn't."

"I don't need the state reviewing my work! That's bullshit."

"Life sucks and then you die."

Fitz scowled at him.

Griffin returned the look calmly. "I want the file. The shooting is connected to the case, ergo, I need to learn the case."

130

"I told you about the case."

"You told me your opinions."

"I'm the lead investigator! I built the goddamn theory of the case, I am the opinion!"

"Then explain this to me: You found Eddie once you started looking at blood drives. And you started looking at blood drives because of the latex strips."

"Yeah, absolutely."

"So why did Eddie, who left behind no hair, no fiber, and no fingerprints, leave behind ten latex strips? Why did he on the one hand learn how to cover his tracks, and then on the other hand leave you a virtual calling card?"

"Because criminals are stupid. It's what I like best about them."

"It's inconsistent."

"Oh Jesus H. Christ. We didn't plant DNA evidence! We did *not* frame Eddie Como!"

"Yeah," Griffin said. "And frankly, Detective, that's what worries me."

13
Griffin

In spite of his words, Griffin didn't head immediately back to police headquarters in North Scituate. Instead, operating on a hunch, he returned to the rue de l'espoir restaurant in downtown Providence. It was 3:30. The three women definitely had had plenty of time to finish their mugs of chai and head out.

Except then he started thinking. Where would they go? They were obviously well experienced in the ways of the media. Surely they realized that as of 9:00 that morning, news teams had descended upon their front lawns, climbed up their front steps, started banging on their front doors. Let alone the number of white news vans trolling the streets, looking for leads, any leads, to give that station the advantage in the evening news race.

If it were him, he decided, he'd simply stay right where he was. With his fellow club members. That way if some earnest reporter did track them down, they'd at least all be together. Safety in numbers. According to Maureen, the Survivors Club had rules about that.

So Griffin returned to Hope Street. And then, operating on another hunch, he checked the license plates in the tiny parking lot. He found Jillian's car in less than a minute. Gold Lexus with license plate TH 18.

"Damn," he murmured, and for a moment, he simply stood there, feeling a rush of sadness that struck too close to home.

Rhode Islanders had a thing about license plates. He didn't know how it had started. Maybe the original colonists had

had a thing about horse brands. But Rhode Island was a small state, so its plates had literally started with one letter, plus a one- or two-digit number. Then the state had gone to two letters with a two-digit number. Now, the state did a straight five numbers, but only cultural outsiders settled for those. A true Rhode Islander, wanting to show off his long-standing ties to his state, personally went to the plate room of the DMV and requested the lowest letter/number combination possible, or, since highly prestigious plates such as A 20 or J 28 were mostly doled out to well-connected insiders, he requested his initials with a low two-digit number. Then he held on to those plates for life. Literally.

TH 18. Trisha Hayes, probably eighteenth birthday. Someone, Jillian most likely, had gone to a lot of trouble to get her little sister the special plates. Had Trisha been excited at the time? Had the plates gone with a new car, just what Trisha had always wanted? Maybe she'd thrown her arms around her sister's neck. Maybe she'd kissed her mother on the cheek. Eighteen-year-old Trisha Hayes, celebrating a new car. Eighteen-year-old Trisha Hayes, about to embark on a whole, brand-new college life.

Griffin doubted that cool, composed Jillian Hayes would ever say much about that day. She'd probably sold the car by now, at the same time she was sorting through her sister's clothes, closing up her sister's apartment, sifting through her sister's things. He could picture exactly what she'd had to do, because not that long ago, he'd done the same. The bureaucracy of death had surprised him. Nearly broken his heart all over again. But you did what you had to do. Get it done, people always advised. Then you can get on with your life.

Driving a car, he supposed, bearing your dead sister's license plates.

"What are you doing?"

Griffin whirled around. Jillian Hayes stood four feet from him, her car keys clutched in her fist and her hazel eyes already starting to blaze. Quick, say something clever, he thought.

He said, "Huh?"

"What the hell do you think you are doing?" She enunciated each word clearly, like steel nails she was hammering into a coffin. He wondered if he should clutch his chest theatrically.

"Would you believe I was in the neighborhood?"

"No."

"Well then, let's not bother with the small talk." He leaned against the side of her car and crossed his arms over his chest. Oh yeah, that definitely pissed her off.

"Get away from my car."

"Nice plates."

"Fuck you."

"Already been told that once or twice today. Apparently, it's time for me to contemplate a new aftershave."

"You really think you're cute, don't you?"

"In all honesty, I hate to think of myself as being cute, but that's just the male ego for you. Handsome, riveting, intimidating, compelling, charming, intelligent, threatening even, all good. Cute . . . Cute, bad."

"I don't really like you much," Jillian Hayes said.

"Is it the aftershave?"

"I'm serious. And I'm not answering any of your questions without a lawyer present."

"So you're taking the Fifth in regards to my cologne?"

Jillian sighed, crossed her own arms and gave him a stern look. "I've had a long day, Sergeant. Don't you have any other women you can go harass?"

"Not really."

"A girlfriend, a sister, a wife?"

"I never had a sister, and I'm not married anymore."

"Let me guess – she stopped thinking you were cute?"

"No. She died."

Jillian finally shut up. He'd caught her off guard. She looked troubled and perhaps fleetingly sad. Then she looked angry again. Jillian Hayes really didn't like being caught off guard.

"I don't think this is an appropriate conversation," she said curtly.

"I'm not the one who started it."

"Yes, you did. You showed up again after we'd already chased you off today."

"Yeah, but tell me honestly – would you really sleep well at night knowing the state police sergeant working your case could be chased off by three women?"

She scowled and appeared even more flustered. Interesting, he thought. Her eyes went gold when she was angry, and brown when she was troubled. What about when she was sad? Or when she was plotting revenge against the man who'd killed her little sister?

"You miss her, don't you?" he asked more softly.

Her voice was stiff, but at least she answered. "I think that's obvious."

"I lost my wife two years ago. Cancer. I still miss her."

"Cancer is hard," Jillian said quietly. She wrapped her arms around her middle, looked away. She did hurt. He could see it in every line of her body, whether she meant him to or not.

"I hated the disease," he continued. "Then I hated the doctors who couldn't make her better. I hated the chemo that robbed her strength. I hated the hospitals that smelled like antiseptic death. I hated God, who gave me someone to love, then took her away from me."

Jillian finally looked at him. "And if you had a high-powered rifle," she said, "you would've tried to kill the disease, too, isn't that what you mean?"

Fitz had been right. She was no dummy.

"Something like that," Griffin said lightly.

She shook her head. "I'm sorry you lost your wife. I'm sorry anyone loses someone they love. But don't try to play me, Sergeant. Don't think that because you've also known loss, you can climb inside my head."

"Your grief is special?"

"Everyone's grief is special."

It was Griffin's turn to look away. She was right, and that shamed him.

"Are you sure it was Eddie Como who attacked you and your sister?" he asked.

"Yes."

"Never had a moment's doubt?"

"Never."

"Why not?" He looked her in the eye. "Everyone has doubts."

"Voice," she said crisply.

"Voice?"

"When I was attacked, the man spoke. So while I couldn't see his face, I definitely heard his voice. And that voice was consistent with Eddie Como's."

"Consistent?" Griffin raised a brow. He caught that nuance right away. "Did they do a voice line-up with Eddie?"

Jillian scowled. "Of course."

"Just you?"

"Carol, as well." More grudging.

"What went wrong, Ms. Hayes?"

"I'm telling you, it was consistent. That means nothing went wrong."

"Bullshit. Consistent is not a positive ID. You couldn't make him, could you?"

"We could narrow it down to him and one other guy."

"Yeah, in other words, not a positive ID." Griffin rocked back on his heels. That was interesting.

Jillian, however, was vehemently shaking her head. "Positive ID is a legal phrase. It's law-enforcement fine print. As far as Carol and I are concerned, we stood in a darkened room, we heard six guys speak and we could pick Eddie out of that bunch. Think of it this way. Four of the guys we were certain *weren't* the College Hill Rapist. And Eddie wasn't one of those."

"A legal breakeven," Griffin mused. "You can't use the voice ID at trial because you didn't really make an ID, but the defense can't afford to bring it up either, because then as you point out, you can argue that you did home in on Eddie. And once again we're back to DNA to break the tie."

She regarded him curiously, her face less obstinate for a change. "You make it sound like that is a bad thing. Last I knew, DNA evidence was a very, very good thing."

"Yeah, generally."

"Generally?"

"Have you ever met Eddie's girlfriend?" Griffin switched gears. "Ever personally spoken to Tawnya Clemente?"

Jillian hesitated a fraction too long. "I . . . I'm not sure."

"You're not sure?"

She sighed. "Did Fitz tell you his theory that Tawnya forwarded Eddie's calls to our homes?" Griffin nodded. "I've also gotten some other calls," she continued. "Someone on the line, just *being* there. I don't know why, but I think the caller might be Tawnya."

"She's very convincing about Eddie's innocence."

"She's a woman with a child to protect. A woman with a child to protect can be very convincing about anything she needs to be."

"Do you like her?"

"I don't know her."

"You sympathize, though." Griffin was sure of this, and it surprised him. Once again there was more to cool, composed Ms. Hayes than met the eye.

"She has an infant son, Sergeant Griffin. Whatever Eddie did or didn't do, it's not her crime, nor the baby's crime."

"But she forwarded his calls to you. Helped harass you. Maybe even called you on her own."

Jillian smiled dryly. "Women in love, Sergeant, have done far worse."

"Call me Griffin."

"No offense, but I think I'll stick to Sergeant."

Now it was Griffin's turn to smile. "Hey, Jillian," he said lightly. "Do us both a favor. Look me in the eye, and tell me you weren't involved in Eddie Como's murder."

Her chin came back up. She looked him in the eye. And she said, "I won't tell you any such thing."

"You understand that we have a second corpse, from the RISD parking lot. Now the bodies are piling up. We can't ignore that, Jillian. The state is in charge of this investigation, and we're manning it with every detective we have. Whatever we learn, whomever we zero in on, we're going to

137

come down on that person very, very hard."

Jillian snorted. Her eyes had gone gold again, about the only warning he got. "Is that supposed to scare me, Sergeant? Is that supposed to terrify my weak little female mind? Because I'm not exactly quaking in my boots. Let's get this straight once and for all. My sister wasn't Eddie's first victim. She was his *third* victim. *Third* victim, Sergeant! And six whole weeks after the first attack. That's how well Providence's 'serious police investigation' was going. And even then, my sister is dead, I'm beaten within an inch of my life and the Providence detectives still didn't have jack shit until we, three *women*, three *civilian women*, got involved in the case. So fuck you, Sergeant. If you cops are so good at your job, you should've been good at it a year ago, when it might have still saved my sister's life!"

She ended harshly, her face red, her breathing coming out in ragged gasps. In the next instant, the full extent of her outburst must have penetrated because she immediately turned away, wrapping her arms tightly around her waist. For a long time, they both simply stood there. Griffin looking at her back, the fallen line of her shoulders, the bowed curve of her neck. Griffin, hearing all her grief and rage still boiling so close to the surface. Calm, controlled Jillian Hayes. Accustomed to single-handedly running her own company while simultaneously raising her little sister and taking care of her invalid mother. Calm, controlled Jillian Hayes, who had probably never felt powerless before in her life.

And then for the first time, Griffin got it. Carol wasn't the member of the Survivors Club closest to falling apart. Jillian was. She merely hid it better than the rest.

"I remember who you are," Jillian said abruptly. She turned around.

Immediately, Griffin's stomach tensed. He forced himself to remain leaning casually against Jillian's car, arms folded over his chest, hands hidden beneath his elbows where she couldn't see his fingers clench. "And who am I?" he asked lightly.

"You led the case. Against that pedophile in Cranston. The Candy Man? Young children kept disappearing, month after month after month. And you were on the nightly news talking about how you were going to find them all. I guess you did, in the end. In your neighbor's dirt basement."

Griffin forced his hands to open, relax. Breathe deep, count to ten.

"Your wife was dying," Jillian said softly. Her voice had changed, not so hard anymore, maybe even sympathetic. Perversely, he found that worse. "Your wife was sick, that's right. I think she had even died – "

"The cancer got her quick."

"And still kids were disappearing and there got to be a bit of a hubbub about whether you were paying enough attention to the case – "

"I did nothing but work that goddamn case. It was all I had left."

"And then" – her eyes were locked on his – "then the police finally found all those poor missing kids. Buried in the basement right next door to your home. The Candy Man was your next-door neighbor."

"It took eleven months, but I caught him."

"You were the one who figured out that it was him?"

"Yeah."

"Why didn't you see it sooner? Were you distracted because your wife died?"

"Maybe. Mostly I think it was because he was my friend."

"Oh." Jillian stopped, blinked her eyes. "I hadn't heard that."

"It wasn't relevant to the case."

"You arrested him?"

"Yes." After he tried to rip him from limb to limb. Down in that basement, with the acrid smell of lime and the deeper stench of death. Down in that basement, with those poor, poor kids. Down in that dark, dark basement, from which he'd been clawing his way back up ever since.

"I learned something that day," Griffin said abruptly.

139

"Not to have friends?"

He had to smile at that. "Maybe. But that's not true. I'll tell you something, Jillian. I'll tell you something about only a dozen other people officially know. For everyone else, it's merely a rumor."

She hesitated, chewed her lower lip, then worried the gold medallion hanging around her neck. He understood her dilemma. Accepting a confidence was like accepting a gift. If she took it, they wouldn't be strangers anymore. Maybe they'd even have a bit of a bond. And he doubted that right now, for a variety of reasons, Jillian Hayes wanted to bond with a cop.

Her curiosity won out. "What?" she asked.

"When I figured out it was David Price, my friend, my neighbor, it was bad. But when I went down to that basement, when I saw what he'd done to those kids, it was even worse. I went a little nuts that day. I went after David, and if I could've gotten my hands on him, I would've killed him. I would've ripped off his head with my bare hands, I would've pummeled him into a bleeding mass of bruised flesh. And I would've felt good about it. I didn't though. Two other detectives got in my way. They took his beating, and they did it because they were professionals who didn't want that son of a bitch to get off on charges of police brutality, and they did it because they were my friends and they understood. It's because of them he's now in prison for the rest of his life. And it's because of them that I still have a job. One friend betrayed me. But two other friends saved me. When all is said and done, it's still very good to have friends."

Jillian didn't say anything. Whether she knew it or not, she was leaning forward slightly, a strange look on her face. Yearning, maybe? Had she trusted anyone since the day her sister died? Even the Survivors Club, did she really trust them?

"But that's not the lesson I learned that day," he said.

"It's not?"

"No. What I really learned is that it's arrogant to be certain of anything. The world is a complex place and only idiots or assholes think they know it all."

Jillian recoiled just as a back door opened and Carol Rosen came walking out of the restaurant into the parking lot.

"Jillian, there you are – " Carol spotted Griffin and suddenly drew up short. Her gaze dashed between the two of them, standing alone together in the parking lot, and it was clear she didn't like what she saw.

"Yes?" Jillian belatedly turned around to face Carol. Her movements were jerky.

"Ummm, Meg . . . We, uh . . . Can I see you inside for a moment?"

"I don't know." Jillian still seemed distracted, but she recovered her bearings quickly, turning back to Griffin. "Are you done accusing me of murder, Sergeant?"

"For now."

"Well then" – she gave him a thin smile – "I think I'll be on my way."

She headed back to Carol, chin up, shoulders square. But then at the last minute, halfway through the restaurant's back door, she turned again.

"You're wrong, Sergeant," she called out to him.

"About Eddie?"

"About the world. You have to be certain of some things. Otherwise you'd go crazy."

It was Griffin's turn to smile. "I wouldn't be so sure of that," he said lightly as she disappeared through the doorway. "I wouldn't be so sure of that at all."

14
Price

Griffin swung by his house a little after 4:30. At the rate things were going, the workday was going to stretch deep into night. Not the ideal first day back for a man who'd gone bonkers just eighteen months ago, but what could you do? As he'd told Fitz, back was back.

Besides, he was increasingly intrigued by this case. Puzzled, confused, fascinated. In other words, in that perverse sort of way homicide detectives had, he was enjoying himself immensely.

Griffin parked outside the little waterfront shack he'd recently purchased in North Kingstown, and went inside to prepare the working homicide detective's Big Case Kit. In other words, a duffel bag containing two fresh shirts, two ties and lots of clean underwear. You could never have too much clean underwear. Oh yeah, he also added a toothbrush and an electric razor – never as good as a blade, but handy in a pinch.

He stopped in the kitchen for a glass of water as he idly went through his mail. Bill, bill, grocery store flyer. Ooooh, oranges for ninety-nine cents a pound. God bless the USA.

He got to the last item, a plain white envelope, and then his heart accelerated in spite of himself. *To: Good Neighbor Griffin.* At Griffin's new address. *From: Your Buddy Dave.* No return address.

David Price never could stand being bored.

Little psychopathic shit.

David had written many times before, mostly to the old house in Cranston, where Griffin had stayed for nearly a year after the Big Boom. He probably should have put it up for sale immediately after he took his medical leave, but who was going to buy the home next to the home where the Candy Man had brutally murdered ten kids? Who was going to buy the home of the dumb fuck detective who'd lived twenty feet away and never suspected a thing?

David Price, who used to pop over and mow their lawn when Griffin and Cindy got too busy. Small, boyish David Price, who looked seventeen even though he was twenty-eight, who could barely lift a forty-pound bag of potting soil but was hell on wheels with electrical wires. Easygoing, neighborly David Price, who helped Griffin lay the pipes for his irrigation system one summer, who liked to come over for barbecued hamburgers and beer, who fixed the light over the sink when the buzzing threatened to drive Cindy mad, who had no family of his own and over the course of three years somehow became part of theirs.

When Cindy had first learned of her cancer, a mere two days after Griffin had landed the Candy Man case, she'd told David about the disease herself. Griffin had an important case, she'd explained. Griffin was going to be very busy. It was so reassuring to her then that David lived right next door.

David had cried that night. All of them had. In the small family room Cindy had painted butter yellow and decorated with pictures of birds in flight. And then David had held Cindy's hand and promised her he'd do whatever she needed. They were going to beat this thing! They were going to win!

Six months later, Cindy was dead.

And five months after that, Griffin was talking to a little girl who had managed to escape from a man who'd tried to pick her up on the school playground. The stranger had been there when Summer Marie Nicholas had first come out, playing on the swings, but when he'd offered to give her a push, she'd gotten nervous.

His pants were "too full," she had said. The little girl had noticed that the man had an erection.

She had run straight back into the school, where she had found a janitor cleaning the gym. And he'd been wise enough to call the police. The man was gone from the playground by the time Griffin had arrived, of course, but seven-year-old Summer Marie had been brilliant.

She announced without hesitation that the man looked exactly the same as the boy in that big eighties movie *Back to the Future*. She liked that movie. That mad professor made her laugh so hard! Plus, when she was old enough to get a car, she wanted one just like that, with the funny doors.

Griffin had stared at little Summer Marie. And through the haze of depression and grief and exhaustion that had kept him half-functioning for months, he had a memory as clear as day: Cindy, Griffin and David sitting on the back porch the first time David had come over. Cindy laughing, saying, "Hey, Dave, anyone ever tell you that you look exactly like Michael J. Fox?"

David, an independent contractor with flexible hours. David, whose electrical jobs took him to different neighborhoods all over the state. David, whose small build, boyish face and easy smile would seem completely nonthreatening to a child. At least until it was much too late.

The girl's description earned them a search warrant. Two hours later Griffin was back in his own neighborhood, leading a small posse of detectives that included Mike Waters into David's home, while his next-door neighbor stood by silently, a strange smile fixed upon his face.

Fifteen minutes later, the first detective opened the door to the basement. The initial waft of odor was so overwhelmingly floral the detective had actually sneezed. And then they'd all caught the smell beneath the smell. The incredibly hard to conceal odor of death.

Down into that basement, with the hard-packed dirt floor and soundproofed ceiling. Down into that basement, with its three harshly glaring bare bulbs. Down into that basement, with a stained mattress and an old workbench covered in handcuffs, dildos and porn. Down in that basement with another corner where the dirt wasn't hard-packed at all. Where instead the dark, loamy soil undulated in ten tiny lime-topped waves.

Ten heartbreaking little white-flecked waves.

David had brought each child down here, down to the odor of death. And he had done unspeakable things to them while they had inhaled the stench of death. Had it made him even more excited?

Or had that come later, when he'd gone next door to mow a state police sergeant's lawn?

Griffin should've killed David Price that day. Most nights, when he awoke drenched in sweat and choking back screams, he still wished that he had. Sometimes when people did the right thing, it was still much too wrong. He'd spent eighteen months in therapy, when frankly, he probably could've cured himself that day with one properly landed punch.

Shrinks just didn't know shit about this job.

Now Griffin looked down at the envelope in his hand. He should throw it away, toss it in the bin like so much garbage. But he didn't. In all honesty, he'd come to consider these little notes the very best in home sanity tests. The state had its fitness-for-duty diagnostic; Griffin had this.

He opened the envelope. It was short by David's standards. Generally he included several pages about his life in maximum-security prison. The carpentry classes he was taking. His newfound love of yoga – good for the body and the mind. Rumors that the ACI might win a contract soon to have inmates make American flags and wouldn't that be a heck of a lotta fun? Oh, and by the way, here's a sketch of a rose to put on Cindy's grave. *I still miss her, buddy.*

In contrast, this letter contained only two lines. It read: *Best wishes with the new case. It's going to be a good one.*

Griffin's blood went cold. He grabbed the envelope, flipped it over. Postmarked Saturday, the eighteenth of May. But that was before Griffin had gone back to work, before Eddie Como had been shot. How could David . . . ? What did David . . . ?

The ringing building in his ears. Heart starting to race, blood starting to pump, sweat bursting from pores.

Griffin took a shaky breath, counted to ten, closed his eyes, and in the next moment, the anxiety attack passed. His breathing calmed. His powers of reason returned.

David was simply fucking with him. He'd probably learned of Griffin's first day back on the job the same way he'd learned Griffin's new address. The power of the prison rumor mill, coupled with way too many big mouths on TV.

And when Griffin returned to work, of course he was assigned a new case. He was a detective, after all. That's what he did. To read any more than that into the note was like giving a psychic all the credit for predicting that "soon, your luck will change."

David Price didn't deserve that kind of credit. And he certainly didn't deserve that kind of power.

Griffin stepped on the foot pedal of the kitchen's white trash bin. The lid popped open and he dropped David Price's letter into the pile of used Kleenexes and sticky eggshells.

"Fuck you, too," he murmured. Then for good measure, he looked at his hands. Not a tremor in sight. Yeah, eighteen months later, he was doing just fine. Eighteen months later, he was fucking fabulous.

Griffin grabbed his Big Case Kit and hit the road.

15
Carol

Carol left the rue de l'espoir shortly after 4:00 but didn't return home until nearly 6:30. First, she spent some quality time at Nordstrom. Dan would scream when he got the bill, but let him scream. It was four in the afternoon on the opening day of her rape trial, which was no longer the opening day of her rape trial, and by God, she would shop if she damn well wanted to shop.

So Carol went to Nordstrom, where a petite young thing helped her select a multitude of designer suits while trying hard not to stare. Carol didn't mind the staring. She'd gotten used to it by now. In the beginning, when Jillian had first proposed the Survivors Club, she had spelled out the side effects of going public. On the one hand, never underestimate the power of three beautiful women standing in front of a crowd of TV cameras demanding that the police ratchet up their investigation and do more to protect the female population of the great Ocean State.

On the other hand, never underestimate the power of the press to descend on three bruised and battered women like vultures on roadkill. *Did they have any idea who was behind these vicious attacks? What about the slow progress of the ongoing investigation? Did they still suffer nightmares? What about their husbands, fathers, sisters, brothers? Did they have any advice for other women out there?*

Jillian fielded all the questions, of course. Jillian was good at that sort of thing. Crisp, professional, never giving too much away.

Now, Carol, if she'd gotten her hands on the mike . . . *Of course I have fucking nightmares! Women, you want to protect yourselves, buy a gun. Shoot first, question later. Fuck 'em all, ladies. It's the only way.*

So, yes, I have nightmares . . . When I sleep . . . Which hasn't been for months . . . And by the way, when I look at my husband I see a rapist's face and when my husband touches me I feel a rapist's hands. And I hate Eddie Como, and open windows and houses that grow too quiet at night. But most of all I hate the fact that when I do fall asleep, I dream of blood and slaughtered lambs, and when I wake up I am so angry I have to press my eyeballs into my sockets to keep them from bursting out of my head.

Other than that, esteemed members of the fourth estate, I am coping just fine.

Carol dropped two thousand bucks. Dan would go ballistic. Good for him. Yes, she was definitely in a mood.

Maybe she should've stayed with Jillian and Meg. Jillian was going to drive Meg home, providing backup in case Meg's father was there and saw his little girl under the influence of not one, but two bottles of champagne. Carol wasn't even sure how Meg had gotten her hands on the second bottle. She'd gone to the restroom, and next thing she knew, a fresh bottle was on the table and half consumed. At least she'd been able to catch Jillian out in the parking lot. Of course, that had been weird, too. Jillian talking to Sergeant Blue Eyes. The two of them standing so close together, so deep in conversation . . . Then the way Jillian had jerked back. Startled. Guilty.

Carol had a strange feeling in the pit of her stomach. Betrayal, though she didn't know why. Suspicion, though she had no proof.

As she and Jillian walked back into the restaurant, Carol had asked her what she had been talking to Sergeant Griffin about. Nothing, Jillian had said. And Carol had wondered what kind of nothing took fifteen minutes to cover in a restaurant parking lot.

Once Jillian was inside, she'd appraised the situation, as Carol had known she would. She'd come up with a plan of attack, as Carol had known she would. Carol could go on her way. Jillian would handle Meg, and by extension, her father, Tom Pesaturo. Go, Jillian.

Personally, Carol didn't like Tom. Based on things Meg said, he sounded overbearing, brutish and chauvinistic to the core. Making his daughter drop out of college. As if denying his child higher education was the secret to keeping her safe. For heaven's sake, was there anything of value in the Y chromosome? One ounce of intelligence to go with all that raging testosterone?

Of course, that made her think of Dan, and the scent of red roses and veal piccata. And that thought sliced through her heady steam of rage, her frenzy of self-righteousness. She was left suddenly empty and bereft, the legs taken right out from beneath her.

She had loved him so much once. Did he ever remember those days? When just the sight of him across the room sent her heart beating rapid-fire with lust? When the thought of seeing him for dinner made her smile all day? When the scent of his cologne was the first thing she wanted to smell in the morning and the last thing she wanted to smell at night? When they used to sleep intertwined like vines, legs and arms coiling, her head planted securely on his chest?

She still remembered those days. Some nights, when she was not busy hating Eddie Como, she stayed awake replaying those first wild, wonderful moments in her mind. She was never sure which set of thoughts hurt her more.

Now she plopped down in the Nordstrom Café, where she had a heaping chicken Oriental salad, and yes, another piece of chocolate cake. Then she ordered a glass of wine. Or two or three or four.

She was still hungry afterward, but that didn't surprise her anymore. She had been hungry for well over a year.

Being raped was an interesting thing. More interesting than Carol would've imagined. Yes, she now suffered from a variety of lovely mental conditions. Post-traumatic stress syndrome that left her with nightmares, cold sweats and irrational mood swings. Generalization that left her hating not just her rapist, but pretty much all men, including her husband, Detective Fitzpatrick and Ned D'Amato. Then there was her "trigger syndrome" – she literally could not turn off the TV because turning off the TV was one of the last things she'd done before being attacked, and thus her mind associated the act with causing the rape. And finally there was good old-fashioned guilt – guilt that she'd been attacked, guilt that she'd survived. Guilt that she'd inconvenienced her husband, guilt that she'd left her window open, guilt that she'd not been able to fend off a grown man. Jillian, whether she would admit it or not, still held the prize in the guilt category, but Carol thought she should get credit for having not just one of the various syndromes they'd read about in rape survivors' handbooks, but pretty much all of them rolled up in a nice, neat, therapy-desperately-needed ball. In her own way, she was an overachiever, too.

So on the one hand, being raped was as traumatic, painful, messy and soul wrenching as Carol had ever imagined. She did not recommend it. Women really should shoot first, and question later.

On the other hand . . .

On the other hand, for lack of a better word, being raped did have its advantages. Take the Survivors Club. Carol now spent the majority of her time with two women whom before this, she probably wouldn't have given the time of day. Meg, after all, was too young for Carol to have ever considered seriously as a friend. And, if Carol was being truly honest, too working class. Assuming their paths ever did cross, it probably would've been in some swanky restaurant where Carol was the patron and Meg the waitress. Neither would have thought of it again.

Jillian was a more interesting case. She was closer to Carol's age and economic status. The type of woman Carol might have met naturally at some society event or charity fund-raiser. They would've exchanged polite chitchat, the normal cocktail party pleasantries. Most likely, Carol would've found Jillian to be too much of a career woman. And most likely, Jillian would've found Carol to be too

1950s, the socialite wife who stayed at home while her husband did the real work.

But now here they all were. Pissy sometimes, mean sometimes, awkward sometimes. Telling each other all the things normal people couldn't understand. Rallying one moment, crying the next. Holding back more confidences still. Carol was sure of this. God knows she had her own things that even a year later she could not bring herself to put into words. And as for Jillian – well, Carol and Meg were certain they hadn't even begun to scratch the surface there. So they had their secrets. But they also had this bond, one that shouldn't exist, and it was sad that it did exist, but here they were. And in all honesty, their weekly meetings were about the only thing that kept Carol going.

Normal people could not understand these things. Normal people, if they were at all lucky, would never have to understand these things.

Carol finished her glass of wine. Then, duly fortified, she finally headed home.

No reporters in sight. That was a welcome relief. They'd probably been camped out most of the day, another reason for her not to hurry home. It was after 6:00 now, however, too late to make the 5:00 news crunch. Or maybe the police were holding a briefing across town. Jillian, Carol and Meg had learned to love police briefings, when the reporters would scurry from their front lawns to police headquarters, leaving the women at least fifteen minutes to breathe. Until the police briefing ended, of course, and the hordes once more came trooping down the street, rows and rows of white news vans carrying legions of question-wielding combatants. On her good days, Carol pictured having a machine gun battened to her roof, which she would use to mow them all down. On her bad days, she cowered in the upstairs bathroom, the only room in the house with no windows, and gobbled pints of Ben & Jerry's ice cream while curled up in the empty bathtub.

Dan's car was parked in the driveway. The hood was cold to the touch; he'd been home for a bit. Not a good sign.

Five minutes later, she found Dan sitting in the family room with only the constantly chattering TV as a source of light. He started when she entered the room, and she would've sworn he made some kind of furtive motion. When she walked around for a better look, however, he was merely picking up a large, round cognac glass for one last sip. She stared at him, waiting to see who would talk first. Then she realized that he still wore a suit and his short, dark brown hair was horribly rumpled – he always ran his fingers through his hair when he was anxious.

On the TV, some blond newswoman was standing in front of the courthouse, talking into her microphone as a barrage of red and blue police lights relentlessly swirled around her head.

"Police have now confirmed that alleged rape suspect, Eddie Como, aka the College Hill Rapist, was shot and killed here earlier this morning. Sources close to the investigation say that twenty-eight-year-old Como was shot once in the head as he was being unloaded from the ACI van at the Licht Judicial Complex around eight-thirty. According to a fellow prisoner – "

"I came home as soon as I heard the news," Dan finally spoke up.

Carol didn't say anything.

"I thought you might want to see me."

Carol still didn't say anything.

"You could've at least called," he said quietly. His eyes rose to meet hers. "I do worry, you know."

"You're dressed for work."

"Dammit, Carol, I canceled three meetings today – "

"You're going back to the office."

"I don't have a choice! Clients pay me to be available at the snap of their fingers. Lawyering isn't a nine-to-five job. You know that."

She said simply, "It will be dark."

Dan's eyes fell. He opened his mouth, then closed it into a grim line and focused instead on rotating the now empty cognac glass between his fingers. He was angry. She read his tension in the tight, bunched line of his shoulders. But he didn't say another word. And the silence went on and on and on.

"I went shopping," she said at last, chin held up defiantly.

"I can see that."

"I bought three suits. Nice ones."

"All right, Carol."

"I spent two thousand dollars," she pushed.

A muscle twitched in his jaw. He spun the fine crystal goblet with even greater concentration. She decided on a new tack. The sun was going down. Dusk descending on their too big, too empty house. And he was leaving her again, proof that no matter what punishment she inflicted upon him, he was more than capable of inflicting it right back.

"The police came to see us today," she announced. "Detective Fitzpatrick crashed our meeting."

"He wanted to be the first to give you the big news?"

"No, he wanted to be the first to ask us if we killed him."

"And what did Jillian say to that?"

"She told him to fuck off. Using bigger words, of course."

"Detective Fitzpatrick should've known better." Dan finally set his glass down on the coffee table. He rose off the sofa. His movements were restless and agitated.

"It wasn't just Fitzpatrick. A state guy came as well."

"The state?" Dan's head jerked around.

"Detective Sergeant Roan Griffin. Big guy. Smart. He claims they'll subpoena our bank records next. You know, to see if they can find any mysterious cash withdrawals or money transfers, anything that might be construed as a payment to a hired gun. He seems very determined about it."

Dan walked away from her, finally halting in front of the mantel around the fireplace. He ran one finger down the scrolling woodwork. Dan had long, lean fingers. He could've been a sculptor or a musician. Or a father teaching his son how to tie his first bowknot.

"Why are they bothering with an investigation?" he asked curtly. "Eddie Como has caused enough damage. He's dead. Let it be."

"I don't care," Carol said fiercely. "Whoever shot him. I don't care."

She was holding her breath, willing her husband to turn around and look her in the eye. She had started this conversation to goad him, but now . . . Now she heard the ache in her voice. She hadn't told anyone, not even Meg or Jillian, but Carol half hoped her husband *had* shot or paid someone to shoot Eddie Como. It would be the first sign she had that he still loved her.

I know where you were that night. I've never told anyone, but I know where you were that night, and it was not working late.

Dan turned around. Dan looked her in the eye with his deep brown gaze. Ten years of marriage later, his face held new lines, darker shadows, grayer hair. The years had been rough on both of them. So many things that had not turned out quite the way they'd planned. And yet she still thought he was handsome. She still wished he would cross the room right now and take her in his arms.

If you would promise to try to touch me, I would promise to try not to pull away. If you would promise to try to reach out to me, I would promise to try not to see you as another Eddie Como. If you would promise to try to love me again, I would promise to try to forgive you. And maybe, if you did try and I did try . . .

He said, "I have to go. The meeting starts at seven and I still need to prepare."

"Dan – " She caught the rest of the sentence. Bit it back. Swallowed it down.

"You'll lock the door behind me?"

"Of course."

"And turn on the alarm?"

"I know, Dan."

"Think of it this way, Carol – the press are bound to be back soon. Then you won't be alone, after all."

He came around the sofa, glanced at her shopping bags and grimaced on his way out of the room. The next sound she heard was the front door opening, then closing behind him. A moment later, his car started up in their driveway.

Carol's gaze went outside, where the sun sank low on the horizon. Dusk falling. Night approaching. The dark coming, coming, coming to find her.

The silence, on the other hand, was already here.

On TV, the perky blond reporter said, *"Eddie Como's family announced this afternoon that they will seek to claim his body from the medical examiner's office no later than tomorrow night, in order to prepare for a Catholic funeral service first thing Wednesday morning. The family, still claiming his innocence, has also said that they would like to start a memorial fund to help other wrongfully accused men . . ."*

Carol locked the front door, armed the security system. Then she went upstairs to the main hallway. She walked down its long, shadowed length to the tightly shut door at one end. She opened the door. And she looked inside the room, the room she had once shared with her husband, the room where she had once made love to her husband, and what she saw now was merely a collection of dusty furniture held captive behind wrought-iron bars.

No open windows. No wet, blood-spattered cotton sheets. No piles of latex strips still littered with pieces of long, blond hair.

Nothing. Nothing, nothing, nothing.

Her hands started to shake. Her heart picked up its pace. He's dead, she tried to tell herself. He's dead, it's over, you're finally safe.

No good. No good, no good, no good.

Carol slammed the door shut, recoiling down the hallway, grabbing blindly at the walls with her bare hands. She had to get away. The TV was still on. Didn't matter, didn't matter. The house was too big, the silence too powerful, and God knows Dan would come home much too late. On her own. Always alone. Run, Carol, run.

She stumbled into the upstairs bathroom. She slammed the door. And then she leaned over the white porcelain sink, where she vomited until she dry-heaved.

Eddie Como's dead. Eddie Como's dead. Eddie Como's dead.

It's over, Carol. You're finally, finally safe.

But her whole body was shivering, trembling, quaking. And she couldn't stop thinking about her empty bedroom. She couldn't stop thinking about that one bedroom window. She couldn't stop thinking that she would swear, she would swear, she would swear that Dead Eddie had been standing right there.

16

Meg

"Jesus, Mary and Joseph, are you *drunk?*"

"I just . . . it was champagne. Only a glass. Maybe two. I swear."

"Mr. Pesaturo, if you would just calm down for a moment – "

"And you!" Mr. Pesaturo swung around on Jillian, beefy face bright red, thick finger stabbing the air. His blue electrician's uniform strained over his gut, two of the white buttons literally quaking with the force of his rage. The effect was rather comical, and now that he was safely yelling at Jillian, Meg started to giggle again. Jillian tried shooting her a warning glance. Meg had had nearly six glasses of champagne. It was hopeless.

"How dare you serve my underaged daughter alcohol!" Tom Pesaturo boomed. "For God's sake, haven't you done enough already?"

Jillian blinked. "Done enough?"

"Daddy – "

"Tom, calm down, have a seat. Meg is home now and that's what's important." Meg's mother, Laurie, intervened, placing her hand on her husband's bulging forearm. She was clearly the voice of reason in the family, thank God. Mr. Pesaturo glowered at Jillian again, but finally, reluctantly, sat.

Meg chose that moment to exclaim, "Holy Lord, I have got to pee!" and go racing from the room.

Mr. Pesaturo renewed his growl of disapproval. Jillian sighed, took her own seat on a threadbare blue recliner and realized she had a raging headache.

"Mr. Pesaturo – "

"Have you seen the news? Do you understand what happened this morning? Our phone has been ringing off the hook since nine A.M. The first news van was here by nine-fifteen. And we didn't even know where Meg was."

"We knew exactly where Meg was," Laurie interjected again, her voice firm. "I told you she was having breakfast with Jillian and Carol."

"That's what Meg *said,*" Tom asserted, with just the right tone of doubt.

Jillian looked at him. "Mr. Pesaturo, do you think we were running around shooting Eddie Como this morning? Is that what you thought we were doing?"

"Hey, I'm not saying I disapprove . . ."

"We were at the restaurant, Mr. Pesaturo. All day, as a matter of fact. With witnesses. Though you should know that the police stopped by. Detective Fitzpatrick and a man from the state, Sergeant Griffin, definitely have us on their radar screen."

"What did you tell them?"

"We didn't tell them anything, of course. We don't have to give them a statement, and personally, I don't want to give them a statement. As far as I'm concerned, they'll have my cooperation the day they bring my sister back from the dead."

Mr. Pesaturo finally stopped scowling. After another moment, he grunted and settled deeper into the loveseat, probably as close as she'd get to praise. "Yeah, well," he said gruffly. Sitting beside him, his wife smiled.

"They will start looking into all of us," Jillian said levelly. She'd been thinking of nothing but that for the last half hour. The state police were on the case. The state police were going to get serious. She wondered what that really meant. Big, bad Sergeant Griffin, who probably could've ripped off that pedophile's head. Big, bad Sergeant Griffin with those penetrating blue eyes. She felt herself getting angry again, then confused. Big, bad Sergeant Griffin . . . She cut off the thought, focused again on the matters at hand. "I'm told that every detective in the state is now working this case. The next order of business will be examining our financial records for any unexplained withdrawals."

Mr. Pesaturo rolled his eyes. "Good luck. I don't have any unexplained withdrawals. I got a mortgage and I got two kids. That pretty much covers it."

"I imagine they'll also want to talk to your brother," Jillian said. "You know, Uncle Vinnie."

The smile vanished from Mrs. Pesaturo's face. She jerked back, looking at her husband sharply. "Tom?"

"Oh come on. Let 'em talk to Vinnie. He don't care."

Mr. Pesaturo was looking at Jillian now. From the hallway, Jillian could hear Meg's voice, followed by a high-pitched giggle. Meg was talking to her little sister, Molly. More laughter floated down the hall.

"You care?" Tom asked Jillian abruptly. Jillian was not an idiot. She understood the nuances of the question.

"I'm all right."

" 'Cause you know, if you needed anything . . ."

Jillian smiled. In his own way, Mr. Pesaturo was a very sweet man. It made it almost tempting, but the problems she had were nothing he could help her with. Now that she'd had more time to contemplate the impact of Eddie Como's death, she figured she had twenty-four to forty-eight hours before she saw Sergeant Griffin again. Life would get tricky. Then again, had it ever been simple?

"I'm all right," she repeated. Mr. Pesaturo was smarter than she'd given him credit for, however, and she could see the open doubt on his face.

"Vinnie . . . he's got a lotta friends."

"I know. In fact, I'm not sure if you know, but I believe Vinnie and my mother have some of the same friends."

"No kiddin'?"

"Do you follow music? My mother used to literally sing the blues – "

"Wait a minute. Hayes. Olivia Hayes. *That's* your mom?"

"She'll be pleased you remember."

Tom Pesaturo was clearly impressed. He rocked back, turning to his wife. "No kidding, Olivia Hayes. You ever hear of her? Pretty little thing about a hundred pounds soaking wet. Then she'd open her mouth and blow the place away. My father used to listen to her records all the time. I probably got a vinyl or two stashed in the attic. Fine, beautiful lady." He turned back to Jillian. "What happened to her anyway? I haven't heard her name in years."

"She retired." Said she was going to finally spend time with her daughters. Had a stroke. Lost her legs. Lost her voice. At least they'd never had to worry about money.

"You tell her I said hi."

"I'll do that."

"Vinnie's gonna flip." Mr. Pesaturo suddenly smiled and sat up straighter. "My daughter is friends with Olivia Hayes's daughter. Vinnie's gonna have a fucking *cow!*"

"Tom . . ." His wife rolled her eyes at his profanity, then glanced at Jillian apologetically. Jillian smiled. She was genuinely pleased that Mr. Pesaturo was pleased. Her mother's time, Jillian's own childhood, was a bygone era not many people remembered anymore. When Trish had been little, stories from the nightclubs had been her favorite ones. The night their mother had sung for Sinatra. How later Frank had let eight-year-old Jillian sit on his knee. Jillian had done her best to tell the tales, though even for her they'd taken on a hazy quality, a life lived so long ago it now seemed more like a distant dream.

The days her mother had had a voice. Jillian had not even heard her hum in years now.

Tom Pesaturo had settled back into the sofa. His face was finally relaxed, his big hands resting comfortably on his knees. Jillian's parentage had done the trick. They were now old friends and he was happy to have her in his living room. It was funny, but during the last twelve months that Jillian's and Meg's lives had been intertwined, she'd never visited Meg's house. Not Carol's home either. By some unspoken rule, the group always met in restaurants or other public places. It was as if after everything they'd told one another, they couldn't bear to share this last little bit.

"I was worried," Mr. Pesaturo said abruptly, maybe even a little apologetically. "When I heard the news on TV, when I couldn't find Meg. I went a little nuts."

"I understand."

"You got kids?"

Jillian thought of Trish and her bright, bright eyes. She thought of her mother, wheelchair-bound since her stroke. "No."

"It's not easy. You wanna keep 'em safe, you know. I mean, you want 'em to go out in the world. Be strong. Make you proud. But mostly, mostly you want 'em to be safe. Happy. Okay."

"She's okay," Mrs. Pesaturo murmured. "They're both okay."

"If I coulda been there, that night . . . That's what kills me, you know. This Como guy," Mr. Pesaturo spat. "He's not even that big. If I'd been there that night, I would've kicked his sorry spic ass."

Jillian thought of Trisha's dark apartment. Her sister's unmoving form on the bed. Those strong, strong hands grabbing her from behind. She said, "I wish you would've been there, too."

"Yeah, well, I guess there's not much I can do about it now. At least the guy's dead. I feel better about that. Hey" – his head jerked up – "think Meg'll be all right now?"

Jillian was puzzled. "I think Meg is already all right."

"No, no. Start remembering. Get her life back. You know."

"I'm . . . I'm not sure. I really don't know that much about amnesia."

"She don't talk about it?"

"What do you mean?"

"Her amnesia. What that asshole did to her. Don't you girls talk about this stuff over coffee or something like that?"

"Mr. Pesaturo . . ." Jillian began, but Laurie Pesaturo beat her to the punch.

"Tom, shut up."

Mr. Pesaturo blinked at his wife. "What?"

"Jillian is not going to tell you about our daughter's state of mind. If you want to know what Meg is thinking, ask her yourself."

"I was just asking," Tom said defensively, but he hung his big head, suitably chastised. Jillian took some pity on him.

"For the record," she told him. "I think Meg is doing remarkably well. She's a strong young lady, Mr. Pesaturo. You should be proud of her."

"I *am* proud of her!"

"Are you? Or are you mostly afraid for her?"

"Hey now!" Mr. Pesaturo didn't like that much at all. But when he found Jillian staring at him steadily, and his own wife regarding him steadily, his shoulders hunkered again. "I'm a father," he muttered. "Fathers protect their daughters. Nothing wrong with that."

"She's twenty years old," Laurie said.

"Still young."

"Tom, it's been years . . ." Laurie said. Which Jillian didn't get. Didn't she mean one year?

Mr. Pesaturo said, "Yeah, and we've been lucky to get her this far."

"That's not fair."

"You're telling me."

Jillian was very confused now, which must have shown on her face, because suddenly both Mr. and Mrs. Pesaturo drew up short. They looked at their guest, they looked at each other, and that was the end of that conversation.

"I should get going," Jillian said at last, when the silence had gone on too long. Meg's parents didn't waste any time getting up off the couch.

"Thank you for bringing Meg home," Mrs. Pesaturo said. "We'll make arrangements to retrieve her car."

"The champagne . . . Well, it seemed like a good idea at the time."

Mrs. Pesaturo smiled kindly at her. "It's been a long, strange day, hasn't it?"

"Yes," Jillian said, and she didn't know why, but at that moment she wanted to cry. She pulled herself back together. Her nerves were rattled, had been all day, and her private conversation with Sergeant Griffin had only made things worse. But her weariness didn't matter. There were probably still cameras outside. You had to wear your game face. Besides, she would need her strength for when she returned home, to where her aphasia-stricken mother had probably already heard the news and was now sifting through her picture book, trying to find an image that could communicate *My daughter's murderer died today and I feel . . .*

Meg was back. "Come on," she told Jillian. "I'll walk you to the door."

Jillian followed her down the narrow hallway. Meg's little sister, Molly, peered out at them from around the corner, a mass of dark corkscrew curls and big doe-brown eyes. *Trish,* Jillian thought. She had to get out of this house.

When Meg opened the door, Jillian was startled to see that it was already dark outside. The night wind felt cool on her face. The street was long and empty. Not a reporter in sight, which made her both grateful and more unsettled. Where were all the flashing lights and rapid-fire questions? Where had the day gone? It was already a blur.

Meg was swaying slightly in the breeze. "Thank you," she murmured.

"For what?" Jillian was still staring into the night. On her right, something moved in the bushes.

"I'm starting to feel better already, you know. The shock's wearing off, I guess. I didn't think it would be this fast, but now . . . I feel like for the first time in twelve months, I can finally breathe."

Jillian just stared at Meg. And then she got it. Meg was talking about Eddie Como's demise. She was thanking Jillian for Eddie Como's murder.

"But you're right," Meg continued expansively. "We shouldn't talk about it. The police will probably still be coming around, at least for a few days. Then the worst will be past. The dust will settle. And we'll be . . . we'll be free."

"Meg . . ."

"Isn't it a beautiful night?"

"Oh God, Meg . . ."

"Such a lovely, lovely night."

"You've had more to drink! Why do you keep drinking?"

"I don't know. The doctors said not to push. The mind will heal itself. But it hasn't, and really, as of today, I thought it should. So I added some bourbon. But you know, it didn't work."

"Meg, you just need rest."

"No, I don't think I do. I think it's all much weirder than that. I've had rest, I've had peace and now I've had closure. But I can still feel the eyes following me. What does that mean?"

"It means you've had too much to drink."

"I want to be happy. I don't think I was. Because if I had been happy, shouldn't I be able to remember it? Shouldn't it come back to me?"

"Meg, listen to me – "

"Shhhh, the bushes."

Jillian stopped, drew up short. She looked at the bushes, still twitching on the right. She looked at Meg. This close, she could see the glassy sheen to the girl's dark eyes, the red flush of bourbon warming her cheeks.

"Whoever is hiding in the bushes, you'd better come out," Jillian called.

"Beautiful, beautiful night," Meg singsonged. "Oh, what a lovely night, just like the last night, that night."

"I'm warning you!" Jillian's voice started to rise in spite of herself as another leaf quivered and Meg rocked back and forth like a giant pendulum.

"A beautiful, beautiful night. A lovely, lovely night . . ."

"*Goddammit!*" Jillian strode over to the bush. She thrust in her hand as if she would drag out the interloper by his ear. She'd yank him out. And then she'd . . . she'd . . .

The gray tiger-striped cat sprang out of the bush with a hostile MEOW and Jillian staggered back, her heart hammering hard in her chest. She had to take a deep breath, then another. Her heart was still racing. The hairs had prickled up on the back of her neck. Oh God, she suddenly wanted away from this house and out of this too-empty street. She couldn't stop shivering.

On the porch, Meg had a beatific smile plastered on her face. "Gone now. He's all gone now."

"Please go inside, Meg," Jillian said tiredly.

"It won't make a difference. He's here, he's here, he's here."

"Who is here?"

And Meg whispered, "I don't know. Whoever's worse than Eddie Como."

17
Griffin

"We got a problem."

Now at the state police headquarters in North Scituate, Griffin finally paused in the middle of five piles of paper. It was a little after six-thirty, and he was trying to get the command post up and running in the vast gray-carpeted Detective Bureau meeting room. It never failed to amaze him how much paperwork could be generated by a single crime. Contact reports, witness statements, detective activity reports (DARs), financial workups and preliminary evidence reports. He was already knee-deep in paperwork and even as he pored over documents, uniformed officers, financial crimes detectives and CIU detectives were breezing through the conference center to drop even more reports on the table. Occasionally, the lieutenant or major or colonel also stopped by, wanting to know if he'd magically solved the case yet. Oh yeah, and the phone rang a lot. Reporters wanting quotes. Local businessmen wanting justice. The AG wanting to emphasize once again that he didn't like shootings in his backyard and that the mayor felt major explosions were bad for tourism.

Now he had Fitz on the phone. "Are you watching this?" Fitz was saying. "Can you fuckin' believe this?"

"I'm not watching anything."

"Then turn on the TV!"

Griffin raised a brow, sifted through the precariously stacked mounds of paper for the remote, then turned on the TV. He was instantly rewarded by a live news feed being shown on Channel 10.

"Ah, so that's where all the reporters went. I kind of wondered when they magically disappeared from the parking lot."

"This is not good," Fitz moaned. "So really not good."

Eddie Como's public defense lawyer, an earnest fellow by the name of Frank Sierra, was now explaining to the equally earnest press corps that a true tragedy had happened this morning on the steps of justice. Why, just last night, he'd gotten a fresh lead that proved once and for all his client's innocence. He'd been planning on introducing the new evidence first thing this morning to clear Eddie Como's name. Another fifteen, twenty minutes, that was all he would've needed, and Mr. Como would have been as free as a bird.

"That doesn't sound promising," Griffin informed Fitz by phone.

"I fucking hate lawyers," Fitz growled.

"Don't worry, I'm sure they hate you, too."

Griffin paused long enough to listen to Sierra's next statement. In the conference room, Waters and a bunch of other Major Crimes detectives had also halted to watch the show. Better than Barnum & Bailey, most of these press conferences.

"Late last night," public defender Frank Sierra was saying, "I made contact with a witness who can place Mr. Como halfway across town on the night and time of the second attack, offering corroboration of my client's activities on the evening in question. Ladies and gentlemen, may I please introduce Lucas Murphy."

Eddie Como's lawyer stepped aside, and a gangly kid who couldn't have been more than eighteen took his place. The kid, all arms, legs and zits, stared at the flashing cameras like a deer in headlights. For a moment, Griffin thought the kid might bolt, and Sierra must've thought so, too, because he grabbed the teenager's arm. Then he remembered his audience, and smiled brightly for all the pretty people.

"A witness," Fitz muttered on the phone. "What the hell kind of evidence is that? For fifty bucks or less even I could conjure up a witness."

Sierra announced, "Mr. Murphy works at Blockbuster Video over in Warwick."

Griffin said, "Uh oh."

"Mr. Murphy, on the night of May tenth, could you please tell these fine people where you were?"

"Oh my God!" Fitz went apoplectic. "He's treating him like a witness. Right here on the evening news, he's launching into his defense. I cannot fucking believe this!"

"I was . . . uh . . . well . . . working," the kid squeaked. "You know, um, at Blockbuster."

Sierra was getting into things now. "And did you happen to see Mr. Como that evening, the evening of May tenth, in your video store on Route Two in Warwick?"

"Um . . . yes."

The reporters obligingly gasped. Fitz swore again. Griffin simply rolled his eyes.

On TV, Eddie Como's lawyer practically rubbed his hands together with glee. "Mr. Murphy, are you certain you saw Eddie Como on the night of May tenth?"

"Um, yes."

"But, Mr. Murphy, because I know the fine members of the press will ask this next, *how* can you be so certain it was Mr. Como who came into your store that night?"

"Well . . . I saw his name. You know, on his membership card."

The press gasped again. Fitz mumbled something along the lines of "Oh my God, someone shut that kid up. Quick, get me a gun."

Griffin told him kindly, "Oh yeah, now you're in trouble."

On TV, Sierra paused, beamed for the cameras again, and prepared to move in for the kill. "Mr. Murphy, isn't it true that whenever someone rents a video at Blockbuster, there is a record of the transaction?"

"Well, yeah . . . you know. People hand over their card. We scan that in. Then, you know, we scan in the video. So the computer has um, the video, and um, who rented it, and oh yeah, at what day and at what time. You know, so we know who has what video and if it's late when they return it, in case, you know, they owe any late fees, that sort of thing. You gotta know that stuff if you're a video store." The kid nodded earnestly. "Also, we got this program now, where if you return a new release right away, like, um, in twenty-four hours, you get a dollar credit on your Block-buster account. So people come inside for the returns to show their card. I mean, a buck's a buck."

Eddie Como's lawyer practically creamed his pants on live TV. "So," he boomed. "Not only did you *personally* see Eddie Como returning a video to your store on the night of May tenth, at ten twenty-five P.M., just five minutes before the alleged attack on Mrs. Rosen, over on the East Side, which Eddie couldn't possibly have driven to in just five minutes, you have a *record* of that transaction. A computer-generated *record!*"

"Fucking computers!" Fitz roared.

While on TV, Lucas Murphy, Blockbuster's new employee of the month, said, "Mmmm, yes."

The reporters started to buzz. In the conference room, Waters shook his head and sighed. Over the phone, Fitz sounded like he was moaning, then came the distinct crunch of antacid tablets.

"Come on," Griffin murmured, staring intently at the TV. "Ask him the next question. Ask him the logical next question . . ."

But Eddie Como's defense lawyer was smarter than he looked. Frank Sierra thanked the press, he thanked the Lord for giving them the truth, even if it was tragically too late, and then he yanked his young, big-eyed witness out of the line of cameras while he was still ahead. The news briefing broke up. Channel 10 cut to a shot of good old Maureen, her blue eyes brighter than ever, saying breathlessly, "Well, it has certainly been a big day in the College Hill Rapist case. New information casts doubt that Eddie Como, shot dead just this morning, was indeed the College Hill Rapist. Ladies, does that mean the real rapist could still be out there – "

Griffin shut off the TV. Waters was looking at him, while

on the other end of the phone, Fitz continued chomping away on Tums.

"Sierra ambushed us," Fitz growled between mouthfuls of antacid. "Didn't give us any warning. Not even a peep about his new evidence, new witness, nada. One minute I'm down at the morgue watching the ME search for viable skin on a deep-fried John Doe, the next I got a call from my lieutenant telling me I'd better turn on the news. What the fuck is up with that? Sierra could've at least given us the courtesy of a phone call."

"Ah, but then you could've prepared a reply," Griffin said.

"This is bullshit," Fitz continued, full steam ahead. "Sierra's client is dead, so now he's carrying out his case on the evening news, where he'll never have to fear being cross-examined. The public will only hear what he wants them to hear." His voice built again. "*Forget* about three raped women. *Forget* about Trisha Hayes, tied up and asphyxiating in her own apartment. *Forget* that Eddie Como irreparably damaged four innocent lives. Let's just focus on the poor little rapist, who was probably potty-trained at gunpoint. For heaven's sake, why didn't Sierra just march over to the women's homes and personally slap them across the face!"

"It's not conclusive evidence," Griffin said, addressing both Waters and Fitz at once. "Saying he could have Eddie's name cleared by afternoon was overstating things a bit. Who's the prosecutor?"

"D'Amato," Fitz grumbled. He seemed to be working on taking deep breaths.

"Yeah, well, that's why Sierra made his case on TV instead of in the courtroom. D'Amato would've eaten this kid alive. Do Blockbuster Video cards contain photo ID? No. Isn't it true that anyone could've come in with Eddie Como's card to return a movie, not necessarily Eddie Como? But he thought the guy did look like Eddie Como? Well then why didn't he come forward before now? Why did he wait a full year to share this news? That's the *real* question."

"He was scared." Fitz played devil's advocate.

"Why? The College Hill Rapist never attacked a man. And don't you have a girlfriend, mother, sister, Mr. Murphy? Didn't you think about them, worry about them? If you really thought Como wasn't the guy, then that means the rapist is still out there. So why didn't you come forward to help catch the real perpetrator and keep your girlfriend/sister/mother safe?"

"I don't know," Fitz said.

"Of course you don't know, Mr. Murphy. That's because it's now been over a year since ten May. How sure can you be after a whole year? Do you remember what you ate that morning for breakfast? What were you wearing? What did you do for lunch? Who did you call? Who were your other customers? What video did you watch that night at work? That's what I thought, Mr. Murphy, you don't really remember that much at all about that night, *do you?*"

"Uh oh, I think I just wet myself," Fitz intoned. "You're right, I am nothing but miserable scum. On the other hand, those fine, magnificent detectives at the Providence Police Department are geniuses, men above men. And that Detective Fitzpatrick, he's a stud. If I had a young, nubile sister, I would send her to him."

"Yeah, but since he's already given his best years to the job, I wouldn't bother."

"Ain't that the truth," Fitz murmured. He took a last deep breath and seemed to come to grips with things. "Computerized records of a rental return. Who would've thought?"

"How sure are you of the time of the rape?"

"It's not exact. Carol Rosen went to bed a little after ten. She thought she'd been asleep about a half an hour when she woke up to a sound in her bedroom. She didn't look at the clock, though."

"So even if Eddie was returning a video in Warwick, that doesn't prove he *didn't* later head into Providence."

"It's not concrete. But if you take this kid's statement and you combine it with Eddie's girlfriend, Tawnya, talking about Eddie's favorite pastime being hanging out with her and their unborn child and watching a few movies . . ."

"Eddie starts looking sympathetic. A quiet family man. Given his fetish, you never checked with Blockbuster?"

"When we asked Eddie what he'd done that night, it was already six weeks later. He thought he might have rented a movie, which was his habit, but when he checked his credit card statement he hadn't. No one thought about a *returned* movie as an alibi."

"Live and learn," Griffin said.

"The DNA evidence is still DNA evidence," Fitz muttered. "God knows, if cops comprised juries, we would send him to the chair. But of course jury boxes are filled with, well, jurors. If Eddie starts looking good . . ."

"The outcome of the trial grows doubtful," Griffin concluded for him. He was quiet for a moment. "You know, if this testimony looked really bad, D'Amato had another option. He could drop the charges pertaining to the second attack. Only try Eddie for Meg Pesaturo, Trisha Hayes and Jillian Hayes. He loses one count of first-degree sexual assault, but life in prison is still life in prison."

"Carol Rosen wouldn't like that much."

"No, she wouldn't," Griffin said meaningfully.

"Even if D'Amato dropped the charges involving Carol so Eddie's lawyer couldn't get Teen Blockbuster in court," Fitz said, "Sierra could still trot the kid out for the press like he's doing now. That makes Eddie start looking good to the public, the ACLU or anyone else who gets off on pitying rapists. And that would piss *all* the women off. Hell, it pisses me off."

"Makes things interesting. Do you think this is what Tawnya meant when she said something was going to come out at trial?"

"I don't know. She's been firm about Eddie's innocence. Seems to me that if she knew about Teen Blockbuster, she would've been shouting this evidence from the rooftop. I had the impression she was talking about something on one of the women."

"Is there something we should know about the women?" Griffin asked sharply.

"Hey, I spent a year with the women, and if there was something we should know, we would know it. Then again," Fitz admitted sulkily, "I'm 'refreshing' my report on them as we speak."

"It provides motive. Particularly for Mrs. Rosen and/or her family."

"Assuming they knew about Teen Blockbuster."

"Which gives us a starting point. How did Eddie Como's lawyer hear about this kid? And how many other people knew about him as well? Assuming, of course, that the kid is telling the truth."

Fitz sighed. "I knew this day was going to end badly. Okay, let's talk it through. Scenario A is that Eddie's lawyer finally got bright and decided to check Blockbuster just in case. Then . . ."

"Kid's probably telling the truth, and never came forward on his own because he didn't want to get involved, or was afraid to get involved, or all of the above."

"All right, so in Scenario A we do have a witness. Which doesn't mean we were *wrong* about what Eddie did after he dropped off the movie," Fitz added testily, "but does make the trial more interesting and the victims/family/friends more anxious about the outcome."

"Agreed."

"Okay, then we have Scenario B, which is that Teen Blockbuster is coming forward now with his own agenda. What might that be?"

Griffin's voice was dry. "Maybe he saw Tawnya. In her own words, she's been beating away the boys since she was twelve. Maybe she decided Eddie needed a little insurance at trial and this was the best way of getting it. Of course, that means someone, probably the kid, had to be willing to mess with Blockbuster's computer system to show a false transaction. I don't know how believable that is."

"Hey, did you see the kid's face? A teenage boy with that many pimples could probably hack into the Pentagon."

"In your own way, you're a real Sherlock, Fitz."

"I like to think so."

"All right," Griffin said. "If it was just the kid's statement, I'd buy into Scenario B. I don't like the computer record, though. That's getting pretty elaborate to be a ruse."

"So we're back at Scenario A, where the kid is legit. Of course, we'll have to pay him a visit to be sure."

"Meaning Eddie Como may have a semblance of an alibi," Griffin filled in.

"No way," Fitz said firmly. "Even if the kid is right, it's just a little confusion over time. So Eddie returned a video in Warwick before he continued on to Providence. There's no rule that says rapists can't run errands. Hell, I'll bet even Ted Bundy tended to daily chores every now and then. But Eddie did it. DNA doesn't lie, and we've got Eddie's DNA. Once, twice, three times. The kid went up to bat, and we have struck him out."

Griffin was quiet for a moment. He had a sense of déjà vu again. For the second time today, he was having a conversation where the evidence against Eddie Como appeared sketchy, *except* for the DNA. And then he finally got what was bothering him about this case. "Hey, Fitz," he said. "How *good* was the DNA match with Eddie Como?"

"Huh?"

"How many points of the DNA matched? A four-point, eight-point, twelve-point match?"

"How the hell do I know? I'm not the guy in a lab coat. The report from the health department said the samples matched. A match is a match is a match."

"Not necessarily."

"Griffin, what the hell are you talking about?"

"I'm not sure yet. But tell me this: Are you absolutely *positive* that Eddie Como didn't have a brother?"

18

Jillian

Jillian got home late. Nearly 9:00 P.M., a late end to a too-long day that had left her jumpy and anxious. She'd checked the backseat of her car four times for interlopers since leaving Meg's house. She'd walked everywhere with her car key sticking out like a weapon from her fisted hand. Once, she had even popped open her trunk, just to be sure. She was protecting herself from overly aggressive reporters, she told herself, but knew that she was lying.

Arriving home, she was grateful to see lights blazing. Since the first phone call from Eddie Como nearly a year before, she had installed motion-sensitive floodlights in the front of her residence, as well as strategically placed spotlights that illuminated each bush and shrub. There would be no skulking around her East Greenwich home. The house also featured a new state-of-the-art home security system with a panic button in every room, and a remote her wheelchair-bound mother kept in her pocket. Jillian hadn't quite convinced herself to buy a handgun yet, but had perhaps gone a little nuts procuring pepper spray. She slept with a canister beneath her pillow at night. Her mom had hers tucked in her bedside drawer. As Toppi had dryly observed, the Hayes women were ready for war.

Jillian pulled into her garage with her car lights on, closed the garage door first, then scrutinized the interior for trespassers before finally unlocking and opening her car door. She once more had her car key protruding like a blade from her fist. She would keep it that way until she entered her home and conducted a brief inspection of the kitchen.

Did you know that approximately one woman is raped every *minute* in the United States? Did you know that women are more likely to be raped in their own homes than anywhere else? Did you know that many intruders bypassed home security systems by simply ducking into the garage behind the woman's car? Did you know that fewer than ten percent of reported rapists go to jail, meaning that an overwhelming number of rapists are still walking the streets, ready, willing and able to strike again?

Jillian knew these things. She read the books. She scrutinized the statistics. Knowledge was power. Know thy enemy. And don't believe for a minute that for some special reason you are entitled to be safe.

Most nights, Jillian went to sleep with a giant knot in her chest. Most nights, around 2 A.M., she jerked awake with sweat pouring down her face and a scream ripe on her lips. It took some time to recover from these things. She had read that, too. In the meantime – and this was her own philosophy – that's why they invented good makeup.

In the garage, Jillian drew a deep breath, squared her shoulders, then raised her chin. Show time, she told herself, and carefully blanked her face as she walked through the door.

In the kitchen, she immediately encountered her mother's live-in assistant, Toppi, who was leaning against the kitchen counter with her arms crossed disapprovingly over her chest.

"Sorry I'm late," Jillian said. She dropped her purse on the desk in the kitchen, took off her jacket, fiddled with her keys.

"Uh huh."

"How is she doing?"

"She lost her voice, not her mind," Toppi said testily. "How do you think?"

"She saw the news?"

"Of course."

"And the press?"

"Phone's been ringing off the hook. At least until I disconnected it. Not like I was worried about *your* call getting through." The edge returned to Toppi's voice. She gave Jillian another stern look, and Jillian obediently hung her head.

At twenty-six, in a wildly colored skirt and with a mass of kinky brown hair, Toppi looked more like a traveling gypsy than a health-care professional. She was cheerful, energetic and, in theory, Jillian's employee. Toppi, however, didn't answer to anyone. Since she had started three years ago, she had turned their stale little household upside down and inside out. She knew not only what was best for Libby, but what was best for Jillian, Trish and the paperboy down the street. She always gave her opinion freely and with great enthusiasm. Jillian's mother adored her. So had Trish.

"You hurt her," Toppi said now. "I know you don't mean to. I know you have other things on your mind. But you hurt her, Jillian. She's already lost one daughter and when you disappear like this, she worries about you."

"I'm sorry."

"It's not me who deserves the apology."

"I'll tell her, too."

Toppi snorted. "Like she hasn't already heard enough sorries from you. Come on, Jillian, she's your mother. She doesn't want your apology, she wants your presence. Come home for dinner. Read her a story. Or better yet, take her to see Trish."

Jillian hung her car keys on the little hook. Then she picked up the mail and started sorting through. Bills, bills, bills. Junk mail. At least there was nothing from him. She didn't even realize that was what had her so worried, until she came up empty. She set down the stack of mail, and Toppi took that as an opportunity to continue her attack.

"That's where you've been, haven't you? You've been visiting Trish."

"I went there."

"Your mom misses her, too."

Jillian didn't say anything.

"She can't tell stories, Jillian. Surely you understand that.

When someone dies, you want to relive their life, and what they meant to you. Share the moments, the laughter, keep them alive a little bit longer by talking about them. Your mom can't do that out loud, but that doesn't mean she isn't doing it in her head."

"I know."

"If you would just sit with her, hold her hand. Let her look at you and tell you everything with her eyes. She does that, you know. In her mind, she is fluent, she does have a voice. If you would just be with her, it would allow her to pretend. She could tell you everything without saying a word. And I think it would mean the world to her."

"I know, Toppi. I know." Old ground. They had been covering it for twelve months now. And Toppi was right and Jillian was wrong, and she wanted to be a better person, but right now, she simply wasn't. At work she had to function, meeting every client's demand or she would lose her business. With Carol, Meg, the press, the police, she had to be capable, always saying and doing the right thing, because she was the leader and she couldn't let anyone down. And then, when she got home . . .

When she got home, she had nothing left. She simply saw her mother, so small and frail and easy to damage. She saw Toppi, hired by Jillian so Trish wouldn't feel guilty about going off to college. And the walls came tumbling down, the barriers eroded and Jillian wasn't ready yet for the woman underneath. Eddie Como had changed her. He'd brought fear into her life, and she would've hated him for that alone. Of course, he'd also done so much worse.

"You bitch . . . I'm gonna get you, even if it takes me the rest of my life. I'm gonna get you, even if it's from beyond the grave."

Jillian opened the fridge. In spite of spending most of her day in a restaurant, she'd hardly eaten a thing. She eyed shelf after shelf crammed with food, but nothing sparked her appetite. Behind her, Toppi was frowning.

"Are you all right?" Toppi asked abruptly. "Lately . . . Jillian, are you all right?"

Jillian closed the door. She started to say, "Of course," but then she saw the look in Toppi's face and the blatant lie died on her lips. She felt her insides go hollow again. The ache, so close to the surface since her discussion with Sergeant Griffin, rose up and pressed back down on her with a heavy, heavy weight. She had lied to the sergeant this afternoon. She had told him she was certain, when in fact she hadn't been certain of anything for a whole year.

"It's been a big day," she said tersely. "I just needed some time to absorb everything. Some time to just be . . . alone."

"With Trish?"

"Something like that."

"Your mom wanted to go there today. I was worried, though, about the press."

"I'm sorry about that."

"It's okay, Jillian," Toppi said gently. "She doesn't blame you. I don't blame you. You reserve that right for yourself."

Jillian smiled. She'd heard this lecture before, too. Many times, really. Where was Trish? She leaned against the refrigerator, took a deep breath. "Does it feel different to you, Toppi? Him being dead. Does it feel different?"

Toppi shrugged. "I'm not losing any sleep over it, if that's what you mean. You lead a violent life, you'll come to a violent end."

"What goes around, comes around."

"Sounds good to me."

"I thought it would feel different," Jillian said quietly. "I thought I'd be . . . relieved. Vindicated maybe. Triumphant. But I just feel . . . empty. And I . . . I didn't know how to come home tonight. How to face Libby. I feel . . . I feel like I failed her."

"You failed her?"

"Yes." Jillian smiled again. "I'm in a weird mood. I've been in it all day. Not myself at all. I should go to bed."

"Jillian . . . the police were here. Two plainclothes officers. They wanted to interview Libby until I explained to them that wouldn't be happening. Is there something I should know?"

"No," Jillian said honestly, then shook her head. "Maybe that's the problem. I didn't kill Eddie. I don't know who killed Eddie. And frankly, that pisses me off. Someone else got to him before I had the chance. Someone else killed him, and in my fantasies I had reserved that honor for myself. Apparently, I'm even more bloodthirsty than I thought."

"I've dreamed of killing him, too," Toppi said.

Jillian looked up in surprise.

"Sure," Toppi said. "Guy like that. After what he did to you, to your mom, to Trish. Death isn't good enough for him. They should've hacked off his penis, then left him to live."

"Castration doesn't work with sex offenders," Jillian said immediately. "In fact, studies suggest that surgical or chemical castration leads them to commit even more violent acts, such as homicide. Because it's not about sex, it's about power. Take away a sex offender's penis, and he'll simply substitute a knife."

Toppi was looking at her strangely. "Jillian, you read too much."

"I know. I can't seem to stop."

Toppi was quiet for a moment. "I don't suppose that reading has included information on post-traumatic stress syndrome?"

"It has."

"Because . . . because that kind of thing would be expected, you know. After what you've been through."

Jillian smiled. "I've earned the right to be a little nuts?"

"Jillian, that's not what I meant – "

"I know I'm struggling, Toppi. I know I'm not quite myself. Maybe I didn't forget everything like Meg and maybe I'm not as aggressively hostile as Carol, but I am . . . wounded. There, that's an accomplishment for me right there. I hate saying that out loud. It sounds so weak. Birds get wounded. Children get wounded. I'm supposed to be above all that. Frankly, I wasn't even raped. What do I have to cry about?"

"Oh, Jillian . . ."

"I know I'm being unfair to Libby," Jillian said quietly. "I'd like to tell you I have a good reason, but I don't know what it is. Right now . . . I just don't feel like coming home these days. Some nights I wish I could go anyplace but here. I'd like to get in my car and just drive. Drive, drive, drive." She smiled again, but it was sad. "Maybe I can work my way to Mexico."

"You're running away from us."

"No. I'm just running. It's the only time I feel safe."

"He's dead now, Jillian. You are safe."

Jillian's shoulders came down. She shook her head and said hoarsely, "But there are so many more just like him, Toppi. I've been reading the books. And you have no idea . . . The world, it is such a bad place." Her shoulders started to shake. God, she was not herself today. And then she was back in that room, that horribly dark room, with Trish needing her, Trish depending on her, and she had not got it done. Far from saving the day, she had nearly gotten raped herself. And now he was gone, and what would give her life meaning without Trisha to take care of or Eddie Como to hate?

And then she was thinking of Meg, *I don't think I was happy,* and she was thinking of Carol, *Let's have some chocolate cake,* and suddenly she knew she had failed both of them. She had turned them into warriors, but long after defeating their enemy, were they really better off? They had nailed Eddie Como, but none of them had managed to heal.

And now Eddie Como was dead and they were unraveling at the seams.

Jillian squeezed her eyes shut, covered her mouth with her hand. Pull it together, pull it together. Her mother was in the next room. And then she was thinking of Sergeant Griffin again, and that confused her even more. Men did not make things better. Just look at Eddie . . .

Toppi had crossed the kitchen. She touched Jillian's shoulder gently as Jillian drew in a ragged breath.

"I'm not an expert," Toppi said quietly. "Lord knows I

couldn't have gone through everything you've been through. But I do know this. When you're really hurting, when you're really feeling low, nothing is as good as crying on your mother's shoulder. You can do that, Jillian. She would like that. And it would do you both a world of good."

Jillian drew in another deep breath. "I understand."

"Do you?"

Toppi's gaze was too penetrating. Jillian looked away. She focused on her breathing, getting to slow, steady breaths. Then she wiped her cheeks with her hands, blinked her eyes clear. She should go to bed soon. Get a good night's sleep. Tomorrow would be another day. She would feel better then. Stronger, in control, ready to take on the press, ready to take on the police because it was only a matter of time . . .

"Well, let me go see her," Jillian said briskly.

"All right," Toppi said. "All right." But it was obvious from her voice that she wasn't fooled.

Jillian went into the living room, where her mother sat in her favorite chair watching TV. At sixty-five, Olivia Hayes was still a beautiful woman. Tiny as a bird, with thick dark hair and big brown eyes. Her hair was dyed, of course, every eight weeks at her favorite salon, with six shades of brown to match her original color as closely as possible. Libby had always been vain about her hair. When Jillian was a little girl, she used to watch her mother brush out the long, thick locks when she came home at night. One hundred strokes. Then would come the saltwater gargle to preserve her vocal cords, followed by a heavy cream to protect her face.

"If you take good care of your body," Libby always said with a wink, "your body will take good care of you."

Jillian leaned over. "Hello, Mom," she murmured. "Sorry I'm late." She hugged her mother gently, careful not to squeeze too hard.

When she straightened, she saw something flash in her mother's gaze. Frustration, anger, it was hard to tell, and

Libby would never say. Since her stroke ten years ago, she had limited movement in the right side of her body, as well as expressive aphasia – while she could understand communication perfectly, she could no longer speak or write back. As one of the doctors tried explaining to Jillian, in her mother's mind she could think fluently, but when she tried to get the words past her lips, her brain ran into a wall, blocking the flow.

Now Libby communicated via a "picture book," filled with images of everything from a toilet to an apple to pictures of Jillian, Toppi, Trish. When she wanted something, she would tap on the picture. Right after Trisha's funeral, Libby had stroked her daughter's photo so often, she had literally worn it out.

"You saw the news?" Jillian asked, taking a seat on the couch.

Her mother tapped her left index finger once, meaning *yes*.

"He's dead now, Mom," Jillian said quietly. "He can't hurt anyone ever again."

Her mother's chin came up. She had a fierce look on her face, but her fingers remained quiet.

"Are you happy?"

No movement.

"Sad?"

No movement.

"Frightened?"

Her mother made an impatient sound deep in her throat. Jillian paused, then she got it. "You're mad?"

One tap.

Jillian hesitated. "You wanted the trial?"

Hard tap!

"But why, Mom? This way you know he's punished. He can't get off because someone in the jury box has a guilty conscience. We'll never have to worry about parole or some kind of prison break. It's over. We won."

Her mother made another impatient sound in the back of her throat. Jillian understood. Why questions didn't work well with this system. To get the right answer, you had to ask the right question. It was Jillian's job, as the person still capable of speech, to come up with the right question.

Toppi had materialized in the doorway. "You didn't see the news conference at six-thirty, did you?"

"No."

"Eddie's lawyer says he has a witness who proves Eddie couldn't have attacked Carol. Instead, he was across town returning a movie at the time."

"You're kidding!" Jillian sat up straight. Beside her, her mother had flipped open the picture book. Her left fingers frantically skimmed away.

"That's ridiculous," Jillian announced. "Carol's not even sure what time he broke into her house. You can't have a definite alibi without a definite time."

"Some of the press is starting to talk of a miscarriage of justice. Maybe Eddie was railroaded. Maybe the police were a little too eager to have a suspect. Maybe . . ." Toppi hesitated. "Maybe you, Carol and Meg applied a little too much pressure."

"That is absurd!" Jillian was on her feet, her hands fisted at her sides. When backed into a corner, her first reaction was always anger, and now she was in a rage. Quick, someone get her a reporter. Any reporter. She wanted to slug one good. "All we did was put together the blood-donor connection between Trisha and Meg. That's it! Eddie's the one who just happened to have access to their home addresses. Eddie's the one who just happened to see two out of three rape victims within weeks of their attacks. Eddie's the one who just happened to have his semen present in their houses. How the hell does the press explain that?"

"They don't. They just flash clean-cut photos from his high school yearbook and use words like *minority, suspected* of rape, *tragically* shot down."

"Oh for the love of God!" Jillian had to sit down again. Her head was suddenly pounding. She thought she might be ill. "They're turning him into a martyr," she murmured. "Whoever shot him . . . He's making him seem innocent."

Libby thumped Jillian's arm. She had found the picture she wanted. A new one, added by Toppi just one year ago to help Libby communicate about the trial. It featured a blind-folded woman holding the scales of justice.

"I know you wanted the trial," Jillian said impatiently. "I understood that."

Her mother thinned her lips. She tapped the photo more emphatically, this time the scales.

"Justice? Not just a trial, you want justice?"

Hard tap!

"Because we don't have it yet," Jillian filled in slowly. "The press is now trying the case in absentia, and they're using Eddie's looks and ethnicity as evidence. And the only way we could counter is with Eddie himself. By actually having the trial and proving beyond a shadow of a doubt that Eddie Como *is* the College Hill Rapist."

Her mother tapped, tapped, tapped.

"You're right, Mom. I'm angry now, too. We were robbed this morning." Jillian's voice grew bitter. "As if we hadn't already lost too much."

Her mother flipped through the pages again. She came to another picture, this one also new. It looked like a child's drawing, a caricature of a monster with big yellow fangs and red bugged-out eyes. Toppi had done the honors, her rendition of Eddie, because there was no way they would permit his real photo in the picture book. They refused to give him that much presence in their lives.

Now Libby's left hand scrabbled with the page of the photo album. She got the plastic cover back. She yanked Eddie's picture from the sticky back. Then she looked at Toppi and Jillian with her chin up, her brown eyes ablaze, and her lower lip trembling with unshed tears. She crum-pled up Eddie Como in her feeble left hand. Then she flung the monster across the room.

Toppi and Jillian watched the paper hit the floor. The wad rolled to a stop five feet away. Then it was still.

"You're right," Jillian said softly. "Eddie Como is gone, so once and for all let's get him out of our lives. Frankly, I'm tired of being afraid. I'm tired of being angry. I'm tired of wondering over and over again what I could've done differently." Her voice rose, gained strength. "Fuck the press, Mom. Fuck the public defender. And fuck some voyeuristic public that has nothing better to do than watch our pain get played out on the nightly news. Eddie Como has taken too much from us, and I'm not giving him anything more. It's over. That's that. We're not talking about him anymore. We're not worrying about him anymore. We're not afraid of him anymore. From here on out, Eddie Como is gone, and we are *done!*"

19
The Victims Club

Ten forty-five P.M.

Carol was not done. She had not gotten Eddie Como out of her life. Instead, she was curled up, fully dressed, in an empty bathtub. The cold porcelain sides gave her a chill, so an hour ago she had pulled down all the towels to keep her warm. It was dark in the upstairs bathroom. No windows, no source of natural light. She didn't know what time it was, but she suspected that it was late. Probably after ten. Things happened after ten.

Dan still wasn't home. The house maintained its silence. Sometimes she hummed to herself simply to make a sound. But mostly she lay in the bathtub, a grown woman who couldn't return to the womb. She rested her head on the hard, cold ledge and waited for the inevitable to happen.

I didn't turn off the TV. I didn't turn off the TV.

It wouldn't matter. It was after ten. She was all alone. And she knew, she knew way down deep, that somewhere in the house, a window was sliding open, a foot was hitting the floor, a man was ducking into her bedroom.

Bad things happened. Women got raped, people got shot, others were blown up by car bombs. Husbands deserted you, wives went crazy, children were never born. Bad things happened. Especially after 10:00 P.M. Especially to her.

Eddie Como had sent her a note. She found it in the day's mail, which Dan had left on the kitchen counter. The pink envelope looked like a Hallmark card and bore Jillian's return address. A nice little note, Dan had probably thought. So had she. Until she'd ripped it open.

I'm going to get you, Eddie had scrawled in red ink across white butcher paper. *Even if it's from beyond the grave . . .*

Carol had bolted back upstairs to the bathroom, but not before first making a stop at the home safe.

I'm going to get you . . .

Not this time, Carol decided. Not anymore, you son of a bitch. Carol reached beneath the towels and, very gently, stroked the gun.

Ten fifty-eight P.M.

Sylvia Blaire was walking home alone from the university library. She had a test tomorrow morning. Final exam for Psych 101. In theory, Sylvia enjoyed Psych 101, but she hadn't kept up on the readings quite the way she should have. Now she was cramming twelve weeks' worth of learning into two nights of studying, a feat she'd mastered in high school, but which was proving far more difficult in college.

Personally, she thought Professor Scalia should cancel the test. As if anyone could study today, with the big explosion just six blocks away, then the sirens wailing all morning long. The air still smelled acrid, a mixture of gasoline, scorched metal and melted plastic. In the student union, all anyone could talk about was the commotion. Frankly, nothing exciting ever happened in Providence. As far as the students were concerned, the school should cancel exam week and let them enjoy the buzz.

No such luck, though. Professors were such pains in the ass. So Sylvia had left the student union in favor of the library, where she'd managed to read six chapters of her textbook before falling asleep and dreaming about chickens scratching out the Pythagorean theorem in return for pellets. Screw it. She was going home to bed.

Sylvia walked down the street to her apartment. Generally there were more people out this time of night, but during finals week most of the students were sequestered away in various study labs suffering massive anxiety attacks. The street was quiet, the old shrouded houses still.

It didn't bother her. The full moon was bright, the lamps cheery. Besides, she knew the drill. Walk with your chin up, your shoulders square and your steps brisk. Perverts sought out meek women who wouldn't fight back, not former track stars like her.

Not that Providence had many perverts anymore. That rapist dude was dead. The women on campus had cheered.

Sylvia finally arrived at the old house that boasted her second-floor studio apartment. She paused on the darkened front steps, then shook her head. Stupid outdoor light had burnt out again. Thing seemed to go every three weeks and the landlord liked to wait another three before replacing it. This one Sylvia had bought with her own money. Like she could see anything tucked inside the covered patio without a light.

She dragged her backpack off her shoulder, and with a long-suffering sigh began digging for her keys. She finally found the heavy metal key chain in the bottom of her bag. The new key ring was a gift from the Rhode Island Blood Center commemorating the donation of her eighth pint of blood just two weeks ago. Way to go, Sylvia, she was now a member of the gallon club.

Sylvia drew out her keys. She flipped through the massive lot that she kept meaning to pare down but never did, until she came to the desired one. She slid her key into the front door lock.

A noise sounded on the right. Sylvia turned her head . . .

Eleven-twelve P.M.

Jillian is dreaming. In this dream, she knows that she is dreaming, but she doesn't care. This dream is filled with warm, happy colors. This dream lifts the weight off her chest and takes her, for the first time in a long time, to a place she wants to go.

Jillian is sixteen years old. She is in a hotel – most of her childhood has been spent in hotels. It is 2 A.M. and Libby is gone. Her gig ended hours ago, but time has never meant

189

much to Libby. Nights are for singing, dancing, drinking, having a good time. Libby has probably met another man by now and is once more falling in love. At this stage of the game, Jillian is used to the drill. Libby falls in love and disappears even more nights of the week. Her singing grows more robust, she wears her nicest gowns and brings Jillian lots of frivolous gifts. Then the bloom goes off the rose. She dumps him, he dumps her, or maybe his wife comes home. Who knows?

Libby falls out of love. They get a new hotel and she promises to spend more time with her daughter. Until, of course, the next handsome man enters the room.

The last time was different, however. The last time had consequences. Jillian now has a baby half sister, whom she was allowed to name. Jillian chose Trisha.

Three-month-old Trisha has fat pink cheeks and big blue eyes. Her head is covered with a downy mist of soft brown hair. She likes to grip Jillian's finger in her tiny little fist. She likes to kick her tiny little feet. And she gurgles a lot, and blows bubbles a lot, and loves big wet zerberts right on her tummy. She also breaks into a wide, smacking smile every time Jillian picks her up.

Now Jillian is cradling baby Trish in her arms and watching her baby-blue eyes grow heavy with sleep. She tickles Trish's chubby cheek with her finger. She inhales the sweet scent of baby powder. She feels her chest expand with the force of her love and thinks that if she cared for Trisha any more, her heart would surely explode.

Libby has never been the perfect mother. There have been times, in fact, when Jillian has grown close to hating her and her careless ways. But as of three months ago, Jillian forgave her mother everything in return for this one, precious gift. Trisha Jane Hayes. Finally, Jillian has someone she can love with her whole heart. Finally, Jillian has someone who will never leave.

The quiet, still night. The perfect weight of Trisha in her arms. The pure beauty of her baby sister, smiling back up at her and kicking her tiny, little feet.

In the dream Jillian knows she is dreaming, she would like to hold this moment forever. She understands, in this dream she knows she is dreaming, that darkness lingers just beyond her sight. That if she turns her head, the beautiful hotel room will spin away and she will find herself in a far different, uglier place. That if she looks at baby Trisha too closely, baby Trisha will spin away and she will find herself holding her grown sister's dying form. That if she thinks too hard at all, she will realize that this moment never happened, that her baby sister cried most nights for her mother, and that Jillian was actually little more than an overwhelmed sixteen-year-old substitute. In this dream she knows she is dreaming, it is only her love for her sister that is real.

A sound intrudes. In the dream hotel room, the dream Jillian turns her head. She listens to the loud, squawking sirens racing down the street.

But then the hotel room falls away. Baby Trisha falls away. And dream Jillian and the real Jillian realize at the same time that the noise is not a siren on the street.

It is in the house. It is in Jillian's bedroom.

Someone has pressed the panic alarm.

Sound. Carol heard it again. A thud in the nether regions of her home. It was followed by a thump.

Someone was in her house. Someone was genuinely inside Carol's home. The panic that held her in its grip all night gained momentum and became suddenly, terrifyingly real.

Carol's breathing accelerated. Very slowly, she straightened legs that had grown cramped and numb while curled beneath her. Then she drew back the pile of towels and slid way down, until just her eyes peered above the rim of the bathtub. More noises down the hall. Maybe the bedroom. That bedroom. The bedroom.

Very carefully, Carol raised the barrel of her .22 and aimed it at the door.

Now the sound was in the hallway. Footsteps, definitely, coming her way.

"Dan?" she called out hoarsely. Questioningly. Hopefully.

There was no reply.

And then the footsteps stopped, two dark shadows coming to rest in the lighted crack beneath the bathroom door. He was here.

Goose bumps rippled up Carol's arms.

Steady, Carol. Steady . . .

The gun in her hand. The breath held in her chest . . .

She watched the brass doorknob slowly begin to twist.

Jillian bolted out of bed. She grabbed her bathrobe, made it to her door, then did an abrupt about-face and raced back to her bed for her pepper spray. The alarm still sounded shrilly through the house.

Running out into the hallway, she found Toppi standing in a white linen nightgown, looking sleepy-eyed and dazed.

"Did you – "

"No."

"Libby!" they both cried and went rushing for her room.

Jillian shoved through the door, leading with her pepper spray and looking around frantically. Libby was lying in her bed. Her face was stark white. She had the security remote clutched tight against her chest.

"Mom, Mom, what is it?"

Libby raised her trembling arm. She pointed to the window behind them. And very slowly, Jillian and Toppi turned.

Eleven thirty-three P.M.

Griffin was still at headquarters sifting through paperwork and rubbing the bridge of his nose tiredly when the officer on duty stuck his head into the conference room.

"Sergeant."

"Officer Girard."

"Sir, 911 just got a report of a disturbance over in East Greenwich. A home security system is going off, and apparently a woman in a bathrobe is now running through the yard. I thought you'd want to know – the house belongs to Jillian Hayes."

"Damn." A disturbance at Jillian's house tonight of all nights could not be a good thing, and he was at least twenty minutes away. Griffin started talking as he headed for the door.

"Do me a favor, Officer, and put in a call to Detective Fitz."

"He's with Providence?"

"That's the one."

"Sorry, sir, but I believe the Providence detectives are out on a call. I heard it on the scanner, though they seem to be keeping the details hush-hush. Some kind of incident on College Hill."

Griffin drew up short. "On College Hill?"

And Officer Girard repeated, "Yes, sir. College Hill."

The bathroom door swung open. Carol closed her eyes, then squeezed the trigger.

Pop, pop, pop. The tiny .22 leapt in her hand. And the dark shrouded form fell flat on the floor.

"Oh my God," the dark shrouded form moaned. "I think you just shot me."

And Carol said, "Dan?"

Jillian was running. She tore through her yard in her baby-blue bathrobe, shoving back tree limbs, pouncing on bushes. Lights were blazing, neighbors gathering, sirens roaring down the street. She was making a spectacle of herself. She didn't care.

"Come out, come out, you bastard!" she cried. She pointed her pepper spray and attacked a shuddering leaf. "You want to play a practical joke? I'll show you a joke, you cowardly son of a bitch. Come on. Show yourself!"

She ran close to the perimeter. Her neighbors shrank back. She ignored them, tears streaming down her face, her nose running from the blowback of pepper spray. He had to be out here somewhere. He couldn't have gone far. And she would find him, and she would grab him by his scruffy, probably teenage neck, and, and . . .

She needed to hurt someone. She needed to inflict violence and pain, and that scared her, too, so she kept running, trampling new budding bulbs and freshly planted pansies. She had to move. She had to fight. She was not in a dark basement anymore. She was not powerless!

There, that bush. It moved. Cowardly son of a bitch . . .

Jillian made a beeline for the trembling sand cherry, and abruptly ran into something hard. "Umph," she said, falling back a few steps, then belatedly raising her eyes to discover Sergeant Griffin's large, unrelenting form.

"Jillian," he said quietly.

"Did you see what he did?"

"The officers told me what happened."

"It was my mother's bedroom. *Do you know what that did to her?* The EMTs had to come, she's having problems breathing. If that sick bastard gave her another heart attack, I swear I'll kill him myself. I'll find him and I'll rip him from limb to limb!"

"Jillian," he said quietly.

"It was my mother's bedroom! What kind of idiot does such a thing? Today of all days. My poor mother. Oh God, my poor mother . . ."

Her shoulders convulsed, then she was swaying from side to side. She looked down to see that her bathrobe had come open and she was standing half-naked in the middle of her lawn. Sirens everyplace, police lights washing her home in violent red light. People everywhere, staring at her, staring at her home, gossiping about her pain.

Eddie Como lives. Scrawled across her mother's bedroom window in red dripping spray paint. *Eddie Como lives.*

"It's not funny," she mumbled. "It's a horrible, horrible practical joke." And then she swayed again and Sergeant Griffin had to catch her in his arms.

"I'm very sorry," he said.

"I hate this!" Her voice was muffled against his chest.

"Jillian . . ." he said gently, and something about his tone finally cut through her haze. Slowly, she raised her head. His blue eyes were somber. So somber. She stared and stared and stared. And then, for no good reason, she was thinking of his dead wife. What had it been like to love this man? To be held in these strong arms, to look up at this steady gaze, and to still feel yourself, slowly but surely, slipping away?

"What happened?" she whispered.

"I'm very sorry. I just talked to Detective Fitzpatrick . . . On College Hill. There's been another incident."

"But there can't be. Eddie . . . he's gone. It's over, it's ended. Even this . . . It's probably just some teenage jerk with a spray can. Please tell me it's just a teenage jerk with a spray can. I *need* it to be just a teenage jerk with a spray can."

Sergeant Griffin didn't say a word. His arms were still around her, supporting her half-crumpled form, shielding her from her neighbors. He wouldn't let her go until she was ready. She understood that now. He would stand here as long as she needed, support her as long as she needed. It was his job, and even back then, on the pedophile case, the reporters had said that he took his job seriously.

She studied his face, broad, hard-planed, firm. She looked into his steady blue eyes. Impulsively, she reached up a hand and touched the raspy line of his chin. She wondered what he would think to know that no one had touched her, and she had touched no one, for well over a year.

Then very slowly, she straightened up, stepped away, and belted her robe at the waist.

"Brunette?" she asked.

"Yes."

"Latex strips?"

"Yes."

"Is she . . . ?"

"Manual strangulation."

Jillian closed her eyes. "All right, Sergeant. Maybe you had better come inside."

*

Twelve twenty-one A.M.

The lights were out in the Pesaturo home. Tom and Laurie slept peacefully on the opposite sides of their king-sized bed. Little Molly was curled up with her head at the foot of her pink Barbie bed. While in her room, Meg began to thrash from side to side in the throes of a dream.

Rich chocolate eyes. Soft, gentle hands. A slow lover's smile. His fingers stroke her hair. His hand drifts down to her breast. She arches her back and aches for him to do more.

"We should stop," he whispers in her ear.

"No, no . . ."

"It wouldn't be right." His thumb flickers over her nipple. His fingers squeeze tight.

"Please . . ."

"This is wrong."

"Oh please . . ."

His hand moves down. She arches her hips toward him, straining. And then . . . His hand presses against her. Her whole body thrums. She throws back her head.

Rich chocolate eyes. Soft, gentle hands. A slow lover's smile.

Meg thrashed again in her sleep. She whispered, "David."

20

The Survivors Club

"I shot my husband."

"You *shot* your husband?"

"Last night, when he came home. I was scared. I'd just received another card from Eddie Como – this time bearing your address, Jillian. And . . . I swear I called out Dan's name first. But he didn't answer. So I pulled the trigger, and I . . . well, I hit him in the upper arm. Pretty good, really. The doctor was impressed."

Jillian frowned. "I thought we agreed no guns."

"No, Jillian, *you* said no guns. I, on the other hand, still reserve the right to think for myself. So how do you like that?" Carol's tone grew hot.

In contrast, Jillian's voice remained particularly cool for this first emergency meeting of the Survivors Club. "I think the real question is," she said dryly, "how did *Dan* like that?"

Meg sighed and slid down deeper in her chair. This was not going well. Carol was so agitated she couldn't even sit at the table they'd reserved in the private room of this intimate Federal Hill restaurant. Jillian, on the other hand, was wearing a navy blue power suit buttoned up to her chin and sitting stiffly enough to do the Queen of England proud. The tension was sky high. Except for Meg, of course. She never knew enough to be tense. Besides, this morning she was too busy nursing her first hangover. At least she thought it was her first hangover.

"In the words of my mother," she spoke up now, "could you two please use your inside voice?"

Carol glared at her. Jillian's look was droller.

"Little slow getting going this morning?" Jillian asked.

"You could say that."

"Did you get to worship at the porcelain God last night?"

It took Meg a moment to get it. Oh, puking. "No. At least I don't think so."

"Well, you'll live."

"Excuse me," Carol interjected curtly. "I was discussing shooting my husband. What do I have to do – kill him? – to get some attention around here?"

"I don't know," Jillian replied. "Is that why you shot him?"

"Oh for God's sake – "

"No, you listen to us for a minute – "

"There *is* no us, Jillian. There's just you. It's always been you. Meg and I are merely window dressing for your holy pursuit of justice. Survivors Club. That's a joke. This club isn't about surviving, it's about vengeance. You just can't use that word in front of the press. Well, here we are now. Eddie Como's dead, I've shot my husband, another girl has been attacked, and the press is crying miscarriage of justice. What are you going to do, Jillian? How are you going to *spin* this one?"

Jillian got up from the table. She walked a small circle, then repeated the motion two more times. Her movements were stiff and jerky. Her face was pale and impossible to read. Meg had seen her in this mood only once before. The first time Eddie Como had contacted them. Meg had honestly been a little frightened of Jillian that day.

"Someone trespassed on my property last night," Jillian said crisply. "Someone loosened all the bulbs in my motion-activated lights, then walked up to my home and spray-painted 'Eddie Como lives' on my mother's bedroom windows. Then he screwed the lights back in. For God's sake, my mom had to receive oxygen to recover from the shock. You think I don't understand fear, Carol? You think I don't know what went on in your head last night as you heard unknown footsteps coming down the hall? If I'd had a gun twelve hours ago, I would've shot someone, too. And I probably would've hit a neighborhood boy, which is why I said no guns."

"Holier-than-thou Jillian . . ."

"Goddammit. You want to have this conversation, Carol? Fine. Detective Fitz and Sergeant Griffin are going to be here in less than ten minutes, so let's get it done."

"There you go again, Jillian. I'm trying to have a conversation and *you're* setting an agenda."

Jillian thinned her lips, then switched her gaze to Meg. "Do you want out?"

"What?"

"*Do you want out?* Have you had enough? Are you sick of this group?"

"I don't . . . No," Meg said more firmly. "I don't want out."

"Why not?"

"Because . . . because we need each other. Look at us. Who else could discuss midnight vandalism and shot husbands without looking at us as if we were freaks? With other people . . . the conversations aren't real."

"But these conversations aren't real either!" Carol said impatiently. "That's my whole point. It's been a year. We're beyond polite conversation, victims' rights or legal strategy. At least we should be. If *we* are the Survivors Club, then it's time we got down to the business of surviving. Or maybe the fact that we're *not* surviving. Except you don't want to have those conversations, Jillian. You're fine about getting the police in here to give us briefings, or getting D'Amato to present legal tactics. But when it's simply us, all alone, ragged, raw, *emotional*, you shut down, Jillian. Worse, you shut us down. And that's not fair. Frankly, if I wanted to be treated like that, I'd go home to my husband."

"Armed?" Jillian asked.

"If I had a brain in my head," Carol snapped.

Jillian finally smiled. The wan expression, however, only made her look tired.

"I'm sorry," she said quietly.

Carol regarded her suspiciously. Meg yawned, wishing they would both just get on with it. Jillian's and Carol's personalities were like oil and water, but they did need each other. They all needed each other, especially now, when a new girl had been raped and murdered. Meg kept thinking it could've been her. And poor Jillian, she had to be thinking of Trish. After a night like last night, how could she not be thinking of Trish?

Jillian's chin had come down a fraction. She regarded Carol steadily. "It's possible . . ." Jillian's voice trailed off. She cleared her throat, tried again. "When I'm under stress, when I'm angry, it's easier for me to remain focused. To outline a plan of attack and implement that plan. I need to keep busy. Keep . . . moving. I suppose I might be forcing that approach onto the group."

"I can't do that," Carol said flatly. "I go home to the same house every night, to the same husband who didn't come home in time, to the same second-story room where a man crawled through a window and took away my life. You can get some distance from things. Meg can get some distance from things. I can't. That night has become like mud, and I'm just spinning my wheels in it over and over again."

"Why don't you sell the house? Why don't you move?" Meg this time. She was curious.

"Dan loves that house," Carol said immediately.

"I'm sure he loves you more."

Carol didn't say anything. The look on her face was enough.

"He shuts you out that much?" Jillian asked softly. The mood in the room shifted. Grew more subdued. And Meg was thinking again, that poor, poor girl. They were fighting with each other, but really, underneath it all, that poor, poor girl.

"Dan shuts me out so much, I don't know why he bothers coming home," Carol was saying. Her shoulders had come down, her angry expression giving way to a pain that was far worse. "He won't talk. He won't fight, grieve or even rationalize. The subject is strictly off-limits. We live in a house with a giant elephant both of us pretend not to see."

"You've never talked about the rape?"

"In the beginning we talked about what the doctors said. Then we talked about what the police said, or what D'Amato said. Sometimes we talk about what our group says. So we talk. About what other people say."

"It's got to be hard for him," Meg spoke up. "I mean, he's a guy. Look at my father. He still hates himself for not being there when Eddie attacked me, and he didn't even live in my apartment. For your husband, that's gotta feel like a hundred-pound weight around his neck. I wonder what other guys say to him."

"Other guys?"

"Well, sure, guys talk. Well, okay, not really. I mean, not like us. But he's a guy and other guys know his wife was raped in his own home. That's gotta make him feel . . . bad. Like a first-class failure. What kind of man doesn't protect the woman he loves? I know if something ever happened to my mom, my father would get out the brass knuckles. Then probably a chain saw. And then my Uncle Vinnie would . . . Well, that's a whole 'nother story."

"He had no way of knowing what was going to happen that night," Carol said.

Jillian looked at her curiously. "Have you told him that?"

Carol hesitated, then shook her head.

"Why not?"

"Because I do blame him, all right? Because I prayed for him to come home that night. I lay there while that man did unspeakable things to me *hoping* that Dan would come home. And it went on and on and on, and still, where was my husband? I *needed* him. How could he not come home?"

"He had no way of knowing . . ." Jillian tried.

"You said yourself he was always working late," Meg offered.

"*But he wasn't at work!* Goddammit . . . Goddammit." Carol sat down hard. She buried her face in her hands. And then in the next moment, her head came back up and her cheeks were covered in tears. "I'd suspected it for months. All the late nights. All his sudden 'meetings.' So I started calling his office. There was never any answer. Never. And then, that night. I called his office at nine-thirty. Nobody was there. Nobody. Face it. My husband couldn't save me from being raped because he was too busy fucking his girl-friend."

"Oh, Carol . . ."

"Oh, Carol."

"So how do you bring that topic up?" Carol demanded thickly. "Huh? Anyone? Hey, Dan, I'll apologize for being raped if you'll apologize for having an affair. Or, Dan, how about I say I'm sorry for being an emotional train wreck if you'll say you're sorry for not coming home in time to stop my attacker. Or, I'll say I'm sorry for not being able to have children if you'll say you're sorry for constantly shutting me out, for putting your job ahead of me, for ensconcing me in some four-thousand-square-foot mausoleum that only reminds me of how much I am alone. And then what hap-pens? We grow old together, always looking at each other and knowing what big failures we are?

"That's the problem with marriage, you know. You start out wanting intimacy, and then when it happens, you remember too late that familiarity breeds contempt."

"Do you still love him?" Jillian asked.

"Oh God, yes," Carol said, and then she started to cry again. For a long time, no one said a word.

A knock sounded at the door. The waitress, an old hand with their meetings, poked her head in.

"Jillian, the police are here."

Jillian looked at Carol. "Do you want to postpone?"

It was, Meg thought, the closest Jillian had ever come to a peace offering.

Carol, however, was already pulling herself back together. She picked up a napkin, worked on blotting her face. "No. Let them in. We have to hear about this girl. We have to know."

"It's probably just a copycat," Jillian said.

"It's not," Meg spoke up.

"We don't know that."

"I do."

"Meg – "

"No, if Carol can have a nervous breakdown, then I should be able to have my feelings, too. And this feels all wrong. This girl, she was one of us. Except we learned about her too late."

Carol and Jillian frowned at her, reunited again over their shared sentiments for flaky little Meg. But Meg stuck to her guns. She was right about this. She knew. This morning the eyes had been following her again. And she had understood for the first time. Eddie Como's death. It was not an end for them, but simply a new beginning.

That poor, poor girl . . .

"Show the police in," Jillian told the waitress.

"I'm sorry, Carol," Meg murmured.

"I'm sorry, too," Jillian said.

Then they all fell silent as Detective Fitzpatrick and Sergeant Griffin walked into the room.

21

Fitz

Taking in the three women for the second time in as many days, Griffin's first thought was that none of them looked nearly as composed as yesterday. Carol Rosen, sitting across the table, bore the red cheeks and puffy eyes of someone who'd recently been crying. Jillian Hayes, standing at the head of the table, had the pale features and dark shadows of someone who hadn't gotten any sleep at night. Finally, Meg Pesaturo, sitting closest to the door, looked pasty around the edges. Hangover, he would guess. From yesterday's champagne. Maureen had included eyewitness testimonies from the rue de l'espoir as part of this morning's news report.

The women didn't know it yet, but they were rapidly becoming the center of a first-rate legal hailstorm. And all this after Eddie Como had been dead for only twenty-four hours. It made Griffin wonder what the next twenty-four might bring.

"Jillian, Carol, Meg." Fitz greeted each woman in turn. Griffin didn't know if Fitz was even aware of it, but he always greeted the women in the same order. By rank, Griffin thought dryly. Or ascending order of victimhood.

The women didn't say anything. They just stared at Fitz and Griffin with the flat eyes of people who were expecting bad news and only wanted to get it over with.

"Thank you for taking the time to meet with me," Fitz said formally, pulling out a chair and preparing to take a seat. "I'm sure you all remember Detective Sergeant Roan Griffin from yesterday. I invited Sergeant Griffin to join us as a professional courtesy – to the extent that last night's activities may be tied in with the death of Eddie Como, the sergeant is also participating in this case."

Griffin smiled at the group, careful not to let his gaze linger too long on Jillian. Professional courtesy. You had to like that. Fitz had just welcomed him to the party while simultaneously putting him firmly in his place. You couldn't get anything past these Providence boys.

"Now then," Fitz said briskly. "I understand there was some excitement at your home last night."

Carol and Jillian both said, "Yes."

Fitz's smile grew tight. "Carol, why don't you start."

"I got a note," Carol said stiffly. "In a pink envelope. The return address was Jillian's. I didn't look at the postmark. When I opened it, however, it was from Eddie."

"Do you still have it?"

Carol's chin came up. "I know the drill."

"All right. What did the note say?"

"It said, 'I'm going to get you. Even if it's from beyond the grave.' I . . . panicked a little. I was home alone and that scared me more. So I got my gun out of the safe. And then, well, unfortunately, I ended up shooting Dan when he returned."

"Taking your marital tensions a little seriously there, Carol?"

"It was an honest mistake!"

"Uh huh. So how is he?"

"He'll survive," she said stiffly. "It's going to take some time, however, for his left arm to heal. And well, probably more time before he'll feel safe walking down the halls of his own home. Of course, I already know all about that."

Fitz ignored that bitter comment and switched his gaze to Jillian. "Your turn."

"Someone spray-painted in big red letters 'Eddie Como lives' on my mother's bedroom window. Then he reactivated the motion-sensitive lights to make sure she woke up and saw it as he was running off my property. Good news, my mother will live. Bad news, graffiti boy won't. Not once

I find him." Jillian spoke in clipped tones.

Fitz grunted. He'd probably already read the East Greenwich police file, which basically said the same. With photos, of course. He turned to Meg.

"And you?"

She shrugged. "Nothing. Let's face it, I'm the boring one."

"Thank God for small favors. You three generate any more paperwork, and the city's going to run out of uniforms to work the cases." Fitz's voice was harsh. He'd been up all night. Working the College Hill scene and catching snippets of the other events on his cell phone. Twenty-four hours without sleep took its toll on a man. Fitz's eyes were red rimmed, his cheeks sallow. His last few strands of graying brown hair stood up wildly on his head, while his rumpled white dress shirt strained over his gut with two new stains. Looked like mustard and ketchup. He'd probably caught dinner/breakfast on the run, grabbing something from the Haven Brothers Diner outside City Hall. Been serving the men in blue for decades, and they all had the cholesterol levels to prove it. Having only slept an hour or so himself, Griffin knew these things.

"Speaking of which," Jillian said levelly.

Carol joined her. "Did he do it? Just tell us that, Detective. Did he do it?"

Fitz leaned back until his chair was balanced on only two legs. He contemplated the room, regarding each woman in turn and taking a long time before answering. "Did he do it? That is the million-dollar question now, isn't it? If by him, you mean Eddie Como, and if by it, you mean attack a girl last night on College Hill, then the answer is no. Hell, no. Eddie Como is dead. I've seen the body. Sergeant Griffin's seen the body. Eddie Como is dead." Abruptly, Fitz slammed forward. "I even understand you ladies drank a champagne toast in his honor."

Carol startled. A moment later, all three of them had the good grace to blush.

"Jillian, Jillian, Jillian," Fitz chided softly, his gaze going to the head of the table. "I thought you were smarter than that. Did you really think the press wouldn't follow up on your whereabouts yesterday morning? Did you really think that in a whole restaurant crowded with people, at least one or two wouldn't be willing to talk?"

"It was my idea," Carol started.

"It doesn't matter," Jillian spoke up. "We all agreed to order the champagne. We all drank it. If people have a problem with that, then it's their problem. We're not public officials running for office. We're not even movie stars or local celebrities. We're just people, and our business is our business."

"Don't be naïve," Fitz said curtly. "You sought out the press on your own last year. The minute you did that, you made your problems everyone else's problems. You can't go back on that now."

"He was our rapist! He died. What the hell did they think we were going to do? Tear out our hair? Throw our bodies on his grave?"

"It would've helped!"

"Helped who? He killed my little sister. Fuck Eddie Como! *Fuck him!*"

"Fuck him, Jillian? Or *kill him?*"

Jillian blew out a breath. She walked away from the table. "Now, now, Fitz. You keep talking and I'm going to want my lawyer present."

Fitz flicked a glance at Griffin. Griffin hadn't planned on bringing this up yet, but what the hell.

"Can your lawyer explain the large cash withdrawals recently made from your savings account?" Griffin inquired.

"You've been busy, Sergeant."

"I try," he said modestly. Both Carol and Meg were staring at Jillian curiously. While Jillian didn't seem surprised by the question, they clearly were.

"I needed the money," Jillian said after a moment.

"Why?"

"Personal reasons."

"What personal reasons?"

"Personal reasons unrelated to Eddie's demise."

"You're going to have to prove that," Griffin said.

"Are you charging me with something, Sergeant?"

"No."

"Then I don't have to prove anything."

Griffin had to nod. He'd seen that coming. Jillian prided herself on appearing cool, and when under pressure, becoming even cooler. Except last night. She hadn't been the composed, corporate woman then. Her long hair had been down, wild and thick around her face. Her movements had been frenzied, her fear honest, her rage unfettered. And her hands, when they had closed upon his shoulders, had been seeking genuine support as her legs collapsed beneath the weight of those red, dripping letters scrawled upon her home. Her mother, he realized abruptly. Jillian was calm when it came to herself. But when her family was threatened . . .

Stupid thought for the day – Cindy would've liked Jillian Hayes. Really bad idea for the day – he was beginning to like her, too.

"Tell us about that attack," Jillian said.

Fitz thinned his lips. "You know I can't discuss an ongoing police investigation."

"Detective," Carol protested.

"Fitz!" Meg chimed in.

Fitz merely shook his head. He was pissed. Even Griffin could see that. If he didn't know any better, he'd guess that the women's cold front had hurt the detective's feelings.

"We could help," Jillian said.

"Drink more champagne?"

"We made a mistake." Carol's turn. "Detective, please. We have to know. Surely you understand. This new batch of mailings, then this vandalism at Jillian's home and then this attack on College Hill. We feel like we're losing our minds."

"Mailings?" Griffin interjected. "As in plural, with an 's'?"

Carol and Meg simultaneously turned to Jillian. "I got one, too. Last Friday. A computer disk, sent to my house with my business address as the return. I didn't look at the postmark, either. You would think we'd all know better by now." She smiled miserably, then got on with it. "The disk contained a video file. A leering picture of Eddie Como, who told me he'd get me for doing this, even if it was from beyond the grave. I should've told you, Detective Fitzpatrick. I know. But at the time, I wrote it off as one last prank before the trial started. He'd already mailed us so much stuff. It seemed silly to bother with one more."

"You still have the disk?"

"Envelope and all. I touched it with my bare hands, though. I should've examined it more closely first. I'm sorry."

Fitz sighed unhappily. He appeared tired and frustrated and fed up with all of them. Perpetrators were bad, but all homicide detectives could tell you that sometimes the victims were even worse. You got to know them more. You grew to care. And then, with the best of intentions, they fucked you royally and all you could do was remind yourself that it wasn't really their fault. People were people. And everyone made mistakes.

"So we got a theme," Fitz said finally. "Eddie Como wants vengeance, even if it's from beyond the grave."

"Interesting choice of words," Griffin commented.

Jillian had caught it, too. "Yes," she said slowly. "It's almost as if he knew he was going to die."

An uncomfortable silence filled the room.

"You don't suppose . . ." Carol said.

"He arranged for his own death?" Meg picked up with a frown. "Why would anyone do that?"

"Could be merely coincidence." Fitz shrugged. "Remember, real life is stranger than fiction."

"Detective." Jillian turned to him with pleading eyes. "The new incident last night. You of all people know what this is doing to us. We understand you don't owe us anything. We understand there is a police protocol . . . But this is so close to home. After everything we've been through. Please . . ."

Fitz hesitated one last time, probably for ego's sake, but the end was never in doubt. He rubbed his red-rimmed eyes, then ran a hand through his thinning hair. "Yeah. All right. You might as well know because the press is gonna come after you, too. We had another assault. A Brown University student. She was attacked in her apartment, tied up with ten latex strips, raped and then . . . strangled to death. She was pronounced DOA at the scene."

"Her name?" Meg asked.

"You really want to know that?"

"I do."

"Sylvia Blaire."

"Her age?"

"Twenty."

"What was she studying?"

"I'm not sure. Psychology, I think. We're still putting together the victim profile."

"Was she pretty?"

"Come on, Meg." Fitz gestured impatiently. "Don't do this to yourself. She's gone now. Learning all this . . . You're just going to torture yourself with it in the middle of the night."

"We need to know," Meg said quietly. "*I* need to know."

"It won't help you, Meg."

Meg smiled gently. "I'm not looking for help, Detective. I'm looking to learn about Sylvia Blaire, a young college student just like Trisha Hayes or myself. This is the Survivors Club, after all. And one of the obligations of survivors is to learn about the other victims and remember them well."

A heavy silence filled the room. Fitz didn't know where to look. Neither did Griffin. And for the first time he got something about the women, their group, this club. They had become a unit. They gave each other strength. And Sylvia Blaire, if she hadn't died . . .

Fitz looked old. Fitz looked like a detective who'd been to one too many crime scenes, and this one, this last one, would be the one he'd never get out of his head. Guys around here liked to retire to Florida, but even there, most of them would say, the images still followed. Too many sad faces staring back up from the tranquil blue waters as they cast their lines and tried to fish.

"In her photos she was very pretty. Long dark hair, big brown eyes. A former high school track star. Got good grades. Donated time to the Boys & Girls Club in Pawtucket."

"A regular blood donor," Jillian filled in.

"Yeah," Fitz said heavily. "Yeah."

"It sounds like him," Carol spoke up. Her gaze went around the room. "You have to admit . . ."

"Too soon to know." Fitz shook his head, his voice picking back up. "Sure, there are common elements, but this isn't exactly a case that's been held back from the public."

"You think it might be a copycat," Jillian filled in.

"It's a possibility. The victim profile – young, brunette, college student – is hardly rocket science. All anyone has to do is flip on the TV and see a picture of Meg or Trish. The connection with the blood drives, also on the evening news, given that Eddie worked as a phlebotomist for the Blood Center. And that latex-ties business came out shortly after Eddie's arrest. So there you have it. One rapist profile, ready to go."

"Was there sign of forced entry?" Jillian again.

"Nah."

"That wasn't in the news."

"Might not be a stranger-to-stranger crime."

Jillian frowned, then got it. "Meaning maybe someone this girl knew – an ex-boyfriend, say – staged this as one of the College Hill Rapist's attacks to cover up what he had done."

"Could be."

"Did she have an ex-boyfriend?"

"It's only been eight hours. Ask me in another two."

"What about fingerprints?"

"We took all sorts."

"DNA?"

Fitz hesitated, shot Griffin a look. Griffin didn't say anything; it was Fitz's party after all. Jillian, however, was too fast for both of them. Her eyes widened. Her face paled. Very slowly, her arms wrapped around her waist.

"No," she whispered.

"Yeah," Fitz said.

"But the douche wasn't in the news. None of the reports *ever* gave out that information."

Carol was picking up on things, looking around the room even more wildly. "Are you saying . . . Was it the same kind?"

"Berkely and Johnson's Disposable Douche with Country Flowers." Fitz sighed again, then brought up his hand and rubbed his bleary face. Griffin had done much the same when Fitz had given him the news. The douche was the kicker. You could spin the scene so many ways, until you got to the douche.

"But . . . but," Meg said. She couldn't seem to get beyond that. "But . . . but . . ."

"Let's not rush to any conclusions," Fitz warned.

"There are still other possibilities," Griffin said.

"Like what?" Jillian cried.

"Like maybe Eddie had a friend," Fitz stated flatly. "Or maybe he liked to brag all about it. Just because *we* didn't give out the details doesn't mean that he didn't."

"He always claimed he was innocent," Carol said, her eyes still dashing all about. "You don't say you're innocent, and then brag all about your crime."

"Sure you do, happens all the time."

Meg had started rocking back and forth. "It's not a friend. It's not a friend. Oh God, oh God, oh God . . ."

"Meg . . ." It was Jillian, her voice hard, trying to restore order.

But Meg was beyond reason. Carol was beyond reason. Only Jillian remained tight-lipped and determined at the head of the table. Her gaze rose to meet Fitz's, to meet Griffin's.

"Eddie Como lives," she whispered helplessly. "Oh God, Eddie Como *lives*."

22
Griffin

Griffin and Fitz stepped outside the restaurant, and the first camera flash exploded in their faces.

"Detective, Detective, can you comment on reports that last night's victim was also tied up with latex strips – "

"Was it true that a man matching Eddie Como's description was seen running from the girl's apartment – "

"Sergeant, Sergeant, will the state police now be taking over the case – "

"What does this latest attack mean for the case against Eddie Como – "

"Detective, Detective – "

"Is it true that someone used blood to scrawl 'Eddie Como lives' on the wall of the new victim's – "

"What about rumors that the man shot yesterday wasn't really Como?"

Fitz and Griffin finally forced their way to Fitz's car. Technically, Griffin had arrived in his own vehicle, but given that it was parked another two blocks away on the crowded street, Fitz's beat-up Taurus beckoned like a godsend. Griffin used his shoulder to muscle back one particularly aggressive reporter, got the passenger-side door open and ducked inside just as a new round of flashes erupted from the herd. A cry went up. The women were now trying to leave the restaurant. The whole pack shifted right and immediately surged forward.

"Shit," Fitz said.

"Shit," Griffin agreed.

They abandoned the Taurus and grimly waded back into the fray.

"Step aside, step aside, step aside."

"Police, coming through."

On the restaurant steps, Jillian stood shell-shocked in front of Carol and Meg as more lights flashed and heated questions started peppering the tiny space. She had probably thought their little rendezvous was safe from the press. In a private room in a restaurant that she knew. She probably hadn't seen the morning news and the public flogging the local news affiliates had delivered to both the Providence Police and the so-called Survivors Club for their aggressive pursuit of Eddie Como. She probably hadn't realized just yet, that last year's press coverage had only been a warm-up. Now, as of this morning, was the real thing. She and Carol and Meg could run. But they could not hide.

Jillian's features had turned the color of ash. A moment later, however, she recovered her bearings and got her chin up. Behind her, Carol had raised a hand in a vain attempt to shield herself from the cameras. Meg simply looked dazed.

"Ms. Hayes, Ms. Hayes, how do you respond to allegations that your group pressed too hard for Eddie Como's arrest?"

"Do you believe this newest attack proves Eddie's innocence?"

"What about the defense attorney's witness? Mrs. Rosen, how sure are you of the time when you were attacked?"

"Ms. Hayes, Ms. Hayes – "

"Did you shoot Eddie?"

"Hey, step aside. State police, don't make me seize your tape."

In all honesty, Griffin couldn't legally seize any of the reporters' tapes, but evidently word of what he'd done to Maureen had gotten around, because three reporters immediately leapt back and snarled at him. He gave them his most charming smile. Then he flung out his massive arms and forced the rest of the jackals back four steps.

Not an idiot, Jillian seized the opportunity to grab Meg's and Carol's hands and bolt from the steps.

"Ms. Hayes, Ms. Hayes – "

"Did you persecute an innocent man?"

"What about his wife and baby?"

"Hey, Miss Pesaturo, remember anything yet?"

The Survivors Club disappeared around the corner and the last question dissipated into the crisp morning air. The press corps took a second to regroup. Then they went after Fitz and Griffin again.

"Who's leading the investigation?"

"What will be your next steps?"

"Is the real College Hill Rapist still out there? What is your advice for all of our young women?"

"Press briefing at four," Fitz barked. "Through official channels. For God's sake, we're just the working stiffs. Now get outta our way."

He and Griffin still had to battle their way back to Fitz's car. This time, they both managed to get inside the Taurus and slam the doors. The reporters tapped on the window. Fitz gunned the engine.

Not doubting for a moment that a Providence cop would run them over, the reporters finally dropped back. Fitz pulled away from the curb while simultaneously digging around his feet for a bottle of Tums. Griffin amused himself by picking up the newest edition of *People* magazine from the dash. Sure enough, Fitz had already inked in half of the crossword.

"You're fucked," Griffin said conversationally.

Fitz had gotten his Tums open. He started chomping. "At this rate, we're all fucked."

"I'm not fucked. I just have a dead rape suspect. Same as yesterday."

"Don't kid yourself. Eddie turns up innocent, we're all fucked. The women'll get heat for applying pressure. We'll get heat for making the arrest. DA'll get heat for building the case. State marshals will get heat for not better protecting one of their transports. And you, the lucky state, will get heat for not stepping in and keeping the rest of us from fucking up. So there."

"You're an optimist, aren't you, Fitz?"

"Tried and true. Goddamn case." Fitz's features grew more haggard. "Goddamn case . . ."

Griffin understood. He lapsed into silence, giving Fitz a chance to pull himself back together as they drove aimlessly around Federal Hill.

"Dr. No," Griffin said finally.

"Dr. No?"

"Forty-eight down. A four-letter James Bond movie. *Dr. No.*"

Fitz grunted, felt around his shirt pocket, then handed Griffin a pen.

"I'm honored," Griffin assured him, and filled in the spaces.

"You went to the Hayes residence," Fitz said. "Last night."

"I did."

"Why?"

"A uniform caught the report on the scanner and let me know. I figured anything happening at Jillian's place the same day as Como was shot couldn't be good."

Fitz looked at him. "You just called her Jillian."

"Mmmm, yes."

"I haven't met a statey yet who doesn't use formal address when working a case. For God's sake, you guys don't even refer to each other by first names. You're like a bunch of friggin' Marines."

"I'm the black sheep?"

"Don't go getting any ideas, Griffin. This case is messy enough."

"You like her that much, Fitz?"

For his answer, Fitz growled and flexed his hands on the wheel. "I am having a really bad day."

"We're both barking up the wrong tree," Griffin told him lightly. "Have you ever asked Jillian Hayes what she thinks of men in our profession? She's not exactly an aspiring groupie. In fact, from what I can tell, she pretty much considers us incompetent morons who are at least indirectly responsible for her sister's death. Hence her total openness and willingness to cooperate with us now."

Fitz grunted, which Griffin took as at least partial acknowledgment of Jillian's point.

"Serial crime is the worst," Fitz grumbled after a moment. "Longer it goes on . . . more victims the perp claims . . . Yeah, maybe I should just be happy I can still find my pants in the morning, 'cause these days I'm sure as hell not finding much else."

"You're riding the case hard," Griffin said. "It's the most a detective can do."

Fitz grunted again. "That incident at Jillian's house, you think it was a prank? Some teenage kid armed with a can of red spray paint and up to no good?"

"It's East Greenwich's call."

"Don't fuck with me, Griffin. Not after the night I've had."

Griffin was silent for a moment. "I don't know," he said finally, then held up a hand to ward off Fitz's snarl. "Honest. The spray paint, graffiti, yeah that fits with a teenage kid. But loosening the bulbs in the motion-sensor lights . . ."

"I wondered about that."

"When you were a kid going to egg someone's house, did you unscrew the outdoor lights?" Griffin shrugged. "Couldn't have done it at night either. The minute someone approached in the dark, the lights would go on. So that means it was done before, during the day, when no one would notice the lights being activated."

"Premeditation."

"Seems very thoughtful. For a kid."

"Ah shit . . ."

"My turn. Off the record, just you and I. Last night, what are you thinking?"

"Christ, I haven't had enough sleep to think." Fitz

rubbed his face wearily, then belatedly grabbed the steering wheel as the car swerved across the street.

"There's still the DNA evidence."

"Yeah, that's what bothers me so much. If it had been merely a circumstantial case, just the fact that he worked for the Blood Center and knew the victims, well then . . ."

"You might have jumped too soon."

"Maybe."

"But you got DNA."

"We got *good* DNA. I went back after our little discussion yesterday evening. Grabbed the report. Given the high-profile nature of the case, we sent the samples out to an independent lab in Virginia in addition to the analysis done by the Department of Health. Both agree. DNA samples from Eddie Como match DNA samples taken from the sheets and the women in all fourteen sites tested. Meaning the likelihood of another person being responsible for the DNA present at the rape scenes is one in three hundred million times the population *of the entire earth*. That's pretty damn conclusive if you ask me."

"Sounds pretty good to me, too," Griffin agreed. "Do the women know this?"

"D'Amato knows this. He's the one who sent it out for the independent analysis, plus it was gonna be the linchpin of his case. He probably went over it with them."

"Meaning they must really, truly feel that they *know* Como was the attacker."

"Hey, I *know* Eddie was the attacker."

"Meaning we're back to a very good motive for murder."

Fitz blew out a breath. "I hate this."

"I know."

"What kind of fucking case is this, anyway? You got me doubting my own victims, and the press has me doubting my own perp. I don't like this. This is not what police work is supposed to be about. You gather the evidence, you put together a theory, you build a case, you nail the SOB. End of story. Eddie Como lives. Christ, it's like being in the middle of a freak show."

"I'm not a big fan of it either."

"I think it's an accomplice," Fitz said abruptly.

"Eddie talked?"

"Yeah. Makes the most sense. Maybe in her own way, Tawnya's right, and all she's ever seen of him is good-boy Eddie. But we know for a fact that there's also a bad-boy Eddie who was running a few more errands than returning a movie to Blockbuster's one night. Now bad-boy Eddie has a need to live on the edge, explore the wild side. And maybe bad-boy Eddie also needs to talk about it later. To some other bad-boy friends that I'm betting Tawnya doesn't even know about."

"Eddie Como led two lives."

"Wouldn't be the first time. And it fits."

Griffin nodded his head. "True."

"Now consider this. Maybe one of those bad-boy friends has spent the last year fantasizing about all those stories he heard from Eddie. Maybe he's even bought a few bondage magazines and gotten heavy into the darker side of porn. But twelve months later, none of it gives him that same secret thrill. Then one day, he turns on the news and lo and behold, Eddie Como is dead. And it comes to him. He could do it. He knows everything from Eddie, so why not? He'll become the College Hill Rapist and *nobody will suspect a thing*. The MO points to Eddie and Eddie can't deny it because he's dead. Eddie can't even say, well I told everything to so-and-so, because again, Eddie's dead. It's the perfect cover."

Griffin regarded him steadily. "Why stop there, Fitz? Maybe the other guy has been fantasizing about the rapes for a year. Maybe he's been thinking he'd like to try that. Except rather than wake up one morning and discover Eddie Como is dead, maybe he decided to ensure the perfect cover, by arranging Eddie's death."

"Shit!" Fitz pounded the steering wheel, and very nearly drove them into a streetlight. "Of course! It's *Single White Female*, except with, well, Freaking Violent Rapists. Why didn't I think of it?"

"Because it's borderline preposterous," Griffin said quietly.

"I don't care."

"I know. Which is the second problem."

"Huh?"

"Off the record. Way off the record. Between two experienced detectives. You need the College Hill Rapist to be Eddie Como."

"Hey now – "

Griffin shook his head. "I know what it's like. I've been there myself. The internal pressure, the external pressure. The media isn't wrong. At a certain point, we all have to get our man."

"You think I'm all wigged out because maybe I gave in to the public's demand for justice and screwed a major investigation?"

"No. I think you're all wigged out because maybe by rushing the investigation, you missed Sylvia Blaire's killer."

Fitz didn't say anything, which they both knew was a yes. If Eddie was innocent, if the real College Hill Rapist was still out there . . . then Fitz had screwed up, and probably the women had screwed up, and not only were two young girls dead, but Eddie Como, Jr. was orphaned for no reason, and someone, probably a victim or a family member, had been driven to murder for no reason. The cost, the carnage, grew very high.

Which was one of the fundamental problems with a long-term investigation. At a certain point, the suspect *had* to be guilty, because everyone involved in the case couldn't afford for it to be otherwise.

Fitz had finally come around the block again and located Griffin's car. He double-parked beside it, ignoring the irate honking that promptly sounded behind him.

"One in three hundred million times the population of the earth," Fitz said. "Think about that."

"I will."

"Hey, Griffin, how much money was missing from Jillian's account?"

Griffin hesitated, his hand on the door handle. "Twenty thousand."

"Enough to hire a shooter."

"Probably." Griffin hesitated again. "Fitz, she's not the only one. Dan Rosen is up to his eyebrows in hock. He took out a second mortgage on his home six months ago for a hundred thousand. Then last week, he liquidated one of his brokerage accounts. The financial guys are still trying to figure out where that money went."

Fitz closed his eyes. "And the day just keeps getting better and better."

"Nothing on the Pesaturo accounts yet," Griffin said, "but I think we all know that they wouldn't need money to hire an assassin."

"They already got Uncle Vinnie."

"Exactly."

"You really think one of them did it."

"I think it's the answer that makes the most sense."

"Yeah." Fitz nodded, sighed heavily, then went fishing for more Tums. "I like them, you know. You're never supposed to get too close, but after the last year, the shit they've been through, the way they've held up, Jillian, Carol and Meg. They're good people. I've been . . . proud . . . to work with them."

"We'll get this figured out."

"Sure." Fitz looked at him. He smiled, but it was bitter. "State's involved now. And the state always gets their man, right, Griff? Not like us hardworking city cops who are only fit for drive-by shootings and other lowbrow gang-banging hissy fits. No, state detectives never make any wrong turns in an investigation. State detectives never succumb to *pressure*."

Griffin's hand spasmed on the door handle. A muscle leapt in his jaw. The buzzing was almost immediate in his ears. Very slowly, he let go of the handle. Very slowly, he took a deep breath and counted to ten.

"You've had a rough night," Griffin said quietly when he finally trusted himself to speak. "So I'm going to do us both a favor and pretend you didn't say that."

Fitz continued to regard him steadily. His pupils were small and dark, his sagging face twisted into a stubborn scowl. For a moment, Griffin thought Fitz would push it anyway. Probably because he had had a rough night, spent at the side of a young girl who never should have died. And now the press was beating up on him, the state was beating up on him, and probably, within the next half an hour, his lieutenant would be beating up on him. And that kind of frustration could build in a man. Build and build and build, until you didn't care anymore. You thought too much about those poor young victims, all the ones that if you'd just moved faster, thought smarter, fought better . . . Until your desire to destroy was even higher than your desire to be saved.

Then you went home and held your dying wife in your arms, so weakened by cancer she couldn't speak, but only blink her eyes. Soon that would be gone, too. You would just come home, sit in an empty house and see images of missing children dance before your eyes.

"Go home and get some sleep," Griffin said.

"Fuck you, Griffin. You know, I may not be young like you. I may not be able to bench-press three times my body weight or whatever the hell it is you do in your free time. But don't underestimate me, Sergeant. I'm old. I'm bitter. I'm fat. I'm bald. And that gives me a propensity for violence you can only dream about. So don't you lecture me about procedure and don't you patronize my handling of a case. Oh, and one more thing. I know where Jillian's money went."

"Fitz – "

"Call Father Rondell of the Cranston parish. Tell him Jillian gave you his name."

"The Cranston parish?" Griffin frowned, then blinked. "Oh, no way."

"Yeah way. I *know* these women, Sergeant. I *know* them. Now get the fuck out of my car."

Griffin shrugged. Griffin got out of the car. "You know, Fitz, these cross-jurisdictional investigations continue to improve relations all the time," he said.

"Yeah, that's my thinking, too."

Fitz peeled away from the curb. Griffin headed for Cranston.

23
Jillian

The waves rolled into the beach, gentle today, peaking low with a cap of frothy foam, then fading back into the dark depths of the ocean. The sandpipers rushed into the retreating wake of low tide, searching frantically for anything good to eat. Slow day on the beach this early in May. Another dark green wave descended upon the sand, and the small white birds took flight.

Jillian continued watching the water long after she heard the car pull up, the engine turn off, the door open, then close. Footsteps in the sand. The thought reminded her of the religious poem she'd read as a child. She smiled, and the pain cut her to the bone.

She had never been good at belief. Never been one for faith. Too many nights alone as a child maybe. Too many promises broken by her mother, until she internalized, somewhere way down deep, that the only one she could depend upon was herself. Yet she had flirted with religion, talked about it with friends, found herself attending the occasional Christmas mass. She loved the sound of a choir singing. She took comfort, during the endless gray days of winter, from going to a cathedral warmed by hundreds of bodies, standing side by side in communal worship.

Trisha had joined a Congregational church when she was in high school. She'd gotten quite into things. Faith in a higher power fit her rosy outlook on life. Conducting good works suited her bubbly nature. Jillian had attended services with her several times, and even she had been struck by the glow that filled her sister's face during prayer. Faith recharged Trisha. Made her somehow even bigger, larger, more *Trisha* than she had been before.

Until the night she had truly needed God . . . or Jillian . . . or even a big, strong policeman intent on doing his job.

If there was a God, and He hadn't seen fit to save Trish, then should Jillian really feel so guilty? Or maybe there was a God, and He had turned to Jillian as His instrument, and by not being up to the task, she had failed Him and her sister both. So many thoughts she could torture herself with in the middle of the night. Or even during bright spring days in May, standing in the warm caress of the sun and watching the ocean break against the shore.

Oh God, Sylvia Blaire. That poor, poor girl. What had they done?

"Jillian."

She didn't turn around. She didn't need to, to know who it was. "Bring your thumbscrews this time?"

"Actually, we're always armed with thumbscrews. Department policy. But I'm a good old Catholic boy – I wouldn't dream of using thumbscrews on a priest."

She stiffened, then finally turned. Sergeant Griffin stood in the sand outside the deck railing. His cheeks were dark and shadowed, the line of his jaw impressively square, his eyes impressively bright. Even ten feet away, she could feel the impact of his presence. The broad shoulders, muscular arms, bulging chest. No different than any other state policeman, she thought resentfully. It was as if the department had a mold, and churned out one well-chiseled officer after another. She'd never been one for brawn anyway. She considered the size of a man's muscles directly inverse to the power of his brain.

"You should've just told me," he said now, his voice quiet but firm.

"Why? I'd already said the money had nothing to do with Eddie's death. If you weren't prepared to believe that, why should I have expected you to believe an even bigger fairy tale?"

"It's not a fairy tale."

She shrugged. "Close enough. I gave the money to Father Rondell in cash, took no receipt, ensured there were no witnesses, and made anonymity the primary condition of the donation. If you want evidence of where the money went, I have none to give you."

"A priest's word is pretty good evidence."

"Yes, but he wasn't supposed to tell you."

Griffin smiled. "I confess, all good Catholic faith aside, I kind of tricked him."

"You tricked a priest?"

"Well, it was for a good cause. I was proving a woman's innocence."

Jillian snorted. "Let's not get carried away."

"Actually, I can't take all the credit. Fitz told me to go talk to Father Rondell. So I approached him, saying that I needed confirmation that you had donated money to help Eddie Como's son. Immediately, he was quite gushing about your twenty-thousand-dollar generosity. It seems that Eddie, Jr. has a guardian angel."

"It's not his fault what his father did. He wasn't even born."

"Tawnya doesn't know?"

"Nobody knows."

"Not even the Survivors Club?"

"Not even the Survivors Club."

"Why, Jillian?"

"I don't know," she said honestly. "I just . . . Trish was gone. Carol's a mess. Meg has lost her past. And I . . . well, I have my own issues, don't I? Last year when the police finally arrested Eddie, I expected to feel better. Vindicated, satisfied, something. But I didn't. Because Trish was still gone, and Carol's still a mess and Meg still has no memory, and now we're seeing pictures of Eddie's pregnant girlfriend and all I can think is here's another victim. A baby who will grow up without his father. One more destroyed life. It seemed too much." She shook her head. "I needed . . . I just needed something good to come out of all of this. I needed to feel that someone would escape Eddie's mistakes. And God knows we never will."

"So you set up a trust fund for Eddie's child."

She shrugged. "I asked Detective Fitzpatrick for the name of someone close to the Como family. He gave me Father Rondell's name. Father Rondell took care of things from there."

"But you kept it secret."

"I didn't know if Miss Clemente would accept the money if she knew where it came from."

"And why not tell Meg and Carol?"

"I didn't think they'd like it. Besides, it's not really their business, is it? It's my money. My decision."

Griffin smiled. "You like to do that. Be a group player as long as it suits you, but revert back to an individual the minute it cramps your style."

She just looked at him. "How did you know I was here?"

"Brilliant detective work, of course."

She snorted again. He raised his right hand. "Scout's honor. Finding you is my biggest accomplishment today. Well, other than tracing your money, but Fitz is the one who connected those dots. After talking to the priest, however, I wanted to confirm the transaction with you. Being of sound mind, however, I figured you wouldn't magically take my call. So I figured I needed to see you in person. And then I started thinking, if I were Jillian Hayes, where would I be today of all days, with the press hot on my heels? I figured you wouldn't go to work, because you wouldn't want to turn your business into a media circus. Then I figured for the same reason, you couldn't go home – it would just bring the press down on your family. Then I confess, I made a wrong turn and tried your sister's gravesite. For the record, three reporters already had it staked out."

Jillian looked at him curiously. "I did try there first. After spotting the reporters, however, I turned away."

"Exactly." He nodded. "Then it occurred to me. Like any good Rhode Islander, you're bound to have a beach house. So I did a search of Narragansett property records. Nothing in your name. Then I tried your mother's. The rest, as they say, is history."

"I see your point. Positively brilliant detective work. So who killed Sylvia Blaire?"

Griffin promptly grimaced. "Touché."

"I'm not trying to be cruel. At least not yet."

"Are you beginning to doubt Eddie's guilt, Jillian?"

"I don't know."

"That's the same as a yes. May I?" He gestured to the three steps leading up to the deck. She hesitated. Nodding would invite him in. He'd take a seat, become part of her last hideaway, and she had such little privacy left. Maybe he'd even sit close to her. Maybe she'd feel the heat of his body again, find herself staring at those arms.

When her legs had given out last night . . . When he had caught her in his arms, and shielded her from her neighbors' voyeuristic stares . . . She remembered the warmth of him then. The feel of his arm, so easily supporting her weight. The steadiness of his gaze as he waited for her to pull herself together once more.

And she *hated* herself for thinking these things.

Jillian moved to the opposite side of the deck from the stairs. She was still in her navy blue suit from this morning, and it was difficult to negotiate the deck boards in heels. She took a seat on a built-in wooden bench. Then, finally, she nodded.

"It's nice here," Sergeant Griffin commented, climbing aboard. "Great view."

"My mother bought it twenty years ago, before Narragansett became, well, Narragansett." She gestured her hand to the oversized homes that now bordered the property. Not beach houses anymore, but beach castles.

"Never thought of expanding?"

"If we built out, we'd lose the beach. If we built up, we'd block the view for the house across the street. And what would we gain? A bigger kitchen, a more luxurious bedroom? My mother didn't buy this place for the kitchen or bedroom. She bought it for the beach and the ocean view."

"You have an amazingly practical perspective on things."

"I grew up with a lounge singer, remember? Nothing

teaches you to respect practicality more than growing up on the New York club circuit."

"Different hotel every night?"

"Close enough." She tilted her head to the side. "And you?"

"Rhode Islander. All my life. Good Irish stock. My mother makes the best corned beef and cabbage and my father can drink a man three times his size under the table. You haven't lived until you've been to one of our family gatherings."

"Large family?"

"Three brothers. Two of them are state marshals, actually. We've probably been policing for as long as there have been cops. If you think about it, it's a natural fit for Irishmen. No one knows how to get into trouble better than we do. Ergo, we're perfect for penetrating the criminal mind." He smiled wolfishly.

Jillian felt something move in her chest. She gripped the edge of the wooden bench more tightly, then looked away.

"Jillian, you said that in the voice lineup, you and Carol could narrow it down to two men. What was it about the two?"

"I don't understand."

"Why those two men? What made you focus on them?"

"They . . . they sounded alike."

Griffin leaned forward, rested his elbows on his knees. His blue eyes were intent now. Dark, penetrating. She found herself shivering, though she didn't know why. "Think back, Jillian. Take a deep breath, open up your mind. You're in the viewing room. The mirror is blacked out, but one by one, men are stepping forward and speaking into a microphone. You are listening to their voices. One strikes close to home. Then another. Why those two voices?"

Jillian cocked her head to the side. She thought she understood now. So she closed her eyes, she tilted her face up to the warmth of the sun and she allowed her mind to go back, to that dark, claustrophobic room, where she stood with just a defense attorney and Detective Fitzpatrick, dreading hearing that voice again and knowing that she must. Two voices. Two low, resonant voices sounding strangely flat as they delivered the scripted line "I'm gonna fuck you good."

"They were both low pitched. Deep voices."

"Good."

"They . . . Accent." Her eyes popped open. "It's the way they said fuck. Not fuck, but more like foik. You know, that thick Rhode Island accent."

"Cranston," Griffin said quietly.

She nodded. "Yes. They had more of a Cranston accent."

"Como grew up in Cranston."

"So it's consistent." She was pleased.

"Jillian, *lots* of men grew up in Cranston. And most of them do butcher the English language, even by Rhode Island standards. We still can't arrest them for it."

"But . . . Well, there's still the DNA."

"Yeah," Griffin said. "There's still the DNA. What did D'Amato tell you about it?"

She shrugged. "That it was conclusive. He'd sent it out to a lab in Virginia and they confirmed that the samples taken from the crime scenes matched Eddie Como's sample by something like one in three hundred million times the population of the entire earth. I gather it's rare to have that conclusive a match. He was excited."

"He told you this. All three of you?"

Jillian brought up her chin. "Yes."

"And that convinced all three of you, the Survivors Club, that Como was the College Hill Rapist?"

"Sergeant, it convinced D'Amato and Detective Fitzpatrick that Eddie was the College Hill Rapist. And if we'd been able to go to trial, I'm sure it would've convinced a *jury* that Eddie was the College Hill Rapist."

"What about the Blockbuster kid?"

"What about him? Carol's never been sure about the time she was attacked. You'll have to forgive her, but while she was being brutally sodomized she didn't think to glance at a clock."

"Jillian . . ." Griffin hesitated. He steepled his hands in front of him. He had long, lean fingers. Rough with calluses, probably from lifting weights. His knuckles were scuffed up, too, crisscrossed with old scars and fresh scratches. Boxing, she realized suddenly. He had a pugilist's hands. Strong. Capable. Violent. "Jillian, did they get a sample from your sister?"

Her gaze fell immediately. She had to swallow simply to get moisture back into her mouth. "Yes."

"So he . . . before you came . . ."

"Yes."

"I'm sorry."

"I was late," she said for no good reason. "I was supposed to be there an hour earlier, but I'd gotten too busy . . . Something silly at work. Then traffic was bad, and I couldn't find parking. So I'm driving around the city and my sister is being . . . I was late."

Griffin didn't say anything, but then Jillian hadn't really expected a reply. What was there to say, after all? She was late, her sister was attacked. She couldn't find parking, her sister died. Running late shouldn't matter. Not being able to find parking in a congested city shouldn't cost someone her life. But sometimes, for reasons no one could explain, it did.

What silly mistake had Sylvia Blaire made last night? Waited too late to head home? Not paid enough attention to the bushes around her house? Or maybe the mistake had been earlier, falling in love with the wrong man or breaking up with the wrong man? Something that had probably seemed completely inconsequential at the time.

Which led her to wonder, of course, what mistakes the Survivors Club might have made with the best of intentions. *Had* they pressured the police too hard? *Had* they believed in Eddie's guilt too quickly? She honestly didn't know anymore, and this level of doubt was killing her. Trish was bad enough. She didn't know if she could stand any more blood on her conscience.

"You didn't see the man?" Griffin asked finally.

Jillian closed her eyes. "No," she said tiredly. "As I've

told Fitz, as I've told D'Amato . . . I didn't see anything that night. My sister had a basement apartment, the lights were turned out . . . He rushed me from behind."

"But you remember his voice?"

"Yes."

"You struggled with him?"

"Yes."

"What did you feel? Did you grab his hands?"

"I tried to pull them away from my throat," she said flatly.

"Were they covered with something?"

"Yes. They felt rubbery, like he was wearing latex gloves, and that made me think of Trish . . . worry about Trish."

"What about his face. Did you go after his face, try to scratch him? Maybe he had a beard, mustache, facial hair?"

She had to think about it. "Nooooo. I don't remember hitting his face. But he laughed. He spoke. He didn't sound muffled. So I would say he didn't have anything over his head."

"Did you hit him?"

"I, uh, I got him between the legs. With my hands. I had knit my fingers together, you know, as they teach you in self-defense."

"Was he dressed?"

"Yes. He had clothes, shoes. I guess he'd already done that much."

"What was he wearing? You said you hit him between the legs, what did the material feel like?"

"Cotton," she said immediately. "When I hit him, the material was soft. Cotton, not denim. Khakis, maybe some kind of Dockers?"

"And higher?"

"I hit his ribs . . . Soft again. Cottony. A button. A button-down shirt, I guess." She nodded firmly, her head coming back up. "That would make sense, right? For that neighborhood. When he walked away he would be nicely dressed, a typical student in khakis and a button-down shirt."

"Like Eddie Como was fond of wearing?"

"Exactly." She nodded her head vigorously.

He nodded, too, though his motion was more thoughtful than hers. After a moment, he twisted around on the bench, looked out onto the water. Sun was high now. The beach quiet, the sound of the water peaceful. Just them and the sandpipers, still trolling the wet sand for food.

"Must be a great place to come on weekends, recover from the demands of owning your own business," he said presently.

"I think so."

"Does your mom still come?"

"She likes to sit on the deck. It's a nice adventure for her and Toppi, once the weather gets hot."

He looked at her sideways. "And Trisha?"

She kept her voice neutral. "She liked it, too."

"Tell me about her, Jillian. Tell me one story of her, in this place."

"Why?"

"Because memories are good. Even when they hurt."

She didn't say anything right away, couldn't think of anything, in all honesty. And that panicked her a little. It had only been a year. May twenty-fourth of last year. Surely Trisha couldn't fade away that quickly. Surely she couldn't have lost that much. But then she got her pulse to slow, her breathing to steady. She looked out at those slowly undulating waves, and it wasn't that hard after all.

"Trisha was mischievous, energetic. She would crash through the waves like an oversized puppy, then roll on the beach until her entire body was covered in sand. Then she would run over to me or Mom and threaten us with bear hugs."

"And what did you do?"

She smiled. "Made faces, of course. Trisha could tell you. I'm not into water or gritty sand. I take my beach experience on oversized towels with an oversized umbrella and a good paperback novel. That's what made it so funny."

She turned to him finally, looked him in the eye. "Tell me

about your wife. If memories are so good, even when they hurt, then tell me about her."

"Her name was Cindy, she was beautiful, and I loved her."

"How did you meet?"

"Hiking up in the White Mountains. We were both members of the Appalachian Mountain Club. She was twenty-seven. I was thirty. She beat me going up Mount Washington, but I beat her coming down."

"What did she do?"

"She was an electrical engineer."

"Really?" Jillian looked back at him in surprise. Somehow, she had pictured this phantom wife as someone . . . less brainy, she supposed. Maybe a blonde, the perfect foil for Griffin's dark good looks.

"She worked for a firm in Wakefield," Griffin said. "Plus she liked to tinker on the side. In fact, she'd just come up with a new type of EKG before she got sick. Got the patent and everything. Cindy S. Griffin, granted a patent for protection under U.S. copyright laws. I still have the certificate hanging on the wall."

"She was very good?"

"Cindy sold the rights to her invention for three million dollars," Griffin said matter-of-factly. "She was very good."

Jillian stared at him. She honestly couldn't think of anything to say. "You don't . . . you don't have to work."

"I wouldn't say that."

"Three million dollars . . ."

"There are lots of reasons to work. You have money, Jillian. You still work."

"My mother has money. That's different. I want, need, my own."

Griffin smiled at her. "And my wife made money," he said gently. "Maybe I also want, need, my own. Besides" – his tone changed – "I gave it all away."

"You *gave* it all away?"

"Yeah, shortly after the Big Boom. Let me tell you, if going postal on a suspected pedophile doesn't convince

234

people that you're nuts, giving away millions of dollars certainly does."

"You gave it all away." She was still working on this thought. Trying to come to terms with a police detective who must make, what, fifty thousand a year, giving away three million dollars. Well, okay, one point five million after taxes.

Griffin was regarding her steadily. She was surprised he was telling her all this. But then again, maybe she wasn't. He hadn't really needed to come to her home last night in person. He really didn't need to clarify her donation to Father Rondell face-to-face. Yet he kept showing up and she kept talking. They were probably both insane.

"When Cindy first signed the deal," Griffin said, "first negotiated selling the rights, it was the most amazing thing. For five years she'd been working on this widget, and then, voilà, not only did she make it work, but she sold it for more money than we ever thought we'd have. It was amazing. Exciting. Wonderful. But then she got sick. One moment she was my vibrant, happy wife, and the next she was a doctor's diagnosis. Advanced pancreatic cancer. They gave her eight months. She only made it to six."

"I'm sorry."

"When Cindy had earned the money, I liked it." He shrugged. "Hell, three million dollars, what's not to like? She took to shopping at Nordstrom, we started talking about a new home, maybe even a boat. It was kind of funny at the time. Surreal. We were two little kids who couldn't believe someone had given us all this loot. But then she got sick, and then she was gone. And the money . . . It became an albatross around my neck. Like maybe I'd made some unconscious deal with the devil. Gain a fortune. Lose my wife."

"Guilt," Jillian said softly.

"Yeah. You can't get anything by us Catholic boys. Probably a shame, too. Cindy wasn't like that. Up until the bitter end, she was thinking about me, trying to prepare me." Griffin smiled again, but this time the smile was bittersweet.

"She was the one who was dying, but she understood I had the tougher burden to bear."

"You had to live after she was gone."

"I would've traded places with her in a heartbeat," Griffin said quietly. "I would've climbed gladly into that hospital bed. Taken the pain, taken the agonizing wasting away, suffered the death. I would've done . . . anything. But we don't get to choose which one of us dies and which one of us lives."

Jillian nodded silently. She understood what he was saying. She'd have given her life to save Trish.

"So here we are," she said at last. "I gave my money to a suspected rapist's son to assuage my guilt. And you gave yours to . . . ?"

"American Cancer Society."

"But of course."

He smiled at her again. "But of course."

"How long has Cindy been gone?"

"Two years."

Her voice grew softer. "Do you still miss her?"

"All of the time."

"I'm not doing a good job of getting over Trish."

"It's supposed to hurt."

"She wasn't just my sister. She was my child. I was supposed to protect her."

"Look at me, Jillian. I can bench-press my own body weight, run a five-minute mile, shoot a high-powered rifle and take out pretty much any shithead in this state. But I couldn't save my own wife. I *didn't* save my own wife."

"You can't fight cancer."

Griffin shrugged. "What is someone like Eddie Como if not a disease?"

"I didn't stop him. I was late, so late. Then I was down in Trish's apartment, seeing her on the bed. And I knew . . . I knew what had happened, what he had done, but then he came at me. Knocked me to the floor, and I tried. I tried so hard. I thought if I could just break free, find the car keys, go after his eyes. I'm smart, I'm well-educated, I run my own business. What's the point of all that if I couldn't break free of him? What's the point if I couldn't save my sister?"

Griffin moved closer. His eyes were dark, so blue. She thought she could drown in those depths, but of course they both knew that she wouldn't. And then she thought that maybe he would touch her again, and she didn't know if that would be the nicest thing to happen to her, or the very worst.

"Jillian," he said quietly. "Your sister loves you."

Jillian put her head in her hands then. And still he didn't touch her. Of course he didn't touch her. For he was still a homicide detective and she was still a murder suspect and it was one thing to catch her as she was falling and quite another to cradle her against his chest. And then there was a new sound in the background. Another vehicle, bigger this time, more guttural, the sound made by a white news van. The press was finally as smart as Sergeant Griffin.

And Jillian cried. She wept for her sister. She wept for Sylvia Blaire. She wept for the grief it had taken her a full year to finally confront. She wept for those moments in the dark apartment, when she'd tried so hard and failed so smashingly. And then she wept for those days, not so long ago, when Trish had run happily along this beach. Days and days and days that would never come again.

And then she heard the guttural engine die. She heard the van door slide open, the sound of feet hitting her gravel drive. She raised her head. She wiped her tears. She prepared to fight the next war. And she thought . . .

Days and days and days that would never come again . . .

24
Maureen

Going around the house to the front drive, Griffin saw good ol' Maureen, already out of the van and adjusting her mike. Griffin knew immediately from the light in the reporter's eyes that they were in trouble. Maureen's gaze shot from him to Jillian and back to him.

"Hey, Jimmy," she called out. "Come out here. I need you to get a shot of this."

Griffin knew better than to rise to the bait. He found himself taking another step forward, positioning himself between the emerging cameraman and Jillian. Not that Jillian required a shield. She'd already wiped her cheeks, touched up her mascara, squared her shoulders. From mini-breakdown to pale composure in ten seconds or less. If he hadn't actually witnessed her crying, he wasn't sure he would've believed it himself. And, frankly, that worried him a little.

"What ya doing, Griff?" Maureen asked with naked speculation.

"Police business."

"Didn't know you made house calls."

"Didn't know you wanted to be arrested for trespassing on private property."

"She can't have me arrested. It's not her property. It's her mother's."

"I have power of attorney over my mother's affairs," Jillian spoke up. "So, yes, I can."

"Oh." Maureen finally faltered. But then she brought up her chin and gave them another dazzling smile. "Then I'll only take a minute of your time."

"No comment," Jillian said.

"I haven't asked the question yet."

"Whatever it is, the answer remains no comment."

"Oh, well, Mr. and Mrs. Blaire will be very sad to hear that."

"Mr. and Mrs. Blaire?"

"Yes, the parents of the slain college student? They flew in from Wisconsin this morning to claim her body. Very nice people. Apparently Mr. Blaire owns a dairy farm which supplies milk for all that wonderful Wisconsin cheese. Sylvia was their only daughter. The real apple of their eye, quote, unquote. They were so proud of her getting a scholarship to an Ivy League school. The first member of their family to get a college degree and all that."

Maureen smiled again. Griffin had to fight back the urge to wring her neck.

"I don't understand what this has to do with me," Jillian said.

"Well, they want to meet you, of course."

"They want to meet me?"

"The head of the Survivors Club? Absolutely!"

"I'm not the head of the Survivors Club. There is no head of the Survivors Club."

Maureen waved her hand carelessly. "Oh, you know what I mean. You are the woman whose face has been in the news. They really do want to speak with you."

"Why?"

"To ask you why you didn't save their daughter, of course." Maureen smiled. Jillian stiffened as the arrow struck home.

"Maureen – " Griffin growled.

"You need to leave," Jillian said.

Maureen ignored them both. "Do you still believe Eddie Como was the College Hill Rapist? What about reports that Sylvia Blaire was also tied up with latex strips? What does this new attack mean for the allegations against Como? And even more importantly, *what does it mean for the safety of the women in this city?*"

Maureen stuck out her microphone greedily. Jimmy homed in with his camera. And Griffin took three steps forward, never raising a hand, never touching a hair on either reporters' head, but effectively blocking their shot with the broad expanse of his chest.

"The homeowner has asked you to leave," he said firmly. Ominously.

"Don't you mean the murder suspect?"

"Maureen . . ."

"What ya gonna do, Griffin, seize my tape?" Maureen dropped her microphone. Far from being intimidated, she stepped right up to him and jabbed her finger into his chest. "I have First Amendment rights here, Sergeant, so don't you go threatening me or my cameraman. I don't care if you think freedom of the press is the root of all evil. As far as I'm concerned, a little fourth-estate action is exactly what we need around here. For God's sake, a man was gunned down at our own courthouse yesterday morning. Now another young college student is dead. And what are you doing about it? What is *she* doing about it?" Maureen jerked her head toward Jillian. "Something about this whole case stinks and I have not only a constitutional right but a civic obligation to do something about that."

"Maureen Haverill, defender of the free world," Griffin drawled.

"Goddamn right!"

"You've been reading your own press briefings again, haven't you?"

"You son of a bitch – "

"I am sorry Sylvia Blaire is dead." Jillian spoke up quietly, unexpectedly. All heads swiveled toward her.

"What?" Maureen said.

"I'm sorry Sylvia Blaire is dead," Jillian repeated. "Her family has my deepest sympathies."

Maureen stepped back from Griffin, motioned furiously at Jimmy, and quickly adopted her most serious reporter's expression. The woman could cry on command. Griffin had seen her do it once by plucking a nose hair. "Do you believe

Eddie Como was the College Hill Rapist?" she asked Jillian, thrusting her microphone forward.

"I believe the police conducted a thorough and responsible investigation."

"Ms. Hayes, another young girl is dead."

"A tragedy we should not lose sight of."

Maureen frowned. "Surely you understand there is a connection between Sylvia Blaire's attack and the College Hill Rapist."

"I wasn't aware that the police had made any such connection."

"You don't *want* the police to make any such connection, isn't that true, Ms. Hayes? Because if the police did make a connection, that would mean the police were *wrong* about Eddie Como. That would mean *you* were *wrong* about Eddie Como. *You and your friends have spent the last year persecuting an innocent man.*"

"I have spent the last year aiding the police and the district attorney with their investigation into who brutally raped and murdered my nineteen-year-old sister, Trisha Hayes. I want justice for what was done to my sister. I think anyone who has lost someone they love can understand that."

"Even at the expense of an innocent man?"

"I want the man who brutally killed my sister. No one else."

"What about allegations that you and your group, this so-called Survivors Club, contributed to a miscarriage of justice by whipping the public into a witch-hunt mentality, desperate for an arrest?"

"I think the citizens of Providence should object to being characterized as an angry mob."

Maureen scowled again. Jimmy made the mistake of choosing that moment to home in on her face with the camera. She furiously waved him off.

"Sylvia Blaire is dead," Maureen said.

Jillian was quiet.

"Eddie Como is dead."

241

Jillian remained silent.

"From the RISD parking lot, the police have another, unidentified body at the morgue. That's three dead people in a space of twenty-four hours."

Jillian still didn't say anything. Maureen changed tactics.

"The day the police arrested Eddie Como, you said you were pleased they had gotten their man. You stood with Meg Pesaturo and Carol Rosen on the steps of City Hall and all but publicly branded Eddie Como as the College Hill Rapist."

"The police had compelling evidence – "

"Another girl is *dead!* Raped and murdered just like your own sister!"

"And I am sorry!"

"*Sorry?*" Maureen trilled, "*Sorry* doesn't help Sylvia Blaire. *Sorry* doesn't give Mr. and Mrs. Blaire their beautiful young daughter back."

"It is not our fault – " Jillian bit back her own words, shook her head. Her composure was beginning to slip, her voice starting to rise angrily. Griffin tried to catch her with his gaze, but she would no longer look at him.

"You pushed for justice," Maureen persisted.

"We were raped! Of course we pushed for justice."

"You told the public they weren't safe until the College Hill Rapist was put behind bars."

"They weren't!"

"You held numerous press conferences, applying enormous pressure on the Providence police to make an arrest."

"Four women had been attacked. The police were already under enormous pressure!"

"You said you were happy with Eddie's arrest."

"*I was happy with Eddie's arrest!*"

"Yeah? Well, how do you feel about his *death?* Need more champagne, Ms. Hayes? It's not every day someone publicly toasts the murder of an innocent man."

Jillian drew up short. Too late she saw the trap. Too late she looked into Jimmy's camera, with her round, dazed eyes, her loose hair wild around her face, her cheeks flushed with outrage.

"Death is not justice," she replied quietly, but her words no longer mattered. Maureen had her clip, and they all knew it. The reporter smiled, genuinely this time, and motioned for Jimmy to turn off the tape.

"Thank you," she said crisply, lowering the mike.

"Do you really think you're helping things?" Jillian asked.

The reporter shrugged. "Can't fuck it up any more than you did now, can I?"

"This is my fault?"

Maureen looked at her. "Are you fucking nuts? Have you ever gone back and watched your old press conferences, Ms. Hayes? Have you ever seen yourself on camera? You spin. Hell, you spin better than most politicians. Always cool, always composed, telling the public what happened to you, what happened to Meg, what happened to Carol. Reminding the public that it might be their daughters next.

"You didn't just insert yourself into a story. You *became* the story. Even I sympathized with you and those other two women. Hell, a bunch of the reporters bought a round of drinks in your honor the day they arrested Como. But that was before Sylvia Blaire. Of course you bear a responsibility for what happened yesterday. Maybe if you hadn't kept the fire so hot, the police investigation could've been more thorough. Maybe if the police hadn't had to spend so much time reacting to your presence on the news, they could've spent more time on the case. The police are vulnerable to public pressure, you know. Just ask your good friend Sergeant Griffin."

"I love you, too, Maureen," Griffin said.

She flashed a smile at him. "That's what makes my job so meaningful."

"There is no conclusive evidence that Eddie Como's innocent," Jillian insisted.

"Tell that to Sylvia Blaire."

243

"It could be a copycat."

"Would you like to go on record?"

Jillian didn't say anything. Maureen nodded. "Yeah, that's what I thought."

She and Jimmy were back in the news van. They had come, they had seen, they had conquered. Maureen waved quite merrily, right before slamming the door shut.

"You shouldn't listen to her," Griffin said shortly, as the news van sped away.

Jillian merely smiled. "Oh, but I will. And Meg will and Carol will. In the middle of the night, we'll think of nothing but what she said. We're women. It's what we do." She turned and headed for her car.

"Jillian . . ." He caught her arm. The contact startled them both. They stared at his hand on her forearm until his fingers slipped away. "Fitz ran a good case. I run a good case. We're going to get to the bottom of this."

Jillian looked out at the sky. "Four hours before nightfall, Griffin. I wonder what young woman will be home alone tonight. I wonder what college student will be hitting the books or daydreaming about her boyfriend or maybe even resting in front of the TV. I wonder what girl is making what small mistake right now that will very soon cost her her life."

"You can't think that way."

"Oh, but I do. Once you've been assaulted, it's very hard to think of anything else. The world is a very dangerous place, Sergeant. And I haven't seen anything to give me any hope yet."

25
Griffin

"Good news," Detective Waters said on the other end of the cell phone. "Eddie Como's dead."

"Now there's something I haven't heard lately." Griffin passed under the Towers on Ocean Road and headed toward Providence while holding the cell phone pressed against his right ear. Traffic wasn't too bad this early in May. Give it another month, and this area of Narragansett would be turned into a tourist-crazed parking lot. Ah, the joys of summer.

"ME confirmed the fingerprints this afternoon," Waters was saying. "Our vic is definitely Eddie Como. In the even-better-news department, Providence just got a hit on the deep-fried DOA, as well."

"No kidding."

"Guy had a military record. Gus J. Ohlsson, formerly of New York. Get this – he served eight years in the Army, as a sharpshooter."

"Ah, so our detective intuitions are right again. Let's face it, the nose knows."

"Yeah, well, you can pat yourself on the back all you want. Providence is still taking the credit. As we speak, they're putting together a subpoena for Ohlsson's military records, plus bank accounts. He has a father listed as next of kin, also out of New York, so you can bet Boz and Higgins are doing the happy dance."

"Road trip," Griffin said. Boz and Higgins had worked in Providence's Detective Bureau for fifteen years. As Providence was a main way station on the I-95 corridor between

New York and Boston, lots of the city's crime ended up tied to New York or Boston case files. Somehow, Boz and Higgins always got the New York trips. Always. The rumor was, they had a thing for Broadway shows.

"Given Ohlsson's military background," Waters was saying, "our hired-gun theory is looking good. Of course, Providence also wants to check out Family ties."

"With a name like Ohlsson?"

"Hey, haven't you heard? It's a global village out there. Everyone has gone multinational, including the Mafia."

"Wow, you take a year's sabbatical and the whole geopolitical landscape of crime shifts on you. Who would've thought?" Griffin came to the exit for Route 1 North and headed up the ramp. "Anything from the state fire marshal's office yet?"

"After only two days? You *are* out of touch."

"I prefer the term optimistic. Hey, Mike, can you touch base with the financial guys for me? Tell them Jillian Hayes donated the twenty thousand missing from her accounts to a Cranston parish. The priest has confirmed the donation, but we need to keep the details under wraps."

"Since you didn't give me any details, that shouldn't be too hard. Aren't you heading back to HQ?"

"No, I'm on my way to see Dan Rosen."

"*You're* on your way to see Dan Rosen?" Waters's voice grew tight, and the silence that followed was immediately tense. Griffin understood. In theory, primary case officers didn't do much legwork. In theory, his job was to remain in headquarters, coordinating and overseeing detectives like Waters, who would handle interviews like Dan Rosen's. And in fact, if Griffin didn't appear at the command center shortly, his lieutenant was probably going to have a few words with him. He wouldn't like those words much.

"What are you doing, Griffin?" Waters asked.

"I have a theory. I need to play it out."

"Tell me your theory. I can play it out."

"You could, but I figured you'd prefer to spend your afternoon in a bar."

246

"*What?*"

"I need you to go to Cranston," Griffin explained patiently. "I need you to identify all the bars/pubs/watering holes in the near vicinity of Eddie Como's house. Then I want you to show the bartenders a picture of Eddie Como and find out if he spent a lot of time there, and more importantly, with whom."

More silence. Long silence. "Griffin . . ."

"I know."

"Fitz finds out about this, he's gonna be pissed."

"Fitz was born pissed. Nothing we can do about that now. Besides, that's why I need you to do it. I'm counting on your charm."

"Ah hell, Griff, nobody has that kind of charm. In a state this small, everything gets around. Providence is going to think we're sniffing at their rape case, and the next thing you know, their lieutenant will be on the phone screaming at our lieutenant. Morelli doesn't like being screamed at or haven't you noticed?"

"Look, we have a body. Our job is to find out who killed that body. Working up a victim profile, complete with names of friends and associates, is not outside the realm of our investigation."

"So you say." Waters wasn't fooled. Neither would Fitz be.

"If anyone asks, just tell them I told you to do it," Griffin said. "I'll take the heat."

"You know that's not what I meant – "

"Cranston accent, Mike. I'm looking for someone who knew Eddie well, who grew up in Cranston, and who was seen on occasion in khaki pants with a button-down shirt. Maybe I'm way off base. But maybe . . . I need you to do this."

"Ah nuts." Waters blew out a big huff of air, which meant he'd do it. "And if I find this mystery man?"

"Then I'm probably going to be even more confused than I am right now, but in a better sort of way."

"Ah nuts," Waters said again, and Griffin could practically see the gaunt detective rolling his eyes.

"I don't like the rape case," Griffin said abruptly.

"So I've heard."

"Something about this . . . I don't know. Something about this feels wrong."

"You know you've been gone awhile. The first case back . . ."

"I should play by the rules?"

"It wouldn't hurt."

"Yeah, but then how would I have any fun?"

More silence. A stranger silence. Griffin didn't like this silence.

"Griff, I got a call from Corporal Charpentier at the ACI," Waters said.

Griffin honestly didn't get it at first. And then, all of a sudden . . . "No!"

"Yeah. I'm afraid so. Good ol' David Price reached out first thing this morning. He claims to have info on Eddie Como and wants to speak with you immediately. I guess we shouldn't be surprised. Your face was on the morning news and God knows he likes to yank your chain."

"Goddammit . . ." Griffin smacked the steering wheel. Thought of his former neighbor. Thought of Cindy. Then hit the steering wheel again; this time his hand stung. He should remain calm. Little psychopathic shit. "Why the hell am I even surprised? The bastard sent me a letter just yesterday, congratulating me on the new case. Of course he wants in on the action."

"He already knew about the case? But he had to mail that letter on Saturday, Griff, *before* Eddie Como was shot."

"Yeah, yeah, yeah. He just wrote congrats on the new case, not the Eddie Como case, not the College Hill Rapist case, just *case*. This is David Price, remember? King of head games. He's bored, he's been waiting for some entertainment. And now that I'm back on the job, he's trying to bluff his way into the party. What could he know about Eddie Como anyway? They were both at the ACI. So are three thousand other humps and they aren't bothering us with calls. Como was held in Intake, right?"

"Yeah."

"And Price is still stinking up Steel City, right?"

"Yeah."

"Ergo, David Price doesn't know shit."

"Roommate," Waters said.

"Son of a bitch."

"Yeah. Eddie Como's former roommate at Intake, Jimmy Woods, already had his day in court. He got sentenced to Old Max three months ago for a B&E job gone sour. Price is claiming that Jimmy Woods has been talking, and for a little *consideration,* Price'll give us the inside scoop."

"Consideration." Griffin spat out the word. "Price murdered ten kids. There is nothing he can give us *ever* that warrants consideration after that. He committed his crimes in a state without the death penalty. He got a big enough break right there."

"Nobody's disagreeing with you."

"Then why don't I feel good about this?"

Waters's tone grew more subdued. "Things are hot, Griff. You haven't been back to HQ yet, but let me tell you. Phones are ringing off the hook from the colonel on down. People are frightened. People with young daughters are freaky-scared. We know David Price. Corporal Charpentier knows David Price. Hell, the lieutenant, the major, the colonel all know David Price. The mayor and the governor, on the other hand . . ."

"First person who wants to open a serious dialogue with David Price gets full-color crime-scene photos," Griffin said coldly. "I don't care if it's the fucking governor. Are we clear?"

Another pause. "We're clear."

"Mike . . ."

"When will you be done with Dan Rosen?"

"I don't know. Six o'clock?"

"I'll be over."

"Mike, I don't need – "

"Yeah, you do. See you at six. And don't worry. This time I'll bring a face mask."

By the time Griffin arrived in the tony Providence neighborhood harboring the Rosen house, his mood had gone south. He was thinking too much. That had always been his problem. He was thinking of Meg's pale features. He was thinking of Carol's brittle smile. He was thinking of Jillian, not even allowed to properly grieve for her sister because some overeager reporter was already pulling into her drive.

And then he was thinking of Tawnya and plump-cheeked Eddie, Jr. He was thinking of lives that had no potential and the kind of people he saw every day, already knowing someplace way down deep that he'd see them again soon enough, in jail, in court, in the back of a squad car. Cycles that went round without end.

And then he was thinking of that goddamn basement, and the lives he could've saved if he hadn't been thinking so much. He thought of Cindy. He thought of David. He thought of the stuff he still hadn't told anyone, not his brothers, not his father, not the nice little therapist assigned to screw his head on straight.

Fuckin' world sometimes. Too much like a boxing ring. You just kept taking the blows, then getting back on your feet. Mike was right. He needed to move. He needed to run. He needed to beat the living shit out of something soon, or the buzzing would return in his ears. His arms and legs would start moving on their own. Instead of eating and drinking like a normal person, he'd turn into a hulking Energizer bunny, churning, churning, churning until five sleepless days passed and his pink fuzzy head blew off.

Some cops got depressed, burnt out. Griffin went to the other extreme. He had hyperanxiety disorder, meaning when he got stressed, he could no longer calm down. The pressure built and built and built until no amount of running, weight lifting, boxing or fucking *anything* did any good. He could break all the bones in his hand without feeling it. He could go without sleep for three days and still be wired when he finally lay down in bed. His hands shook, his knees trembled and he appeared downright manic. Then six, seven days later, his body would simply give out beneath the strain. He'd come down hard, like someone who'd been mainlining cocaine.

Then he'd enter the true danger zone. Physically and emotionally he had nothing left in reserve, but the pressure was still there. His wife gone, his neighbor a baby-killer, his job intense. His family had helped out the first time. His brothers had taken turns staying at his house so he was never alone. They had got him through the worst. He'd taken over from there.

He was learning now how to manage his stress from the start. Eat well, sleep well and get a good aerobic workout four to five times a week. That way he tapped off steam every day, instead of letting it build. Not always that easy, but not really that difficult. Besides, on the bad days, he simply thought of Cindy. She had fought so damn hard to live. Even after the cancer started shutting down her internal organs, took away her voice and sapped away her flesh. Even at the bitter end, when she could communicate only by blinking her eyes and her hands had not even the strength to hold his. She had fought. How could he do any less?

Breathe deep, he told himself now. Count to twenty. You can't change the world, but you can improve a bit of it a little at a time.

He got out of his car. Shut the door. Breathed in, breathed out. Thought of reopening his door and slamming it, but got hold of the impulse. *Just breathe*. He boarded the front steps of the Victorian home and knocked on the dark-stained door slightly harder than necessary, but not too bad. No one answered, though he heard voices coming from inside.

He knocked again, counted to ten, then knocked again and made it all the way to thirty before he heard the click of someone drawing back the brass cover from the peephole. A moment later, Carol Rosen stood in front of him. She wore blue-checkered flannel pajamas buttoned up to her neck, even though it had to be nearly sixty outside. Her cheeks were flushed. Her eyes held a glassy sheen.

Drunk, he thought immediately, though when she swayed forward he couldn't catch the scent of any booze on her breath. Vodka then.

"I don't . . . talk to you," she said, gripping the door tight.

"Is your husband home?"

"Nope."

"His office said he wasn't at work."

"Well, he's not at home."

"Mrs. Rosen – "

"Try his girlfriend's." Her eyes grew brighter. She stabbed a finger at him and for the first time he saw the knuckles on her right hand. They were bleeding. He looked at her sharply, but she didn't seem to notice. "Not here. Not there. Must be at his girlfriend's."

"Your husband has a girlfriend?"

"That's what I said."

"What is her name?"

"I don't know. I betcha she was never raped. What do you think?"

Griffin was quiet for a moment. "Would you like me to call someone for you, Mrs. Rosen? Maybe a friend or relative who could come stay with you for a while?"

She waved her finger, falling forward, then getting a better grip on the door. "Not a reporter. I hate them! Phone ringing . . . all the time. Tell us about Eddie! What about that poor college student? Sylvia Blaire. Pretty Sylvia Blaire. Eddie's dead, and still the women suffer."

"How about I call Miss Pesaturo or Ms. Hayes?"

"Meg doesn't know shit. She's so young." Carol sighed. She tilted her head to the side, her long blond hair sweeping down her shoulder. "Young and sweet and innocent. Do you think I was ever that young and sweet and innocent? I don't remember. Even before Eddie . . . I don't remember."

"Ms. Hayes?" he asked hopefully. No dice.

"She hates me," Carol announced. "I'm too broken, you see. Jillian only loves people she can fix. Improve yourself! Get with the program! Take control of your life! Jillian is really Oprah Winfrey. Well, she's not black."

"Are you going to be all right, Mrs. Rosen?"

"I can't have children," she said mournfully. "I bet Dan's girlfriend can have children. I bet she can turn off the TV anytime she wants. I bet she's never slept in an empty bathtub or compulsively checked all the bars on the windows. She's probably never shot at Dan either. It's hard to compete with that."

"Mrs. Rosen . . ." She was definitely drunk. He took another deep breath, then acknowledged that it didn't matter. He still had a job to do, and frankly, her inebriation made his life easier. He said, "Does Dan ever talk to you about money?"

"No."

"A home like this must be very expensive."

She singsonged, "New plumbing isn't exactly cheap, you know."

"So things have been tight?"

"'Jesus Christ, Carol, someone has to pay for all this.'"

"Very tight."

"Meg and Jillian think we should sell this house. I picked out almost everything in it. This door, I selected this door." She stroked it with her hand. "This molding, I selected this molding." She touched the doorjamb tenderly. "So much of it was gone before. Rotted out, yanked out. Replaced with cheap pine trim. I read books. Scoured old pictures of Victorian homes, talked to experts in historical restoration. No one could have loved this house more than I did. God, I wish it would just burn to the ground."

"Mrs. Rosen, we know Dan liquidated his brokerage account. Do you know where that money went?"

She shook her head.

"We're going to have to look into that, Mrs. Rosen."

She smiled and leaned her head against the door. "You think he hired an assassin? You think he spent that money to kill my rapist?"

"I would like to ask him that question."

"Sergeant Griffin, my husband doesn't love me that much. Try the girlfriend. Maybe she also likes expensive old homes."

Griffin brought up his hand. Too late. Carol Rosen had already closed the door. He tried knocking, but she wouldn't respond. After another minute, he returned to his car, where he sat behind the steering wheel and frowned.

He didn't like leaving Carol Rosen alone in her current state of mind. Last night she'd shot her husband, and that was *before* she'd learned about Sylvia Blaire.

He picked up his cell phone and gave Meg Pesaturo a try. No answer. Next call, Jillian's beach house. Also a dead end. Then he dialed her East Greenwich residence, where he finally got a person.

"Hello," Toppi Niauru said.

Jillian wasn't in, so Griffin told Toppi about Carol Rosen. She said that she and Libby would be right over.

Carol's historic house didn't have wheelchair access, so Griffin hung out in the driveway. Forty-five minutes later, Toppi pulled up in a dark blue van. She opened the side door and operated the wheelchair lift to lower Olivia Hayes to the ground.

Jillian's mother had put on makeup for the occasion. She had her dark hair piled high on her head, and greeted Griffin with a kiss.

At 5:00 P.M., he carried Libby up the front stairs while Toppi followed with her wheelchair. At 5:01, they all knocked on the door.

At 5:10, they stopped knocking, and Griffin took down the door with his shoulder. At 5:11, they found Carol sprawled on the rug in front of the blaring TV, her hand still clutching the empty bottle of sleeping pills.

Griffin started CPR, Toppi called for an ambulance and Dan Rosen, with his usual sense of timing, finally came home.

26
Carol

Jillian arrived first. She forcefully shoved her way through the pack of reporters clogging the hospital parking lot, then bustled through the emergency room doors.

"Goddamn vultures!" she cried as the electronic doors finally slid shut, but not before some earnest reporter shouted out, "Ms. Hayes, have *you* ever thought of committing suicide?"

Meg and her family were shortly behind Jillian. A uniformed officer had located their vehicle outside Vinnie Pesaturo's home and passed along the news. Arriving in the hospital parking lot, Vinnie shouted, "Outta my way, you rat bastards," and the reporters, recognizing an armed man when they saw one, let the family through.

The moment they were inside the ER, Meg homed in on Jillian. "Where is she? Is she okay? What have you heard?"

"I don't know. We need a doctor. There. You in the white coat. What can you tell us about Carol Rosen?"

"Jillian! Over here. Jillian!"

Jillian and Meg turned in time to see Toppi waving at them from the other side of the waiting room. Next to her sat Jillian's mother. Next to Olivia, sat Sergeant Griffin.

"Why is your mother here?" Meg asked.

"Is that really *the* Olivia Hayes?" her father breathed.

"I'm going to kill Sergeant Griffin," Jillian said.

They rushed across the emergency room, where Toppi rose to meet them. "How is she? Is she going to be all right?" Jillian's hands were shaking. She didn't even realize it until Toppi reached out and clasped them in her own.

"We don't know yet."

"Oh God – "

"Her husband is talking to one of the doctors now. Maybe he'll know something soon."

"What *happened?*"

"It looks like she overdosed on sleeping pills. Maybe some alcohol as well."

"Oh no." Meg now. She had started to cry. "I didn't realize . . . I mean, I knew she was upset, but I didn't think . . ."

"No one could know," Jillian said, but the words were automatic, lacking genuine conviction. They were Carol's friends; they'd seen her just this morning. Maybe they should have known. Meg's mother put an arm around her daughter's shoulders.

"And where was the husband during all this?" Uncle Vinnie boomed.

Toppi shrugged and looked at Griffin. He said simply, "Out."

"Figures," Uncle Vinnie snorted.

"I can't take this," Jillian said. "I'm going to find a doctor."

She headed for the receptionist's desk, and wasn't surprised when Griffin followed.

"How could you?" she railed at him the moment they were out of earshot of the others. Her hands were still shaking. She felt sick to the bottom of her stomach with worry for Carol.

"How could I what?"

"Get my mom involved in all of this!"

"Oh don't you start!" Toppi had just caught up with them, and she barreled into the conversation fiercely. "Look at her! Glance over your shoulder and just look at her!"

Jillian thinned her lips mutinously, but did as she was told. Her mom now had Meg's father and uncle literally at her feet. The two men were talking animatedly. Her mother was smiling.

"She looks pretty good to me," Griffin said.

Jillian stabbed his overpumped chest with her finger.

"*You* are not allowed to speak." Then she turned back on Toppi. "She's fragile – "

"She's fine."

"EMTs put her on oxygen just last night!"

"She had a shock."

"And finding Carol on the floor of her home wasn't shocking?"

"Probably, but I imagine it was still worse for Carol."

"Oh!" Jillian was so mad she yanked on her gathered hair. "I don't want her involved!"

"Too late. She's your mother. She's involved."

"She'll just worry more."

Toppi snorted. "She was already worried. This finally gave her something to do."

"Toppi!"

"Jillian!" Toppi mocked. "Look, I'm being serious now. When Sergeant Griffin called, I asked your mom what she wanted to do. She didn't hesitate for a second. Carol is your friend. Libby was delighted to help her in any way we could. And it's a damn good thing, too." Toppi's voice finally quieted. "I know she wasn't around much when you were a child, Jillian. But you're not a child anymore. You grew up. Have you ever stopped to consider that maybe she did, too?"

Toppi walked back to the group, where Meg was now leaning her head against her mother's shoulder and Libby was flipping rapidly through her picture book to the apparent delight of Tom and Uncle Vinnie. Jillian turned back to Griffin. "Don't say it," she warned.

"Haven't muttered a word."

"She's wrong, you know. Toppi's the one who doesn't get it. I know my mom has changed. But I've never had a father, and I no longer have a sister. Libby . . . She's all I have left."

At the receptionist's desk, no one would help her. She wasn't family, and in the eyes of medical protocol being a fellow rape victim didn't count. They knew who Jillian was, of course. The nurse in charge was even kind. And then for the first time, Jillian realized the full implication of where they were. Women & Infants. One of Providence's best hospitals and where each one of them had been at least once before . . . On those nights, that night, the night.

She turned away, no longer so steady on her feet. Of all the strange bonds . . . And then she suddenly realized that she couldn't lose Carol. She just couldn't. Carol had to survive and then it would be Jillian, Carol and Meg again, sitting in the back room of some restaurant, and arguing or laughing, or being petty or being genuine, but certainly helping one another cope.

She had started the Survivors Club with so much purpose, but maybe at the end of the day, the group had worked even better than Jillian had thought. Because standing here now, she couldn't imagine not seeing Carol. She couldn't imagine even a week going by without it being her, Carol and Meg.

"Sit," Griffin said quietly. "Wait."

"I can't sit. I don't know how to wait. That's my whole problem." Her fingers had closed around his sleeve. She didn't know when that had happened. "Oh God, I just want to know that Carol is all right."

A door on the left suddenly swung open; Dan Rosen walked through. His features were ashen. His dark hair stood up in a rumpled mess on top of his head, while his left arm stood out prominently in a white sling. He wore a tan jacket with a gold tie, as if he'd once been on his way to work. Now he didn't seem to know where he was.

Jillian took one look at his face and felt the world tilt again beneath her feet. "Oh no . . ."

"Mr. Rosen," Griffin said quietly.

"Huh. What?"

"Dan?" Jillian whispered more urgently.

He finally seemed to register their presence. "Oh. Hello, Jillian."

"Is she? Please, Dan?"

"They're pumping her stomach. Treating her . . . an activated charcoal slurry, I think the doctor said. She took all her Ambien. Booze, too. Not good, not good at all. Ambien plus booze equals a coma, that's what the doctor said." Dan looked at Griffin shakily. "He said . . . he said if you hadn't gotten to her so soon, she'd probably be dead."

"She's been drinking?"

"I guess. And her throat . . ." His fingers touched his own. "Her esophagus is . . . aggravated. I think that's how the doctor said it. And her back teeth show signs of erosion. From bile, he told me. When she makes herself sick."

It took Jillian a moment. "Bulimia?"

"He thinks. So my wife, it appears, spends her free time eating too much and maybe drinking too much and then making herself sick. Over and over again. I swear I didn't know." He looked at them, still dazed. "Jillian, did you know?"

"I didn't know."

"You should've, though." Meg had come over while they were speaking. Now she had her hands placed authoritatively on her jean-clad hips while she regarded Dan with an imperious stare. "We were her friends, but we only saw her once or twice a week. You *lived* with her. How could you not know what she was doing?"

"I've been . . . working."

"Meg," Jillian tried. She was too late.

"Working?" Meg said. "Or playing with your *girl-friend*?"

"What?" Dan's head popped up. "What?"

"Oh don't play innocent with us." Meg was on a roll now, and everyone, including Sergeant Griffin, was watching with great interest. "Carol told us all about it. Your pathetic excuses of late-night meetings and overburdened workload. She called your office, you know. She knew you weren't really there. That night she was raped – she knew what you were *really* doing."

"Carol thinks I'm sleeping with another woman?" Dan asked in a strangled voice.

"Oh come on – "

"I'm not. I swear I'm not. I wouldn't do that to Carol. My God, I love my wife!"

"You're never home!" Meg cried.

"I know."

"You're never at work!"

"I know."

"Then where the hell are you?"

Dan didn't answer. He simply looked stricken. And then another voice spoke up from across the hushed waiting room.

"Foxwoods," Uncle Vinnie announced. "Danny boy's not a cheater. He's a gambler. And if you don't mind me saying, he's a really bad one, too."

Next to Jillian, Dan Rosen nodded his head miserably. "I love my wife," he said again. Then he turned away and slammed his one good hand into the wall.

"You're going to have to tell me everything," Griffin said to Dan ten minutes later. He had commandeered an empty exam room in an attempt at privacy. Of course, Jillian, Meg and the rest of their entourage had immediately followed him and Dan into the room, and were now looking at them both as if they had every right to be there. Griffin considered kicking them out but figured what the hell. Vinnie Pesaturo obviously had relevant information, and Jillian and Meg seemed to be the interrogative equivalent of brass knuckles. All they had to do was look at Dan, and he gave up the store.

"I never meant to hurt Carol," Dan started off weakly.

"You know, Dan, she did shoot you."

"That was an accident! I should've announced myself the minute I got home. It was late . . . She gets nervous after dark." His lips twisted. "After what happened to her that night, can you really blame her?"

"Yes, that night. Let's talk about that night." Griffin took out his Norelco Pocket Memo, turned on the mini recorder and got serious. "You told the police you were working late."

Dan hung his head.

"I gather you told your wife the same?"

"Yes."

"But you weren't really at work?"

Dan didn't look up. Vinnie smacked his arm. "For God's sake," the bookie said. "Stop being such a whiner and stand up for your wife."

Dan shot the bookie a look, but seemed to get ahold of himself. "I, uh, I was at the Foxwoods casino."

"You lied to the police?"

"Yes."

"You do that a lot?"

"I was embarrassed! It was bad enough to be gone when my wife needed me. But then, to have to admit that I was sitting at a blackjack table while she was being viciously assaulted . . ." He groaned. "My God, what kind of husband does a thing like that?"

Griffin let the question hang, which was answer enough. "So you lied to the police, and you lied to your wife. All to cover up one night at the gaming tables. Do you gamble a lot, Mr. Rosen?"

"I don't know. Is four, five days a week a lot? Is liquidating my business a lot? Is second-mortgaging my home?" Dan's face gained some color. He looked at Griffin hotly, as if daring him to state the obvious.

"You tell me," Griffin said quietly.

That quickly, Dan folded again. His shoulders slumped. His chin sank against his chest. "I think . . . I think I have a gambling problem." And then, "Oh God, Carol is going to kill me!"

"How long has this been going on?"

"I don't know. Three years, maybe. I went to Foxwoods one night with some friends. Business associates, really. And I . . . I had a *really* good night. Seriously." Dan's features perked up again. "I quit the blackjack tables ahead ten thousand dollars. And back then, ten thousand dollars . . . Wow. I was just about to open my own law firm, and God knows the house needed some kind of something. Ten thousand bucks helped out. Felt good. Easy money."

"Uh huh," Griffin said knowingly.

Dan smiled thinly. "Exactly. So I opened my own law practice, except instead of taking with me five loyal clients, I only took three. Money was tighter than I thought, and things got off slower than I thought, and health care cost more than I thought . . ."

"You started taking on debt."

"I didn't want to tell Carol. We'd talked about me starting my own practice so many times. She wasn't as sure. That house, those mortgage payments, my God. But it was my dream. I had to have my own practice. Trust me, I told her. Trust me. So she did."

"But you got behind in payments. And then you . . . ?"

"I remembered Foxwoods. Ten thousand bucks. Easy money, right? I'm a smart man, I've read all the books on blackjack, memorized the odds tables. Hey, it's not like betting on horses. That's pure luck. Now blackjack, that takes strategy."

"Hence all the blackjack millionaires out there," Griffin observed dryly.

"I've won," Dan said immediately. His face held that flush again. "Hey, I've won a lot!"

"How much are you down, Mr. Rosen?"

The lawyer faltered. He didn't seem able to meet anyone's eye. After several moments, when the silence ran long, Vinnie raised his arm to smack the man again. Griffin waved the bookie off.

"Mr. Rosen?"

"I owed eighty thousand dollars," Dan said gruffly. He ran his right hand through his hair, leaving the brown strands standing up on end. "Only twenty now. I, uh, I liquidated my brokerage account. Otherwise, they weren't going to give me any more money. And then . . . Well, then I wouldn't have any chance of getting ahead, would I?"

"Who's they, Mr. Rosen?"

"Why don't you ask Mr. Pesaturo?" Dan said bitterly.

Griffin looked at Vinnie.

"Not with that tape on," Vinnie said.

"I'm working on a murder here – "

"Not with that tape on."

Griffin sighed, shut off the Pocket Memo. "Let's hear it."

"I might be aware of Mr. Rosen's predicament."

"You think?"

"Hey, man needed money, and I happen to know people who don't mind loaning a few bucks every now and then."

"Percentage?"

"Well, you know how it is in banking. The interest rate on the loan is dependent upon the level of risk. Look at him." Vinnie shot Dan Rosen a disparaging glance. "Eighty grand down at jack? He's high risk."

"You're charging him a hundred percent?"

"Fifty. We're not completely unsympathetic."

"Wait a minute." Jillian raised a hand, finally interjecting herself into the conversation. "You mean to tell me that you – "

"My associates," Vinnie amended.

"Fine, *your associates* are loaning Dan money for his gambling habit with an interest rate of fifty percent?"

Vinnie nodded. She turned to Dan. "And you are *taking* the money at that rate?"

"One good day," he said immediately. "That's all you need. One good day, and the loan is repaid and I can get the credit cards down, maybe even make an extra payment on the mortgage. One good day."

"Oh God," Jillian said. "Poor Carol."

Dan deflated again. Griffin turned the recorder back on. "Is it correct to say, Mr. Rosen, that you used the sixty thousand dollars you liquidated from your brokerage account to repay loan sharks?"

Dan nodded. Griffin gave him a look. "Yes," Dan said belatedly into the minirecorder.

Griffin turned to Vinnie. "And can you, Vincent Pesaturo, verify – through *sources* – that such a transaction took place?"

"Yeah. My *sources,* they say such a thing took place."

"Vinnie Pesaturo, did you order a hit on Edward Como? Did you arrange for him to come to harm in any way?"

The questions came out of left field, but Vinnie didn't blink an eye. He bent lower, so his mouth was directly above the recorder. "No, I, Vincent Pesaturo, did not order a hit on Eddie Como. If I, Vincent Pesaturo, wanted that piece of garbage dead, I would've done it myself."

"Or ordered a hit in prison," Griffin muttered. Vinnie smiled, looked at the recorder and didn't say a word.

"Tom Pesaturo," Griffin spoke up again. "Did you order a hit on your daughter's suspected rapist, Edward Como?"

Tom looked a bit more defensive. "Nah," he said slowly. "I decided against it."

"Tom!" his wife gasped.

"Daddy!" Meg seconded.

He shrugged. "Hey, I'm a father. After what that bastard did to my daughter, I'm allowed to think these things. But I didn't do anything." He shrugged again. "I don't know. Sounded like the police had a good case. That DNA and all. And I figured . . . I figured the trial might be better for Meg. She could face down her accuser and all. I, uh, I read some-place that sometimes that's better for the victim, you know. Gives her some sense of power back, control. That kind of thing."

"You read about rape victims?" Meg asked.

"Kinda. I saw this article . . . in *Cosmo*."

"*Cosmo?*" Vinnie exclaimed.

Tom Pesaturo huffed his shoulders. "Hey, she's my daughter. I want what's best for her. 'Sides, there was a long line at checkout, and you know they got all those women's magazines just sitting right there, decorated up with half-naked cover models. Of course I started looking. And then, well, I saw the title for the article. And then I kind of opened up the magazine. And hey, it was a really long line and, and . . . It was a good thing to read."

"You are a sweet man, Tommy Pesaturo," Meg's mother said. She slipped her hand into her husband's and squeezed.

"Ah well," he said. Everyone was looking at him now. He turned bright red.

A tapping sound came from the back of the room. Heads

turned to Libby, who was staring at Griffin expectantly.

"Oh," he said belatedly. "Um, Olivia Hayes, did *you* hire someone to kill or harm Edward Como?"

Olivia made a motion with her hand, which he took to mean no. She was using her left hand to flip through her picture book. Toppi came closer, leaning over her shoulder as Libby tapped on one picture, flipped several more pages, then tapped on two more pictures.

"She's pointing out Jillian, Carol and Meg," Toppi said. She looked at Libby. "The Survivors Club?"

Libby tapped once, flipped through the book, tapped again.

"The number one," Toppi said. "The Survivors Group, plus one?"

Single tap.

"That means yes," Toppi translated for the group. She knelt down. "I don't know what that means, Libby. Do you mean the other victim? Sylvia Blaire?"

No response.

"Do you mean the Survivors Club should be four people?"

Libby frowned, then tapped once. This tap was clearly reluctant, however. The statement still wasn't quite right.

"Why four people?" Meg asked.

"It can't be an open-ended question," Jillian spoke up. "She knows what she wants to say, but you have to help her find it by using yes or no questions."

She was studying her mother now as well. It was hard to read the look on her face. Some compassion, some yearning, some resignation. Then Libby looked at her as well. The softening of her features was immediate and obvious. A mother looking at her daughter. A mother, looking at the only daughter she had left.

"Yes or no question," Tom muttered.

"Four people, four people," Vinnie was saying.

"A bigger Survivors Club," Meg mused.

Then all of sudden, Jillian's eyes grew wide. "I know what she means. Oh my God, why didn't we think of it before?"

265

In her wheelchair, Libby leaned toward her daughter, waited for her daughter to speak the words from Libby's head.

"Sergeant Griffin asked all of us if we were involved in Eddie's death, because we're Eddie Como's victims. We have the best motive."

Tap, tap, tap.

Jillian turned toward Griffin now. Her cheeks were flushed, her eyes dazed. "But what's the other major statistic in rape cases, Griffin? That rape is a largely unreported crime. That in fact, something like only one in every four rapes is ever brought to the attention of the police."

Griffin closed his eyes. He understood now as well. "Ah, no."

And in her wheelchair, Libby went tap, tap, tap.

"Ah, yes," Jillian said softly. "Meg, Carol and I are the women who came forward, the women who called the police. But that doesn't mean we were the College Hill Rapist's only victims. It is quite feasible, it's very probable, that there's at least one other woman out there. Another woman, another family, and a whole host of other people who wanted Eddie Como dead."

27
Griffin

By 6:30, there was still no word on Carol, but Griffin had to go. Waters was waiting for him, plus he had work to do. He left the subdued group inhabiting one corner of the waiting room, an odd sort of family. Dan had started off slightly apart, but then Jillian, of all people, had moved to the seat beside him. Maybe Dan was grateful. It was hard to tell. He should be, Griffin thought. He gave Jillian one last glance, then headed out the door.

In the parking lot, he was immediately assaulted by the gathered press.

"Any word on Carol Rosen's condition?"

"Are you prepared to make an arrest?"

"Is Carol Rosen's attempted suicide connected with Eddie Como's murder?"

Griffin ignored them all and climbed into his car. In all honesty, there weren't as many reporters present as he would've thought. Then he turned on the radio and found out why.

Tawnya Clemente was holding a press conference in downtown Providence. At a law firm. Where her new attorney was announcing the fifty-million-dollar wrongful-death suit he was planning to bring against the city of Providence and the Providence Police Department on behalf of the Como family.

"As recent evidence indicates," the lawyer boomed, "Edward Como never should have been arrested by the Providence Police Department. Indeed, the premature and irresponsible indictment of Edward Como as a serial rapist set in motion the events leading to the tragic death of this young man, shot down in front of the very courthouse where he would've shortly been found innocent. Yesterday was a dark, dark day in the halls of justice. The city of Providence turned on one of its very own sons. Now the city must make restitution. The city must make amends."

On cue, Griffin's cell phone rang.

"Are you listening to this?" Fitz yelled into his ear. "Holy mother of God, I am having a heart attack. My heart is literally fucking exploding in my chest. I'm gonna die on this thankless, shitty, fucking nuts job, and then my wife is gonna sue this city for seventy-five million just so she can stay ahead of the Comos. Jesus H. Christ. I should've arrested Tawnya when I had the chance."

"You have a wife?" Griffin said.

"Eat my shorts, Sergeant!"

"I take it you had another lovely afternoon."

"Blockbuster," Fitz moaned. "Goddamn kid seems legit. Showed us the computer records of Eddie's transaction, then practically cried as he told us how he'd been too scared to come forward earlier. His sister goes to Providence College and he was so sure Eddie was guilty, he didn't want to do anything that might set the College Hill Rapist free."

"So on the one hand, the kid from Blockbuster did see Eddie that night, but even he's still convinced that Eddie is guilty?"

"The DNA. Some people really do believe in that stuff. Why the hell aren't any of them ever on juries?"

Griffin had turned onto the highway. The lack of sleep the night before was starting to catch up with him. So much information, and he couldn't seem to get his brain to process half of it.

"Is this kid the basis of Tawnya's claim?"

"Maybe. I'm guessing, though, her lawyer's mostly focusing on last night's assault on Sylvia Blaire. That case is consistent with the College Hill Rapist attacks and since that happened *after* Eddie was dead, Eddie couldn't have done it, meaning he couldn't have done any of them."

"Meaning the heat is on to resolve what happened to Sylvia Blaire."

"Would you believe the mayor just gave us carte blanche on the Blaire case?"

"Oh, you big boy you."

"Yeah, apparently you can spend a small fortune on manpower and high-priority forensic tests without coming close to the expense of a fifty-million-dollar lawsuit."

"I take it you're fast-tracking the tests on the DNA sample?"

"Oh yeah. We're trying to get results by first thing tomorrow morning. Please let it be an ex-boyfriend. About the only thing that will save our asses now is for it to be an ex-boyfriend. Oh, and when we pick him up, he's gotta confess that it was a copycat crime and he learned all the details from reading some Internet site, www.IWannaBeARapist.com, or something like that. Ex-boyfriend. Confession. Yeah, that's about what it's going to take to salvage my career."

"I think you stood a better chance of having the heart attack," Griffin said.

"Probably." Fitz sighed again. He still hadn't gotten any sleep and it showed in his voice. "Hey, Griffin, did Carol Rosen really try to commit suicide?"

"We found her passed out with an empty bottle of prescription sleeping pills. I understand that she'd probably been drinking as well."

"Ah, shit."

"I'm sorry, Fitz."

"It's the Blaire case, isn't it? Has everyone wigged out. Press is going nuts, people are phoning nine-one-one if the bush outside their house moves . . . It's a copycat. How hard is that for people to grasp? Sometimes you get copycats." Fitz sounded desperate. He knew it, too. He sighed again, then said gruffly, "It's not her fault, you know. Whatever happened, whatever mistakes we may or may not have made . . . It's not her fault, not Jillian's fault, not Meg's fault. We're big boys over here. We handled the case the way we handled the case."

"Fitz, did you guys ever try to find any additional rape victims?"

"What do you mean?"

"Jillian and her mom raised an interesting point. Rape is a largely unreported crime. Sure, we have three known victims of the College Hill Rapist. But that doesn't mean they were his only victims."

Fitz was silent for a moment. "Well, we ran the details of the case through VICAP to see if we'd get any hits. No crimes matching these descriptions came up in any other states. Of course, that's not exactly foolproof. Another victim might not have filed a police report. Or maybe she did, and the police department still hasn't gotten around to entering it into the database, etc., etc. D'Amato waited six months before going to the grand jury, just in case we could find any other women willing to come forward and add their charges to the package. That's one of the reasons he didn't mind Jillian and her group going on TV all the time. He figured if anything would influence another victim to come forward, it would be seeing Jillian, Carol and Meg standing tall."

"But no one came forward?"

"Not that we ever heard of."

"But that doesn't rule out the possibility . . ."

"Griffin, there is no way of ruling out that possibility. You could interview every woman in this state, point-blank ask her if she was ever raped, and still not rule out the possibility because one of them might lie. We're cops. We can't focus on the impossible. We have to focus on the probable."

"I can account for everyone's money," Griffin said abruptly.

Fitz was clearly stunned. "No shit."

"Yeah. I even asked Vinnie Pesaturo if he arranged for a hit. He said no. And call me crazy, but I actually believe him."

"In other words, you just ran out of suspects."

"I ran out of suspects for this theory," Griffin said.

"Meaning?"

"Meaning maybe it wasn't a vengeance case. Maybe it was about something else. You tell me, Fitz. Why else would someone want Eddie Como dead?"

Griffin had no sooner set down his cell phone from that call than it rang again.

"Sergeant Griffin," he said.

"Where the hell are you?"

"Lieutenant Morelli! My favorite LT. Have I told you how lovely you look today?"

"You wouldn't know how lovely I look today. You haven't bothered to see me today. Funny, but my memory of the primary case officer's job is to keep the higher-ups informed. To actually be at headquarters overseeing information, generating theories and keeping the ball rolling. What is your memory of the primary case officer's job, Sergeant?"

"Good news," Griffin said hastily. "We're making lots of progress."

"Oh really? Because I've been listening to the news, Sergeant, and it seems to me that this case is going to hell in a handbasket."

"It's the fifty-million-dollar lawsuit, isn't it?"

"That's one problem."

"And the fact that the public is now convinced there is a serial rapist on the loose, and they're all about to be raped and/or murdered in their sleep?"

"That would be another problem."

"The mayor is getting calls, and the colonel is getting calls and the media is having an absolute field day at our expense?"

"Very good, Sergeant. For someone who's never around, at least you're keeping up-to-date. Detective Waters taking pity on you?"

"Yes, ma'am," Griffin acknowledged.

"Well, that speaks highly of Detective Waters. Whom, I

understand, you have running around Cranston looking for associates of Eddie Como. That sounds an awful lot like you're poaching on Providence's rape case. Are you poaching on Providence's rape case?"

"I'm being thorough," Griffin said carefully.

"Sergeant, don't make me kill you."

Griffin smiled. He'd always liked Lieutenant Morelli. He took a deep breath. "Here's the problem. We started out with a basic theory. Eddie Como is an alleged rapist, ergo the most likely suspects in his murder are the rape victims."

"I remember that conversation."

"Pursuant to that angle, the financial crimes detectives did a full workup on the three women and their families. That yielded two good leads: Jillian Hayes and Dan Rosen have both made substantial cash withdrawals with no identifiable recipient."

"They could've hired the gunman."

"They could've. Unfortunately they didn't. Jillian Hayes donated her money to a Cranston parish, as confirmed by the parish priest. And Dan Rosen blew his money at Foxwoods, as corroborated by Vincent Pesaturo. It appears Mr. Rosen has a gambling problem."

"Which means you now have a problem."

"Yeah. At least as it stands now, none of the known victims and their families make good suspects, not even Vinnie Pesaturo."

"Where are you going with this, Sergeant?"

Griffin laughed. It was the hollow, stressed-out laugh of a detective watching his case go down the tubes. "Well, we have two angles left. First, we hold with the vengeance theory, and pursue the possibility that there were *other* victims of the College Hill Rapist. Ones that have never come forward to the police."

The lieutenant was silent for a moment. "That's an interesting theory."

"Isn't it? Jillian Hayes and her mother came up with it. Remember, rape is a drastically underreported crime. I checked with Fitz, and they did some initial legwork. Ran the rape profile through VICAP, etc. No hits, but that doesn't mean much. If there are other victims, they may never have gone to the police at all."

"Did they try the rape hotline or a rape-crisis organization?"

"Uh, no . . ."

"Well, maybe you'd like to send out some detectives, Sergeant. A rape-crisis organization won't give you names, but they can tell you if they received calls from someone who suffered a similar attack. Then at least you'll know if you're on the right track."

"Ummm, good point."

"That's why my name starts with the initials LT. Now what's your second theory?"

"It involves the Sylvia Blaire case. Fitz is hoping it's a copycat, praying really, that it's a copycat, but there are some problems with that theory."

"The douche."

Griffin scowled. "For a neglected lieutenant, you're keeping well informed."

Morelli said, "I'll have you know, I do look very good today. Plus, it just so happens that Lieutenant Kennedy from Providence has the hots for my sister. Which is, by the way, the only thing that is keeping Detective Fitzpatrick from wringing your neck. Well, that and the fact that Detective Fitzpatrick has his own problems at the moment."

"I appreciate that," Griffin said seriously. "Well, okay. So Fitz and I had an interesting discussion on the Sylvia Blaire case this morning. One possibility is that Eddie Como led two lives, one as the loving fiancé, and the other as a sexual deviant. And maybe Sexual Deviant Eddie had some friends to whom he liked to brag."

"Drinking buddies?"

"Maybe."

"Who knew all the details of what he did, including the douche?"

"That's the thought."

"Another interesting thought," Morelli concurred. "But

why just a drinking buddy? Why not an actual accomplice? We've seen rape duos before."

Griffin shrugged. "Only one semen type was ever recovered from the vics. Plus, Carol and Jillian only reported seeing one man."

Morelli was silent for a moment. "What if the second person was more of a passive partner? Maybe a lookout?"

Griffin pursed his lips. "Oh," he said. "Ooooooh."

"I'm good, aren't I, Sergeant?" she said knowingly.

"You're good," he agreed. "The times! That would explain the times. See, it would appear that the first vic, Meg Pesaturo, was a quick in and out. Like the rapist was afraid of being discovered. But he spent a lot of time with Carol, who was always considered a last-minute substitute. Why wasn't he worried about someone coming home? And it would appear that the rapist had been in Trisha Hayes's apartment for a while, too. He'd already completed the rape before Jillian arrived, but he hadn't left yet. And even though in theory Jillian walked in on him, he was aware she was coming. He hid and jumped her from behind. Now, part of his lingering at the Rosen and Hayes crime scenes probably had to do with his escalating appetite for violence. He needed more and more to get the same thrill. But maybe he also had a lookout, or gained one as he went along. Someone whose job was to give him the security to stay as long as he liked. Except in Trisha Hayes's case, when someone did unexpectedly appear, it was a basement apartment with only one point of entry/exit. So he couldn't bolt without being spotted. His better move was to ambush her instead, which he then prepared to do."

"And now this accomplice is no longer just a lookout?" Morelli said.

"That could be. Huh, that might explain the incident last night at the Hayes residence. Someone spray-painted 'Eddie Como lives' across a bank of windows. Maybe that's what this guy thinks he's doing. Carrying on the tradition of Eddie Como."

"But this person would also have reason to kill Como,

correct? Both to protect what he'd done in the past and what he was thinking of doing in the future."

"Yeah, maybe. When Fitz brought it up this morning, I thought he was pushing the limits. But then again . . ."

"It assumes a shift in behavior." Morelli was thinking out loud. "Perpetrator number two was willing to be just a lookout, and now has graduated to actually committing sexual assault – and murder."

"A graduating level of involvement is not uncommon in sex crimes, though," Griffin added. "Most rapists start with bondage fantasies, then commit lower-level acts of violence against women – battery, assault – before moving to rape. In this case, we have a perpetrator who's definitely interested in rape. He's hanging out with a rapist, taking some role in the crimes. To have his first solo incident involve a high level of violence, homicide . . ." Griffin scowled. "That doesn't fit the pattern as well, but there could be mitigating circumstances. If Sylvia Blaire was attacked by Como's partner, the guy had gone a whole year without doing anything. Maybe the tension had built too high. He saw a potential victim. He went nuts."

Lieutenant Morelli was silent. He could tell she had to think about it, too. "It's worth pursuing," she said at last. "So I can tell Lieutenant Johnson that you're searching for associates of Eddie Como as possible suspects in our murder case?"

"You can say that."

"I think I will say that. Providence has enough problems without feeling as if they're at war with us, too."

"Providence has problems," Griffin agreed.

"Speaking of which . . ."

He knew what was coming next. His grip tightened on the phone, but at least he kept his breathing steady.

"Sergeant, have you spoken with Corporal Charpentier at the ACI?"

"Not yet. I've heard of the issue, though."

"No one here is taking him seriously," she said quietly.

"I appreciate that."

"On the other hand . . ."

He didn't say anything.

"This case is growing hot," Morelli said evenly. "It's getting a life of its own. You know what happens when a case gets a life of its own."

"I'm on top of it."

"Speed, Sergeant. We need to close this one. Quick. Before the public gets more frightened. Before Tawnya Clemente's lawyer gains more ammunition. And before the press realizes there is a man in the ACI who claims to have information relevant to the case. You understand?"

Griffin closed his eyes. He understood perfectly.

He was pulling into his driveway now. Waters's blue Taurus was already parked to one side, the detective sitting behind the wheel.

"I gotta go," Griffin said.

"First thing in the morning – "

"I'll have a report on your desk."

"Damn right, you will. And in the meantime?"

"I'll put detectives on the rape-crisis organizations and others on the Cranston bars."

"Good luck, Sergeant."

"Yeah." Griffin flipped shut his phone, thought about Carol lying in the hospital and Price sitting behind bars. "Good luck."

28

Waters

Detective Mike Waters got out of his car already wearing a pair of gray sweats and a white T-shirt bearing the emblem of the Rhode Island State Police. He swung a dark blue gym bag over his shoulder, and waited for Griffin to unlock the front door. Both were parked in the driveway; Griffin had his weight set and boxing equipment set up in the single-bay garage.

"Nice place," Mike said, eyeing the small, teetering white bungalow warily.

Griffin smiled. "You see any places in the floor that look mushy, trust me. Don't step there."

He opened the door and led the way in. He'd purchased the house six months ago, needing a fresh start and finding a new hobby. The home sat on prime real estate. North Kingstown. Waterfront access. On a clear day, he could sit on the back deck and see well past the Newport Bridge. Peaceful place. Lots of birds, a few gorgeous hundred-year-old beech trees. In other words, the house itself was an absolute shack. A real person – i.e., one with money – would've bulldozed the place and started over. After his generous donation to the American Cancer Society, however, Griffin didn't have that kind of money. Besides, he liked to live dangerously.

"I heard you were fixing it up." Mike's tone was more dubious now. He stepped over the threshold with a critical look at the water-stained hardwood floor, then the plaster ceiling that was literally peeling away in foot-long sheets.

"Full-time for six months," Griffin said.

"No way."

"I started with wiring, then moved on to plumbing, then did the roof. Now I just have the kitchen, bathroom, the ceilings, the floors and three bedroom walls to go. Oh, and the back deck. Oh, I think something may have crawled in and died beneath the garage."

"So . . . sometime before the extinction of man?"

"That's my plan." Griffin directed Mike into the tiny kitchen. The floor was a dirt-brown vinyl, straight out of the seventies. The stove was olive green, also from the seventies. The refrigerator, on the other hand, was a tiny, domed icebox circa 1950. He pulled on the metal lever-handle and gave a sigh of relief when the door actually opened. "Beer? Soda?"

"Afterward."

"Suit yourself."

Griffin disappeared into the first-story bedroom, changed into sweats himself, then led Mike to the garage. He had a nice free-weight system. Not from his brief days of money, either. No, he'd been carefully acquiring these pieces since he graduated from college. His first purchase, of course, had been the Everlast heavy bag hanging from a heavy-duty swivel and chain in one corner. Next to it was a twin pair of small, leather-covered speed bags with specially inserted rubber bladders for greater recoil. If you blinked at the wrong time, those things could knock you out – or give you one helluva black eye. Don't ask Griffin how he knew.

They headed to the boxing corner first. Mike had done some lightweight work in college. He looked too skinny for the sport, but what he lacked in bulk he made up in reach and speed. First time he and Griffin had squared off, he'd nailed Griffin four times before Griffin ever saw him coming. Of course, with an extra fifty pounds behind him, Griffin only had to land a single punch to end the sparring. They'd stuck to the bag after that. Pretty much.

Waters unzipped his blue canvas tote. He took out an ump's face guard, and matter-of-factly slipped it over his head.

Griffin froze. He got the hint and wasn't sure how to respond. He finally settled on a smile. "I'll just batter the rest of you," he warned and was secretly relieved when Mike smiled back.

"I don't think so," Waters said. "I've been practicing. You know how much shit a guy gets when his best friend breaks his nose?"

"Ahhh, they all figured out that you were slow?"

"Slow? Hell, they left a Ronald McDonald nose in my locker. I even wore it one day just to make them feel guilty."

"Did it work?"

"Nah. Next day they left me his shoes. Detectives have way too much time on their hands."

Mike stood. He left his face guard on, and positioned himself behind the heavy bag.

"Any luck with the bar search?" Griffin asked.

"Not yet. But I only made it to six joints. Ask me again tomorrow."

Griffin grunted and got on with it. He started slow. Warmed his muscles and thought that for the first time back with Mike it would be good to show a little control. But the day had been long, the case hard. He was thinking too much about Eddie Como and was he or was he not perpetrator number one and then was there or was there not a perpetrator number two. Then he thought of Carol, still no news. And then he thought of Jillian Hayes, the way her eyes turned molten gold when she was mad, the way her fingers had curled around his arm just an hour before.

He pummeled the living shit out of the heavy bag. Even Waters was breathing hard when he was done. The detective didn't say a word. He motioned with his head, and they changed places.

Holding a bag for Mike wasn't too difficult. He didn't have the mass to hit that hard. But he liked to thoroughly work over the target; Griffin had watched him do it before. Turning the bag into a human proxy, then going after various points. Kidney, kidney, kidney, right uppercut. Stomach, stomach, stomach, left chin.

Griffin relaxed, let his body do the work on setting the bag, and allowed his mind to drift. It had been a while since he'd worked out with anyone else. Brought back a certain measure of comfort. The smell of chalk and sweat. The heat of bodies working hard. The silence of men who didn't need to talk.

Afterward, Griffin hit the weights while Mike amused himself with a jump rope. Then Griffin played with the speed bags while Mike used the weights. Then an hour had passed, neither one of them could move, so they grabbed two beers, a gallon of water and headed for the back deck.

Sun was down. In the distance, the lights of the Newport Bridge twinkled like stars while the breeze came in off the water and covered their sweat-dampened skin with goose bumps. Mike dug out a sweatshirt. Griffin retrieved a fleece pullover.

They still didn't speak.

Cell phone rang. Griffin went back inside to get his phone off his bed. It was the hospital calling. Carol Rosen had been moved to the ICU. Her stomach had been pumped, but she had yet to regain consciousness. The doctors wanted to keep a close eye on her.

When he came back out, Waters had finished off the H$_2$O and cracked open both beers. He held out the red-and-white can of Bud to Griffin as he took his seat.

"I see you still only buy the best," Mike said.

"Absolutely."

They lapsed back into silence. Finally, ten, twenty, thirty minutes later, it didn't really matter, Mike said, "You still miss her?"

"Every day."

"I miss her, too." Mike looked at him. "It was hard, you being out. It was as if I'd lost both of you."

Griffin didn't say anything. He and Mike went back fifteen years now. Mike had been there for Griffin's first promotion to detective. He'd been there when Griffin came back from a hiking trip raving about this woman he'd just

280

met. He'd served as best man at Griffin and Cindy's wedding, and then one bright spring afternoon, he'd been a pallbearer at her funeral. It was hard sometimes for Griffin to remember that the pain was not his alone.

"David Price was a piece of shit," Waters said abruptly. "And he hid it really well, not just from you. It's over, though. He took enough. Don't give him any more."

"I know."

"Good. She'd want you to be happy, Griffin. She never wanted less for you than you wanted for her."

"It wasn't fair, you know," Griffin said.

"I know."

"That's the hardest part. If I think about that . . ." He spun the can of beer in his hands. "If I focus on that, I start to go a little nuts again."

"Then don't think about that."

Griffin sighed heavily. He went back to studying the dark depths of the ocean at night. "Yeah. Things happen as they happen. People who think they're in control of life – they're just not paying attention."

"Amen," Waters said. He went back inside and fetched them both another can of beer.

Later, Griffin said: "Did you follow up with Corporal Charpentier?"

"Yeah."

"And?"

"David Price doesn't know anything."

"You're sure?"

"Corporal Charpentier tracked down Como's former roommate Jimmy Woods, the guy now serving time in Steel City. According to Woods, Eddie Como was a first-class whiner even behind bars. All he ever did was go on and on about how he was innocent, and this was all some horrible mistake."

"This is what Woods said?"

"That's what Woods said. Just for the sake of argument, Charpentier followed up with Price. Price said Woods was lying, but Charpentier wasn't impressed. Charpentier even asked Price if he knew who had done Sylvia Blaire. You know what he said?"

"What did he say?"

"He said Eddie Como. And then he laughed."

29

The Survivors Club

Nightfall. Meg sat on the floor of her little sister's room, ostensibly braiding the hair on her sister's new Barbie doll, but really trying to pretend she didn't notice the thick darkness gathering outside the second-story window – or the sound of her parents' voices, arguing down the hall.

"The pink dress," five-year-old Molly announced. She'd been going through her shoebox of Barbie clothes for the past ten minutes, trying to pick the perfect outfit for Barbie's upcoming wedding. Molly didn't own Ken, so Barbie was going to marry Pooh Bear. Pooh seemed very excited about the whole thing. He was wearing a new pink cape for the occasion. Molly loved the color pink.

Molly handed over the long, sequined dress, more appropriate for receiving an Oscar than, say, a wedding, but Meg dutifully tugged it up over the doll's feet.

"Maybe we should tell someone," her mother was saying down the hall.

"Absolutely not!" her father's muffled voice replied.

"What about Jillian – "

"No."

"Sergeant Griffin?"

"Dammit, Laurie, this is a family matter. We've made it this long, we're not getting strangers involved now."

"Shoes," Molly declared. She looked at Meg and promptly frowned. Matching shoes were hard to come by for the real people in this house, let alone the tiny plastic pairs that went with Barbie.

"She could have a barefoot wedding," Meg said.

"No!" Molly was shocked.

"Pooh doesn't have any shoes," Meg pointed out reasonably.

Her little sister rolled her eyes. "Pooh is a bear. Bears don't wear shoes, *everyone* knows that."

"Bears wear capes?"

"Yes, pink capes 'cause pink is Barbie's favorite color and her husband has to know that her favorite color is pink."

Purple, Meg thought idly. The color of royalty. His favorite color. Who was he? How did she know that?

"I'm worried . . ." Her mother's voice was rising down the hallway.

"Now, honey – "

"No! Don't honey me! For God's sake, Tom. The doctors told us her memory would come back shortly. Trauma-induced amnesia isn't supposed to last this long or be this complete. But she doesn't seem to remember anything. *Anything*. What if she's doing worse than we thought?"

"Come on, Laurie. You've seen her. She's happy. So what if she doesn't remember anything. Hell, maybe we're all better off that she forgot."

"Or maybe she hated her life that much. You ever think of that, Tom? Maybe what we did . . . Oh my God, maybe we scarred her that badly!"

"*Shoes!*" Molly squealed. She triumphantly dumped out her box of Barbie clothes and fished out a pair of bright red platform heels that had probably come with Barbie's flower child outfit or a killer pair of jeans. Now Molly took Barbie out of Meg's hands and used the shoes to finish up Barbie's hot-pink wedding ensemble. Outfits that would not be appearing in a Mattel commercial anytime soon, Meg decided. But Molly was very pleased.

"It's time for the wedding," Molly said with a big smile. "Dum-dum-de-dum, dum-dum-de-dum . . ."

"*I'll marry you.*"

"*No . . . no . . .*"

"*It's them, isn't it? Well, fuck them! I'll take you away.*

I'll make you happy. Come on, Meg, sweet Meg, my pre-cious little Meg . . ."

"I'm scared."

"Don't be scared. I won't let anyone hurt you, Meg. Not anyone. Ever."

"I'm scared," her mother was saying. "What if one day it suddenly comes back to her? Bang. Just like that. What if she's not ready?"

"The docs said if she did remember, then she'd be ready."

"Oh please, the doctors also said there was no reason for her to have forgotten this much. Face it, Tom, they don't know anything. It's amnesia. A brain thing, a mental thing. They're making this up as they go along."

"Laurie, honey, what do you want?"

"I want her to be happy! I want her to be safe. Oh Tom, what if *we* were the ones who had come home today to find Meg passed out from an overdose of sleeping pills? If the trauma of being so viciously raped is too much for a grown woman, what do you think it must be doing to Meg?"

"Meg?" Molly asked.

Meg blinked her eyes. Her sister's pink-painted room came back into focus. She was sitting once more on the floor. Her little sister was beside her, peering up at her anxiously.

"Meg doesn't feel good?" Molly asked. She was still clutching Barbie in her right hand.

"I'm, uh, I'm . . ." Meg touched her cheek. Her face was covered in sweat. Her skin had grown cold and clammy. "Just a little headache, I guess." She smiled at her sister weakly, trying to get her bearings back.

"Marry me."

"I can't – "

"Marry me."

Her stomach rebelled. For a moment, she thought she might be sick. And then suddenly, in the back of her head:

"*Fucking brat. Run home to your mommy and daddy. Go hide behind their narrow little minds and fucking subur-ban panacea. You don't want my love? Then I take it back. I hate you, I hate you, I hate you . . .*"

"Meg?"

"Just . . . a minute."

And then again from down the hall. "I don't want her to end up like Carol. I couldn't stand it if she ended up like Carol. Oh Tom, what if we've failed her?"

"M-M-Meg?"

"I hate you, I hate you, I hate you . . ."

"The doctors still aren't sure Carol's even going to make it. Meg's honestly grown close to the woman. What if she dies, Tom? What will happen then? My God, what will happen then!"

Meg bolted off the floor. She stumbled out of Molly's room.

"M-M-Meg?"

She careened down the hall.

"I hate you, I hate you, I hate you."

"What if Carol dies, what if Carol dies . . ."

Meg got the toilet seat up. She leaned over . . .

Nothing. She'd never eaten lunch. She'd forgotten about dinner. Her stomach rolled and rolled and rolled, but there was nothing present to throw up. She moved over to the sink. Turned on the cold water. Stuck her head under the faucet and let the icy flow shock the distant images from her brain.

Minutes passed. Long, cool minutes while the water sluiced over her sweaty skin and dampened all the voices in her head. Cool, cool water bringing blessed nothingness back to her brain.

When she finally looked up, her parents were standing in the doorway. Her father appeared his usual stoic self. Her mother, on the other hand, had one arm wrapped tightly around her stomach, while her right hand fidgeted with the gold heart dangling around her neck.

"Meg honey?" her mother asked.

Meg straightened. Strange voices, faint rumblings returned to the back of her mind. Like faraway scenes, threatening to come closer, closer, closer.

Meg found a towel and used it to methodically blot her face.

"You okay, sweetheart?" her father asked.

"Just a little queasy. All that time in the hospital, you know." She offered a faint smile.

"I'm sure Carol will be all right," her mother said briskly. Her right hand was now furiously twisting the dangling gold heart.

"Sure." Meg turned off the faucet. Rehung the towel. Ran a comb through her long brown hair.

"If there's anything you need . . ." her father tried.

"I'm fine, Daddy."

"We love you, sweetheart." Her mother this time.

"I love you, too."

What were they doing? Saying so many words, but none of the ones that mattered. Lies. She had never realized it before, but sometimes love produced lies. Big lies. Whopping lies. Gigantic lies, all packaged prettily and offered up with the best of intentions. Protection through falsehood. That's right – a suburban panacea.

Her parents were still standing in the doorway. She was still standing at the sink. No one seemed to know what to do.

"I, uh, I have a wedding," Meg said.

"A wedding?"

"Barbie and Pooh Bear. Didn't you get the invite?"

"Oh, Molly's marrying off Barbie again." Her mother finally relaxed. Her hand stilled around her neck. "The hot-pink dress?"

"Absolutely."

"Red platform shoes?"

"The kid's got style."

"Well, by all means." Her mother moved to the side, gestured for Meg to pass. "We wouldn't want to stand in the way of true love."

"I hate you, I hate you, I hate you."

"Okay then." Meg pasted the smile back on her face. She made it down the hall, where Molly sat uncertainly in the middle of her room, still clutching Barbie on her lap.

"Let's have that wedding!" Meg said with forced cheerfulness.

Molly looked up at her and positively beamed.

Hours later, the Pesaturo family went to sleep. One by one, the tiny rooms of the tiny home went dark. Meg turned off her own light. But she didn't go to bed. She went to her window. She stood in front of her window.

"I hate you, I hate you, I hate you."

She stared at the night outside her window, and she wondered at the darkness waiting for her there.

Those rich chocolate eyes. That gentle lover's kiss.

"David," she whispered, then licked her lips and tried out the name once more. "David. Oh no. David Price."

At midnight, Jillian finally left the hospital. Carol had yet to regain consciousness. Her stomach had been pumped, her body purged. Now she lay peacefully beneath stark white hospital sheets, her long golden hair a halo around her head as a heart monitor beeped in rhythm to her pulse and a respirator pumped air into her lungs.

Coma, the doctors said. She had ingested nearly 125 mg of Ambien, or twelve times the recommended dose. Combined with the alcohol, it had shut down her system to the point where she responded only to painful stimuli. The doctors would test her again in the morning, see if she began to pull out once the levels of sleeping pills and alcohol in her bloodstream came down. In other words, they would poke and prod at her poor, peaceful body. See if they could inflict enough pain to jar her back to life.

Dan remained in the room. He had pulled up a chair next to Carol, where he had finally fallen asleep with his head on the edge of her bed, his hand cradling her wrist. From outside the ICU door, Jillian had watched a nurse drape a blanket around his shoulders. Then Jillian had turned to go.

The night was cold, a sharp slap against Jillian's cheeks. She still wore her suit from this morning, no coat, no scarf. She hunched her shoulders beneath the tailored blue jacket and shivered as she walked. The parking lot was nearly empty this time of night. Certainly no reporters anymore. In the news world, Carol's suicide attempt was already old.

Been there, done that. As of six this evening, the hot story had become Tawnya Clemente's lawsuit against the city.

God, Jillian was tired.

At her car, she went through the drill. Peered through the windows at the backseat. Glanced at neighboring cars to make sure no one loitered. Unlocked her door with her left hand. Held her canister of pepper spray in her right. Preparedness was nine-tenths of the battle. If you don't want to be a victim, then you can't act like one.

She got straight into her Lexus, immediately locked all the doors, then finally started the engine. She glanced again at her backseat. Nothing but empty, shadowed space. Why did she have chills running up and down her spine?

She got her car in reverse, turned to back out and nearly screamed.

No. Eddie Como. *No*. It was all in her head, all in her head. The backseat was empty, the parking lot was empty. She turned back around, shoved her automatic in park and sat there shaking uncontrollably, the fear still rolling off her in waves.

Panic attack, she realized after a moment, trying to regain her breath. In the beginning, she'd had them all the time. It had been a bit since the last one, but then again, today had been a bad day. First Sylvia Blaire. Then Carol.

Oh God, Carol . . .

Jillian rested her head against the steering wheel, and suddenly started to cry. Second time for her in one day. Had to be a new record. She couldn't stop, though. The sobs came up from the dark pit of her, angry and hard and desolate, until her stomach hurt and her shoulders ached and still she choked out rough, bitter tears. This is why she didn't cry. Because there was nothing dainty or tragic about her grief. She cried like a trucker, and afterward she looked like a disaster, with red, blotchy cheeks and mascara-smeared eyes.

What if Sergeant Griffin saw her now? The thought made her want to weep again, though she didn't know why.

She could call him. He would probably take her call,

even though it was after midnight. He'd probably even let her go on and on about her sister and the ache that wouldn't ease and the grief that knew no end. He would listen to those things. He seemed to be that kind of guy.

She didn't pick up her cell phone, though. Maybe she wasn't that kind of woman, the kind who still believed in Prince Charming. Or maybe she was, but Meg was right and she wasn't ready to stop punishing herself for her sister's death.

Or maybe it was all a bunch of psychobabble bullshit, and the bottom line was that she just wasn't ready. She did still miss her sister. She did still ache. And she did hold too much in and she did suffer too much guilt. And now she was worried about Carol, and as always she was worried about her mother, and then there was this thing with another poor dead college student and who knew what was really going on out there in that pitch-black night?

Shit. Jillian put her car back in drive. She got out of the dark parking lot.

At home, outside lights fired up her home like a suburban landing strip. She'd had three new spotlights added first thing this morning and God knows her neighbors had probably put on sunglasses just to go to bed. Good for them. May that be the worst tragedy they ever had to face.

Jillian drove by the patrol car parked down the street. The two officers sitting inside nodded at her. She waved back. So Griffin had kept his word as well.

She pulled into her garage with the normal drill. Car doors still locked. Gazing out the rearview mirror and watching the opening until the garage door had closed all the way. Checking out the shadowy depths of the garage for other signs of intruders. The coast appeared clear. She finally unlocked her car door, and entered her home.

Toppi had left her a plate covered with plastic wrap on the kitchen counter. A chicken sandwich in case she was hungry. Jillian put the plate in the refrigerator, poured a glass of water and made the rounds. Doors still locked. Windows secure. Nothing out of place.

The house was quiet this time of night. Just the ticking of the hallway clock, and the occasional fluttery snore from behind Toppi's bedroom door.

One A.M. now. Jillian should go to sleep. She kept prowling the house, driven by a compulsion she couldn't name.

Had she failed Carol? In the past, Carol and Meg had accused her of carrying too much guilt. Then, just this afternoon, Griffin had implied she took too much responsibility for things. No one could keep everyone safe.

It was her job, though. For as long as she could remember. Libby had led the wild life. Jillian held things together. Baby Trish required stability. Jillian made them a home. Her mother's health declined. Jillian took her in as well. They were her family, she loved them and with love came responsibility. So she did everything she could for them. She just never let them get too close.

Just as she had done with Carol and Meg.

For the first time, it occurred to her – was she feeling guilty that Trisha was dead, or was she feeling guilty that she had not loved her more when she was still alive? All those summers with Trisha racing along the beach and Jillian alone beneath an umbrella. Why hadn't she run out into the sand? Why hadn't she splashed through the waves with her sister? What had she been so afraid of?

Strong, responsible Jillian who had never had a serious relationship. Independent, serious Jillian who focused on work work work, all of the time. Proud, lonely Jillian who marched through life as if it were a battlefield and she didn't want anyone taking her prisoner. Not her mother. Not her sister. Not Eddie Como and not the Survivors Club.

Poor, stupid Jillian who, at the age of thirty-six, still knew so little about what was important in life. Griffin had been right before. Trisha had loved her. And it shouldn't have taken Jillian nearly a year to remember that.

Jillian moved into the hallway. She thought of Trisha again, and the days that would never be. And then she thought of her mother, and all the years still to come. Proud, fierce Libby tapping, tapping, tapping. Sad, silent Libby who so longed to visit her daughter's grave. Jillian walked down to her mother's bedroom. She pushed in the door. She spotted Libby, lying upon her bed, bathed in the icy blue glow of a night-light. Libby's eyes were wide open. She'd been watching the door and now she stared straight at Jillian.

"You've been waiting for me to come home," Jillian said softly, with genuine surprise, genuine wonder.

Her mother's finger tapped the bedspread.

"You wanted to make sure that I got home safe."

Her mother's finger, rising and falling on the bedspread.

Jillian went farther into the room. "You can rest now. I'm home, Mom. I'm . . . safe." And then, a heartbeat later, "And I love you, too, Mama."

Her mother smiled. She held out her arms. And for the first time since she was a little girl, Jillian went into her mother's embrace. And it didn't hurt so much after all. All of these years, all of these miles later, it finally felt right.

While the clock ticked down the hall. And the spotlights lit up the house. And the uniformed officers sat in their patrol car, waiting to see what would happen next.

30

Griffin

Four A.M., Wednesday morning, Detective Sergeant Roan Griffin drove to state police headquarters in North Scituate. He was early. Very early. Good thing, too. He had contact interviews to review, witness statements to consider and detective activity reports to analyze. Then he needed to prepare a time line of events. Oh, and he wanted to produce a chart, filling in the recent findings on their key suspects. That ought to make Lieutenant Morelli happy.

Yep, Griffin had gotten a whole five hours of uninterrupted sleep last night. No new rapes, no new shootings, no new lawsuits. Now he was feeling downright chipper. He should've known better.

Walking into the Investigative Support Service building, he was immediately greeted by the uniform on duty. Griffin nodded back, then proceeded down the narrow, yellow-lit hallway to Major Crimes. The ISSB, a flat, dull-brown 1960s building that could've passed as any government office, was divided into a series of wings. The Criminal Identification Unit took up the back right corner of the building, with one large office space for the five CIU detectives to share and a series of smaller rooms to house their toys – the lie detector room, the two Automatic Fingerprint Information System (AFIS) rooms, the significantly sized evidence-processing room, the photo lab.

In contrast to the CIU suite, the Major Crimes detectives were granted a small corner in the front of the building, where they had five gray cubicles crammed into one blue-carpeted space. Of course, they considered themselves to have the nicer room. The ten-foot-high drop ceiling only had a fraction of the yellow water stains found in the rest of the building. Plus, the detectives kept their tidy desks free of paperwork and openly displayed nicely framed family photos. A few detectives had brought in plants over the years, and now massive green vines draped cheerfully down the cubicle walls. All in all, the place could've been an accountant's office – if accountants had a back wall covered with "Most Wanted" photos and a front wall bearing a white board with homicide notes.

Griffin liked the Major Crimes office. Not nearly as dreary as other law enforcement facilities, say, for example, the Providence station where Fitz worked. That place ought to be condemned, and maybe would be once the new headquarters was completed across the highway. It was a thought.

Griffin stuck his head across the hall, where Lieutenant Morelli had her office. Nobody home. Perfect. He'd sit down, whip the case notes into order and know exactly what was going on in the Eddie Como homicide file by 8:00 A.M. Just like a good case officer. Hell, maybe he'd surprise them all and actually have the case solved by 9:00 A.M. Oooh, he was a cocky son of a bitch.

Griffin's optimism lasted until 7:00 A.M., when his cell phone rang. It was Fitz, and he didn't sound good.

"You gotta get down here," Fitz said without preamble.

"Where's here?"

"Providence," Fitz said tensely. "Hurry."

"Has there been another attack?"

"Just get here. Now. Before the press finds out."

Fitz hung up the phone. Griffin sat there a moment longer, staring at his silent cell phone. Ah, shit.

He grabbed his jacket and headed for the door. Halfway down the hall, he ran into Waters, who was just getting in for the day. Mike was moving a little stiffly this morning, which under other circumstances would've made Griffin proud. Now, however, he simply swapped notes.

"I gotta run to Providence. Something's up."

"Another attack?" Waters asked immediately.

"I don't know. Have you heard the morning news?"

"Drive time was quiet."

"Well, then, whatever it is, we're still one step ahead. That's worth something. Listen, can you follow up with the other detectives? See if they're making any progress with the rape-crisis groups. Oh, and take a few more bodies with you to the Cranston bars. I'm guessing we're going to need progress, mmmm, now."

"Got it. You'll let us know?"

"When I know what I know, you'll be the first I'll let know." Griffin headed down the hall.

"Hey, Griffin," Waters called out behind him. Griffin turned. "I'll call ACI. Just in case."

Griffin hesitated a fraction of an instant. "Yeah," he said more slowly. "Just in case."

He went out the door, no longer feeling so good about the day.

The Providence Police Department was located right off I-95 in downtown Providence. The rapidly aging building took its role as an active urban police station quite seriously. Ripped-up gray linoleum floors, water-stained drop ceilings, scuffed-up walls, exposed pipes. The Providence detectives liked to joke that their offices were straight out of *Barney Miller*. For interior decorating, their color options were dirt, dirty and dirtier.

Definitely a far cry from the state police's White House in North Scituate. Not that there was any resentment or anything.

Griffin arrived shortly after seven-thirty. He parked his Taurus in the tow-away zone near the front entrance. A Providence uniform would ticket him out of spite. Fitz would make it go away. Every organization had its rituals.

He walked through the exterior glass doors, passing three black youths in baggy jeans and sleeveless sweatshirts who glared at him balefully. He stared back and, by virtue of size, got them to look away first. Inside was a small dark foyer. Griffin took the door to the left into another small dark foyer, where three receptionists sat behind bulletproof glass. This room was crowded with various people pleading various cases. "Man, I gotta see so-and-so." "Hey, this parking ticket's bogus!" The receptionists didn't have the power to do anything, of course, but that didn't stop the masses from trying.

Griffin pushed to the front, flashed his shield and was promptly buzzed through the main doors, into the heart, or rather, bowels of the police station. Lucky him.

He took the stairs up. He'd tried the elevator only once and it had groaned so badly and moved so painfully he'd vowed never again. The way Griffin saw it, the Providence police would be lucky to get out before the whole building came down on their heads.

The Detective Bureau was on the second floor, adjacent to the Bureau of Criminal Identification. Griffin tried the main room, didn't see Fitz, then moved down to the locker room. Still no Fitz, but plenty of artwork; the detectives liked to hang photos of their more interesting cases on their lockers. The victim who was folded in half when hit by an oncoming train. The badly decomposed body of a victim who wasn't found for several weeks. A pair of hands, covered in marijuana leaves, found in the trunk of a car after it was pulled over for a routine traffic stop. The body, found a day later, that went with the hands . . .

Griffin continued through the labyrinth of tiny gray rooms until he came to the end of the hall. There, Providence had their evidence-processing center, basically two adjoining rooms, each the size of a coat closet, crammed full of cabinets, tables, gear and AFIS. Fitz was standing in front of the folding table, deep in hushed conversation with a sharply dressed black man whom Griffin recognized as Sergeant Napoleon, head of the BCI. Both men looked up the minute he filled the doorway.

" 'Bout time," Fitz muttered.

"You rang, I ran," Griffin said lightly. Fitz's face had an unhealthy flush. His eyes had sunk deeper into the folds of his face and his sparse hair stuck up in unusual disarray. He'd finally changed clothes since yesterday, so he'd obviously managed to make it home. Unfortunately, the break didn't seem to have done him any good.

"Griffin, Napoleon, Napoleon, Griffin." Fitz made the introductions.

"We've met," Griffin said as he and the sergeant obligingly shook hands. In contrast to Fitz, Napoleon appeared excited. He had a light in his eyes, a fervor to his face. Oh no, Griffin thought immediately. When the forensics guys got excited . . . Oh no.

"You got the reports back," Griffin said abruptly.

"Uh huh," Fitz said.

"The DNA?"

Fitz looked at the open door. He dropped his voice to nearly a whisper. "Uh huh."

Griffin leaned forward. He lowered his voice as well. "And?"

"We got a match," Fitz whispered.

"A *good* match," Napoleon emphasized.

"We know who raped Sylvia Blaire," Fitz said grimly. "According to the Department of Health, it was Eddie Como."

"This has got to be a mistake," Griffin declared five minutes later. He, Fitz and Napoleon had commandeered the lieutenant's office, shut the door and resumed their earnest huddle. They kept their heads together and their voices down. In a police station, there were eyes and ears everywhere.

"Of course it's a mistake!" Fitz snapped, then immediately dropped his voice again. "A dead man did not rape and murder Sylvia Blaire. Now do you want to tell me who did?"

Griffin turned to Napoleon. "Could it be a family member? What about an uncle, a cousin, a father? Hell, what about a long-lost brother?"

Napoleon shook his head. "We got a preliminary match in seven out of seven sample sites. We'll send it out for further analysis, but we're looking at a dead-on hit."

"Okay, a long-lost identical twin brother."

"Identical twins don't have the same DNA. It would be close, yeah, but again, seven out of seven sample sites . . ."

Griffin raked his hand through his hair. "Shit," he said.

"It is not Eddie Como," Fitz muttered. "It is not *fucking* Eddie Como."

"Okay, okay, okay." Griffin held up his hand. "Let's be logical about this. Assume for a moment that the DNA from the Blaire crime scene really does match the sample taken from Eddie Como. What if someone else had somehow saved semen from Eddie Como and smeared it at the scene?"

He and Fitz promptly stared at Napoleon, who at least seemed willing to consider the possibility.

"Swabs are first tested for semen, to see if we have something for DNA testing," Napoleon mused. "Now, spermatozoa only tests positive for seventy-two hours, so if someone had gotten a Como 'sample,' so to speak, it would have to be fresh. Otherwise the spermatozoa would be dead, the swabs would test negative for semen and nothing else would be done."

"The man's been behind bars," Fitz growled. "How do you get a fresh sample from a man in prison?"

Griffin just looked at him.

"Hey," Fitz said. "I know there's more sex in prison than in most bordellos, gimme a break. But we're not talking about someone smuggling out a stained sheet and dropping it at the scene. The match was seven out of seven sample sites, meaning they found matching DNA on the sheets, the night-gown, vaginal swabs, etc., etc. You wanna explain that scenario to me?"

"That makes it trickier," Griffin confessed. "Eddie could've preserved a sample somehow. I don't know, jacked off in a Dixie cup and sent it out?"

It was Fitz's turn to stare at him. "Now why the hell would he do that? This is a guy who's been swearing to anyone with a microphone that he's innocent. Wouldn't he kind of wonder about a request for, gee, seminal fluid?"

"Conjugal visits?" Napoleon tried.

"Not at Intake," Griffin said.

"This is crazy," Fitz muttered.

"This is nuts," Griffin agreed. "Okay, what if we're going about this backward? What if the swap wasn't made at the scene? What if the swap was made with Eddie Como's sample?"

"What do you mean?"

"I mean, the samples from the crime scenes are showing a match with another sample *labeled* Eddie Como. But what if *that* is where we have the mistake?"

"No way," Fitz said immediately.

"Couldn't happen," Napoleon seconded. "Standard operating procedure for executing a search warrant for DNA samples: Detective Fitzpatrick and Detective McCarthy picked up Eddie Como and brought him to the Reagan Building, where two clinicians and I were waiting. The clinicians drew two vials of blood, plucked several strands of hair from Como's head, then took additional combings from his pubic region. *I* personally packaged each sample and labeled it as evidence to preserve chain of custody. So that's what, five people who can vouch that Eddie Como was in the room – "

"I'm not saying you guys had the wrong man," Griffin interrupted.

"And four *samples*," the BCI sergeant continued relentlessly, "all properly sealed and labeled that you would have to swap. What are the chances of that?"

"It would be difficult," Griffin said grudgingly.

"Try impossible," Fitz countered hotly. "Try fucking impossible. We know how to do our goddamn jobs!"

"Then how did we get this match?" Griffin's voice was rising.

"I don't know! Maybe it was Eddie Como. We haven't seen his body."

"Eddie Como is dead! The ME already confirmed his fingerprints. The guy is dead, deader and deadest. So once again, how the hell did his DNA wind up at another rape-murder scene?"

"I don't know!"

"Someone is fucking with us," Griffin said. "Someone is playing a game." And then, on the heels of that thought. "Shit!"

"What?" Fitz asked wildly.

"Shit! Shit! Shit! I gotta make a phone call."

"*Now?*"

"Yeah, now. Where's a landline? How the hell do I dial out?"

"Who are you calling?"

"The Easter Bunny, who do you think?" Griffin impatiently punched in the number. "Detective Waters," Mike said thirty seconds later.

"Mike, Griffin. You talk to ACI? What did he say?"

"Price said . . . Price said, he told you so, and he's still waiting for your visit."

He told you so . . . Who murdered Sylvia Blaire, David? Eddie Como.

Ah shit. Griffin hung his head. The room simultaneously closed in on him and fell away. Eighteen months later. Eighteen painful, careful, deliberate months later, here he was again. Knee-deep in some strange, twisted David Price game. Griffin took a deep breath, struggled to pull it together. A dead man couldn't have killed Sylvia Blaire. Something else had to have happened. Something else that put Como's DNA at the scene.

And then he was thinking back to Monday afternoon and his conversation with Fitz: "*So why did Eddie, who left behind no hair, no fiber, and no fingerprints, leave behind ten latex strips? Why did he on the one hand, learn how to cover his tracks, and then on the other hand, leave you a virtual calling card?*"

Fitz had angrily declared that the Providence police had *not* framed Eddie Como. Now, Griffin finally, horribly, had an idea who had.

Games. Games didn't sound like Eddie's style. But

Griffin knew another man, a young man with an even younger face, who loved to play games. Who also sent notes and made phone calls, except they never declared his innocence. A man who had spent two days now claiming insider knowledge and had even graciously sent Griffin a note welcoming him to the case.

And then Griffin was back to thinking about that stupid DNA, the *only* evidence that had pointed at Eddie Como. DNA that was supposed to have been washed away by Berkely and Johnson's Disposable Douche with Country Flowers . . . Except . . . What's the worst thing a detective could do? Make an assumption. And what was the major assumption they had all made? That the douche had been used in an attempt to *remove* DNA from the scene. Son of a bitch.

The final pieces started clicking into place and for a moment . . . For a moment, Griffin was so mad, he couldn't speak.

"What's going on?" Waters was asking on the other end of the phone.

"Who? Who?" Fitz was saying beside him.

"What day was the first reported rape?" Griffin asked harshly. "When was Meg Pesaturo attacked?"

"Eleven April, last year," Fitz replied. "Why? What do you know?"

April eleventh. Five months after David Price's November arrest. Five months after Griffin's little meltdown. It seemed impossible. And yet . . .

"He's playing us."

"What do you want to do?" Mike asked on the other end of the line.

"Who? What?" Fitz was still parroting wildly.

"The guy who saw this coming." Griffin closed his eyes. "The guy who somehow knows more about this case than we do."

"Who saw this coming?" Fitz pleaded.

"David," Griffin said quietly. "My good old sexual-sadist neighbor, David Price."

31

Price

Griffin was dialing his cell phone, navigating his way furiously through tiny Providence streets to the I-95 on-ramp while Fitz clutched the dashboard and continued cursing colorfully under his breath. Jillian answered the phone, and Griffin immediately started talking.

"Jillian, I need you to tell me something and I need you to be honest."

"Griffin? Good morning to you, too – "

"I know you're angry with the police," he interrupted steadily. "I know you think we failed your sister and I know you haven't had a lot of incentive to cooperate with us. But I need your help now. I need you to tell me if you ever met a man named David Price. And don't lie, Jillian. This is deadly serious."

Silence. He gripped the wheel tighter, wondering what that silence meant, and wishing that his stomach wasn't beginning to turn queasily while the ringing picked up in his ears. Breathe deep, release. Eighteen months of hard work. Don't lose sight of the ball now.

"The name sounds familiar," Jillian said finally. "Wait a minute. Wasn't he your neighbor? Griffin, what is this about?"

"Did your sister ever mention his name?"

"No, not at all."

"Ever get any correspondence? Maybe something in the mail?"

"No. Wait a minute." There was a muffled clunk as she moved the receiver from her ear. Then he heard her voice shout out, "Toppi. Have you ever received anything from someone named David Price? Check with Mom." Another muffled thunk, then Jillian was back on the line. "They both say no. Griffin, you arrested him, right? You sent him to jail . . . a long time ago. Why are you asking about him now?"

Griffin ignored her question, and instead asked one of his own. "What are your plans for the day?"

"I told Mom I would take her to see Trish. Griffin – "

"Don't."

"Don't?"

"I want you to stay close to home. Or better yet. Load up Toppi and your mom and take them to the Narragansett house. I'll arrange for a pair of uniforms to meet you there."

"Did he get out of jail?" Jillian asked quietly.

"No."

"But you're targeting him. Is he involved in all this? Did David Price somehow hurt my sister?"

"That's what I'm trying to find out. Any word on Carol?"

"I was just about to call the hospital."

"I should send uniforms there as well," he muttered out loud, then wished he hadn't.

Jillian's voice grew even more somber on the other end of the line. "Something's happened, hasn't it? Something bad."

"I'll be in touch," Griffin told her. "And Jillian. Be careful."

He flipped shut his phone. Mostly because he didn't know what else to say. Or maybe because he did know what he wanted to say, and now was not the time or place, especially with Fitz sitting red-faced and haggard beside him.

He took the on-ramp for 95 South, headed for the ACI and simultaneously tossed his cell phone to Fitz. "You're up."

Fitz dialed the Pesaturo residence. Thirty seconds later, they both heard Meg's mother pick up the phone.

"Detective Fitzpatrick here," Fitz said roughly, then cleared his throat. "I, uh, I need to speak to Miss Pesaturo, please."

"Detective Fitzpatrick!" Meg's mother said warmly. "How are you this morning?"

Fitz kept his tone gruff. "Mrs. Pesaturo, I need to speak with Meg."

Laurie Pesaturo faltered. From the driver's seat, Griffin could hear the confusion in her staticky voice as she asked Fitz to wait one moment. It was several more minutes, however, before she was back on the line. "I'm sorry," she said stiffly. "Meg seems to have stepped out."

"She's not home?"

"Not at the moment."

"Do you know where she is?"

An even stiffer reply. "Not at the moment."

Fitz cut to the chase. "Mrs. Pesaturo, have you ever heard the name David Price?"

A pause. "Detective, what is this about?"

"Please, just answer the question, ma'am. Do you know, or have you ever known, a man named David Price?"

"No."

"Meg has never mentioned his name?"

"Not that I recall."

"Has he ever sent anything to your home? Perhaps called?"

"If he had done that," Laurie Pesaturo said crisply, "then I would know the name, wouldn't I? Now I'm asking *you* again, Detective. What is this about?"

"I would like you to find Meg, Mrs. Pesaturo. I'd like you to keep her close to home today. In fact, it might not be a bad time for your husband to take a day off, spend the afternoon with his family. Perhaps you could all pay Uncle Vinnie a visit, something like that."

"Detective . . ."

"It's just a precaution," Fitz added quietly.

Another pause. And then, "All right, Detective. Thank you for calling. Will you call again?"

"I hope to touch base again this afternoon, ma'am."

"Thank you, we would appreciate that."

"Find Meg," Fitz repeated, and then they were turning

into the vast facility that comprised the ACI.

Griffin found the red-brick admin building that housed the prison's Special Investigation Unit as well as the state police's ACI unit. He turned the car into a parking space, cut the ignition. He no longer looked at Fitz. He was focusing on the growing tension in his shoulders, that steadily building ringing in his ears. Breathe deep, release. Breathe deep, release.

"Hey, Griffin baby, you think this is bad? Let me tell you about your wife . . ."

Fitz got out of the car. After another moment, Griffin followed suit.

The ACI "campus" spreads out over four hundred acres of land. With brick towers and barbed-wire fence visible from the freeway, the facility is actually half a dozen buildings nestled among half a dozen other government institutions. Nearly four thousand inmates reside in the ACI at any given time, and they generate enough internal and external complaints to employ six ACI special investigators and two state detectives full time. The special investigators are the first responders, handling all inmate-to-inmate complaints. In situations, however, where there are criminal charges – serious assault, murder for hire, drug trafficking, etc. – the state police are brought in to lead the inquiry.

In between these cases, the state detectives spend their time receiving calls from various inmates looking to flip on various other inmates in return for various considerations. The detectives get plenty of calls. Very few of them, though, ever lead to anything.

That's what Griffin had been hoping for when he'd first learned of David Price's outreach. Now Griffin wasn't so sure anymore.

Corporal Charpentier met Griffin and Fitz in the lobby of the admin building, then led them down the one flight of stairs to the state's basement office. Griffin immediately wrinkled his nose at the stale air, while Fitz actually recoiled.

"I know, I know," Charpentier said. "In theory, the building is now asbestos-free. As the people actually inhaling, however . . ." He let the rest of the thought trail off. Griffin and Fitz got the picture. They were also both getting a headache.

Charpentier came to the end of the hall, opened the door and led them into a tiny office. Two desks were set up face-to-face, topped with computer terminals, manila folders and a variety of paperwork. The remainder of the cramped space was taken up by two desk chairs and a wall of gunmetal-gray filing cabinets. No cheery office plants here. Just cream-painted cinder-block walls, gray industrial carpet and dim yellow lights. Police officers led such glamorous lives.

"They're bringing him down to the rear hall," Charpentier said, taking a seat and gesturing for them to do the same. "They need another ten minutes."

"All right," Griffin said. He didn't sit. He didn't want anyone to see that his body was beginning to twitch.

"Personally, I don't think he knows jack shit," Charpentier added, then gave Griffin an appraising look.

"How is he adapting?" Griffin asked.

"Better than you'd think." Charpentier leaned back, shrugged. "He's young, he's small, he's a convicted pedophile. Frankly, he's got jail 'bitch' written all over him. But I don't know. I heard this story from one of the corrections officers. Six guys surrounded David Price in the prison showers. Were going to give him a little prison indoctrination, show him the way this place works for small, flabby-muscled baby-killers. Then David started talking. And talking and talking and talking. The guards were running to the scene, of course, expecting to find carnage, and . . . And David Price was now surrounded by six laughing guys, not hitting him, not pummeling him, but slapping him merrily on the back. Basically, in three minutes or less, he'd turned them into six gigantic, brand-new friends." Charpentier shook his head. "I don't get it myself, but in another year, he'll be running the place, the world's smallest prison warlord."

"He's good with people," Griffin said.

Charpentier nodded, then slowly leaned forward. His gaze went from Griffin to Fitz to Griffin again. "You want to hear something wild? Assaults in maximum have doubled since David was assigned there. I was just looking at the stats again this morning. Code Blue nearly every day for the last nine months. It's been open season over there. And the only new variable I can see is a man who could still buy his clothes from Garanimals."

"You think he's responsible," Fitz said bluntly.

Charpentier shrugged. "We can't prove anything. The guys always have their reasons for why they did what they did. But . . . David talks a lot. All the time. He's like some frigging politician, working the yard, passing notes along the cell block. And the next thing you know, we'll have trouble. A lot of trouble. Guys ending up in the infirmary impaled with sharp metal objects kind of trouble. I don't know what the hell Price says or does, but there's something scary about him."

"He's very good with people," Griffin said again.

"Let me tell you about your wife . . ."

The corporal's phone rang. He picked it up. "All right. They're ready for us."

ACI's maximum-security building, aka Old Max, is a singularly impressive building. Built in 1878 from thick gray stone, the three-story structure is dominated by a gigantic white-painted center dome. In the old days, a light would burn in that dome, green light if everything was okay, red light if something was wrong. The folks in Providence would then send a horse and buggy to check things out.

The prison also boasts one of the oldest working mechanical systems in the nation. Most prisons are electronic these days. Push a button to buzz open cell door A or cell block B. Old Max still has working levers for operating the thick steel doors. The inmates probably don't appreciate these things, but it lights a fire under the history buffs.

Mostly, Old Max has sheer charisma. The thick stone

walls look like prison walls. The heavy, steel-constructed six-by-eight cells, stacked three tiers high and thirty-three cells long, look like prison cells. The black-painted steel doors, groaning open in front of you, snapping shut behind you, sound like prison doors. The steady assault of odors – sweat, urine, fresh paint, ammonia, BO – smell like prison odors. And the rest of the sounds – men shouting, TVs blaring, metal clinking, radios crackling, water running, men pissing – sound like prison sounds.

Tens of thousands of men have passed through these gates in the past hundred years. Rapists, murderers, drug lords, Mafiosi, thieves. If these walls could talk, it wouldn't be words at all. It would be screams.

Griffin and Fitz signed in at the reception area. Civilians were required to pass through a metal detector. As members of law enforcement, however, they got to skip that honor, and they and Corporal Charpentier were immediately buzzed through a pair of gates into the main control area. Security was still tight. They had to wait for the gate to close behind them. Then a corrections officer who sat in an enclosed booth gestured for Griffin and Fitz to drop their badges into a metal swivel tray. The officer rotated the tray around to him, inspected the IDs, nodded once, dropped in two red visitor's passes and swiveled the tray back around.

Only after Griffin and Fitz had fastened the visitor's passes to their shirts did the white-painted steel gate in front of them slowly slide back and allow them to proceed into the bullpen. There they stood again, waiting for the gate to close behind them before a new set of gates opened in front of them. Then they had finally, officially arrived into the rear hall of Old Max.

Half a dozen guards sat around the red-tiled, white-painted space. Directly to the left was the door leading to the left wing of cells. Ahead of that was the lieutenant's office, where two corrections officers were monitoring the bank of security cameras. Straight ahead was the corridor leading to the cafeteria. And to the right was a visiting room, used by corrections officers for official business.

Today, David Price sat shackled inside. Two other corrections officers sat outside. They looked up at Griffin, nodded once, then made a big show of looking away.

Did they think he was going to attack the kid again? Was this their way of saying that if he did, they didn't care? It sounded like Price had been keeping the whole facility hopping, whether the officers could prove anything or not. Even in maximum, inmates got a good eight hours a day outside their cell – eating, working, seeing visitors, hanging in the yard, etc. In other words, plenty of opportunities to mingle with other inmates and plenty of time to cause trouble.

This place really was too good for Price.

Corporal Charpentier opened the door. Griffin and Fitz followed him in.

Sitting in a tan prison-issued jumpsuit, David Price didn't look like much. He never had, really. At five eight, one hundred and fifty pounds, he wouldn't stand out in a crowd. Light brown hair, deep brown eyes, a softly rounded face that made him look seventeen when he was really closer to thirty-two. He wasn't handsome, but he wasn't ugly. A nice young man, that's how women would classify him.

Maybe that's even what Cindy had said, that first day he'd stopped by: *"Hey, Griffin, come meet our new neighbor, David Price. So what's a nice young kid like you doing living in a place like this?"*

David Price was smiling at him.

"You look good," Price said. He didn't seem to notice either Corporal Charpentier or Detective Fitz. They were irrelevant to the matters at hand. Griffin understood this, probably they did, too. God, please keep him from killing David Price.

David was still smiling. A nice, friendly smile. The kind a kid might give his older brother. That was Price's thing. He never challenged directly, particularly larger men. He'd play the sidekick, the loyal student, the good friend. He'd be respectful but never gushing. Complimentary but never insincere. And at first you simply dismissed him, but then he kind of grew on you, and the next thing you knew, you were looking forward to his company, even eager for his praise. And things started to shift. Until it was never really clear anymore who was in charge and who was the sidekick, but you didn't think about it much anyway, because it seemed as if you were doing what you wanted to do, even if you didn't really remember wanting to do those kinds of things before.

Men liked David – he was the perfect unassuming friend. Women liked David – he was the ideal nonthreatening male companion. Children liked David – he was the favorite uncle they never had.

Man, Griffin should've just killed him when he had the chance.

"Have you replaced Cindy yet?" David asked conversationally. "Or is no other woman good enough? I imagine it can't be that easy to find another soul mate."

"Shut the fuck up," Fitz snarled.

"Tell us about Sylvia Blaire," Griffin said. He pulled out a chair but didn't take a seat.

David cocked his head to the side. He wasn't ready for business yet. Griffin hadn't thought that he would be. "I miss having dinners at your house, you know. I used to love watching the two of you together. Cindy-n-Griffin, Griffin-n-Cindy. Gave me faith that there was something worthwhile in life. I hope someday I get to fall in love like that, too."

"What's his name?"

"Hey now, Griff, that's sorta rude, don't you think?"

"I want the name of the man who raped and murdered Sylvia Blaire." Griffin placed his hands on the table and leaned forward pointedly.

David merely smiled again and held up his shackled hands. "Hey now, no need to get physical, Griff. I'm quite helpless. Can't you see?" Another one of those goddamn sugary smiles.

Griffin's voice rose in spite of himself. "Give me the name."

Instead, David looked at Fitz. "You don't look the type

to bail a guy out," he said matter-of-factly. "Now Mike Waters, he was a guy. Leapt forward and took the hit, so to speak. And your buddy Griff here, he can pack a punch. Have you ever seen the pictures of Mike's face?" The kid let out a low whistle. "You would've thought he'd gone ten rounds with Tyson. I imagine he got some first-rate plastic surgery when all was said and done, and probably at tax-payer expense. You might want to bear that in mind, Mr. Providence Detective. You look like you could use a little plastic surgery, or at least some liposuction here and there. And there and here. Say, I don't suppose french fries are your favorite food or anything?"

"Give us the fucking name," Fitz snarled.

David sighed. Blatant hostility had always bored him. He returned to Griffin. "I thought you'd at least write."

"You're going to tell us what you know," Griffin said quietly. "We both know that you will. Otherwise, you can't have any fun."

"Did you get my letters?"

Griffin shut up. He should've done this sooner. For David to play his game, he had to have input. Take away your participation, and there was nothing left for him to manipulate. No more happy reindeer games. No more jolly schoolboy fun.

"It's not so bad in here, you know," David said, switch-ing strategies. "Food's actually pretty good. I gather the fuckers in charge have figured out it's best to make sure the animals in the zoo are well fed. Keeps us from sharpening our fangs on one another – or maybe on them. I'm learning inner peace through quality time in a lotus position, and wouldn't you know it, I have a natural gift for carpentry. I know, I'll make you a table, Griff. Carve your initials in the base. For old times' sake. Come on, any size."

Fitz opened his mouth. Griffin shot him a look, and the detective frowned but fell silent.

"Ooooh, just like a trained seal," David said. He was smiling joyfully, all smooth round cheeks and big brown eyes. Back with his favorite kind of audience, he was happy.

He was horrible. Jesus Christ, he looked like he was barely sixteen.

"Who raped and murdered Sylvia Blaire?" Griffin said quietly.

"Eddie Como."

"How did you meet?"

"Griff, buddy, I never met Eddie. That's what I keep saying. It's his roommate, Jimmy Woods. We've spent some time together here in good ol' Max."

"I'm not interested in your patsy, David. I want to know about the real College Hill Rapist. Tell me, which one of you thought of the douche?"

For the first time, Price faltered. He disguised it well, recovering swiftly and smiling again. On his lap, however, his fingers were beginning to fidget with his shackles. "You like this case, don't you, Griffin? It's complicated. Clever. You always appreciated that. Which one of the three women do you think hired Eddie Como's assassin? Or was it a member of their families? Personally, I got my money on the cold one. What's her name? Oh yeah, Jillian Hayes."

"David, you have ten seconds to say something useful, or we're all walking out that door. Ten, nine, eight, seven, six – "

"I know who the real College Hill Rapist is."

Griffin shrugged. "I don't believe you. Five, four, three – "

"Hey, hey, hey, don't be too hasty, man. Haven't all those months of therapy taught you anything? Slow it down. Take it easy. It wasn't my idea to yank your chain. He came to me."

Griffin finally paused. "The College Hill Rapist came to *you*?"

"Yeah. Sure."

Griffin already knew he was lying. "Why?"

"I don't know. Maybe he heard about my rep. Maybe he just desired a decent conversationalist. I can't read some guy's fucking mind. But he came to me, and we, uh, we talked about a few things."

"How to commit a crime?"

"We both had an interest."

"How to fuck with the police."

David Price smiled. "Oh yeah. We both had an interest."

"Congratulations, Price," Fitz spoke up. "You just became an accessory to multiple rapes and murders. Now you're going to have to keep talking just to save your dumb-ass hide."

David shot the detective a look of disdain. "Save my ass from what? The life in prison I'm already serving? Hey, buddy, haven't you heard about me? I'm the guy who befriends little kids on the playground. I hand them some candy, I push them on the swings. And then I take them home, down into my soundproofed basement, where I strip off their cute little clothes and – "

"You still haven't said anything new yet," Griffin said. "Three, two, one – "

"He puts Como's little swimmers into each douche."

"Fuck it, David. *I* told you that."

"It was my idea," David said seriously. "That DNA is troubling stuff. Hell, that's why I had to bury my pretty treats. Let decomposition do its nasty work. And then it occurred to me. DNA so likes to be up there in those deep, dark places . . . Why not let it have its way, man? Why not go with the flow? Don't hide DNA, own it. Man, bring it to the fucking game."

Griffin stood up. "Thanks for repeating my own theory back to me. You're a shithead, David. Always have been. Always will be."

Griffin headed for the door. And behind him, David Price said, "He knew Eddie Como. Eddie probably didn't know him. But he met the great Eddie Como. Met him one afternoon, probably for no more than ten minutes, just enough time for poor dumb Eddie to mention that he worked for the blood center. After that, my friend, his fate was sealed. The College Hill Rapist had his man."

Griffin turned slowly. "He stalked Eddie Como?"

"He did his homework."

313

"And what, stole old condoms out of Eddie's trash can?"

David had that sly look back on his face. "I won't answer that. But it is the key question, isn't it? How do you steal a man's mambo jambo? It's not like we lose track of it."

"I don't believe you."

"What's so hard to believe, Griff? That I'd help someone attack young college coeds? Or that you still can't do a thing to stop us? You got a serial rapist on the loose, Detective Sergeant Roan Griffin. Someone who looks like Eddie Como, sounds like Eddie Como and tests as Eddie Como. In other words, you have absolutely no fucking idea who he really is. So *you* sit down. And *you* listen up. Because I do know his goddamn name, and you're going to give me something for it. You're going to give me whatever I want, or you'll get to see my face on the five o'clock news, telling the frightened public how some overpumped, overranked state trooper is willfully disregarding critical evidence which could stop the bastard murdering their precious daughters. Now how do you like that?"

Griffin came forward. Then he took another step, and another step. Breathe deep, part of his mind said. The rest of him didn't give a flying fuck. His hands were fisted, his muscles were tensed and his face was mean. He should've killed David that day. He should've pounded his own friends into the ground, just so he could've gotten to David and ripped off his too-cute, too-smart, lying head.

"You're not getting out," he said harshly. "No matter what you say, you're not getting out."

"College coeds are dying – "

"Ten kids are dead!"

"I can guarantee you a new body by tonight. Count on it."

"And I can guarantee you a transfer to Super Max. No more carpentry classes, yoga or cafeteria hours. Just the rest of your life, rotting alone in a six-by-eight cell."

"Do you want to punish me, Detective Sergeant, or do you want to stop the man preying on pretty brunettes? Think carefully before you answer. The parents of all the

College Hill Rapist's future victims breathlessly await your reply."

"You little fucker – " Fitz snarled.

Impatiently, David cut him off. "Six o'clock," he said crisply, eyes on Griffin's face. "Standard hardship leave for three hours. I get to have street clothes, you get to put me in shackles. I get to go into the outside world, you get to supervise. That's the deal."

"No."

"Oh yes. Or I go straight to the press and tell them that the same detective who tried to break my face eighteen months ago, now won't protect their precious little girls out of spite. Think about it, man. You don't deal with me, and another girl dies. You don't deal with me, and the public will eat you for dinner." David glanced at the overhead clock. "It's ten A.M. now. You have until noon to decide."

"We don't make deals with pedophiles."

"Sure you do. You make deals with whoever has the fucking information. Now ask the question, Griff. Come on, man. Ask me what you really need to know." David leaned forward. He stared up at Griffin with that wide beaming smile, that round choirboy face.

"You didn't hurt her," Griffin said abruptly.

David Price blinked.

"You like to think you did. But you didn't. Cindy was better than you, David. Let's face it. She was better than me."

"Ask the goddamn question!" David barked.

"Why do you want a three-hour leave, you little psychopathic shit?"

David finally sat back. For the first time since the interview started, he appeared satisfied. He glanced at Fitz, he glanced at Charpentier and then he looked at Griffin. "I want to see my daughter. No prison suits, no interview rooms. Just her and I, face-to-face. It's probably the only time I'm ever going to see her, so I want it to be good. Let's face it, man, her grandparents are never bringing her here."

"Her grandparents?"

315

"Tom and Laurie Pesaturo. Or didn't Meg tell you? Molly Pesaturo is my kid. See, I didn't kill all the little girls, Griff. Some I let breed."

Five minutes later, Griffin, Fitz and Charpentier were back in the parking lot. They were all taking in huge lungfuls of crisp, outside air. Later, they would shower until their skin was raw.

"He doesn't get out," Griffin said flatly. "Not at six P.M., not at any time, not for three hours, not for any hours. The man doesn't get out, period!"

Griffin's arms were moving on their own volition, his left leg twitching, ears ringing. Yeah, ringing, ringing, ringing. Fuck it all, he might as well go crackers. Insanity was probably what it took to deal with the likes of David Price. He turned on Charpentier.

"I want lists, lots of lists. Names of anyone who visited, wrote, called David Price. Names of all the inmates who could've come into contact with David in any way, shape or form. Names of all known friends, families and associates of said inmates, especially those with a criminal past. And then I want a list of which of those inmates have recently been released. Got it?"

"It's going to take some time," Charpentier said grimly.

"You have two hours. Commandeer whatever resources you need."

Charpentier nodded. He got into his car and headed for his dank basement office. That left Griffin and Fitz alone in the parking lot.

"He doesn't get out," Griffin said again.

"We'll work on it."

"He doesn't get out!"

"Then find the fucking rapist!"

"Then I fucking will!" Griffin thumped the top of his Ford Taurus. Fitz pounded it right back.

Griffin yanked open the driver's-side door. "He's got a plan."

"No shit."

"He's thought of this. Set it all in motion. Don't be deceived by those peach-fuzz cheeks. He doesn't give a rat's ass about his daughter. He has something else in mind."

"You think?"

"He doesn't get out," Griffin said again. "Not now, not ever." But as they pulled out of the maximum-security parking lot, they both saw the white Channel 10 news van roll in.

32

Molly

Fitz drove. Griffin worked the phone. He dialed Waters first.

"Here's the deal. David Price is claiming he knows who the real College Hill Rapist is, and he'll give us that information in return for a personal visit with his long-lost daughter, Molly Pesaturo. We have two hours to decide."

"Huh?"

"No kidding. Look, are you still in Cranston?"

"Trolling the bars as we speak."

"Perfect. Get a picture of Tawnya Clemente. Fuck Eddie Como. Start shopping her picture around."

"Tawnya's picture? You think the loyal girlfriend is in on this?"

"Half of everything David says is a lie, but he's right about one thing: Eddie Como was innocent. The real College Hill Rapist set him up, used him as a patsy to commit the perfect serial crime. Now, to do that, the real rapist had to get Eddie's semen from somewhere. Tawnya's the logical place to start."

"She conspired against the father of her child?"

"Fifty-million-dollar lawsuit, Mike. Think about it. All she has to do is sacrifice one guy. Then she – and Eddie, Jr. – never have to worry about anything, ever again."

"Well, when you put it that way . . ." Waters said.

"Yeah. Now, remember, you got two hours. Have fun!"

Griffin hit end, then promptly dialed the next number. Thirty seconds later, he had Sergeant Napoleon on the phone.

"Sergeant! I'm calling on behalf of Detective Fitzpatrick. He'd like you to run a few tests."

"Uh oh," Napoleon said.

Griffin pretended he hadn't heard him. "Detective Fitzpatrick has brilliantly deduced the source of the Eddie Como DNA. He believes Como's semen was injected into the rape victims via the douche. What do you think?"

There was a moment of silence. Fitz was rolling his eyes at the thick praise. Then Napoleon said, "Well, shit on a stick. That makes some sense."

"It could be done?"

"Sure. You inject the semen into the douche, give the douche a little shake, then expel the contents into the body cavities. The resulting linen stains, vaginal swabs, etc., would test the same as if the douche was being used to flush the semen out. Of course, that assumes the rapist did use a condom, otherwise we'd pick up a second DNA sample as well."

"Yeah, I'm pretty sure he used a condom. You still have the douche bags in evidence?"

"Well, you know us Providence detectives. Every now and then we do practice proper evidence handling and storage."

"Really? Huh. Well, so much for that rumor. Okay, so you could test the inside contents of the bag, right? If there's a DNA sample *inside* the douche, then definitely . . ."

"Oh yeah. I'll look into it. For Detective *Fitz*, of course."

"One last question. You said the semen sample would have to be fresh for it to test positive for spermatozoa. What about if it had been frozen?"

"You mean frozen at time of ejaculation, then thawed at time of use?"

"Okay."

"Sure," Napoleon answered promptly. "As long as the semen sample was frozen within seventy-two hours, the spermatozoa would be preserved until thawed again. Sperm banks do it all the time." Then Napoleon got the full implication. "Ooooh," he said. "How interesting. And the dead come back to life."

"And the dead come back to life," Griffin agreed blackly. Then muttered, "Even from beyond the grave . . . Thanks, Sergeant. Fitz'll be in touch."

He flipped shut his phone just in time for Fitz to say, "We're in Cranston. Meg or Tawnya? Who do you want to hit first?"

"Meg," Griffin said immediately. "I want to give Detective Waters time to complete his inquiry into Tawnya's social life. With any luck, he'll provide the ammo, then we'll go in for the kill."

Fitz glanced over at him somberly. "Have I told you lately that I love you?"

"No. But just for that, I'll let you go after her first."

"Ah, I just love this job!"

"Come two hours, remember that, Fitz. Remember that."

Griffin and Fitz pulled in front of the Pesaturo house shortly before 10.30. Already down to an hour and a half and they'd barely made progress. Why, then, Griffin thought, was he surprised to knock on the Pesaturos' door and have Jillian Hayes answer it.

"Sergeant," she started.

He didn't give her time to finish. He shouldered past her and stormed down the tiny hall toward the back family room as Fitz followed suit. "I want to speak with Meg. Now!"

"She's not here," Jillian called out behind them, scrambling to catch up.

"Where is she?"

Griffin burst into the family room. Meg's parents, Tom and Laurie, were sitting side by side on the sofa. Tom appeared sullen, Laurie had her arms wrapped protectively around Molly and had obviously been crying. Sitting opposite them were Toppi and Libby Hayes. One big happy family. Christ, just what he and Fitz needed.

He whirled on Jillian, who was apparently the only speaking member of the party. "Where is Meg?" he demanded again.

"We don't know."

"You *lost* her?"

"She . . . We don't know."

Griffin thought of a word, remembered that Molly was in the room, and bit it back. He homed in on the Pesaturos, jerking his head at their *granddaughter*. "Get her out of the room."

"I don't really think – " Laurie started vaguely.

"Get her out of the room!"

"I'll do it." Toppi stood, crossing over to take Molly's hand, but not before giving Griffin a reproachful look. He glared right back at her. No more friendly Sergeant Griffin. Friendly Sergeant Griffin had gotten royally screwed. Now it was time to put the fear of God into these folks.

"You," he gestured at Jillian, who had her chin up and her feet planted for battle. "If you want to remain in this room – "

"I am a guest of the Pesaturos. They asked me to come here – "

"*If* you want to remain in this room – "

"Probably because they knew you were going to be pig-headed and hostile about this."

"I will arrest you for obstruction of justice."

She snorted. "Oh get over it. We're all worried about Meg."

"Jillian, sit down and shut up. The Pesaturos have some talking to do, and unless you're their attorney, I don't want to hear a single peep out of you."

Jillian gave him a look. But after another moment, she crossed stiffly to the wingback chair next to her mother. She sat down. She seemed to shut up. Just in time for Libby Hayes to stick out her tongue at him. Oh for heaven's sake . . .

"You." Griffin stabbed his finger at Tom, because he couldn't keep yelling while looking at Laurie Pesaturo's tear-stained face. "Start talking."

"It was a long time ago. We didn't think it was relevant – "

"Your daughter had a relationship with a known

pedophile, and you didn't think it was *relevant?*"

"The man's behind bars!"

"No thanks to you, and not in another few hours!"

Tom fell silent. All at once, his massive shoulders slumped. He appeared miserable. "I swear to God, Sergeant, we didn't know. We never dreamed of a connection until you called . . . Oh God, Meg . . ."

Griffin and Fitz gave him a moment. Griffin needed to count to ten anyway. So much ringing in his ears. He knew if he looked down now, his hands would be shaking. If he tried to sit, his knee would jog up and down with a mind of its own. Reel it in, reel it in. Whatever these people had done, they were suffering for it now. And he needed to play it cool a little longer.

"Maybe if you started from the beginning," Jillian spoke up quietly. She had obviously been briefed on the situation, and she was gazing at Tom and Laurie compassionately. Griffin resented that. He didn't know why, but he did.

"Meg was only thirteen," Laurie murmured. "We had no idea. None at all. Not until I found her one day, curled up weeping on the bathroom floor. She'd just taken a pregnancy test and it was positive. We didn't even know she was dating."

"How did Meg meet Price?" Fitz asked. Griffin turned toward Tom, though he already knew the answer. His former next-door neighbor, the electrician . . .

"Work," Tom said predictably. "We were on the same job, wiring a new CVS. He was such a nice kid. I remember thinking that. What a nice kid. Did good work, too. And he mentioned one day that he didn't have any family. Parents were dead, I don't remember why. And I felt kinda bad for him. He couldn't have been more than twenty-four, twenty-five. So I started inviting him over for dinner."

"He was always so polite," Laurie murmured. She couldn't seem to get over that. "Please, thank you, yes ma'am. Even helped with the dishes." She finally looked up. "I knew Meg had a crush on him. He was a nice-looking young man and of course at thirteen, she was beginning to notice that sort of thing. But I thought of it as a schoolgirl's crush. The kind you have on your father's hired hand, or the bag boy at the grocery store. She was still so young. I never imagined . . ."

"You never saw them together?" Fitz again.

Both shook their heads. "Never," Tom said. "She snuck out at night. I didn't even know she'd think of doing such a thing. I'm sure he must've suggested it to her. I'm telling you, she'd never been a problem. She was a good girl, got good grades. Oh Meg . . ."

"So you found out she was pregnant," Griffin fast-forwarded. "She tell you he was the father?"

"She was upset," Laurie said. "She told us everything."

"Did you confront him?"

Tom made a small, uncomfortable motion that led Griffin to understand there had been a confrontation, but it hadn't involved much talking. Tom's fists and David's face, however, had spent some quality time together. Griffin understood completely.

"If Meg was only thirteen," Fitz said, "that's statutory rape. Why didn't you file a report? Get the kid arrested?"

Tom and Laurie exchanged miserable glances. "We were embarrassed," Laurie said softly. "Meg was humiliated – and frightened and confused and heartbroken. She seemed to think she really loved him. According to her, he'd even proposed marriage. We just . . ." She took a deep breath, got herself together. "It all seemed a horrible mistake. We hadn't been paying enough attention. Meg didn't show good judgment. Going to the police would just bring it all out in the open and make things worse. You have to understand, we didn't know David had done this kind of thing before, or have the wildest idea what he'd go on to do next. Seducing a thirteen-year-old girl isn't right, but still . . . We never would've guessed." She looked at Griffin earnestly. "Please, you have to believe us. We never would've guessed."

"You covered it up," Griffin said bluntly, harshly. She wanted forgiveness from him? What about the ten other families David had victimized?

"I have relatives," Laurie whispered. "Upstate New York. We sent her there for the duration. I started telling people I was pregnant. And then, when the time came, I, we, had a beautiful baby girl. We love her, Sergeant." She looked up earnestly. "The circumstances were horrible, but Molly is perfect. I have been proud to have her as my daughter, and we've been saying that for so long, as far as I'm concerned, she *is* my daughter. And I will do anything in my power to protect her."

"He wants to see her," Griffin said.

"No!"

"Price has information on the College Hill Rapist. In fact, we're coming to believe that he helped create the College Hill Rapist, and set this whole thing in motion – "

"Eddie Como is dead," Jillian said firmly from across the room.

Griffin pivoted and glared at her. "Yeah, but he's not who raped and murdered your sister."

There was silence. Even Libby's hands were perfectly still on her picture book. How to absorb, what to say? Griffin and Fitz had had more time with the thought than the others, and they were still reeling themselves.

Fitz finally spoke up, "We, uh, we got DNA results back from Sylvia Blaire. They match Eddie's."

"What?" Jillian again, her face still pale, her voice bewildered. "But that's impossible!"

"We're working on the assumption that Eddie's DNA was introduced as a red herring at the rape scenes. The douches were not being used to wash semen out, but to inject semen into the body cavity." Fitz paused for a moment. He said out loud, without seeming to realize it, "Well, that would explain why Eddie was so willing to give a DNA sample. Poor bastard honestly thought he hadn't done it."

"But the notes," Jillian insisted. "All those phone calls and letters . . . He harassed us!"

"Claiming his innocence," Griffin said. "Wouldn't you,

if you were behind bars for a series of crimes you knew you didn't commit?"

Her mouth worked. "But that tape!" she said finally, firmly. "The tape he sent me on Friday. *That* was threatening. And the letter to Carol's house. All that, 'I'll get you from beyond the grave.' What was that all about?"

"Do you know they came from Eddie?"

"I . . . well . . ." She frowned. "The tape that contained his picture."

"A video file, right? Of a man whose image has been broadcast all over TV for nearly twelve months." Griffin looked at her. She closed her eyes.

"It could be faked," she whispered.

"Part of the setup. In the interesting-but-true department, the first time you mentioned the tape, I thought immediately of David Price. It sounded like something he would do."

"Oh my God!" Jillian covered her mouth with her hand. "Poor Eddie Como. Oh that poor man . . ."

"I don't understand," Tom Pesaturo spoke up. "You're saying this was all done by some other guy?"

"It's the theory of the day."

"Well, who the hell is he?"

"If we knew that, Mr. Pesaturo, we wouldn't be here right now."

"But David Price is helping this guy?"

"It would appear that way."

"Why?"

"To get out of prison, Mr. Pesaturo. To return to the real world where he can rape and murder small children. Why do you think?"

"No!" Laurie's voice shot up. Her face was wild. "You can't let him. You can't let him out."

Griffin just shrugged. "He says it's the only way. We have a sexual-sadist predator running around who for all intents and purposes *is* Eddie Como. We don't have prints, we don't have DNA, we don't even have a description. And according to David Price, the real College Hill Rapist will kill another girl by tonight unless we let David have a three-hour hardship leave to visit your granddaughter."

Griffin turned abruptly on Tom. "For God's sake, Mr. Pesaturo, why didn't you and Vinnie kill the little prick when you had the chance? He impregnated your thirteen-year-old daughter. That wasn't enough for you?"

"We didn't know." Tom was positively moaning. "And Meg was so confused, believing that she really loved him, I worried about what it would do to her if he suddenly disappeared. Then after his arrest . . . when we all learned what he was really like . . . Meg locked herself in her room and cried until she was sick. Couldn't eat, couldn't sleep, had horrible nightmares. We just wanted to get her through. So we vowed never to mention his name again. We would pretend it had never happened. David was going away after all. The papers said he'd never get out, never see the light of day . . ."

"We started lying," Laurie murmured. "And in our lie, there was no David Price. There was just Molly, our new daughter. Everything was so nice that way. So much easier to believe."

"Well, welcome back to the real world, Mrs. Pesaturo. Where there is a monster named David Price. And he probably is working hand in hand with a serial rapist. Why do you think Meg was the College Hill Rapist's *first* victim?"

Tom moaned again. "David wanted revenge. After what *he* did to Meg, he wanted revenge . . ."

"Yeah, Mr. Pesaturo. And knowing Price, he's just getting started."

33
Jillian

Sergeant Griffin and Detective Fitz went upstairs to look through Meg's room for any hint of where she might have gone, while Tom and Laurie remained sitting in the family room, their bodies drained, their faces shell-shocked.

"It's going to be all right," Jillian said firmly. "The police are starting to make genuine progress now. It's going to be all right."

"Meg," Laurie whispered.

"We'll find her. She probably just ran out to do some errands, maybe grab some lunch." But that didn't sound like Meg, and Jillian knew it. Conscientious Meg always told her parents where she was going. Cautious Meg never spent much time out alone.

"He can't see Molly," Tom muttered. "Can't. Just . . . can't."

"It's going to be all right," Jillian repeated. "Everything will work out fine." She turned to her mother. "Mom, maybe you can show Tom some more pictures from your singing days. I need to go upstairs and talk to Sergeant Griffin."

Her mother tapped her left finger somberly, a soldier accepting her mission. The look on her face made Jillian's heart tighten in her chest. She gave Libby's hand a quick, reassuring squeeze. Funny how in the last twenty-four hours, Jillian felt that she had finally taken the first step forward with her life. Funny how in the last twenty-four hours, it would appear that Griffin had taken at least three steps back.

There was an air about him now. A crackle of barely concealed anger. If he stood in front of a punching bag, she thought, he would easily tear it to shreds. And then he would stomp on the torn, tortured bits while the tendons corded in his neck and the menace in him grew and grew and grew.

He'd said he'd tried to kill David Price the day of his arrest. Two fellow detectives had gotten in Griffin's way. Seeing his fury now, she wondered how they could've been so brave. And she wondered what those two men had looked like five minutes after the encounter.

She squared her shoulders and headed up the stairs.

She heard Detective Fitz's voice first. He was down the hall, apparently asking Toppi some questions in Molly's room. Jillian bypassed that door and headed to Meg's bedroom, where she found Griffin standing in front of Meg's small, white-painted desk. His powerful shoulders filled the window, blocking the light.

In spite of herself, Jillian couldn't take another step forward. She remained in the doorway, where she cleared her throat.

He turned slowly, Meg's calendar held between his hands. "This is an official police investigation, ma'am. Get out of the room."

"I'm not in the room."

"Jillian," he growled.

"Griffin," she replied, and now she did step forward. She came right up to him, where she could see that his hands were shaking, his blue eyes had turned jet black and his jaw was set so tight, he had to be grinding his teeth.

"They were just trying to protect their family," she told him quietly. "Laurie and Tom, they never meant anyone any harm."

"Tell that to the ten other families. The mothers and fathers who had to file through the morgue, looking at videotape because the real remains of their children were too gruesome for even seasoned professionals to see. Tell that to the detectives who went through peer counseling just to get those images out of their head."

"They didn't know, Griffin. Nobody knew. Isn't that why you're so angry? Because their mistake reminds you of your own, and that just pisses you off all over again."

He literally snarled. She had never seen a human being do that before. He snarled at her, raw and savage, and in the depths of his rage, she also saw his pain. It gave her the courage to raise her hand and place it gently on his chest.

"It's different this time. It's going to be okay."

"How do you know? You've never met Price. You don't know just how much he enjoys a good game. And that's all this is to him: a game. Another way to pass the time until he gets his ass out of jail. Which I think he's going to do shortly after six this evening if I don't magically figure everything out."

Jillian didn't say anything.

"What do you know, anyway?" His tone picked up in hostility. "You and your little Survivors Club. What a joke that name turned out to be. It's the Liars Club, that's what it is. Each one of you hoarding your precious little secrets, and in the meantime real people are out there dying. Real people are getting hurt because you women won't tell the police everything."

She still didn't speak.

"What do you even know about Meg, anyway?" he went on relentlessly. "According to her own parents she once considered herself in love with a man who's a convicted serial killer. How do you know she isn't *still* in love? Ever think of that? Her rape was the least traumatic. Hardly a bruise on her. You always considered her lucky, but maybe she was simply in cahoots with Price all along. Her rape was staged, her amnesia is staged. She's part of Price's game, too, and right now, she's off doing things to help good old lover boy."

"No."

"No? You're sure? Absolutely, positively sure?"

"Yes."

"Why, Jillian, you suddenly have that much faith?"

And she replied firmly, "I do."

He closed his eyes. "Goddammit," he muttered hoarsely.

"I know," she whispered. "I know. She needs you, Griffin. I don't know where Meg is. But she's not helping David Price. She's not in cahoots with the College Hill Rapist. She's a young girl who's already had two very bad breaks in life, first being seduced by a pedophile, then being attacked by a sexual predator. And maybe her rape was the least violent, but the police have said all along that's not uncommon for the first attack. The College Hill Rapist used her as a trial run, and unfortunately for all of us, it went so well, he unfettered his anger even more. Also, based on what her parents just said, her total amnesia finally makes some sense. How is she supposed to remember the truth when her life doesn't have any? Her sister's really her daughter, her first love is a perverted killer, and her parents are also grandparents. For God's sake, I can't even keep that all straight."

He opened his eyes, peered at her curiously. "You care for her that much, Jillian?"

"Yes," she answered honestly. "I do."

He stepped away, placed the calendar back on the desk, and seemed to stare at the clean surface without seeing much. Was he thinking of David Price again? Except further back, to the days they had once been friends? It sounded as if he had genuinely liked David Price once. Maybe he had believed in him, too.

"How is Carol?" he asked abruptly.

"The doctors took her off the respirator this morning. Apparently that's a positive sign her body is starting to recover. Of course, no one will know how much she will recover until we see how much she has recovered."

"Has she regained consciousness?"

"No."

"Dan?"

"They say he hasn't left her side."

"Probably can't," Griffin muttered. "Minute he leaves the hospital, some of Vinnie's boys are due to break his legs."

"I had a conversation with Vinnie about that."

He looked at her in surprise. "Trying to save the world, Jillian?"

"I protect what's mine," she said evenly. "Though I have it from good sources that I can't protect everyone all of the time. I've decided, however, that it's still good to try. Besides, Libby asked me to."

"You bailed Dan out? Paid his debts at your mother's request?"

"No. I convinced Uncle Vinnie that my mother would consider it a huge favor if he forgave the rest of Dan's debt. Then she smiled at him, and that took care of that. Then I told him *I* would consider it a huge favor if he arranged it so Dan could never borrow money again. Vinnie thought that was cruel, so naturally he liked the idea." She hesitated. "Griffin . . ."

He looked at her.

She took a deep breath. "I know no one wants to say it, but what if . . . What if negotiating with David Price is the best idea?"

"No way!"

"Please! Hear me out. You said yourself he knows the College Hill Rapist's real identity. Are you sure of that?"

"The man is a natural-born liar and a natural-born predator. So, no, I'm not sure of anything."

"But you're taking his allegations seriously."

"He knew about the DNA," Griffin said curtly. "He knew when we got the DNA analysis back on Sylvia Blaire it would point to Eddie Como. Plus there's Meg. It's too much of a coincidence that the rapist's first victim would also be Price's first conquest. And there's me, of course, the detective who put David Price away, and who is now leading the supposed College Hill Rapist homicide investigation. Well, shit!" Griffin's eyes widened. "Of course, an assassination at the state courthouse. Hey, good news everybody, three days later, I finally know why poor Eddie Como is dead."

"Why?"

"To bring me in on the case, of course. Because if Como dies *at* the courthouse, it's automatically state police jurisdiction." Griffin smiled bitterly. "Leave it to David to send only the bloodiest invite to his party."

Jillian closed her eyes. Oh God, she had never heard of a man as evil as David Price. It pained her, then, to say what she had to say next. She opened her eyes. She peered at Griffin intently, trying to get him to see the truth, even if it hurt. "So David Price must be involved. And if he does know the name of the College Hill Rapist . . . Griffin, I know you don't want to deal with him. I know *I* would give anything to keep such a man away from Molly. But as you said, real people are dying out there. And if you're not any closer to knowing the real identity of the College Hill Rapist . . . David only wants three hours," she whispered. "Surely saving even one life is worth giving David Price three supervised hours on the outside. Won't you at least consider it?"

Griffin's hard-lined face was no longer mottled red. Instead, his expression went dangerously cold.

"The press is going to agree with you," he said softly. Menacingly.

"The press is not always wrong."

"And the public will call the mayor, and the mayor will call the governor and the governor will call my superintendent, and David Price will get his way."

"But you'll get the College Hill Rapist!"

"Do you really think so, Jillian? How will we know if the name Price gives us is the right one? How will we know it's not another patsy? And even if it is the right man, how will we build the case? We have no prints, no hair, no fiber, no DNA. We could arrest him today, only to let him go tomorrow."

"D'Amato is good. He'll come up with some sort of charge to buy you time. You can put things together. It worked before."

"When Providence arrested an innocent man?"

She lost some of her composure. Poor Eddie Como. The true impact of his innocence hadn't sunk in yet. She wasn't ready for it to sink in. She tried again. "At least an arrest will start the ball rolling."

"Price has offered us nothing," Griffin argued quietly. "It's what he does best. He gives you ashes, but makes it sound like prime rib. Face it, he's the perfect criminal for this day and age – sound-bite ready for network news and cable TV."

"Griffin, all those girls, those poor, poor girls . . ."

Griffin was silent. She thought maybe she'd finally gotten through to him, and then he started to speak.

"I'm going to tell you something, Jillian. Something very few people know. I'm going to tell you, and then I don't want you to mention it ever again. Do you agree?"

Jillian got a chill. She had a feeling she should say no. She had a feeling this is how it felt to make a deal with the devil. She nodded helplessly.

"Eighteen months ago, when we arrested David Price, I went down into the basement of his home. I saw ten tiny mounds where he buried his victims beneath the dirt floor. I saw the mattress where he raped them and I saw the paraphernalia he used to torture them. But I still didn't attack him. I called CIU to process the scene. I ordered him put into handcuffs, and I got on with the business at hand. This was a big arrest in a big case. We were all taking it very seriously."

Griffin's eyes were locked on hers. "Price started talking. Making conversation really, as he stood there cuffed between Detectives Waters and O'Reilly. How he met the kids, how he kidnapped the kids, what he did to them. It was hard. We were professionals, but what he said, and so calmly, too, it wore on you. But it was also incriminating, a bona fide confession, so we let him talk while Waters started recording him. And then, then Price switched topics. He stopped talking about the kids. He started talking about Cindy."

Griffin paused. Jillian simply stared at him. She had the horrible thought she was going to wish she had never heard what he had to say next.

"In the last two weeks of Cindy's life," Griffin said quietly, "it was obvious she wasn't going to make it. The cancer had eaten her from the inside out. She couldn't walk, couldn't sit up, couldn't even raise her hand. I brought her home as we'd agreed, set her up in a special bed in the family room, and got a hospice worker to come over and help out. Cindy could still blink her eyes, and that's how we would talk. I would ask her questions and she would blink once for yes and twice for no. Much like your mother. I, uh" – he swallowed, his voice finally growing husky – "I used to ask her if she loved me, at least ninety times a day, just so I could see her blink. Just so I would know she was still that much alive. I was working the damn Candy Man case, of course. I could make a lot of the phone calls from home, process the paperwork . . . But sometimes I'd have to go out, and sometimes the hospice worker also needed a break, and sometimes, sometimes David would come over.

"That's right." He nodded. "Our good friend and helpful neighbor, 'we're going to beat this thing' David Price, would come over and sit with Cindy. As the saying goes, it seemed like a good idea at the time.

"But now we're down in the basement, with that mattress and that workbench and those dark, tiny waves. Now we're down in the basement and David is telling me exactly what he did those afternoons he sat with Cindy. Exactly what he did to my wife."

Griffin saw the look on her face and immediately shook his head. "No, nothing like that, Jillian. Cindy was a grown woman and David's into little kids. She provided something even better for him. An audience. Yeah, a fucking audience. For over a year, see, Price has been involved in this incredible crime spree, kidnapping and murdering small children. And no one suspects a thing. Which means he has no one to talk to, no one to brag to. That kind of thing only gets you in trouble anyway, and David knows it. But now, here's Cindy. Helpless, dying, unable to speak a word. So he goes over there and tells her everything. Every tiny, terrible detail of how he finds the kids and stalks the kids and abducts the kids and hurts the kids and strangles the kids and buries the kids in his basement. On and on and on, an unending litany of depravity. And Cindy can't escape. Cindy can't repeat a word.

"You have to wonder how she must have felt, David told me, as she watched me greet him so gratefully each time I returned home. You have to wonder how desperate she must have been, he said, for me to see something in her face, or in his face. If I would just ask the right question . . . My smart, brilliant wife, he mused, knowing all about his horrible crimes, and unable to do a thing to stop them. My compassionate, gentle-hearted wife, he postulated, dying with all those murdered children on her conscience. And all the while, her husband never suspected a thing. All the while, her husband was so grateful to have David come visit . . .

"That's when I broke, started swinging my fists. I don't remember much of it after that, honestly. They tell me Waters and O'Reilly got in my way. And they tell me that David Price never stopped smiling.

"That's the kind of man we're dealing with, Jillian. He makes friends purely so he has people to betray. He seeks out children purely to have life-forms to destroy. And he is very smart, in an ingratiating, awful sort of way. He is brilliant."

Griffin bent over the desk. He picked up the plain desk pad, and from beneath it, a piece of paper fluttered to the floor. It landed by Jillian's feet, so she picked it up first. It was a page from a notepad, and written all over it in Meg's large, round script were the words: *David Price, David Price, David Price. Oh no, David Price.*

"Well," Griffin said after a moment. "Apparently Meg has finally started to remember."

Five minutes later, Griffin and Fitz were striding out of the house, their faces carefully shuttered, but the line of their mouths grim. Tom and Laurie remained inside. They couldn't seem to move, couldn't seem to digest this new, dreadful turn of events.

Jillian was the one who followed the two detectives to their car, watched them climb in, slam the doors.

At the last minute, she knocked on the driver's-side window. Griffin lowered the glass.

"Were you with your wife the day she died?" she asked him.

"Of course."

"Did you ask her if she loved you? What did she say?"

Griffin's voice softened. "She blinked yes."

Jillian nodded, stepped back. "Remember that, Griffin. If David Price does get leave from prison, if you do catch up with him, remember that. He didn't win. You did."

Griffin finally nodded. Then his window was back up, the car in gear. He and Fitz peeled away from the curb and hit the road.

34
Meg

Griffin and Fitz had made it only four blocks from the Pesaturo home when Fitz shouted, "Stop!"

Griffin obligingly slammed on the brakes, and Fitz obligingly hit the dash. "Ow, shit, Jesus, over there!" Griffin followed the detective's pointing finger to a mini-mart on their right. Three cars were gassing up at the pumps. Fitz, however, was fixed on a small brown Nissan parked in front of the mini-mart's glass doors. "That," he declared, "is Meg's car. Check out the plates."

MP 63. Griffin swung them into the parking lot.

They circled the car first. It held the usual clutter – Kleenex box, hairbrush, discarded mail, plus a variety of hair scrunchies looped over the parking brake. Griffin noted the expired Providence College parking sticker just as Fitz placed his hand on the car's hood and declared it cold.

The two men exchanged frowns. If the engine had already cooled, the car had been there a bit. They walked into the mini-mart. Two women and a clerk were in the store. The first woman, with graying hair and an oversized navy blue sweatshirt, was deep in consideration at the ice cream case. The second woman, over in the snack aisle, had bright blond hair. Definitely neither one was Meg. Fitz and Griffin exchanged more concerned looks.

They approached the cashier, a pimple-ridden teenager who could've doubled as Teen Blockbuster. Fitz badged him.

"Where's the driver of the Nissan?"

Kid gaped at Fitz's badge, swallowed audibly, gaped at

the badge some more. "Don't know," kid squeaked.

"What do you mean, you don't know?"

"I mean, she's not here. Sir," the kid added belatedly.

"Did you *see* the driver of the brown Nissan?"

"Yes, sir! I mean, she was pretty, sir!"

Okay, that woman sounded like Meg. "Did she come inside, say anything to you?"

"No, sir."

"She didn't come inside?" Fitz glared at the kid.

"No, sir. I mean, I think she was going to, sir. But then her friend pulled up and she went with him."

"Him?" Griffin asked sharply.

The kid flicked a glance at Griffin for the first time, noticed the state detective's imposing size and promptly blanched. "Y-Y-Yes."

Fitz leaned on the counter. Both of the female shoppers had stopped eyeing food by now and were shamelessly eavesdropping on the conversation. Fitz ignored them. He focused his amiable tone on the kid.

"Can you describe exactly what you saw for me? Take your time. Think about it."

The kid took a deep breath. He thought about it. "Well, I saw her get out of her Nissan. And then, well, I looked again 'cause, well, she was *very* pretty."

"What was she wearing?"

"Umm, some kind of brown jacket. Suede, you know, and this big purse swung over her shoulder and jeans, I guess. I don't know. Nothin' special."

"Okay, so she's out of the car with her coat on and her purse over her shoulder. Did she close the car door?"

"Yeah. She did that."

"And then?"

"She took a step forward, like she was coming inside. But then she suddenly stopped and turned. I saw another car pull up and this man get out. He seemed kind of urgent, you know. He ran up to her, said something, then they both got into his car."

"Describe the man," Fitz ordered.

338

"Ummm, not too tall, I guess. Maybe your height. Brown hair. Just . . . a guy, an average guy." The kid shrugged.

Fitz looked at Griffin, who nodded slightly. An average guy. Everyone's favorite description of Eddie Como. Shit.

"Age?" Fitz asked.

"Ummm, older, I guess. I couldn't see him real well from here, but I remember thinking that he was too old for her. I don't know why I thought that."

"Did you see his car?"

"Not from here. It sounded big, though. Big engine. Old. Sputtered when he pulled out. Probably needs new plugs," the kid added helpfully.

Griffin spoke up. "Did he touch the girl?"

The kid's gaze shot toward him, then promptly plummeted to the countertop. "Umm . . ."

"Touch her arm, shoulder, anything?"

"Oh yeah! When he first came up. He put his hand on her arm. And he escorted her to his car, you know. Got the door for her. A girl like her probably has a thing about manners." The kid nodded, then sighed morosely. At his age, he probably understood how life worked, and that guys like him never won a girl like Meg.

"Was he still holding her arm when he got the car door?" Griffin pressed.

"Well, now that you mention it. He had his left hand on her arm, and he got the door with his right."

"He never let go of her?"

"I guess not."

Griffin and Fitz exchanged new glances. This did not sound good. Griffin glanced at his watch. Eleven forty-six A.M. Shit, they were never going to make Price's twelve o'clock deadline.

"What time did she pull up?" Fitz's gaze had followed Griffin's to the watch, and his tone held fresh urgency.

"Oh, a while ago. Wait – a big Suburban had just filled up both tanks. That was a couple of pennies. Let me check the receipts."

The kid opened his register and started slowly turning over pieces of paper. Griffin and Fitz began shifting restlessly. The clock was ticking, ticking, ticking. The kid idly turned over one receipt, said "Huh," then moved methodically to another. Then another. Then another. Just when Griffin thought he couldn't take it anymore, Fitz snapped.

The detective snaked his arm across the counter and grabbed the kid's wrist. "Listen, just estimate. Eight, nine, ten A.M., *what*?"

"Uh." The kid looked down at the detective's whitened knuckles. "Nine A.M., sir!"

"Fine, thanks. You've been great." Fitz was motioning at Griffin furiously. He said to the kid, "A uniform is going to come by shortly to take your statement. I want you to tell him everything you've told us, plus anything more you remember. Can you do that?"

"Um, yes, sir."

"This is important. We appreciate your help. Okay?"

"Okay, sir!"

"Good man. We'll be in touch." Fitz headed out the door, working to catch up with Griffin, who was already on his hands and knees beside Meg's car. Ten seconds later, Griffin spotted a silver flash and fished out a key ring from beneath the vehicle.

He and Fitz stared at the mass of keys, complete with a green plastic parrot from a Jimmy Buffet concert.

"She probably still had them in her hand," Griffin mused. "Then when the guy grabbed her arm . . ." He released his hold, and the keys dropped just about where he'd found them.

"I don't think she met a friend," Fitz said quietly.

"No."

"Why do you think he grabbed her now?"

"Because nobody can crack a case in two hours and David Price knows it." Griffin reached down to recover the keys, then glanced up at Fitz. "Price is betting he's going to get his little hardship leave at six P.M. And when he makes his break for it, he doesn't want to be alone."

"Poor Meg," Fitz murmured. "Poor Molly."

Griffin glanced at his watch. Five minutes before noon. He said, "If David Price gets out of prison, poor all of us. Let's go."

Griffin and Fitz had no sooner gotten back into the car than Griffin's cell phone chirped. It was Waters.

"My two hours are up. Sorry, Griff, I have nothing."

"How many bars?"

"We've hit two dozen and counting. You know, this entire city is nothing but one giant tavern. Several places reported knowing Tawnya, but they mostly recognized her picture from the five o'clock news. One place said she used to come in, but that was before she got pregnant."

"Get more uniforms and keep trying. Someone had to see something."

"Will do."

"Mike . . . Meg Pesaturo is missing. She was last seen being led into a car by a strange man. Whatever's going down, it's already started. We have to catch up, Mike, and we have to do it now."

"Griffin, it's already twelve – "

"I'll take care of Price's deadline. You just keep on looking for information on Tawnya Clemente. Got it?"

Griffin hit end, then started punching a fresh round of numbers.

"Calling God for a miracle?" Fitz asked glumly.

"Nah, even better. Corporal Charpentier."

Griffin got Charpentier's pager, punched in his number followed by one for urgent, and in thirty seconds had Charpentier ringing back.

"Where are you?" Griffin asked. He could hear lots of noise in the background.

"Parking lot of Max. Maureen Haverill of Channel Ten just finished up with David Price's lawyer. Now she's demanding to speak with Price. Visiting hours for his cell block officially start at noon. Sergeant, I think the jig is up."

"Got my lists?"

"Detective James is downloading names as we speak. We're talking nearly a hundred men, though. I don't see how it's going to help."

"I have a new theory. Cull out names of people David Price met when he was still at Intake, *before* he got sentenced. And of those names, guys that didn't end up going to jail. Maybe they were found innocent, or got off on a technicality, anything."

"Why those guys?"

"Because after the first rape happened, Detective Fitz says they rattled the sex-offender tree and nothing fell out. So maybe the real rapist isn't a convicted sex offender. He was arrested but not convicted."

"Meaning his DNA is in the system," Corporal Charpentier filled in slowly, "taken at the time of his arrest. The rapist himself, however, is still a free man."

"A free man in need of a new way to do things," Griffin said.

"Which David Price helped him find," Charpentier concluded. "Why not? As long as you're in jail, why not pick the brain of a master?"

There was more noise in the background. Charpentier's voice grew muffled, as if he was covering his mouth with his hand. "Sergeant, I can get you the list, but it will probably be another hour and it looks like this media circus is about to begin. The director of the department of corrections wants to examine the cameraman's equipment, but he can't keep the press out. It's visiting hours, Price's lawyer has sanctioned the interview . . . We're screwed."

"How long will examining the equipment take?"

"Fifteen minutes at most. We might stretch it to twenty."

Griffin glanced at his watch. They were almost at the Como residence, but fifteen minutes would never be enough time to break Tawnya Clemente. And once Maureen stuck her microphone in front of Price and he began his pathetic spiel . . .

"Code," Griffin said suddenly.

"Code?"

"Yeah. Code Blue or Code White, I'll settle for any color.

If there's a code, they have to shut down the whole prison, right? Clear everyone out, even lawyers and aspiring news anchors?"

"That's right," Charpentier said, his voice picking up.

"And it could take a while to sort it all out and let everyone back in, right? Prisoners have to be searched and escorted back to the visiting areas. Maureen and Jimmy would have to go back through security . . ."

"It could take a while," Charpentier agreed happily. Then he hesitated. Griffin understood. A Code Blue only happened if there was a major disturbance, a guard down, a fight between two inmates. A Code White, on the other hand, was sounded in case of a medical emergency. Either way, something had to happen in the prison first. "The director isn't wild about a news team entering the prison," Charpentier said finally. "I could talk to him. Maybe now would be a good time for a drill. You know, as a favor to the state police."

"We would appreciate that favor," Griffin said.

"Hang on a sec." There was a pause, the muffled sound of footsteps, then some definitely muffled talking. Moments later, Charpentier was back. "You know what? It turns out Max hasn't had a drill in quite some time. The real thing, sure, but not a drill. And you know how it goes, if you don't practice every now and then . . ."

"You're golden, Corporal, and tell the director we always approve of good practice. One more thing – "

"Yeah?"

"If the interview does go down . . . ask the director not to return Price to his cell. Escort him anywhere else, but *not* to his cell."

"You don't want him picking up anything he might have stashed there."

"It's never too early to take precautions."

"I'm sure the director will see your point. And gee, the cell block is probably due for a surprise inspection, as well. What a wonderfully educational day for the corrections officers."

"Practice makes perfect. Work on that list, Corporal. I'll be in touch."

Griffin flipped his phone shut just in time to turn down Tawnya's street.

Twelve-ten P.M. He parked his Taurus in front of her house.

"You go first," he told Fitz.

The detective positively beamed.

35
Tawnya

They went around to the back door again. Given that you never knew what bushes were hiding what kind of cameramen, it seemed the thing to do. This time Tawnya appeared after their first knock. In her normal good humor, she took one look at Fitz through the door's window and spat.

Griffin wagged a finger at her playfully. Maybe his charm was returning, because she grudgingly opened the door.

"If you pigs are here about the lawsuit," Tawnya said, "go fuck a goat. My lawyer says I'm not supposed to talk to you."

"Colorful," Griffin observed to Fitz.

"I got more. Keep talking and you'll hear them all."

"Hello, Mrs. Como." Fitz eased into the kitchen behind Griffin, keeping the state detective's larger bulk between him and Tawnya. Mrs. Como stood in front of the stove again. Today's culinary adventure seemed to be simmering black beans. The wafting odors of garlic gave the kitchen a homey touch. Not that the bleaching baby diapers had been lacking.

Eddie, Jr., was awake this time, nestled in a baby carrier on top of the kitchen table. He studied Griffin with big brown eyes, then stuck a multicolored teething ring into his mouth and drooled away. Griffin tucked his hands in his pockets before he did something stupid like tickle the baby's pudgy cheeks. He was supposed to be big bad detective here. Clock was ticking, ticking, ticking. Man, babies were cute.

"Maybe we should talk in the family room," Fitz said and jerked his head toward Eddie, Jr.

"I don't got nothin' to say to you," Tawnya said.

"Let's go into the family room," Fitz repeated, more firmly. Tawnya scowled at him, but went.

The minute they were out of the kitchen, Fitz opened fire. "We know what you did, Tawnya. Come clean now, before another girl dies, and maybe we can still work something out. Eddie, Jr., has already lost one parent. You want him to grow up completely orphaned?"

"What the fuck are you talking about?"

"Fifty million dollars. For that kind of money, people sell out their own mothers, let alone some boyfriend who's knocked you up but still not walked you down the aisle."

"Are you talking about my lawsuit? Because I'm not talking about my lawsuit. My lawyer told me I don't have to tell you pigs one damn thing. You killed my Eddie. Now it's your turn to pay!"

"There won't be any lawsuit, Tawnya," Griffin spoke up quietly.

"Not one red cent," Fitz emphasized, "not once the public knows what you really did to Eddie."

Tawnya was good. Real good. She looked at them first in bewilderment, then drew herself up for battle. She bared her teeth. She flashed those long hot-pink nails. "Get out of my house."

"You need to listen to us, Tawnya. Work with us now, and you can still salvage something for Eddie, Jr."

"Miserable, fucking, shit-eating, donkey-humping, flea-repelling, toad-hopping jackasses. *Get out of my house!*"

Fitz and Griffin didn't move a muscle. Fitz glanced at Griffin. "You're right, the language is very colorful."

"Goes with the nails."

"Think she'll attack soon?"

"That'd be nice. Then we can arrest her now, and she'll never see the light of day."

"Too bad for Eddie, Jr."

Griffin shrugged. "You know what they say. You can't pick your parents."

Tawnya foamed at the mouth. Griffin promptly went in for the kill.

"You have thirty seconds to start talking," he told her, his voice low and intense. "We know you framed your boyfriend. We know you're an accomplice to four rapes and two murders. You come clean right this moment, and Eddie, Jr., still has a chance at having a mother. You jerk us around one more second, however, and we're arresting you. We'll shackle you in front of your kid. We'll drag you out of this house and you'll never see your baby again. Thirty seconds, Tawnya. Twenty-nine, twenty-eight, twenty-seven . . ."

Tawnya wasn't into negotiating. She growled once, then launched herself at Griffin's massive form. He grabbed her raking hands, slipped his foot behind hers, and neatly face-planted her onto the worn shag carpet. Fitz produced the cuffs. They didn't have time for fooling around. They hauled her, spitting and sputtering, back onto her feet and were preparing to march her out the door when Mrs. Como stepped into the room, dried her hands on a kitchen towel and uttered a single word.

"Stop," the old woman said.

Some instincts ran deep: they froze. Griffin recovered first. "Mrs. Como," he said firmly, "we have reason to believe that Tawnya helped frame your son for rape – "

"I did not!" Tawnya screeched. She started squirming again, then kicked out at Fitz, who deftly stepped aside.

"Tawnya is a good girl," Mrs. Como said.

"Good girl, my ass!" Fitz sputtered, still dodging.

"Good girls have done far worse for fifty million dollars," Griffin reminded her tightly, and tugged Tawnya away from Fitz.

"Tawnya no do lawsuit," Mrs. Como said. "I do lawsuit. I want money. For my grandson."

"The lawsuit was your idea?"

"*Sí.*"

"But Tawnya was the one on TV," Fitz spoke up.

347

"I no like TV."

Fitz and Griffin exchanged troubled looks. They pulled back from Tawnya, but only slightly. She, of course, took the opportunity to spit at both of them. "I would never do anything to harm Eddie! I loved Eddie, you stupid, miserable – "

"Yeah, yeah, yeah," Fitz interrupted, holding up his hand and glancing at his watch. "We got the picture."

"My son was framed?" Mrs. Como asked from the doorway. "My Eddie no do bad things?"

Griffin looked at Fitz's watch, too. Nearly twelve-thirty now. Shit. "Mrs. Como, are you aware that another girl was attacked last night?"

Mrs. Como nodded.

"We got DNA tests back from that victim, Mrs. Como. They match samples taken from Eddie."

"But that's impossible!" Tawnya burst out. "Eddie's dead. What, you pigs are so desperate you're going after corpses now? Not even dead Latinos are safe from you. Miserable, fucking – "

This time Griffin held up a hand. He studied Tawnya's red, outraged face. He looked at Mrs. Como, and her much-harder-to-read expression. Something was wrong here, he could feel it in his bones.

And that damn clock was still ticking, ticking, ticking.

"Tawnya," he said, "are you aware that when detectives searched Eddie's and your apartment last year, they found all sorts of books on forensics and police procedure? Some clippings, too, right, Detective? News articles from another rape case that had happened in Rhode Island."

"I told the police, that stuff wasn't Eddie's!"

"Whose was it?"

"I don't know! A box came in the mail to Eddie. The note said it was from a friend. He didn't know what that meant so he stuck it in a closet. He figured someone would call about it later or something. I told that to the detectives. I *told* them."

"When did you get the box?"

348

"I don't know. A long time ago. Last year. Before . . ." She frowned. "Before the bad things started happening. I don't understand. How can you think Eddie killed that woman last night? Eddie's *dead*."

"Did the box have a return address?"

"I don't know. I didn't open it. It came to Eddie."

Griffin glanced at Fitz. "No," the detective told him. "It was just an old cardboard box with a mailing label on it. Frankly, it looked to us like he'd used the box for storage of the materials. When we found it, it was shoved in the back of a coat closet."

" 'Cause it wasn't his stuff!" Tawnya cried again. "Eddie didn't know why it had come in the mail!"

"Have you ever heard the name David Price?" Griffin asked Tawnya.

"Who?"

"Did Eddie ever mention the name David Price?"

"Who the fuck's David Price?"

"Have you ever heard of the Candy Man?"

"The pervert who hurt all those little kids," she said immediately. "Now there's a dude who deserves to have his little weenie whacked off – or the electric chair!"

Griffin studied her again. Her brown eyes were clear, earnest. If she was lying, she was very, very good.

"Tawnya, did Eddie have another girlfriend?"

She instantly erupted again. "Eddie loved me! Why is that so hard to believe? Eddie loved me and I loved Eddie, and we were gonna be all right. He had a good job, you know, and after Eddie, Jr., was born I was gonna go to beauty school. And then, and then . . . Ah, fuck you all!"

Her shoulders sagged, the first tear slid down her cheek and she immediately turned away. Crocodile tears? Or the saddest display Griffin had ever seen? He'd been lied to so much lately, it was getting hard to tell. But he had the suspicion he was getting a lesson in irony here. In this case, the victims and their families had lied – with the best of intentions, of course – while the prime suspect and his family may have been telling the truth.

"Tawnya," Griffin said quietly, "we're running out of time here. I need you to tell me the truth, I need to hear it now."

"I *told* the truth!"

"Tawnya, did you give someone a . . . sample, from Eddie? Maybe it seemed like you were supposed to, or it was a favor for a friend."

She stared at him in bewilderment. "A sample? You mean a *sample*? Are you fucking nuts? Who gives out a thing like that?"

"Tawnya, Eddie's semen ended up in a murder victim the day *after* he died. You tell me, how could that have happened?"

And all of a sudden, she must have figured it out, because her eyes went wide. "Oh no," she said. "Oh no, oh no, oh no . . ."

"What, Tawnya? What is oh no? What did you and Eddie do?"

Her face crumpled, her voice grew hollow. "We needed the money," she whispered. "I was pregnant, and Eddie wanted to get me something special, you know. Plus, we had to start saving more . . ."

Ah no. Griffin glanced at Fitz and saw from his face that he'd finally gotten it, too. It made so much sense, but who would've thought to ask the question? Who asks a question like that?

"Eddie was in good health," Tawnya was saying. "Gave blood every eight weeks so you know he didn't have any diseases. And he's nice-looking. They like guys who are nice-looking, you know."

"Who likes guys who are nice-looking?" Griffin prodded. She had to say it. And then she did.

"The sperm bank. Eddie donated at the Pawtucket sperm bank. A couple of times. Right after I found out I was pregnant. They pay cash, you know." Tawnya looked at them helplessly. "They pay cash."

Fitz and Griffin were out of the house and walking fast.

Twelve forty-five P.M., starting to make progress but still running out of time.

"We need a couple of uniforms," Griffin said.

"Someone to keep her under lock and key until we can verify her story," Fitz agreed. They piled into Griffin's car and he picked up the radio for the request.

"Ever get the impression we're dumb as skunks?" Fitz muttered.

"I don't know, how dumb are skunks?"

Fitz finally unleashed a little, and whacked the dash with his hand. "Goddammit! Sergeant Napoleon nailed it this morning. 'Sperm banks do it all the time.' Why don't we just get the full frontal lobotomy and be done with it!"

"And miss having all this fun? Come on, clock's ticking. Let's talk it through."

"Eddie makes a donation at a sperm bank," Fitz said as Griffin pulled away from the curb.

"In theory, donors are anonymous."

"To the recipients. The sperm bank knows who they are, the sperm bank's gotta clear them first. I don't know, how much vetting do you do before you hand a guy a plastic cup and send him into a porn-filled room? Lucky bastard."

"Someone inside," Griffin prodded.

"Someone who would have access to the frozen samples."

"And Eddie's name."

"David Price said the guy had met Eddie. Eddie probably didn't remember him at all, but the guy had met him."

Griffin rolled out his neck, shrugged his shoulders. He hated to give weight to anything David Price had said, but they had to start somewhere. "Maybe he's a technician, then. Someone who worked one of the days Eddie donated, made small talk with him. Maybe he noticed that Eddie was roughly his same size and build, and had that same Cranston accent. He decided here was a good candidate."

"So he was already in the market for a patsy," Fitz said.

"Meaning he had already met David Price."

"Meaning he'd probably been to prison. At least held in Intake on some kind of charge."

"He's already in the system," Griffin said slowly. "Isn't that the key issue? He's a sex offender, he knows he's a sex offender, and even if he didn't get found guilty, he at least got caught. So now he knows his prints and DNA are in the system, just as he knows he won't stop, because sex offenders never stop. They just get more creative with their attacks."

"He knows when he gets out, if he gets out, it's still only a matter of time."

"So he befriends David Price."

"Who must've thought that was funny as hell."

"Except then Price realizes maybe he can get something out of this, too. Someone on the outside, working for him. Someone he can someday cash in for a get-out-of-jail-free card."

"And then a partnership is born."

"So who do we have?" Griffin demanded. "Someone who's at least been charged with a sex crime. Someone who's been held at Intake during the same time Price was there, so that's what, November through March. He's gotten out and gotten a job at a sperm bank."

"Unlimited access to porn," Fitz muttered. "Where else would a sex offender go?"

"Can't be a technician, though," Griffin countered. "They'd investigate someone like that, find out about his criminal past and get nervous."

"Someone lower level then, but with unlimited access. Has keys to the rooms with the freezers and doesn't look suspicious moving about at strange hours."

They got it at the same time. "Janitor!" Fitz shouted.

"Or cleaning crew," Griffin said grimly. "Something like that."

He flipped open his phone and got Waters on the line.

"Sorry, Griff – " Waters started.

"We know who it is," Griffin cut him off. "I mean, we know how it was done. We just need a name. Meet me at the Pawtucket sperm bank in ten minutes."

"Where?"

"The sperm bank. Where the College Hill Rapist works."

"All right," Waters said, but he didn't sound as excited as Griffin thought he would. And then he finally heard the sounds coming from behind Waters in the busy bar. A woman's voice talking. Maureen Haverill, introducing David Price to the general viewing public on the bar's big-screen TV. One P.M. Griffin and Fitz had just run out of time.

36
The Victims Club

It was dark. Meg kept squinting her eyes, trying to peer into the gloom. It didn't do her any good. The dark was a thick, tangible presence, as smothering as any wool blanket, as pervasive as an endless sea.

She twisted her body, straining against the ties that held her hands captive above her head. The latex bindings dug into her wrists cruelly. She felt a fresh trickle of moisture running down her arm and guessed that it was blood. At least she didn't feel much pain anymore. Her hands had gone numb hours ago, her bound feet shortly thereafter. She still had a dull ache in her shoulder blades from the awkward position. She imagined that would be gone soon, as well. And then?

She shifted her bound feet again. Tried to find leverage against the corner wall, as if she could climb her way up the vertical surface, slog her way through the ocean of black and burst out the top, gulping for air. Of course, she could do no such thing. She remained a captive twenty-year-old girl. Peering into the dark, inhaling the stomach-churning scent of latex, and feeling the blood drip down her arm.

Sound. She shifted, trying to guess the direction of the noise. Footsteps. Above her. From the right? From the left? She never realized how much the darkness echoed before she had been tied up in this musty basement.

Closer, definitely, closer. Humming now. The man, she thought, recoiling reflexively, then holding her breath.

He had called her name in the mini-mart parking lot. She had stopped on instinct, even though she hadn't recognized

354

the car or the driver inside. Not recognizing someone was hardly new at this point, and mostly she remembered feeling faintly curious. Who was this stranger and what stories from her past would he know?

Instead, he'd told her there'd been an accident. Molly needed her right away. While she was still absorbing that shock, he'd hustled her into the passenger's side of his car. At the last moment, something inside her had balked. She'd seen him open the driver's-side door, watched his body bend down to slide inside and something had stirred in the dark pit of her mind. Not a memory, per se. But an emotion. Fear, stark and raw and instantaneous. She'd grabbed for the door handle at the same time he'd hit the lock button and flashed his gun.

She'd known him then. She'd stared at his face, and while the individual features still sparked no recognition, she had a clear image of a body laboring above hers in the dark. The grunting, the groaning, the endless noises to accompany her endless shame. How the ties, the horrible latex ties, kept her body exposed, vulnerable and there for his taking.

And just when she thought it would never end, she could take no more, and her body would be ripped in half, he had finally collapsed on top of her, heavy with sweat.

The man had laughed low in his throat. And then he'd murmured, "David said you liked it rough. Need a brother or sister for Molly, Meg? Or maybe I'll just wait a few years and give little Molly a try instead."

She had started screaming then. But the gag smothered the sound, forced it back into her lungs, where it built and built and built. A scream without end.

"David misses you, Meg. David wants you, Meg. You never should've turned him down. Now he's sitting in prison, surrounded by beasts eager to learn your name. We all get out sometime and we all know where you live."

The man rolled off of her, reached for his shirt. "Oh yeah," he said casually. "David sends his love."

The scream had grown too big then. It had exploded up her throat and ripped through her mind. It had burst out of her eyeballs and wiped out her brain. It had gone on and on and on, a sonic boom of a scream. And still she never made a sound. No one heard a thing.

And then as violently as it had started, the scream recoiled, turned in on itself, sank back into her body and took her with it into a dark, velvety abyss.

She had spent a year wanting to remember. Now, in the car with this man, Meg wished she could forget.

He had driven her to a section of town she didn't recognize. Remote. Desolate. The kind of place where only bad things happened. Pulling into a side alley, he took her hands in a surprisingly strong grasp. She smelled the latex before she saw it. Her stomach roiled. She thought she would be sick. He slid the figure-eight ties over her wrists, tightened the bindings, then placed his hand on her breast.

So this was it, she'd realized.

Absurdly, she thought of Jillian. The classes they'd taken in self-defense, the books they'd read on surviving assault.

Women do not have to be victims.

But then why did they make men with such strong grips?

"We have a few hours," he said lightly. "I have some things I need to do first. But once I've completed my chores . . . Don't worry, Meg. I remember how you like it." He flicked his thumb over her nipple. He gave her one last cruel smile, then tied a rolled black T-shirt around her head.

She had been living in darkness ever since.

More sounds now. Banging. Cupboard doors opening and closing. The rattle of pans. Her stomach growled and she suddenly knew what he was doing. He was making lunch. The monster had brought her to his lair, tied her up, captive, terrified for her life, and now he was fixing himself a goddamn cup of soup.

She jerked her arms painfully. Pulled hard on the bindings looped through a metal anchor above her head. Nothing, nothing, *nothing!* She wanted to scream in frustration.

Women are not victims! She was not a victim! Dammit, she had read the books, she had taken the courses. She had listened to Jillian and she had *believed.* How could one girl be so damn unlucky? How could she have spent the last year coming so far, just to wind up here?

She yanked on the bindings again. Felt the concrete hold strong while her own flesh tore, and her wrist once again began to bleed.

And then she just wanted to weep.

He would finish eating soon. He would open the door at the top of the stairs. He would descend into the basement with its musty smell of decay and fresh-turned earth.

And then?

Jillian had told them that they could control their own lives. Jillian had told them that if they tried hard enough, they could win. They could be confident and independent and strong.

But Meg couldn't think like Jillian anymore. She was just a twenty-year-old girl. And she was tired and she was hungry and she was terrified. And soon, very soon, something bad was going to happen. Something worse than even the College Hill Rapist.

Very soon, the man had promised her, David would be here.

In the intensive care unit, Dan sat reading a book. *Recovering from Rape: A Guide for Victims and Their Families*. He had bought the book two weeks ago. He was now on the chapter "The First Anniversary and Beyond – When You Are Not 'Over It.' "

Monitors beeped in steady rhythm to his wife's pulse. Down the hall, some other machine started to beep frantically and a nurse boomed, "Code, code, code!" The words were swiftly followed by the clatter of wheels and metal as someone raced a crash cart to the rescue.

Carol never stirred. Her chest rose and fell peacefully. Her head lay serenely on a golden pool of hair. The white sheets remained smooth and unmussed over the faint mound of her chest.

Every now and then, her right hand would twitch. In the last twenty hours, it was the closest they'd gotten to any sign of consciousness.

Dan finished the chapter from the survivor's point of view. Now he moved on to "The Significant Other – When She's Not 'Over It.' "

He read, and though he was not aware of it, sometimes he cried.

Down the hall, the doctors and nurses fought desperately to save a life. While in Carol's room her heart beat steadily, her lungs worked rhythmically, and her very peacefulness threatened to steal her away.

Dan finished the chapter. Now he gazed at his sleeping wife, his elbows planted on his knees, his head bent. His left arm still ached where Carol had shot him. He barely noticed it anymore.

Twenty hours of vigilance. Twenty hours of hoping and praying and wishing and cursing.

He thought of all the years and all the ways fate had been unkind. He thought of all the things Carol had done and he had done. He wondered why we always hurt the people we love. And then he wondered why it took an emergency room visit to understand what was really important in life.

He would turn back the clock if he could. He would forget the lure of blackjack; he would find a way to be happy at a corporate law firm. He would come home more, ignore his wife less, concentrate on all the little things that used to make her smile. He would be the perfect husband, a man who came home in time to stop the vicious attacker, a man who didn't drive his wife to bingeing, purging, booze and pills.

Of course that wasn't an option. All he could do now was slog messily on, with his injured arm and massive debts and drowning sense of guilt. Carol was broken, he was broken. According to the rape book, such feelings were natural and it would probably be a while before either one of them felt whole – if they ever felt whole. You just had to keep going, the book advised. Wade through the pain, keep looking for the other side.

There had to be another side.

"I love you," he said to Carol.

He got no response.

"Dammit, Carol, don't let him win like this!"

Still no response.

Down the hall, things took a turn for the worse. No more frantic noises. Just a far eerier silence. Then a doctor's voice penetrated the hush. "Time of death," the doctor announced.

"Fuck it!" Dan cried. He threw down the book. He climbed onto the white hospital bed. He negotiated wires and tape and tubes until he could gather up his wife. Her head lolled against his shoulder. Her long blond hair poured down his chest.

Dan got his arms around Carol. He pressed her against his body, and he held her as close as he could.

While down the hall, the crash team wearily retreated to the break room, where they turned their attention to the TV.

"Hey," someone said. "Isn't that David Price?"

Still sitting in the Pesaturos' living room, Jillian didn't know what to do. Tom was staring at the floor, as if the worn carpet held the secret to life. Laurie had disappeared into the kitchen, where, judging from the distinct smell of Pine-Sol, she was waging a holy war against dirt. That left Libby and Toppi to entertain Molly. The little girl now had Libby picking through a shoe box of Barbie clothes while Toppi was in charge of getting a hot-pink cape onto a stuffed Winnie the Pooh. Jillian couldn't begin to fathom what that was all about.

Tom stared, Laurie cleaned, Molly played, and Jillian . . . ? She didn't know what she was supposed to do. The Survivors Club was fractured. They had careened away from one another, whether they had meant to or not, and alone they definitely weren't as strong as they had been together. Bitter Carol had given in to her self-destructive rage. Flaky Meg had vanished when her family needed her the most. And Jillian? Grim, determined, holier-than-thou Jillian? She had no troops to lead into battle. She sat next to her mother, slowly twisting Trisha's gold St. Christopher pendant, and tried to rein in her scattered thoughts.

If Griffin was right, the Survivors Club had been doubly victimized. First the rapist had battered their bodies. Then he'd duped them into wreaking not their vengeance, but *his* vengeance upon some poor guy who'd tried to tell them better. Poor Eddie Como, proclaiming his innocence right up to the bitter end.

If Jillian thought about that too much, thought of the man, Eddie, them, Trish, she was afraid she would start with yelling and end with breaking every object in the room.

If she thought about it too much, she would be down in her sister's dark apartment again. The man would be squeezing her throat, calling her vile names. And while he did these things, he would be laughing on the inside, because he already knew that when she tried to seek justice later, she'd only be serving his needs once again.

While Trish died on the bed.

One year ago, she had called Meg, she had called Carol. She had told them that they had been victimized once, but it never had to happen again. She had told them they could reclaim their lives. She had told them they could win.

She had lied.

Is this what life came down to in the end? You tried and you failed, you tried and you failed. The opposition was not just physically stronger than you but smarter as well? You could struggle as hard as you knew how, but still your sister died. You could finally arrest a murdering pedophile, and the man would simply smile and tell you exactly what he had done to your wife.

David Price. David Price. It all came down to David Price. Charming, seemingly harmless, perfect neighbor, David Price.

Jillian gripped Trisha's medallion in her hand. It wasn't so hard to transfer her rage after all. She wanted David Price dead. And then, for the first time, she truly understood Griffin. And then, for the first time, she had an inkling of an idea.

The front door opened and shut. Laurie, who had gone

out to get the mail, walked into the family room, sifting through the pile.

She came to the middle. Meg's mother started to scream.

37

Maureen

"This is Maureen Haverill, reporting live from the Adult Correctional Institutions, Cranston. Today, startling new revelations in the College Hill Rapist case, which gained fresh intensity last night with the brutal murder of Brown College student Sylvia Blaire. Was twenty-eight-year-old Eddie Como, tragically shot down Monday at the Licht Judicial Complex, the real College Hill Rapist, as he was charged? Or was Como merely another victim in a sadistic game? I am here with ACI inmate David Price, a convicted murderer, who claims to know the real identity of the College Hill Rapist but tells us that state police have repeatedly ignored his offers of assistance. Mr. Price, what can you tell us about the attack on Sylvia Blaire?"

"Good afternoon, Maureen. May I call you Maureen?" He kept his voice friendly, then gave her his most neighborly smile.

"If you'd like. Now, Mr. Price – "

"Please, call me David."

"David, you claim to have information on a very serious case. How is it that you know the College Hill Rapist?"

"Well, we're kind of like pen pals."

"Pen pals?"

"Yes. See, the man, the real rapist, he's been sending me letters."

"Letters? As in more than one?"

"That is correct."

"Interesting. How many letters have you received from the man alleging to be the College Hill Rapist, David?"

"I'd say six or seven."

"And when did you get the first letter?"

"Over a year ago, shortly after I was sentenced to Max. Of course, in the beginning I didn't take them very seriously. I mean, why would some rapist write to me? It wasn't until the past few days I figured out the man might be legitimate."

"Can I see these letters, David? Do you have them? Can you show them to our viewers?"

"Well, I do have them, Maureen . . ."

"Yes?"

"Well, they're evidence, aren't they, Maureen? Letters from a rapist. I don't think we should be handling something like that. I should just keep them safe for the state police. This is an important investigation. I don't want to do anything that might mess it up." He smiled at her again.

She frowned. "But you said the state police aren't taking your claims seriously, isn't that right, David?"

"The state police don't like me very much."

"Why is that?"

"Well, the head of the current investigation, Sergeant Griffin, used to be my next-door neighbor. Sergeant Griffin never liked me much. He was always working, you know – those state police detectives have very important jobs. But that meant his wife was home alone a lot. We became good friends, and I think . . . well, I think Sergeant Griffin might have been threatened by that. Not that he had any reason to be! His wife was a lovely lady, very nice. I don't have any family, and she was very sweet to keep me company. She was really a wonderful, beautiful, sexy lady."

"David, isn't it true that Sergeant Griffin was the arresting officer in your murder case?"

"Well, yeah. And that makes him mad, too. I mean, it took him nearly a year to catch me, Maureen, and I lived right next door. When you're a state police detective, I think that's a little embarrassing."

"This was the infamous Candy Man case, was it not?"

"I heard that's what they called me."

"You were found guilty of murdering ten children, isn't that correct, David?" She regarded him sternly. "The bodies of the children were found buried in your basement, and you are now serving ten consecutive life sentences with no hope of parole. Isn't that correct?"

David Price humbly bowed his head. Sitting once more in the private interview room of ACI's rear hall, he practiced looking contrite. "It shames me to say it, Maureen, but you are correct. I've done some bad things in my time. On the other hand, I think that's why the College Hill Rapist latched on to me. He seems to regard me as some kind of hero."

"The College Hill Rapist is *impressed* by you?" She looked dubious, maybe it was disgusted.

"I believe so, Maureen. He said that in the first letter. He was doing something he thought only I would understand."

"He told you about the rapes?"

"In the most recent letter. He provided very graphic detail, Maureen, including things only the real rapist could know. Which is what I've been trying to tell the police."

"Can you give us an example, David? What is something only the 'real rapist' would know?"

David switched from looking contrite to looking troubled "I don't know, Maureen . . . It's an official investigation. Maybe I should keep quiet. Sometimes the police don't like the public to know everything. It compromises the investigation. I wouldn't want to do anything like that . . ."

Maureen took the bait. "Authenticity, David," she responded instantly. "If you give us just one detail, one little thing that only the *real* College Hill Rapist would know, that would prove the authenticity of your letters. And that would be a huge break in the investigation. People would be very proud of you."

"You think?"

"One little detail, David. Just one little detail."

"Well, I can think of one. But, it's kind of graphic . . ."

Maureen leaned closer with the mike. "This is a serious crime, David. The women of Providence are scared. We need to hear what you know."

"Well, okay. He, um, well, he uses douches on the victims. That's a detail. He's used it on all of them, when he was done. The police think it's because he's trying to remove . . . well, you know. I can't say it in front of a lady."

"Semen, David?"

"Well, yes." David squirmed in the orange plastic chair, then looked right into the camera and blushed charmingly. "So he uses a douche when he is done with each woman. But the police are wrong, Maureen. He's not removing semen. Instead, according to his letters, he's . . . well, he's putting stuff *in*. He's using the douche to spray another man's sample, Eddie Como's DNA, at the scene. And that's why the police can't catch him. All the evidence points to another guy. Let's face it, four attacks later, the police are no closer to identifying the real College Hill Rapist. They haven't a clue."

Sitting across the table, Maureen was clearly breathless. "This man thinks he's invented the perfect crime, doesn't he, David?"

"Oh, absolutely. He's proud of what he's done. And he has no intention of stopping. His letters are very clear. He enjoys hurting women. Honestly *likes* it. And he's going to keep going and going and going – "

"You've told this to the state police?"

"Maureen, I've been calling the police ever since Eddie was shot, poor guy. The minute I heard he was gunned down at the courthouse, I knew the letters were for real. This guy, you see, he framed Eddie and then he killed Eddie so it would look like a dead man was attacking Providence's coeds. He's smart, Maureen. Very smart. That's what I've tried to tell the police."

"You've actually spoken with the police?"

"Sergeant Griffin finally met with me this morning. It didn't go well, though, Maureen. He threatened me with interfering with a police investigation. Then he got mad and started going on about his wife. I'm telling you, we were just friends!"

"Did you show Sergeant Griffin the letters you received?"

"He never gave me the chance. From the beginning, it was obvious he thought I was lying."

She leaned forward intently. "Are you lying, David?"

David looked straight at the camera, and deep into the eyes of the viewing public. "No, Maureen. And the fact that I know about the douches should be proof enough. Call the ME, call a Providence detective. They'll tell you that a Berkely and Johnson's Disposable Douche with Country Flowers was found at every rape scene, even this last one. Now how could I know that if I hadn't learned it from the real College Hill Rapist?"

Maureen turned toward the camera. She said somberly, "In fact, I learned just this morning from an inside source that douches are considered a signature element of the College Hill Rapist's attacks, something that has never before been revealed to the general public. Also, police found a used douche in the home of slain college student Sylvia Blaire, raising the theory that she is the College Hill Rapist's latest victim." She turned back to David, her expression grave. "David, I don't think you're lying. The viewing public doesn't think you're lying. So tell us the real name of the College Hill Rapist."

And David Price, reformed sinner for the day, said, "I'm sorry, Maureen, but I don't think I should tell you that."

"Come on, David. You want to make good. You want to help the public. Here's your chance."

"I should tell the police and only the police."

"But according to you, David, the police don't believe you."

"I know. And it's sad, very sad, Maureen, because I received a new letter just this morning. The College Hill Rapist went a whole year without attacking a woman because he wanted to kill Eddie first and wrap up his plan. Now he's done that. Now he's ready to make up for lost time. I'm pretty sure . . . No! I'm *absolutely certain* he's going to attack another girl tonight."

"He's going to strike again, *tonight?*"

"I think so, Maureen. Yes, ma'am, I'm *sure*."

Maureen leaned across at the table.

Her blue eyes were blazing. She was gripping the microphone so tightly her knuckles had gone white. She was jazzed. Her cameraman was jazzed. In the small room, they radiated pure energy. David amused himself by picturing them both dead. "David, tell us his name. You did a horrible thing once. You kidnapped little kids, you hurt children, you damaged a lot of families out there. People still remember that. There are people watching this right now, wondering why they should believe any word spoken by a monster such as you. Tell those people the College Hill Rapist's real name. Show those people that you're ready to make amends."

"I can't."

"What do you mean you can't?" Maureen was nearly shouting now. "Do you or don't you know the name? Speak to me, David. Help us! According to your own words, another innocent college student is doomed to die!"

David finally let loose. "I know his name! I want to help!" reformed sinner David wailed. "But . . . but look at me! I'm living in maximum security, Maureen. I'm living in the middle of Steel City, surrounded by the worst of the worst. And look at me! I'm only five eight. I weigh a hundred and fifty pounds. For God's sake, do you know what it means to be so small in a place like this? Do you?"

"What are you saying, David?"

"Information is power, Maureen. In prison. In life. This is the only information I have. It's my only chance at power in a place like this. God forgive me, but I can't just give it up. I need something in return."

Maureen finally drew back. For the first time, she sounded genuinely disappointed. "You'll only give up the name of the College Hill Rapist in return for something else? That's what you're saying, isn't it, David? You'll only help us if there's something in it for you."

This was the tricky part. David bowed his head, then he sneaked a humble peek at his audience. "I'm sorry, ma'am. I'm sorry to everyone out there, too. I know it's not right.

But that's how the system works, and I'm part of this system now. I have to play by these rules."

"Are you hoping to get out of prison? You raped and murdered babies, David. You buried their bodies in your basement. No matter what you know now, people are going to be uncomfortable with you getting any kind of consideration."

"I know."

"You're a murderer, David. Let's be honest. You're in maximum security for a reason, and most people are grateful that you're there."

David took a deep breath. "I'm a father."

"You're a father?" Maureen was so shocked, she actually blinked her eyes. It was probably the first genuine emotion she'd ever shown on camera.

"Yeah. I'm a father. I have a little girl. Five years old. Maureen, I've never gotten to see my little girl. Never even . . . gotten to say hi."

Maureen's face grew serious again, her tone intent. "What do you want, David?"

"I want to see my little girl, that's all. Look, I'm not denying what you say. I know I'm never getting out of prison. I've made my peace with that. After the things I did, I should be grateful just to be on God's green earth. I've seen the chaplain. I'm reading the Bible. While I can't change what I have done, Maureen, I can try to be a better man from this day forth – "

"Tell us the name of the College Hill Rapist, David."

"I have a daughter," he continued relentlessly, "and she's getting to that age where she's noticing that she doesn't have a father like other kids. I want her to know that it's not her fault. I want her to know that someone loves her. I want her to know that *I* love her."

"What do you *want*, David?"

"Three hours, Maureen. That's what I want, all I want. Three hours, fully supervised, in street clothes, to go see my daughter. For the first time. For the only time. So I can tell her that I love her. So I can tell her that she's a good girl. So I can tell her that I can't be her father, but it's not her fault."

"You want the state to release you from prison for *three hours*. To turn a convicted killer loose on the outside?"

David held up his hands. "Supervised hardship leave, Maureen. Like the corrections department does for funerals, things like that. I'd be shackled, wrists and ankles. Escorted by corrections officers at all times. The police can pick where we meet, they can pick how we get there. I'll do whatever I'm told. Greeting my daughter in leg irons with a security escort is still better than making her come here. Let's face it, no little girl belongs here."

Maureen finally sat back. She was frowning but for the first time she seemed willing to consider his proposal. And if she was willing to consider it, others would be willing . . .

"A three-hour hardship leave, fully supervised. And in return you'll provide the name of the College Hill Rapist?"

"Yes, ma'am."

"Who is your daughter, David?"

"I won't tell you."

"This daughter you love so much?"

"My daughter exists, Maureen. Just ask any prison official. But I'm not announcing her name on public TV. I wouldn't do that to my little girl."

Maureen made one last play. "Why don't you give us the rapist's name now, David, and in return I'll go to work on securing a three-hour leave as you have requested. In return for doing the city such a big favor, I'm sure something could be arranged."

"You're a nice lady, Maureen."

"Thank you, David."

"But I'm not that dumb."

"What?"

"I get my three hours. I see my little girl. And when it's done, I'll turn to the first police officer I find and tell him the College Hill Rapist's name. That's the deal. I hope it happens, and for all of our sakes, I hope it happens soon. The College Hill Rapist is a hungry man. Come nightfall, he'll strike again."

"David – "

"Oh, and Sergeant Griffin, if you're listening, I'll say it again. Your delicious wife and I, we were honestly just friends."

38
Griffin

Griffin was having a hard time controlling his rage. He leaned his massive frame across the gleaming, cherry-wood desk, homed in on the young man who had the misfortune to be the sperm bank's business manager and didn't waste any time on words.

"Janitor. Name. *Now*."

"I'm trying to tell you, we don't have a janitor."

"Who cleans?"

"A service."

"Their name. *Now*."

"I need to look it up."

"Then look it up, dammit!"

The man turned hastily toward a cherry file cabinet, manicured hands fumbling with the wooden handle while he sweated through his Armani suit. Apparently there was money in infertility treatments. Lots of it.

Fitz stood behind Griffin. Waters stood next to Fitz. Both were eyeing him carefully, but neither of them intervened.

"Korporate Klean," Mr. Management Money announced two minutes later.

"Address?"

The man handed over the manila file. Griffin flipped through the pages.

"There are no names of which individuals actually handle your building."

"Our contract is with Korporate Klean. They figure out the staffing."

"How often do they come?"

"Every night."

"What about daytime?"

"When they have special projects. The inside of the windows, polishing the brass railings in the elevators and stairs. Oh, and laundry. They bring in fresh loads of linens, towels, etc., a few afternoons a week. We, uh, we like to make our patrons feel like they're at home, and not in a clinical environment."

"How thoughtful of you. Who brings in the laundry?"

"I don't know."

"How big is the crew that works this building?"

"I don't know."

"Same people all the time?"

"I don't know!"

"Mr. Matthews – "

"Our contract is with Korporate Klean, Sergeant. I'm sorry, I'm honestly trying to help. But we don't worry about those details. You'll have to talk to them."

"Thanks for the file," Griffin snarled, and stalked out of the building.

In the elevator, Fitz took the folder. "I've heard of them. Korporate Klean."

"The PPD has cleaners?" Waters drawled mildly. "I never would have guessed."

Fitz shot the skinny detective an impatient glance. "No, we investigated them once. You numbnuts should've heard of them, too. Korporate Klean hires mostly ex-cons."

"What?" Griffin stopped pacing the brass-trimmed elevator and stared at Fitz.

He shrugged. "It's a 'second chance' company, you know. Run by a couple of Ben & Jerry liberals who believe people really can reform their evil ways. Guy serves his time, gets out of prison, he's gotta start somewhere. He goes to Korporate Klean and re-enters polite society as a janitor. We've checked into them a few times but never found any funny business. Everyone makes good, everyone works hard, everyone plays well with others. At least that's what the owner, Sal Green, says."

"Companies are willing to be serviced by a cleaning crew of former inmates?" Waters asked.

"I don't know how much the companies know. You heard Mr. Sperm Bank. Their contract is with Korporate Klean. Korporate Klean takes care of staffing."

"Oh great," Griffin muttered darkly. "So when we ask them for a list of employees with past records, that's going to be their entire damn company."

"Yeah, but not everyone's cleaning the sperm bank."

Griffin's cell phone rang. He snatched it up as the elevator hit ground floor and dumped them into the lobby. "Griffin."

"You saw the news?" Lieutenant Morelli asked.

"I listened to the radio."

"Sergeant, we'd like you to return to headquarters – "

"We're onto him, Lieutenant. According to Tawnya, Eddie made several donations to a local sperm bank, which just happens to be serviced by a cleaning company comprised of ex-cons. We're on our way to Korporate Klean as we speak. One hour, two hours, we're going to have the perp's name."

"Sergeant, in light of David Price's involvement . . ."

"I'm fine, Lieutenant."

"We appreciate your efforts, and we think it would be best – "

Griffin thrust out his phone to Waters. "Tell the Lieutenant I'm fine." He probably shouldn't have growled when he said that. Waters took the phone while Griffin rolled out his neck.

"Afternoon, Lieutenant. Uh huh, uh huh. Yeah. Uh huh."

Waters handed the phone back to Griffin. "She doesn't like you much."

"I'm telling you, I gotta try a new cologne." Griffin tucked his phone against his ear and opened the door to his car. "Lieutenant, we're going to get him. Before six o'clock, and without David Price. We're going to nail the son of a bitch."

And Lieutenant Morelli said quietly, "We're making plans for a three-hour release."

"*What?*"

"Target time is six P.M. We're working hand in hand with the department of corrections, the state marshals and SWAT. I'll be leading the team."

"Lieutenant, don't do it. It's what he wants. Don't do it!"

"Do you think I can't handle the team, Sergeant?"

"It's not about you," Griffin said, closing his eyes. "It's not about me. It's about David Price. Listen, the rapes started over a year ago. Think about that. That means Price has been in on this for over twelve months, twelve months of thinking, planning and scheming for this day. He's got another agenda. And he's had ample opportunity to get it into play."

"Do you think I can't handle the team, Sergeant?"

"The Pesaturos will never allow it," he tried again, more desperate now. "They're not about to have their five-year-old granddaughter serve as bait."

"The Pesaturos have personally requested the meeting. It was their call to the superintendent, not the other hundreds of calls," the lieutenant added dryly, "which influenced the final decision."

"What? How? Why?"

"They found a note in their mail. If David Price doesn't see Molly, they don't get to see Meg. The note came with a picture. Do you understand now how serious this situation has become?"

"He's covering all the bases," Griffin murmured. "If the public outcry isn't enough, pressure from the victim's parents will definitely get the job done. Oh, and now we can't hurt him either. You can position all the snipers you want at this *meeting,* but none of them can take a shot. Something happens to David at any time, and we lose Meg. Think about that, Lieutenant. He has already set up a human shield, without the human even being present. It's fucking brilliant. *That's* what one year of planning can do."

The lieutenant didn't say anything right away, so she

probably agreed. Sometimes, even when you knew you were being manipulated, you couldn't avoid it.

"It's three P.M. now," Morelli said quietly. "I'm starting preparations for the cover team as we speak." And then, even more quietly, "Griffin . . . we know who we're dealing with. *I* know who we're dealing with. I'm getting the best people, I'm demanding the tightest security. I don't want Price out of prison any more than you do. But if it does happen, if it comes to that, I'll make sure it goes down right."

"We're going to get the man's name," Griffin said.

"I look forward to that call. And Sergeant – if you find the College Hill Rapist first, remember what you've spent the last year learning. Remember, we still need Meg."

39

The Victims Club

The man entered the basement. Meg heard the protesting groan of the old wooden stairs, then his out-of-tune humming. He'd paid her a visit earlier. Skipped down the steps, told her to smile and turned on a bright light right before she heard the whir of an instant camera. She'd still been tilting her head up, trying to peer beneath the bottom edge of her blindfold, when he had summarily clicked the light back off and thumped back up the stairs. She was left alone in the endless dark, her arms pulled painfully over her head, the muscles in her rib cage beginning to protest.

Now she heard him approach once again and unconsciously shrank back against the concrete wall, as if that would save her.

"How is pretty, pretty Meg?" the man whispered. He cupped her cheek. She turned her head and he chuckled, running his fingers down her throat, dipping them beneath the collar of her shirt. "My, my, you've been working up a bit of a sweat."

With the latex gag cutting into her mouth, she couldn't say anything and didn't bother to try.

"Tsk, tsk," the man scolded, "I don't think David's going to like that much. Maybe before he comes, I should give you a bath. You, bound and naked in a tub. I haven't tried that before. I think I might like it."

His hands were inside her shirt, on her lace-covered breasts. He didn't squeeze, didn't stroke. Just let his hands rest on her chest as if to prove his point – he held the power to do anything he wanted to her body. And there was nothing she could do to stop him.

"Well," the man said briskly, "I have one last chore to attend to. A little present for David, one not even he's expecting. Should be lots of fun for everyone, especially me. Wish me luck, dear. If all goes as planned, I should have a few moments to come back and play."

Now his fingers did move. She pressed her cheek against the dank wall. She did her best not to vomit.

The man chuckled. "See you soon, Meg." He kissed her on the neck. Then he resumed his toneless humming as he ascended the stairs.

The moment she heard the door click shut, Meg released her pent-up breath. She sagged against the hard-packed dirt floor, her legs trembling, her arms screaming with savage pain. She cried a little, but her tears were short-lived. He hadn't given her any water since her kidnapping, and she couldn't afford the loss of moisture.

She sniffled, she took a deep breath and then she tilted her head up toward a wall anchor she couldn't see. When she pulled forward, nothing happened. But as she'd twisted away from the man's fingers, she was sure she had detected the slightest wobble. If the anchor moved a little now, then maybe, over time, it would move a lot.

It wasn't much, but it was all she had. Meg, the human pendulum.

David Price was coming. David Price was coming. Meg started swaying.

Lieutenant Morelli sat in the living room of the Pesaturo home. Toppi had whisked Molly upstairs the moment the lieutenant had arrived. Now Lieutenant Morelli spread out a map on the living room floor and went straight to business. She gazed at Tom, Laurie, Jillian and Libby somberly. She told them, "This is what we're going to do. We want the meeting in public, so we can properly monitor it, but we also want it semiprivate to reduce the risk of pedestrian interference."

"You mean hostages," Jillian murmured.

"We like this residential park." The lieutenant tapped the green square on the map. "Direct street access that can be easily monitored. We close off all the side roads, of course, and shut down the park to the general public. The park itself is an open, green space, meaning it's easy to monitor with few places to hide – "

"You mean in case the College Hill Rapist is setting up an ambush," Jillian said.

This time, the lieutenant paused long enough to give her a stern look. Apparently, in the state police officer's world, civilians were to be seen, not heard. Well, that explained Griffin. "We can also position snipers on rooftops here, here and here," the lieutenant continued curtly. "In other words, we will have a bead on David Price at all times during the three hours."

"If you shoot him, what happens to our daughter?" Tom asked.

"Given the situation, our snipers will have to radio for permission to use deadly force."

"What does that *mean*?" Laurie asked.

"It means we understand Price holds valuable information and we'll do our best to conduct the operation accordingly."

Jillian spoke up. "But under some circumstances, you would authorize use of deadly force."

"We're professionals," Lieutenant Morelli said firmly. "We know what we're doing."

Jillian, Tom, Laurie and Libby exchanged glances. They thought they knew what that meant. The snipers wouldn't kill David Price if he still appeared controllable. But if it looked like he was getting away . . . If the state police had to weigh the life of one woman against a convicted serial killer who would definitely return to his murderous ways should he ever get free . . .

"The state marshals will be in charge of transferring Price from the ACI to the park." Lieutenant Morelli resumed speaking. "Transporting prisoners is their job and they know it best. Given the extreme situation, we will provide police escort and we will follow a predetermined, secured route. Upon arrival at the park, the state marshals will turn Price over to two state detectives for the duration of the meeting."

"He'll be in street clothes?" Laurie asked.

"Price's lawyer will deliver clothes for the visit by four this afternoon. We will thoroughly inspect the articles of clothing, of course, as well as conduct a full search of David Price."

"His wrists and ankles will be shackled?" Tom asked.

"Absolutely. His ankles will be bound. His cuffed hands will be secured to his waist with a chain. His mobility will be extremely limited, I assure you. Now then, I want to talk about Molly – "

"I don't want him to touch her!" Laurie cried.

"We plan on keeping them ten feet apart at all times."

"How about the length of the park," Tom growled.

"We may increase that distance at our discretion," the lieutenant replied.

"In other words, if David is acting hinky . . ." Jillian murmured.

"We won't let Molly anywhere near him," the lieutenant finished for her.

Tom sighed heavily. His big shoulders sagged, his face was haggard. It was obvious he hated the idea of what was to come, and it was obvious he felt he had no other choice.

"Now," Morelli said briskly. "About Molly's escort – "

"We'll take her!" Tom said instantly, head popping up.

"We would prefer that you didn't – "

"Hell, no! Not an option. This is our daughter . . . granddaughter we're talking about. Molly needs us, she depends upon us. We will be there at her side every step of the way."

"Mr. Pesaturo, we understand your concern. But this is a potentially volatile situation. We feel it would be best to minimize the number of civilians involved and maximize the number of experienced professionals."

"Too bad. I'm her father. I'm not leaving her side."

"Mr. Pesaturo, it would be my honor to escort Molly – "

"*I'm her father!*"

"And I have two daughters of my own!" Lieutenant Morelli's voice finally rose angrily. She caught the emotion, leveled her tone. "Mr. Pesaturo, we don't know what Price's true intentions are. We suspect, however, that they involve a great deal more than simply saying hi to his long-lost daughter. If he springs something, what are you going to do?"

"Kill the bastard." Tom saw her look and hastily added, "In self-defense, of course."

"And what about Meg?"

"I don't . . . I don't know." His shoulders sagged again. Meg had been missing nearly six hours now. Six long, uncertain, fearful hours. Tom whispered, "What would you do?"

"I don't know," the lieutenant answered gently. "I suspect none of us will know what to do until the moment it is asked of us. But the point is, there may be split-second decisions that need to be made, and as someone experienced in these matters, I'm better equipped to make them."

"This is ridiculous." Laurie again. "We're doing exactly what he wants."

Lieutenant Morelli didn't say anything.

"Isn't there something else you can do? Some way you can *force* him to tell you where Meg is? To give us the rapist's name?"

"He's in prison for life," Morelli said. "That's already the maximum penalty this state allows."

"But prisons do have punishments," Jillian spoke up. "Protocols, procedures for when prisoners get out of line."

"Inmates can be LFI – locked and fed in, meaning they must remain in their cells even during mealtimes. It's ACI's version of solitary, except the inmate remains in his original cell. Or, in cases where an inmate routinely disrupts prison life, he can be reassigned to Super Max, where inmates are confined to their cells twenty-three hours a day. In other words, they lose all the perks still offered in Old Max."

"Then threaten him with reassignment!" Tom boomed. "Tell Price you're going to send him to this Super Max place."

"Sergeant Griffin already did. Price didn't care." Morelli leaned forward. "I'll be honest with you, Mr. Pesaturo. If we had more time, we could try some different tactics, place Price in Super Max and see if the pressure got to him. But I suspect Price knows that. That's why he's given us an aggressive timetable. That's why we have only a matter of hours. If we don't do what he wants, something could happen to Meg, or something could happen to another innocent young girl. Yes, what we're doing is not ideal. But we're going to do it with the best of our abilities. I'd like to escort your granddaughter, Mr. Pesaturo. I promise you I will do my best to keep her safe."

"What will Sergeant Griffin be doing?" Jillian asked.

Morelli gave her a wary glance. "The sergeant is pursuing another avenue of the investigation."

"I would think you would want him at the scene," Jillian pressed, giving the lieutenant a steely glance of her own. "Isn't he the one who knows David Price the best?"

"Sergeant Griffin feels he has a good lead. We thought it was best to let him pursue it."

"Does he think he knows where Meg is?" Laurie spoke up hopefully.

The lieutenant didn't say anything, and then Jillian got it. "Griffin thinks he might be able to identify the real perpetrator," she said slowly. "He's trying to find the College Hill Rapist, *without* David Price."

"We are doing everything in our power to avoid granting David Price's request," the lieutenant said.

"Oh, thank God," Laurie said. Sitting next to Jillian, Libby tapped her finger.

"But," the lieutenant reminded them firmly, "the meeting Price is demanding may still happen. We need to be prepared. I would like permission to escort your granddaughter – "

"No!"

"Mr. Pesaturo – "

"No," he said again. Tom looked at his wife, then took her hand. Together, they turned toward the state lieutenant. "We've raised Molly as our daughter. She needs us now. We'll do this together. As a family."

"And if Price tries something?"

"Then we'll see how good your snipers are, won't we, Lieutenant?"

Four P.M. Griffin, Fitz and Waters finally found the Korporate Klean world headquarters. In other words, a decrepit old warehouse in south Providence, amid a bunch of even more decrepit old buildings. Apparently cleaning companies didn't make as much money as, say, sperm banks.

The front doors were locked. Griffin started punching buttons on the mounted intercom system while Waters gazed up at the security camera. It took four or five rings before a scratchy female voice crackled through the box.

"*What?*"

"We're looking for Korporate Klean," Griffin said.

"*Why?*"

"We're dirty and we need a good scrubbing, why do you think?"

"*You cops?*"

"Worse," Griffin announced. "We're IRS."

That did the trick. The doors instantly buzzed open. A bunch of ex-cons would have nothing but disdain for law enforcement. Everyone, on the other hand, fears the IRS.

Up on the fifth floor, the office "suite" of Korporate Klean was a pleasant surprise compared to the rest of the building. Sure, the gray carpet was threadbare, the bone-colored walls boring, but the place was spic-and-span. Even smelled like ammonia and Pine-Sol. This must be where the recruits practiced their new trade.

The three detectives came to an empty front desk in the tiny entryway, gazed down a long narrow hallway behind it and waited impatiently for someone to appear. Griffin's leg was starting to jiggle again. He clasped his hands behind his back so no one would see them shake. When he glanced back up, Waters was staring at him, so maybe he wasn't fooling anyone after all.

Four-oh-three P.M. Not much time. Christ . . .

A door down the hall finally opened. A girl with jet-black hair walked out, wearing way too many piercings and not nearly enough clothes.

"May I help you?" she asked, and gave them a very direct glance for someone half-naked in front of three men.

"We're looking for the owner of Korporate Klean."

"May I ask what this is regarding?"

"Taxes."

"IRS agents don't make house calls."

"How would you know?" Griffin gave up on the staring contest. He flashed his ID. "This is official business. Find the owner. Now."

The girl raised a silver-studded brow, gave them a dismissive look just so they'd know that they hadn't scared *her*, and then retreated down the hall.

Griffin's other leg got a tremor. He paced around the room while Waters and Fitz watched.

Another minute, a long, interminable minute. One of so many minutes, ticking, ticking, ticking. Didn't anyone understand the urgency of time?

The girl finally returned. Mr. Sal Green would see them now. The last doorway on the left. Try not to break anything on their way there.

Too late. They stormed down the hall, stormed into the room and arrived as a definite physical presence.

"Officers." An older, trimly built man in faded jeans and a graying ponytail greeted them as they burst into the office. He belatedly rose to his feet, then waved his hand vaguely at the two empty chairs.

"Sergeant," Griffin corrected him sharply.

Green wasn't impressed. He shrugged, then commented, "I'd say I'm surprised by your visit, but of course I'm not. What happened this time, gentlemen? A paper clip is missing from someone's lobby, and you're here to follow up with your favorite scapegoats?"

"The state police doesn't get involved in missing paper clips."

"Oh, you're right, you're right. So one of my crews was speeding instead. You know, it really is safe to hand them the ticket. Not all ex-cons bite."

Griffin's blood pressure jumped another fifty points. He turned to Waters, who got the hint.

"We need a name," Waters said.

"No kidding."

"We need to know who works the sperm bank up in Pawtucket and we need a record of their date-of-hire."

"Then I would need a subpoena."

"Then you're going to need a cast," Griffin growled.

"Oooh, good cop, bad cop." Green turned to Fitz. "What are you, the comedic sidekick?"

Fitz said, "I'm the corroborative witness who'll testify that the first two didn't really hurt you."

"Oh spare me." Green sat back down behind his desk. "Look, I run a good company, with good guys. You people run screaming through my personnel records once a month, and you haven't found anything yet. Whatever it is this time, get a subpoena. If you finally have proof someone in my employ has done bad, then you shouldn't have any trouble getting a judge to agree."

"We don't have time," Waters said tightly.

"And I don't have a million dollars. Welcome to life."

Griffin had had enough. He planted his hands on the desk, leaned in until his face was inches from Green's and held the man's stare. "It involves the College Hill Rapist, got it? Have you been watching the news? Do you understand what we're talking about?"

Green finally paused. He looked away from Griffin, then frowned. "My guys work at night – "

"Not every night."

"I vet them myself. We have no one with a history of sex crimes. The women on my crews would object – or hurt him."

384

"This guy was never convicted."

"Then how do you know he's one of mine? Look, Sergeant, I'm just a beleaguered small-business owner, and you're not making a very good case."

"We have our reasons. We have *compelling* reasons – "

"Then tell them to a judge," Green interrupted firmly. He picked up his phone, as if to signal that he was done.

Griffin slammed the phone back down. "If another girl is hurt – "

"Then you know where to find me, don't you, Sergeant?"

"You son of a bitch," Fitz snarled.

Green shot him a look, too. He was angry now and it showed in his face. "Gentlemen, it's called due process. You're the police, you ought to know about it. Now if I were you, I'd find a judge. Because it's getting late, and frankly I plan on going home at five."

Griffin almost went for him then. Blood pressure so high. Ringing so loud in his ears. Waters touched his arm. He reined himself back in. Breathe deep, count to ten. Count to twenty. Man was an asshole. The world was filled with them.

"We'll be back," Griffin said.

"You and Schwarzenegger," Mr. Green said dryly and picked up his phone.

They exited the building fast. Four thirty-two and counting. "We need a judge, a friendly judge," Griffin growled. "I'm out of the loop."

"I know one," Waters said immediately.

"Okay, you and I will get the warrant. You" – Griffin turned to Fitz – "watch the building. I don't want to come all the way back with paper just to find Mr. Bleeding Heart gone."

"Oooh, me and all the ex-cons. I can hardly wait."

"Neither can they. Come on, Waters. Let's roll."

Fitz went back inside the building. Waters and Griffin climbed into Waters's car. The sky was still light, dusk three hours away. But it would come, and it would come quick, and Price would be out of prison, walking toward his five-year-old daughter. While some young college student walked out of the student union, headed for her apartment.

And Meg? And Jillian? And Carol?

Griffin had failed his wife once. He had failed ten help-less children. He had failed himself. He was supposedly older and wiser now. He didn't want to fail again.

"Are you going to make it?" Waters asked tightly.

"I'm holding it together."

"Just barely."

"See?" Griffin said lightly. "I've made progress."

Four forty-six.

A corrections officer stopped outside the solitary-confinement cell where David Price had been temporarily placed.

"Hands," the guard said.

"You're going to shackle me already? Wow, you guys really aren't leaving anything to chance."

"Hands," the guard repeated.

David shrugged. He knew the drill. He stuck his hands through the slit in the cell door. The corrections officer slapped on the cuffs. David withdrew his shackled wrists, and his cell door was finally opened. The guard pulled him out by the shoulder and led him over to Processing.

"Can I stop by my cell?" David asked.

"Why?"

"I like that toilet better. You know, it's hard to relax in a new cell."

"Eat more fiber," the guard told him and pulled him down the hall. At the end was a room where three more guards waited. One saw him coming and snapped on a pair of gloves.

"Full cavity search?" David arched a brow. "Why this is just my lucky day."

The guard regarded him stonily. David shrugged.

"Oh, the price of freedom." He went into the room,

where his favorite shirt and pants were stacked on the table. The clothes had probably already been searched. Now it was his turn.

David turned away from the stack of clothing, trying not to smile too brightly.

"Free at last," he murmured as he raised his hands above his head, "free at last. O Lord Almighty, free at last."

Five P.M.

David Price bent over.

Griffin and Waters pleaded their case before a judge.

Fitz stared at a half-dressed receptionist.

Tawnya fed a crying, fussy Eddie, Jr.

Meg swayed from side to side.

Carol's right hand started to twitch.

And Jillian sat in the Pesaturo home, thinking of Meg, thinking of Carol, thinking of her sister, thinking of Sylvia Blaire and then thinking of David Price's game plan. Something was wrong here, she thought, then rubbed her temples as she tried desperately, quickly, to think of what.

Molly sat on the floor of her bedroom and waited.

40
Price

"We need a subpoena – "

"We have probable cause – "

"The College Hill Rapist Case – "

"Como donated sperm to a Pawtucket sperm bank – "

"The rapist had to have access to those samples in order to plant evidence at the crime scenes – "

"We need to see some personnel records. Now!"

It wasn't the most elegant arguing Griffin and Waters had ever done before a judge, but it did the trick. At five-eleven, they received their subpoena. They promptly drove ninety miles per hour back to Korporate Klean, burnt some rubber making the hard right turn into the parking lot and squealed around to the front doors.

First thing they saw was Fitz, standing outside, hand on Mr. Green's arm, talking furiously. Green was obviously trying to make good on his threat to go home at five. Fitz was obviously making good on his vow to stand guard.

Griffin screeched to a halt directly in front of them, while Waters thrust the subpoena out his open window.

"We require access to your files, *now!*" Waters announced.

Sal Green sighed and shook his head at their persistence. Then he turned back toward the building.

Five minutes later, he kicked an old gray metal filing cabinet three times, jerked the lower drawer open, then gestured to the emerging row of files. "These are my current employees."

Griffin eyed what appeared to be forty to fifty names.

They didn't have that kind of time. "People who work the sperm bank," he said curtly. "Past and present."

"I rotate the crews – it keeps everyone on their toes."

"Date of hire November through April, Mr. Green. *Move it!*"

For a moment, it looked like Green might protest. Griffin's hands started itching at his sides. He was trying to remember what Lieutenant Morelli had said. For that matter, what his therapist, his brothers and Waters had said. Mostly, however, he felt himself descending down, down, down into that dark basement with its neat rows of sad little graves.

Green started pulling files. Griffin figured it was the best decision the man had made all day.

He, Waters and Fitz began skimming. Ten minutes later, Fitz won the prize. "I know this man! Ron Viggio. I arrested him myself, several years back. A regular Peeping Tom. The woman was embarrassed though, and wouldn't press charges."

"Peeping Tom," Waters said. "That sounds like a budding rapist to me."

"Hey, all I know about was an arrest for B&E," Green protested immediately. "Viggio told me about it up front. It was all some misunderstanding, he was trying to plant a surprise in his girlfriend's apartment and a neighbor took it the wrong way."

"He was caught breaking into a woman's home?" Griffin asked sharply.

Green shrugged. "He was charged, not tried. At least that's what I was told."

Griffin was already dialing his cell phone. "Sergeant Griffin here. I need you to run a name through the system. Ronald Viggio. V-I-G-G-I-O. Yep. Uh huh." And two minutes after that. "Current address?"

"All right." He grabbed the file. "Let's go."

"Hey now!" Green started to protest again, but no one waited around to hear.

*

Five-thirty P.M.

The state marshals appeared and led David to the waiting transport van. Courtesy of his lawyer's timely delivery, David was wearing his own clothes for the first time in a year and a half – a pair of tan khakis, a dark blue button-down shirt and dark brown loafers. The clothes had been searched and run through the metal detector, of course. So had he.

Now his hands and ankles were shackled. A state marshal walked on either side, both heavyset faces grim. David smiled at his escorts. He smiled at the assembled corrections officers. He smiled at the waiting blue van. He was in a good mood.

They loaded him up.

"Try anything, buster," one of the state marshals said, "and we'll grind you into dust. *Capisce?*"

"I don't speak Italian, you English-challenged hump."

The marshal growled at him. David smiled back.

The van doors closed. Soon the prison gates would open.

Five thirty-five P.M. So close to freedom, David could taste it on his lips. Five, ten more minutes, and the gates would open. Five, ten more minutes, and his real journey would begin.

Thank you, Sergeant Griffin, he thought. And of course, thank you, Meg.

"Apparently, Ron Viggio didn't feel the need to tell his employer about his entire criminal history," Griffin said as he hurtled his car onto the interstate and Waters called for backup. "Turns out he wasn't arrested for B&E, but for first-degree sexual assault. He also spent three years behind bars in the mid-nineties for breaking into a woman's home."

"So first he's a Peeping Tom, then he's breaking into women's homes, then he goes for assault. Wow, he's positively textbook."

"Yeah. Unfortunately, the sexual-assault charge didn't stick. The woman had had a prior relationship with

Viggio – they'd dated briefly – and since she'd slept with him willingly in the past, she got worried the jury wouldn't believe her claim. Or maybe she just got freaked out at the thought of the trial. It's not exactly a walk in the park."

"Why try the defendant when you can beat up the victim?"

"Exactly. Viggio entered Intake in December, his accuser dropped the charges in January. His probation officer can probably tell us even more stories." Griffin came to the Cranston exit, flashed his lights at the sluggish traffic, then whipped around them, cursing. Some jerk pulled out in front of him. He slammed the brakes hard and swore, and Waters grabbed the bullhorn. "*To the right. NOW!*"

That put the fear of God into the asshole. Of course the driver shot them a dirty look as they went barreling by. Civilians.

"Viggio had four weeks at Intake during the same time as David Price," Griffin said, breathing hard, his palms dampening with a combination of adrenaline and anticipation. He found the proper side street, his speedometer over eighty and his attention focused on the wheel.

"Oooh, is it just coincidence?"

"Or is it probable cause? By December, Viggio had probably figured out that it was only a matter of time until he attacked a woman again. But he also knew his DNA and prints were already in the system, so the first time he gave in to impulse, he'd have two detectives knocking on his door. Then he remembered good ol' David Price, who lived next door to a cop and still got away with killing ten kids. Good ol' David Price, who's conveniently locked up with him in Intake."

"Even rapists need role models," Waters said.

"Unfortunately for us. And now, unfortunately for Viggio. Hang on a sec, we're here." Griffin saw the street sign belatedly, hit the brakes and let the momentum of the car's back end whip them around the turn. He promptly killed the grille lights and eased up on the gas. He didn't want to spook Viggio by racing down the street, lights flashing. First, they would conduct a casual drive-by to assess the home.

They neared the address and immediately spotted a man walking out the front door, heading for his car in the driveway. The man wore dark blue pants, a light blue chambray shirt and, from the back at least, could've been a double for Eddie Como. Hello, Ron Viggio.

"Jesus Christ," Waters murmured in awe.

"He's gonna bail!" Griffin warned. He grabbed the radio. "Everyone, greenlight, greenlight, *greenlight!*"

Griffin whipped his car sideways onto the driveway, blocked Viggio's vehicle and slammed on the brakes. Viggio's head popped up. He registered the two unmarked cars and one police cruiser bearing down on him. And then he ran.

"Move, move, move." Griffin was out of his car. Up ahead, he saw Fitz swerve his Taurus into another driveway in an attempt to stop the fleeing suspect. Viggio leapt onto the Taurus's hood, jumped down the other side and kept moving.

Shouts now. Waters bellowing, "Police, stop!" Residents peering out of their homes and yelping in surprise at the commotion. Officers yelling as they tore out of their cruisers and prepared to give chase.

Griffin had the lead. He scrambled over Fitz's hood and thundered down the sidewalk. He'd show Ron Viggio what a five-minute mile meant. Vaguely he was aware of Waters racing right along beside him. Fitz panted somewhere in the distance.

Viggio glanced frantically over his shoulder and saw them closing the gap. He darted right, headed between two small houses and leapt a low wooden fence. A woman shrieked. A dog barked. Griffin heard it all from far away as he vaulted the fence, homed in on Viggio and dove for the man's legs.

At the last minute, Viggio spun left, avoiding the tackle and reaching a tall chain-link fence. Griffin went down, rolled into the fall and was back on his feet in time to see

Viggio and Waters disappear over the barrier. He jumped onto the chain link and resumed pursuit.

They had arrived in someone's personal version of a salvage yard. A small white house sat forlornly in the middle of a pile of twisted, burnt-out wrecks. For a moment, Griffin couldn't see anyone at all. Then he heard a clatter as Viggio darted past a pile of rusty hubcaps, and Waters went careening around another gutted car.

Griffin watched Viggio's line, saw the obvious destination – a kid's bike by the home's front door – and raced around the other side of the house.

He burst into view twenty feet in front of Viggio. "Boo!" Griffin roared.

A startled Ron Viggio drew up short.

And Waters took him out with a flying tackle.

Ten minutes later, Ron Viggio sat handcuffed in the back of a Rhode Island police cruiser, sullenly refusing to talk. They let him be for now and descended upon his home. In the bathroom, Waters found the neatly stacked boxes of latex gloves. In the kitchen pantry, Fitz bagged and tagged three rows of Berkely and Johnson Disposable Douches, all Country Flowers. Then, of course, there were the vials they found in the freezer.

The kitchen table held an open package of model rocketry igniters and was covered with some sort of gray clay. Griffin sniffed the gray material suspiciously, then left it for Jack-n-Jack to figure out. They checked the upstairs bedrooms, the downstairs bathroom and all the closets. Still no sign of Meg.

Griffin finally found a door beneath the staircase, a door leading to the basement. He took a deep breath, motioned to Waters, and together they descended into the depths.

"Meg?" Griffin called out. Something grazed the top of his head. The end of a pull chain for an overhead light.

Still no sound in the dark.

Steeled for the worst, he yanked the chain and turned on the light.

Thirty seconds later, he and Waters had walked the entire length of the dank, empty space.

"Floor doesn't even looked disturbed," Waters said. "I don't think anyone's been down here for a bit."

Griffin thought about it. "Car?" he asked with a frown.

"Gotta be."

"Shit."

They were back up the stairs and out of the house. Car wouldn't be good. Trunk of a car would be even worse. Hold it together. Remember the lessons of the past year.

The driver's-side door wasn't locked. Waters opened it with gloved hands, while Griffin ran around to the trunk. He had his firearm out, just in case. On the count of three, Waters popped the trunk.

Griffin leveled his gun.

"Hey," he said a split second later. "Isn't that a bomb?"

Carol had started to move. Dan didn't know if it was good movement or bad movement. At first, just her right hand twitched. He'd taken that as a good sign, stroking her fingers, trying to talk his wife back to life.

Then, her left leg had started to twitch, and she had developed a hitch in her breathing. He wasn't sure what that meant. The doctors had told him that the high dosage of Ambien and alcohol in her bloodstream had effectively shut down her system. In theory, however, her kidneys would do their job, removing the impurities from her bloodstream, and she would respond by waking up. At least that's what they hoped.

Was twitching the same as waking? Did people regain consciousness by first suffering labored breathing?

Dan was standing now. He patted Carol's hand, smoothed back her hair from her pale, cool forehead.

"Come on, honey," he murmured. "Come back to me, love. It's going to be all right. I promise you, this time, things are going to be better."

Her left leg twitched again. Her breathing hiccupped.

Dan leaned forward. He gazed down at his wife's quiet,

peaceful face, as beautiful now as the first day he had met her.

And he realized for the first time that her chest was no longer moving. Her breathing had not returned.

A machine started to beep. Dan dropped his wife's hand. He raced into the hallway, his voice already frantic.

"Help, help! Somebody, help us, *please!*"

Five forty-five P.M.

The massive ACI gates swung open. The blue transport van pulled forward. David Price, still grinning, was on his way. In the Pesaturo home, Lieutenant Morelli finished up last-minute details of the meeting, including handing Tom and Laurie bulletproof vests.

They had told Molly they were going to play a game. They were going to a park for a police officers' picnic. They would have some punch, eat some cookies and she could watch all the police officers do their jobs. A man might come and play pretend, too. But not to worry. He was just part of the game.

Molly regarded them solemnly. Children always knew when adults were telling a lie.

They were walking out the front door, faces somber, moods grim, when Morelli's cell phone rang.

It was Griffin. "We got him, we got him, we got him! We've found boxes of latex gloves, plus the douches. Ron Viggio, former cleaner of the Pawtucket sperm bank, is definitely the College Hill Rapist."

"And Meg?" Morelli asked sharply. Tom and Laurie froze, stared at her.

"Not here."

"Where the hell is she?"

"We don't know yet. Viggio's not talking. But we can apply some pressure, retrace his steps. We'll find her, Lieutenant. It's only a matter of time."

Morelli looked at Tom and Laurie. "We have a man who may be the College Hill Rapist," she told them quietly, "but we haven't found Meg."

"Do they have any leads?" Laurie asked.

"Sergeant Griffin believes it is only a matter of time."

"How much time? Does she have food, does she have water? What if she's being held somewhere outside? We want our daughter, we need our daughter to be safe."

"Don't let him go, Lieutenant," Griffin was saying excitedly into the phone. "Don't let Price out. We can do this on our own. We don't need Price anymore."

Morelli looked again at the Pesaturos' anxious faces. She glanced at her watch. Five fifty-five P.M. She said, "I'm sorry, Sergeant. It's too late."

41
The Candy Man

Meg was frightened. Her arms and shoulders hurt seriously now, throbbed with a low keening ache. Her fingers, however, she barely felt at all. They were slow, sluggish, like a separate entity that no longer belonged to her.

Sometimes she felt moisture in her hair, a slow, steady drip. At first, she thought the ceiling had developed a leak. Now she realized it was more blood from her torn, shredded wrists.

She still swayed back and forth, slower now, with less force. Sometimes the wall anchor moved. More often than not, it remained rigidly fixed. She was slightly built, admirably thin. In other words, she didn't have the mass to get the job done. And now she was feeling tired beyond tired. She had strange spells where she couldn't tell whether she was asleep or awake. Her lips were dry and cracked. Her tongue felt glued to her mouth.

Perversely, her bladder had finally given out on her. She hadn't gone to the bathroom since first thing this morning and she simply couldn't hold it any longer. The shame was worse than the discomfort. To be a grown adult with urine-soaked pants; it wasn't right.

And now, to add insult to injury . . .

She missed her captor. She genuinely wished, way down deep, that he would return to her. Maybe, her fuzzy, fatigued mind reasoned, he would cut her down, ease the ache in her shoulders. Maybe, she fantasized, he'd give her a bath, let her feel human again.

And if he did touch her after that, if he did demand some kind of payment . . .

She wouldn't be in the dark anymore. She wouldn't be lost with wet jeans and bleeding wrists. She wouldn't be alone in a musty basement that felt too much like a grave.

These thoughts were bad, she realized in the saner corner of her mind. These thoughts let him win. She had to hold tough, be strong. She had to ignore her pain. To focus her anger, as Jillian liked to say.

We are not victims. The minute we believe that, we let the rapist win. When it boils down to brute strength, ladies, perhaps we can't protect our bodies. But we can always control our minds.

Oh please, oh please, oh please let her get out of this. Before her arms gave out completely. Before she did anything she'd regret. Before . . .

Before David Price arrived.

David couldn't see out of the van very well. The transport vehicle offered no side window, and there was a mesh screen between him and the two state marshals, which blurred the front windshield.

That was okay: he didn't need to know where he was or where he was going. That was not relevant to matters at hand.

David leaned forward and pretended to stretch out his back. Then he shifted restlessly from side to side, his fingers slipping along his left shirtsleeve until he found the slim wooden shape sewn into the cuff.

The bulk was barely noticeable. The quarter-inch-thick, heavily lacquered wooden lock pick was tucked inside the top seam of the cuff, where the heavy chambray fabric already formed a ridge. If nothing else, Viggio was very good at following instructions. Then, in a move he'd spent the past four months practicing, David leaned forward and bit the hem of his right pant leg. Inside the pant cuff, his tongue found the waiting treasure – what appeared to be crumbled bits of white chalk. Pieces of Alka-Seltzer – too small to be easily noticed, and like the wooden pick, guaranteed not to set off a metal detector.

Sometimes, the simple things truly worked the best.

David eased the pieces of tablet out of the pants cuff and into his mouth. Then, he started to chew.

Forty seconds later, he made a gurgling noise in the back of his throat.

The state marshal glanced in the rearview mirror.

"What the hell?" he said.

In the back of the transport van, David Price was foaming at the mouth.

Griffin was in Ron Viggio's face. "Where is she?"

"I don't know who you're talking about."

"Don't play dumb with me. *Where is she?*"

"My grandma's been dead for years, but thanks for asking."

"We have you, Viggio. We know all about how you stole semen samples from the sperm bank, then injected them into douches. You're already looking at two counts of murder, let alone four counts of first-degree sexual assault. You're a little beyond minimum time behind bars, Ronnie boy. Start talking now, and maybe you have some hope of ever seeing daylight."

Sitting in the back of the police cruiser, Viggio yawned.

"Are you trying to protect David Price? Because he's already sold you out. Three hours from now, when he's done meeting with his daughter, he's going to give your name."

Viggio laughed.

"We caught you because of him, Viggio. If he hadn't told us that you'd personally met Eddie Como, we wouldn't have thought to check personnel at the sperm bank."

Viggio frowned.

"Yeah, that's right. You were doing so well, too. You had the perfect setup, a great little plan. Except for David Price. He was your weak link. He's who got you into this mess. Here you thought he was helping you, when really he was playing you all along. You're not a brilliant criminal mastermind. You're just David Price's pawn."

Viggio thinned his lips. Despite his best intentions, he was starting to look pissed.

Griffin's turn to shrug. He straightened, crossed his arms over his chest and gave Viggio a dismissive glance. "Pawns can be sacrificed, Viggio. Guys like Price do it all the time. Why do you think we're here? Price wanted to buy his freedom, so he sold you out. Now he gets to meet his little girl, while you go to prison for the rest of your life. Hardly seems fair. Where is Meg, Viggio? Talk now, while you still have a chance."

"Go to hell."

"Come on, Viggio. David isn't going to help you. You're fucked, you're screwed. Whatever you thought you had coming, it's over. What do you still owe him?"

Viggio's gaze flickered toward his car, now cordoned off in the driveway. Griffin caught the look. He stared at Viggio's vehicle, and then he got it.

"That's another car bomb, isn't it, Viggio? Except, instead of using it on a hired gun, you were going to use it on David Price. You were going to hook it up, then watch your favorite partner-in-crime go boom. Well, I'll be damned. So there really isn't any honor among thieves. Wait a minute." Griffin's voice changed. He leaned forward intently. "That means David Price was going to get into a vehicle. What the hell do you know, Viggio? *What the hell does David Price have planned?*"

Jillian was pacing the living room of the Pesaturo home while Libby and Toppi watched. Her right hand twisted Trisha's medallion relentlessly. Her left hand was clasped behind her back.

"This isn't right," she told Libby and Toppi, though they had probably grown bored with her tirade by now. "Tom and Laurie need us. Meg needs us. We should be *doing* something!"

"Jillian," Toppi said firmly, patiently, "we're not professionals. Sometimes the right thing to do is to wait."

"But David Price is getting exactly what he wants! Surely

there's got to be another way! God, why can't I think of another way?"

Libby sighed. Toppi stared at Jillian.

"How do we even know he will give up the rapist's name?" Jillian quizzed them. "Griffin is right. After meeting with Molly, Price can say anything he likes. It's too late to do anything about it then."

"They could send him to Super Max," Toppi said. "Or punish him with this LFI thing."

"Oh, like David Price cares about that. It's games he likes, getting the upper hand, controlling all the moves on the board." She stopped abruptly, frowned. "Huh."

"What?" Toppi asked.

"David likes to control everything," Jillian said slowly. "But this meeting . . . He let the police pick the place and the route for getting there. He only set the time. If he were planning something, you'd think he'd want to choose the location. Someplace he knew well, or had an opportunity to booby-trap. Or have the College Hill Rapist booby-trap. That would make sense. David helps the College Hill Rapist come up with the perfect crime. In return, the rapist helps David get out of jail."

"Maybe he's not planning anything," Toppi said firmly. "You heard Lieutenant Morelli. The police are focusing all of their resources on this meeting. Price can hardly just exit the van and keep walking."

Jillian glared at her irritably. "Of course he's planning something! If he really wanted to see his daughter, he would've pressed the issue *before* going to jail. So this isn't about Molly. It's about getting out of prison." She paused, still thinking out loud. "And it's about revenge. Arranging things so that Meg would be the first victim, then setting up the assassination of Eddie Como so it would bring Griffin onto the case. His actions are personal, almost autobiographical – same victim, same detective. But he didn't pick the place. Why didn't he pick the place?"

And then, her eyes flew open. "Oh no!"

"What?"

"It's not going to be at the location! Don't you get it? All the snipers, the lieutenant and Molly . . . That's just a cover, something to distract the police. He didn't pick a place, *because he has no intention of getting there!* Whatever he's going to do, it's going to be en route. Quick, where's the phone, where's the phone? I've got to call Griffin!"

Driving down Route 2 in Cranston, State Marshal Jerry Atkins urgently radioed the state police cruiser in front of him. "Something's wrong with Price. He's foaming at the mouth. Jesus Christ, I think he's going into convulsions! What do you want us to do?"

Pause.

"Well we can't just let him die . . . He's supposed to give up the damn rapist. Wait a sec. Whooooa! He's out. He's on the floor. Jesus, I think he's choking on his tongue. He needs immediate medical attention. Quick, pull over!"

Up ahead, the police cruiser abruptly turned right, heading into a restaurant's parking lot. This part of Route 2 was nothing but an endless strip mall, not a great place for an emergency stop with a violent felon on board. But then, from the back of the van, came another loud crash as Price's shackled ankles jerked violently.

A second police cruiser pulled in behind them and tried to fashion a barricade in the back of the lot. The parking lot wasn't crowded. It was the best they could do.

Jerry jumped down from the driver's side of the van. He had a small first-aid kit, and only the faintest idea of how to proceed.

"Radio for an ambulance," he yelled.

"We're talking to the lieutenant!"

"Does she know first aid?"

"Don't unshackle him!"

"Jesus Christ, do I look like an idiot?"

Jerry threw open the side door. His partner was right behind him. Apparently, the state police did think they were idiots and their escorting officer, Ernie, shoved them both aside. He peered in first with his holster unsnapped and his hand on the butt of his firearm.

"Holy shit."

Jerry and his partner pushed past Ernie and promptly drew up short. David Price's scrawny body seemed to have folded in on itself, a jumbled tangle of shackled arms and legs that could not be natural. As the three men stared in shock, his body spasmed again and his head lolled back, giving them an eerie image of a man trying to stare out through the whites of his eyes.

Jerry was galvanized first. "Quick, quick, get him straightened out. We gotta get a stick in his mouth before he bites off his tongue." He jumped into the van, grabbing at David's shackled feet. Ernie went for his shoulders.

Jerry had a strange thought. Price's hands – they weren't where they should be. What had happened to the thick belt that should be shackling his hands to his waist? His gaze fell to the floor, he saw a small wooden sliver. Almost like a lock pick. And then . . .

Jerry's head came up.

David's magically freed hand grabbed Ernie's Beretta.

Jerry yelled, "N – "

The bullet slammed into his brain.

Crackle, confusion. In the cordoned-off park in Cranston, Lieutenant Morelli strode away from the Pesaturo family with her cell phone in one hand and her radio in the other. She was sweating heavily beneath the weight of her Kevlar vest, and her gaze kept going to the surrounding rooftops, checking on her snipers.

"What do you mean Price is having some kind of fit?"

"No, don't pull over. What? You've already pulled over? Whose dumb idea was that?"

Her cell phone rang. She flipped it open first ring and while still listening to Brueger's muddled explanation on the radio, barked, "Morelli."

"He's going to do something on the way," Griffin yelled over the phone. "He was never planning on meeting Molly.

It's a ruse. Viggio was going to tamper with his getaway car!"

"Griffin . . ." And then to the radio, "I know you can't let him die!"

"Lieutenant, where is the transport van? Tell me where to find the transport van."

"Dammit, Brueger, where are you? Griffin's yelling that Price has some kind of escape plan. Don't touch him. You hear me? Nobody touches David Price. Brueger?"

Shots. Sudden, sharp, coming over the airwaves. Lots of them. And then men swearing, and more gunfire, and then a gurgle. Close. In the receiver. A man choking on his own blood.

"Brueger? Brueger, do you hear me? Brueger, what is happening?"

"Where is the van, where is the van?" Griffin was yelling. *"Brueger!"*

Silence. Total silence. Even Griffin had finally fallen quiet. Seconds ticked away. The sweat trickled hot from Morelli's forehead to the tip of her chin. She turned around slowly. She stared at Tom and Laurie Pesaturo, who were watching her with shocked, frightened eyes. Her gaze fell. She looked at Molly. Pretty little Molly, who, if there was any justice in this world, would never know her real father.

And then. A voice.

"Send Griffin my love," David Price said over the radio. *"Oh, and somebody might want to send an ambulance. Wait, on second thought, I believe the coroner will do."*

Griffin swore once, stunned, as the radio clicked off.

Lieutenant Morelli hung her head.

Griffin shut his cell phone. It promptly rang again. For a moment, he simply stared at it. Waters did, too. They had heard everything coming over Morelli's radio into Griffin's phone, and now their faces were white, drained. Fitz appeared shell-shocked. The assembled officers were shattered. Sometimes life was like being submerged twenty miles beneath the sea. All sounds were muted. Your limbs felt too heavy to move. You drifted in the dark, the surface too far away, the pressure about to collapse your chest.

Griffin's phone rang again.

He flipped it open and steeled himself for Price's smirking voice.

"He's going to do something along the way!" Jillian exclaimed. "He's never going to make it to the park!"

"I know," Griffin whispered.

"Think about it," she continued excitedly. "He let the police pick the location. He never would have done that if that's where he was planning on making his escape."

"I know."

"And with the snipers and the SWAT team and all that coverage . . . It would be impossible to do something there. En route, on the other hand, when it's just him and some drivers – "

"Jillian, I know."

"You do? Well, then, stop him!"

He didn't say anything. He didn't have the words to voice what he had just heard. How many men had been involved in the escort? Four, six, eight? How many had wives? How many had children? Waters had turned away. Fitz sat down hard on Ron Viggio's driveway, staring bleakly at a streetlight. Somewhere in the neighborhood, a dog howled.

"Griffin?" Jillian said, her voice suddenly uncertain. "Did he? Is it . . ."

"It just happened."

"Oh my God. What did . . ."

"I can't."

"Meg?"

"We don't know."

"Griffin, he can't get away."

"You think I don't know that?" His body finally came alive. He kicked the tire of the police cruiser. Then kicked it again and again. Sitting in the back of the car, Viggio gazed at him balefully. The prick had probably heard it all and still didn't give a damn.

Griffin's vision started to cloud over. He could see his hands so clearly. He could envision them fastening on Viggio's neck, squeezing, squeezing, squeezing . . .

Breathe deep, exhale. Breathe deep, exhale. Don't give in. Picture yourself in a happy place. He wanted to dance on David Price's grave. Was that a happy place? Or did that simply mean that one year later, he hadn't learned a goddamn thing?

"Griffin," Jillian said, "Lieutenant Morelli claimed you had a lead on the rapist."

"Found him."

"But he doesn't have Meg?"

"Nope. And he doesn't seem to be in the mood to talk about it."

"Griffin, I know where she is."

"What?" He perked up. Waters and Fitz caught the change in his demeanor and glanced at him sharply.

"David's self-centered," Jillian said in a rush. "Self-absorbed. This has all been about him. He picked Meg to be the first victim again. He picked you to lead the case again. And now, for the grand finish . . ."

"No!" Griffin breathed.

"Yes. He has one more grave to dig, don't you see, Griffin? He started with Meg. And now he's going to do what he probably thinks he should've done six years ago. He's going to kill Meg. And he's going to bury her in the basement. He's going back to your old neighborhood, Griffin. He's going back to his old house!"

Griffin looked at Viggio. The rapist tried to blank his features, but was too late. The look of amazement on his face said enough.

"How did you get access to Price's former home?" Griffin barked.

"My mother bought it."

"*What?*"

"Price recommended it. Face it, who wants to buy a home that used to have murdered babies in the basement? The real estate agent gave up months ago, and my mother bought it cheap. She's on fixed-income, so hey, she's happy."

"You involved your *mother* in this?"

"Of course not! She's in Florida. I surprised her with a free trip."

"Son of a bitch!" Griffin motioned furiously at Waters and Fitz. "Jillian, thanks. We're on our way there."

Griffin's car was blocked by the police cruiser. They ran for Fitz's Taurus while Griffin started yelling into the radio.

David had a ten-minute head start and they were a good fifteen minutes away. Once more the clock was ticking. For Meg's sake, Griffin hoped they weren't too late.

In the Pesaturos' living room, Jillian hung up the phone, grabbed her coat, grabbed her purse and then grabbed her pepper spray.

"This is insane," Toppi said immediately. "You're not a cop!"

"It's Meg."

"Let them handle this."

"Because it's gone so well thus far?" Jillian turned to her mother. "May I have your pepper spray? I'll take as much as I can get."

Libby frowned, gazed at her reproachfully.

"I can't sit around and wait anymore, Mom! Meg needs me. I have to try."

Libby didn't budge.

"Oh for heaven's sake, I'm not going to just barrel into the house! I did that once before and I know as well as anyone that it didn't work. I'll be careful. I'll . . . I'll think of something along the way."

Libby's expression started to waver. Jillian bent down and looked her mother in the eye.

"I have to do this," she said quietly, intently. "I didn't save Trisha, don't you see? You miss her terribly, I know you do. But I *failed* her, and I have to live with that every day of my life. Yes, he was stronger than me. Yes, you should blame the rapist and not the victim. It all sounds so well and good. But I was there. I saw her. And I . . . I didn't get to her in time. I didn't save her.

"I don't want to lose someone else, Mom. I don't want to lose you or Meg or Carol. So I need to do this. Maybe I can't change the world. But I'm finally learning that, for me at least, it's important to try. Please, Mom, may I have your pepper spray?"

Libby reached into her pocket. She held out the canister with a trembling, liver-spotted hand. She looked at her last daughter with open concern. Then she sighed and dropped the canister into Jillian's palm.

Jillian kissed her mother's cheek.

Then she turned and ran for the door.

42

The Survivors Club

Meg had drifted off again. She was at home, in Molly's pink-colored room. They were preparing Barbie for her big wedding day, except this time Pooh's cape was blood red. Meg was trying to get the cape off when she looked down to see that Pooh's fuzzy cheeks had morphed into David Price's smirking face.

"Daddy!" Molly cried in delight.

Meg jerked awake with a scream. Her legs had given out beneath her, and her arms screamed at the sudden impact of her dead weight. Hastily she scrambled to get her footing on the rough dirt floor. Perversely enough, her arms and shoulders ached worse.

A sound. Up above. A door opening. Footsteps moving quickly across a wooden floor.

Meg couldn't help herself. The College Hill Rapist was back, and she was grateful. Her bloody wrists stung, her bound ankles hurt. She couldn't stand the feel of her urine-soaked jeans plastered against her skin. She wanted down. She wanted out. She wished . . . she wished so badly to feel human again.

She turned her head to where she believed the staircase was, and held her breath in anticipation of his approach.

Another click, the door opening at the top of the stairs. And then, "Hi, honey," David Price's voice sang out clearly, "I'm home!"

Through her gag, Meg started to scream.

Five blocks from Griffin's old home, Fitz hit the brakes.

Adrenaline demanded that they roar up to the front door and leap out, guns blazing. Prudence advised a different course. The three men gazed studiously around the neighborhood for any sign of David Price while Fitz drove a grid.

Up one street, down another. Around this block, around another. Clock ticking, tension mounting. Griffin could feel the knots bulging in his shoulders, while Waters cracked his knuckles incessantly.

The streets were quiet. The sun was beginning to sink and firing the sky bright orange and deep crimson.

They got within one block of Griffin's former home, where he had lived and loved and lost his wife. Then Fitz pulled over.

"How many points of entry?" he asked quietly.

"Three. Front door, side patio door and basement bulkhead."

"We split up," Waters murmured.

"Finesse job," Griffin said. "David's armed and he won't hesitate to use Meg as a shield. Basically, it's a hostage situation that, given the neighborhood, could rapidly grow worse."

"Contain him," Fitz muttered.

"Yeah. Meg is bad enough. We don't want him to end up in another home, with an entire family to torment."

No one asked the next logical question – at what point did they sacrifice Meg to contain Price? They had to hope it wouldn't come down to that.

"All right," Griffin said.

They got out of the car, got out their firearms, and one by one disappeared into the fiery dusk.

The doctors poured in. Kids, really, in oversized lab coats raced into Carol's room and surrounded Dan's wife. Her left leg was twitching, her right arm thrashing. The machine beeped and the doctors shouted strange codes to the nurses, who were already pushing Dan aside as they scrambled for more equipment and one helluva big syringe.

"Carol, Carol, Carol . . ."

"You need to leave, sir."

"My wife . . ."

"A doctor will be with you shortly, sir."

"Carol – "

The nurse shut him firmly out of the room. He stood outside, alone in the hallway, while the doctors yelled, the machine beeped and his wife's body convulsed on the bed.

David touched her. His fingers stroked Meg's cheek and gently feathered back her hair. She tried to turn away, but she couldn't escape. He had taken off her blindfold first thing. All the better to see you, my dear, he'd crooned. The sudden glare of the bare overhead light hurt her eyes.

"You grew up," David said now. "Pity."

He ran one finger up her arm, then raised it to his lips and sucked her blood off his fingertip.

"You've been busy, my dear. Look at the mess you've made. It didn't help you at all, but it's sweet that you tried. Did Ronnie tell you I was coming, Meg? Did you work yourself into such a state, simply for me?"

She still had the gag in her mouth, so she didn't bother to reply.

"Well, I really can't delay too long," David said briskly. "So let's get you unhooked and down to business."

Meg eyed him warily. She could see the butt of a gun sticking up from the waistband of his pants. One side of his shirt carried a red stain, and his right cheek was flecked with blood. He reeked of gunpowder and death. She had no illusions what that meant.

He slipped his hand behind his back. It emerged with an ugly, black-sheathed knife.

"Courtesy of Jerry," he told her, though she didn't understand whom he meant.

She watched him unsnap the leather sheath. She watched the large, serrated hunting knife slide into view, the overhead light caressing the menacing edge. She should've worked the wall anchor more. She should've tried harder. Who cares that her arms and shoulders had ached. Whatever

David did to her now was going to hurt far, far worse.

He rested the tip of the blade against her collarbone. It felt cool and sharp against her sweat-soaked skin.

She closed her eyes, pressed her back against the wall and tried to tell herself it couldn't hurt forever. Everything, even pain, had to end. Poor Molly. Poor Mom and Dad. Poor Jillian and Carol . . . Poor Meg. She had been getting things together. Really, even without a memory, she had been looking forward to getting on with her life. And now . . . The knife moved. She whimpered helplessly . . .

And David cut her down.

Her arms fell forward abruptly, her bound hands hitting her stomach like a rock. In the next instant, blood flow returned to her strained limbs, prickling nerve endings to sudden life, and she nearly screamed at the sudden whomp of pain.

Watching her, David laughed. "Yeah, sometimes the recovery is worse than the injury. You know, I've spent the last year getting into yoga. Take it from me, if you had conditioned your muscles properly to begin with, it wouldn't hurt so much now. Jesus, Meg, did you wet your pants?"

She wanted to hit him. She couldn't move her arms. They felt strange and rubbery, as if they no longer belonged to her. And her shoulders felt different, overly loose. Parts were assembled, but someone hadn't done the wiring right.

"I had planned on playing here for a while," David announced matter-of-factly, "but the fact that Ronnie's absent leads me to believe he might have been detained, and if Ronnie's been detained, then this house is no longer safe. In the good-news department, I see he's already procured a car. What do you say, Meg? Let's go for a ride. For no reason at all, I'm going to have you start the engine first."

He stepped toward the stairs and when she didn't automatically follow, he looked back at her with a frown. "Come on, don't be shy." Then his gaze fell and he finally noticed her bound ankles. "Well, well, looks like Ronnie didn't like to leave anything to chance. Believe me when I say I know exactly how you feel. Come on, I need you to walk."

David got the knife back out. He bent and started sawing through the latex ties. The material finally snapped free. He looked up at her with a smile.

Meg smiled back. And then she drove her knee as hard as she could into the underside of his chin. His jaw cracked sharply. His face went bone-white as the pain ricocheted up to his forehead. David stumbled back, still gripping the knife.

Don't give him time to recover, their self-defense instructor had told them. Don't give your attacker time to think.

Meg lashed her foot out at David's groin; he blocked her with his thigh. She drove her foot down into his tender instep. He made a funny noise in the back of his throat. She went after the side of his kneecap and he finally went down.

She wanted his gun. She wanted his knife. She wanted to stick her fingers in his eye sockets and dig for his brain. But her fingers wouldn't move, her arms wouldn't obey.

Meg whirled toward the wooden staircase with her useless, bloody arms. She started to run.

Behind her, David yelled, "One more step, you fucking bitch, and I will blow you away!"

Meg didn't stop.

David opened fire.

Griffin was easing along the front of the house, approaching the front door, when he heard the first gunshot. It was quickly followed by many more. He ducked low, grabbed the doorknob with his left hand while holding his Beretta with his right. Twist, turn, he rolled into the front entryway and came up in time to see David Price standing at the top of the basement stairs only four feet away. David was bellowing, "I'M GONNA KILL YOU, BITCH!" and brandishing a gun that matched Griffin's own – apparently David had armed himself courtesy of his state police escorts.

Griffin squeezed the trigger just as David spotted him, dodged right and returned fire. Shit! Griffin hurtled himself into the room on the left, getting off a few wild shots while David splintered the floorboards at his feet. Another shape suddenly appeared on Griffin's left – Fitz, emerging through the side patio door.

Griffin yelled: "Down!"

David raised the barrel and squeezed off another shot as Fitz hit the ground.

Griffin fired again. David whirled around the corner into the kitchen, where he had access to the next flight of stairs.

"Damn!" Fitz swore into Griffin's ear, crawling to his feet. "I think he took out the last of my hair."

"Where's Meg?"

"I don't know, but he shot the hell out of something in the basement."

"You go down, I go up."

"And let you have all the fun?"

"You get the girl."

"Oh yeah. Enough said."

Griffin scrambled across the floor, on his hands and knees now and finding the shattered flooring the hard way. He drove four splinters into his forearms before he finally arrived at the entranceway to the kitchen. He reached in with one hand, toppled a small table onto its side and dove behind it for cover.

Then he waited, letting his eyes readjust to the gloomy interior. A light glowed from the bottom of the basement, but apparently that was the only light on in the tightly shuttered house. Griffin blinked, worked on catching his breath, then turned his gaze to the ceiling above him.

Not a sound from overhead. Not a footstep, a scuffle or a muttered curse.

Seven-oh-five P.M. The house was deathly still as the sun began its final descent, and the combatants prepared for round two.

Jillian was trying to drive and read a printout from maps.com detailing how to get to Price's former address, which she'd found listed in old news stories detailing his arrest. The first time she drove right by the street. She went to do an illegal U-turn, then realized it was better this way; she would have a better chance at surprise if she approached the house on foot.

She had one canister of pepper spray in her hand, another in her pocket. Spray worked best up close. Go for the eyes and nose, get it in the mucous membranes. For someone like her, that would require stealth. David was looking for the police, after all. He probably had his hands full battling seasoned professionals like Griffin. Maybe he was even having difficulty controlling Meg. They would be the distraction.

She thought of Trish's apartment again. The man's weight pressing her to the floor, pinning her in place while her sister suffocated and died on the bed. The man laughing at her futile efforts. The man promising to fuck her good.

But she needed to keep those memories at bay. She needed to focus on the sidewalk beneath her feet, the cool metal canister in her hand and the house looming near.

Trish had died, the man had won. You couldn't change the past. Time to move forward. Focus on Meg. Think of the lessons she had learned.

And then return home to her mother, who truly needed her.

Jillian homed in on the house. She was still trying to figure out how to approach, when she heard a low moan, then a male voice shouted, "Jesus Christ, Waters. Oh man. Oh . . . Jesus . . . Hang in there, buddy. Oh man, we need a doctor *quick!*"

Meg was breathing hard. Her body had started trembling uncontrollably and she had to remain plastered to the bedroom wall or she was afraid she'd shatter into a million pieces. As she'd raced up the basement stairs, she'd heard gunfire behind her. At first she'd ducked instinctively, dodging imaginary bullets, then she'd realized that even more gunfire came from behind David. Someone had penetrated the bulkhead. For one moment, her spirits had soared. She *was* being rescued! The cavalry *had* arrived. Then she had heard a man's sudden, sharp exclamation. A stranger's voice. Someone else, not David, had been hit.

She had run and run. And still she had heard shots, coming steadily closer and gaining fresh intensity in the foyer. Then, just as abruptly as it had started, it was over. No more shots, just David's harsh exclamation as he careened up the first-floor stairs.

If the police had come, then he'd shot them all. Because David didn't seem to be running away. Instead, from what she could tell, he was now on the second floor with her. Somewhere down that shadowed hallway, he was looking for her.

Her gaze went around the dusky bedroom, now searching for some means of escape. The blinds were pulled, casting the room into a deep gray pall that made every shadow sinister and every piece of furniture a hulking monster waiting to attack. She spotted the bed in the room's far corner. Her first temptation was to crawl underneath, push herself to the back and curl up her legs and hide. He would look under the beds, of course. And once he found her, she'd be trapped, helpless. He'd grab her by the ankles and drag her out, his knife already in hand.

She couldn't get boxed in. She needed to preserve her options. She was trying to think: *What would Jillian do?*

The bathroom. Maybe she could find a razor or hairspray. Of course, a razor didn't exactly compete with a hunting knife and hairspray hadn't been known to checkmate a gun. Halt or I'll spritz you to death!

She almost giggled, then realized she was becoming hysterical and bit her lower lip. The movement pressed the gag deeper into the corners of her parched mouth. Her eyes teared.

What if she could make it to the bedroom window? She could open it, maybe get onto the roof. Or if the house didn't have a first-story overhang, she could always just jump. It would probably hurt. She might break a leg or worse. But given the alternative . . .

She heard a sound. It was a whisper, slithering down the long dark hall.

"Oh Meg, pretty Meg," David crooned softly. "Come out, come out, wherever you are."

Fight or flight? Not much time left . . .

Poor beaten Meg made her decision.

Griffin had to get up to the second story. He wasn't sure how. As in so many small New England homes, the staircase was narrow and steep. With his build, he'd be a walking target all the way up. All Price had to do was hear him coming, turn the corner and open fire.

Then again . . .

Floorboards creaked up above. Price was on the move.

And then Griffin heard another sound. More old wood groaning, then the telltale squeak of a window finally giving way. But this noise came from the opposite corner from the first noise.

There was a second person upstairs. Oh no, Meg . . .

Griffin didn't have a choice anymore. He abandoned the cover of the table and made his move.

Jillian came around the side of the old house. The first thing she saw was Fitz on the ground, kneeling over another man. "Come on, buddy, come on, hang in there."

"Detective Fitzpatrick?" she called softly.

He jerked around sharply. It was hard to see his features in the rapidly growing dusk, but his movements appeared dazed.

"Jillian, what are you . . . Never mind. Got a cell phone? I need it now!"

"Is he . . ."

"That son of a bitch David Price shot him as he opened up the basement bulkhead. Guess David was already waiting in the cellar."

"Meg . . ." the man on the ground murmured. "Price . . . going to shoot . . . her."

"Shhhh, Griffin's got her."

"She's still in the house?" Jillian dropped down on her knees next to Fitz, then dug in her purse for her cell phone. The downed detective didn't look good. She could see the stain growing rapidly along his left side. His thin face was abnormally pale, sweat beaded his brow. He was going into shock.

"Here." She thrust her phone out to Fitz, then took off her long coat and draped it over the man's chest. He was starting to shake now. The cold grass wasn't good for him, but she didn't know if they should move him. She glanced nervously around the bare yard. They were five feet from a house with an armed killer and the damn landscaping didn't even offer a bush or tree for cover.

Fitz was on the phone. In a quiet, controlled rush he was demanding backup, demanding an ambulance, demanding assistance for an officer down. "Detective Waters has been shot," he said. "Repeat, we require immediate medical assistance."

Jillian took Waters's hand. His fingers felt cold and clammy to the touch. "M-M-Meg."

"Meg's fine," Jillian lied. "Please don't worry."

"Got up . . . basement stairs. I . . . distracted . . . Price."

"Shhhh, it's going to be all right, Detective. Relax now. You heard Fitz. Griffin's inside. Griffin will take care of Meg."

Fitz was done with the phone and was now looking from her to Waters frantically. Jillian understood his dilemma.

"I'll stay with him," she said. "You go help Griffin."

"He's a good guy," Fitz said gruffly, still torn as he looked at a downed fellow officer.

"I have Detective Waters," Jillian repeated firmly. "You help Meg."

Fitz gave Waters one last look. The detective wearily, blearily waved him off. "G-G-Go."

Fitz turned. He ran back around to the front of the house, where David Price waited with a gun, where Griffin stalked a killer and where Meg fought for her life.

Jillian sat down in the cold, damp grass. She clasped Waters's hand in hers. "Stay with me, Detective," she murmured. "We're going to get through this. I promise you, we're all going to get out of this alive."

*

Meg was at the window, exposed and vulnerable to the partially open doorway. She could hear movement now, creaking down the hall, growing rapidly closer. David was coming. Slowly but surely, he was checking out each small, bare room.

Not much time, not much time. Come on fingers, work!

She had her arms up, her elbows bent. Sensation was returning to her swollen fingers, and though they felt clumsy and sluggish, she finally had some movement. She'd gotten the blinds up. Now she fiddled with the metal half-moon window clasps until she finally got them turned.

Finally, the tricky part. Her arms were all wrong. Her shoulders still felt strange and disjointed. She didn't think she could push anything up, let alone an old window stuck in its casing. But there was only one way out of this house at the moment. Only one way to circumvent David.

I am not a victim. I am not a victim.

Meg was weeping. Her breath was labored, her whole body hurt. She thought of how much she loved her parents. She thought of how much she loved Molly. And then she shoved her arms beneath the window, sank her teeth into her bottom lip and pushed with all her might.

The window squeaked, her arms screamed, and then . . . The window rocketed up. She stuck her head out into the crisp night air. And found herself looking straight down at none other than Jillian.

David heard the squeak of a window opening. Meg! She was trying to bail on him. He took two quick steps down the hall, leading with his gun, then he heard another sound, also up ahead, but this time to the right. He halted immediately, straining his ears.

Griffin, he deduced, trying to sneak up the stairs. Goddammit, why couldn't he have just died in the foyer? David was running out of time for these little games. Dammit, he'd had a *plan!*

He frowned, caught the expression and forced his brow to smooth back out. Think. What could Meg really do from a second-story window? Fall? Break her back? All the easier to kill her later. Griffin posed the more immediate threat. He would deal with Griffin first.

David moved to the right side of the hallway. He pressed his back against the wall and brought his gun up to his chest in a two-handed grip. Griffin would be coming up the stairs low, trying to be less of a target. He might also be wearing a flak vest. So David would also go in low and aim for the head.

He bent his knees, sinking down to the hall floor. He felt fluid, smooth as silk, even after picking the locks of his shackles, divesting himself of his chains, and taking out a fully armed escort. In some ways, prison had been the best thing that had ever happened to him. He'd entered the ACI a physically weak man with a gift for charm. He'd emerged with a finely honed, absurdly flexible physique and a whole new understanding of human nature. Old David had preyed on kids. New David would prey on the entire world.

But first, he would kill Sergeant Griffin.

David eased steadily into the shadows.

"You can't jump," Jillian was saying, low and frantic from the yard.

Meg shook her head desperately and leaned out the window.

"Dammit, Meg, it's too high – "

Meg couldn't speak through the gag, just show her bound, bloody wrists.

"Oh, Meg . . ."

Meg took a deep breath, then threw one leg over the windowsill.

"Wait, wait, wait!" Jillian cried. "Quick, I have an idea!"

Flat on his belly, Griffin slithered his way slowly up the hardwood stairs. He held his gun just in front of his face as he peered warily into the dark void waiting at the top. He grew closer and closer, knowing that at any time Price could strike.

Five steps from the top.

Groans down the hall. Squeaky floorboards, the sound of glass vibrating. He couldn't think about those things yet. He had to keep his attention on the top of the stairs.

Four steps from the top. Three, two . . .

And then.

Suddenly, quickly, David Price's face materialized in the gloom. A burst of fire. BOOM, BOOM, BOOM.

Griffin squeezed the trigger even before he felt the first bullet graze his forehead. He rolled sideways, hitting the unforgiving wall as he fired desperately, trying to hit a man he could no longer see. Rings of light exploded in front of his eyes, the muzzle flash temporarily breaking into his dark, dusky world and blinding him.

Blood. Pain. His head.

Griffin kept firing. Then he came up the stairs with an enraged roar.

David ran across the hall. He heard Griffin still firing. Good, good, good, blow your fucking wad, shoot up the staircase. David didn't have many shots left; he certainly wasn't going to waste them.

He darted into the bedroom, already looking for Meg.

A cool breeze immediately hit his cheeks, accompanied by a relatively brighter flash of fading daylight. He forced his gaze to readjust and realized that the blinds were up and the bedroom window was open. In the next moment, he heard a thump out in the yard.

David rushed to the open window. He stuck out his head in time to see a woman's shadowy figure scramble to her feet and run across the lawn.

No, no, no. It wasn't possible. Meg should be hurt. She couldn't just get away like that. She was his, his, HIS.

David raised his gun to fire. Just as a second shape suddenly materialized from behind the closet door.

"I hate you, I hate you, I hate you!"

David whirled around. "Meg? What the – "

She caught him in the side with her shoulder and they

both went smack against the wall as Griffin roared into the room.

David was tangled. He had to get to his feet, find his balance and regain control. He got one hand around Meg's neck and shoved her brutally aside. Just in time to encounter Griffin's fist.

David's left cheek exploded. He went down hard, registered the new threat in the room and rolled left. He came back up with his gun, squeezing off one wild shot before Griffin had his hand in his massive grip and started twisting his arm behind his back.

David cried out at the sudden pain. Then he grew royally pissed off. This was not according to his plan! This had not been part of his equation!

He went still, sagging forward and letting the sudden impact of his weight drag Griffin off-balance. They both fell forward. David rolled clear first and sprang up onto his feet. This time he had out the hunting knife. That was better.

He went for Griffin's ribs, just as his old friend and neighbor threw up his arm. David sliced through Griffin's shirt and had the satisfaction of drawing first blood. He danced back, watching Griffin rise thunderously to his feet. Griffin didn't appear to have a gun anymore. He had probably run out of bullets on the staircase, then thrown down his gun in disgust. Griffin always acted on impulse. All the better for David.

"I've learned a few things since we last met," David said, bouncing around on the balls of his feet, flashing his knife. He'd lost track of Meg. He decided it didn't matter. What could a girl do?

"Needlepoint?" Griffin drawled.

"I'm not going back, no fucking way. I'm going to kill you, then I'm going to take out every goddamn cop along the way. I've already racked up at least six today. What's a few more?"

"I think you should take the car in the driveway," Griffin

said, circling warily. "You know, Viggio went to a lot of trouble to set it up just for you."

"Shit! He rigged it, didn't he? Well, that just curdles my cheese. I'm the one who told him where to go on-line for the bomb-making guide, you know. Without me, that low-level turd would be *nothing*."

David leapt forward, slashing at Griffin's unprotected thigh. Griffin, however, saw him coming, stepped neatly left and slammed him with a fresh uppercut to his left eye. David's head snapped back. He saw stars but didn't go down. Instead he spun away and worked to regroup. Griffin was bigger, all right. But David was smarter, and better armed.

Griffin didn't lunge again but just kept circling. He appeared strangely calm, almost curiously patient.

"Without you, Viggio could've been the College Hill Rapist forever," Griffin said. "No one could ever rat him out – like you were planning on doing."

"I wasn't necessarily going to turn him in. What do I care if he's running around this state terrifying college coeds? I sort of considered him a going-away present for you, Griff. Your job would never be boring. Now I'll just have to kill you instead."

"So you keep saying."

"What the fuck are you doing, Griffin? Where's the rage, where's the holy war? Don't you remember what I did to Cindy? Do I have to tell you again what her last moments were like?"

"Cindy died surrounded by the people who loved her. We should all be so lucky."

"I told her *every little detail*."

Griffin didn't say anything. David frowned. He didn't like this. Where the fuck was Griffin's rage? He needed his old friend's anger. He fed on Griffin's rage. Griffin's beautiful, dark, mind-fogging hate, which always lured the over-sized detective into doing something stupid.

"She tried to close her eyes, Griffin. I held her eyelids open with my fingers. It's not like she could fight me."

Griffin still didn't say anything. He appeared to be looking behind David at the doorway. David whirled around sharply, saw only the shadowed hall, then had to quickly twist again before Griffin jumped him from behind.

"What you looking at?" David demanded. He was getting the heebie-jeebies again, feeling his control of the situation slip away, though there was no logical reason why.

"I'm not looking at anything."

"There's no one left, Griffin. I shot your stupid friend, the skinny one, Waters. 'Fraid you can't break his nose anymore, Griffin. He interrupted me in the basement, so I killed him."

Griffin remained silent.

David waved his knife. "Do you hear me! You're all alone! I killed your friend, I tormented your wife. I murdered ten kids and *you didn't do a thing*. And now, my good friend, I'm *out of jail*. Yep, you helped me with that, too. Welcome, Great Sergeant Griffin. Welcome, the aspiring criminal's best friend."

"Where's Meg?"

"What?" David drew up short again. Something was wrong. None of this was going according to the usual script. He had sweat on his forehead. And he felt . . . he felt strangely tired. All this effort. He was putting on a good show. What the fuck was up with his audience?

"Where is Meg?" Griffin asked again, circling, circling, circling.

"Meg's irrelevant."

"You think?" Circling, circling, circling.

"What do you mean?"

"Well, you haven't exactly gotten away yet, David. Think about it. You went to a lot of trouble to get out of prison, only to become trapped in your former home. That's a lot of running, I would agree, but not much progress."

"Shut up."

Griffin shrugged. "If you say so."

"What the fuck is wrong with you!" David screamed. "Goddammit, *yell at me!*"

Griffin didn't say a word. Just circled, circled, circled.

And David . . . And David . . . Something went. In his head. Behind his eye. He felt a little pop, as if all of his homicidal fury had just exploded like a neutron bomb. And then his arm was above his head. And then he was running, because he had to kill Griffin. He had to kill this man with his calm face and steady voice and knowing, knowing eyes. Goddammit, after all of this planning, he deserved a better audience.

David screamed at the top of his lungs. He charged forward . . .

And Griffin pulled his gun out of the small of his back and shot him point-blank in the chest. Pop, pop, pop. David Price went down. He didn't get back up again.

Thirty seconds later, Fitz stepped into the room from where he'd been sheltering Meg in the hall. He approached David's body while Meg peered in cautiously from the doorway. The detective leaned down, discovered no pulse, and looked back up at Griffin.

"That was expertly played," Fitz said grimly.

And Griffin said, "I learned from a master."

He came out of the house, Meg and Fitz in his wake. Ambulances had arrived, their lights blazing, their sirens piercing. Funny how he had never heard their approach. In the bedroom, his world had been small, just comprised of David and the lessons of his past. Now it was lights, camera, action.

Jillian came around the house, fresh from her cameo as a fleeing Meg Pesaturo. Her cheeks were flushed, her hair was a long, tangled mess, her clothes were stained with blood. He thought she had never looked better. She glanced at him once, her chin up, her gaze curiously open and proud. Then Meg was flying into her arms and she was holding the girl close, stroking her hair.

Griffin went to the ambulance where they were loading up Waters on a stretcher. An oxygen mask was over Waters's face, but his gaze was alert, focused.

"How is he?" Griffin asked.

"Gotta get to the hospital," the EMT said.

"He gets the best."

"Men in blue always do."

"Mike . . ."

Waters tried a halfhearted thumbs-up. Then the stretcher was in the back, the doors were closing and the ambulance was pulling away.

More cruisers came screeching down the street. More lights, camera, action.

Griffin stood in the middle of the chaos of his old neighborhood, his old life. He looked at Meg. He looked at Jillian. He looked up at the bedroom where a dead David Price now lay.

And he whispered, "Cindy, I love you."

The night wind blew down the street and carried his words away.

In the intensive care waiting room, Dan sat with his elbows on his thighs and his fingers digging into his hair. Thirty minutes had passed. It might as well have been a year.

A door opened and closed. Dan finally looked up to see a white-jacketed doctor standing before him. He tried to read the man's face, tried to steel his body before he heard the words.

"Your wife would like to see you."

"What?"

"Your wife . . . She suffered an episode. But the good news is, she's now regained consciousness."

"What?"

"Would you like to see your wife, Mr. Rosen?"

"Oh, yes. I mean, *please.*"

Dan went down the hall. Dan went into the room. And there was Carol, pale but conscious, lying on the bed. His feet suddenly stilled. He couldn't remember how to move.

"Honey?" he said.

"I heard your voice," she whispered.

"I thought I'd lost you."

"I heard your voice. You told me that you loved me."

"I do, Carol! Oh I do. There has never been anyone else. You have to believe me. I've made so many mistakes, but Carol, I have never stopped loving you."

"Dan?"

He finally got his feet to move. He took tiny, meek little steps toward the bed. She was awake now, capable of remembering all that he'd done, all of the ways that he had failed her. She was awake and he had not been a good husband, and . . .

Carol took his hand. "Dan," she told him quietly. "I love you, too."

EPILOGUE
Jillian, Carol and Meg

"What about this dresser? Coming or going?"

"Going."

"And the lamp?"

"Definitely going."

"I don't know, I kind of like it."

Carol rolled her eyes at Meg, then looked at Jillian for support. "I don't think French country quite goes with anything in a college dorm," Jillian told Meg. "Maybe it's the heavy gold fringe."

"Hey now, *anything* can coordinate with beanbag chairs and lava lamps. I believe it's called *eclectic*." But Meg dutifully tagged the lamp for Dan and Carol's upcoming furniture auction. She'd been cheerfully trying to scam items for two hours now. Fortunately, not many of Carol's heavy French antiques were small enough for Meg's soon-to-be new address – the Providence College dorms.

"Next room?" Jillian asked.

"Next room," Carol agreed.

"Are you sure?

"I'm sure."

All three of them exited the bedroom and journeyed down the hall. Passing the staircase, they could hear the voices of their families floating up the stairs. Dan and Tom were busy sorting through the toolshed, but Laurie, Toppi and Libby had staked out the kitchen. Last Jillian saw, they had Griffin retrieving all of the high objects from the cupboards. As fast as he got an item in one box, they'd want it placed in another. He kept wiggling his eyebrows at Molly, then doing as he was told. Molly thought the whole project was loads of fun, and even now they could hear her shrieks of laughter as Griffin performed his latest Herculean task.

Molly was doing extremely well these days, and had surprisingly few questions about her strange sojourn to the park six months ago. Meg, on the other hand, was looking paler, thinner. She had recovered physically from her abduction, as had Detective Waters. But with Meg's newfound memories had come nightmares, night sweats, panic attacks. She was holding up, pushing through. She had her life back, she'd told Jillian and Carol at their last Survivors Club meeting, and she was determined to get on with it. Just next month, she'd return to Providence College for her degree. Her father was still negotiating for the right to call her every night and provide armed guards, but that was to be expected. And in his own way, Tom was really sweet.

Jillian, Carol and Meg came to the closed door at the end of the hall. The last room to be tagged for auction. The room.

"Are you sure?" Jillian asked again. "Meg and I could do this."

"Dan offered as well," Carol said quietly.

"Maybe you should accept his offer."

"I thought about it. He'd like to help more."

Jillian and Meg didn't say anything.

Carol shook her head. "I'll tell you the same thing I told him. I *need* to do this. It's just a room, after all. Just a room in a house that's not even mine anymore. The new owners arrive next week. They'll fill this place with their things, their kids, their dreams. If they can handle this room, I can, too."

Jillian didn't think that was quite the same, but it wasn't for her to say. She opened the door to the musty, shadowed space, then gave Carol a moment to marshal her resources.

The master bedroom had been unused for over a year and a half. The air smelled stale, the corners were draped with long, intricate cobwebs. The hardwood floor held a fine coating of undisturbed dust. Old ghosts fit in comfortably in a space like this. Jillian could look at the dusty wrought-iron bed, and for the first time picture perfectly what Carol had gone through. A man coming through that window under cover of night. A man pouncing, hitting, gagging, tying. A woman screaming, and still not making a sound.

A woman victimized in a place where she had every right to feel safe.

Meg had unconsciously taken Jillian's hand. Then Carol walked right in, snapped on a light, and that easily the spell was broken. The room was just a room after all. One, as a matter of fact, in need of a good cleaning.

"Everything in here," Carol said briskly, "goes."

Twenty minutes later, they retired to the hallway. Carol sat on the floor with a sigh. Jillian and Meg followed suit, leaning their heads against the wall.

"Any regrets?" Jillian asked softly.

Carol opened her eyes. "Honestly? Not as many as I thought I would have."

"It's a beautiful home," Meg said. "You should be proud of what you did with it."

"I am. But you know, it is just a house. And for as much love and attention as went into renovating it, a lot of not so loving things happened here. It's good to get out. I can get a fresh start. The money will help Dan make a fresh start. And you know, our new home is nice, too. Just on a much smaller scale. But that back family room, I'm already thinking . . . Take out a wall, add a few more windows, and we'd have the perfect sunroom right off the kitchen. Put up some plants, polish the hardwood floors . . ."

She broke off. Jillian and Meg were smiling at her.

"You're hopeless," Jillian said.

"I like houses. All houses, I guess. Oh, hey. I'm a house slut!"

She beamed proudly and they laughed.

"Dan's taking to corporate life?" Jillian asked.

Carol shrugged. "As well as can be expected. Being on payroll again means less freedom, but it's also a lot less stress than running his own practice. Plus, let's be frank, we need the money."

"The auction will help," Meg said.

"Sure. Between downsizing the house, getting Dan a real job, getting me a part-time job, hey, we might actually be debt-free by the end of the year." She smiled, though it was chagrined. "Not exactly what we were expecting as we hit our mid-forties. No savings, no retirement funds. No white picket fence."

"Is he going to his Gambler's Anonymous meetings?"

"He goes to his meetings, I go to my shrink. Ah, yuppie love."

"You put the new house in your name?" Jillian checked.

"He insisted upon it himself. The car's in my name now, too, and get this, we have only one credit card, which is owned by me. Even if he does slip, there's not much damage he can do."

"He's trying very hard, Carol."

"Actually, I'm proud of him. Maybe life isn't what we were expecting. But maybe that's the way it's supposed to be. When we had everything we thought we wanted, we were miserable. Maybe by having nothing we'll finally learn to appreciate one another. Own less, but have more. I think . . . well" – her tone grew brisk again – "we have to start somewhere."

"You love him?" Meg asked.

"Absolutely."

"Then you're very lucky."

Carol smiled. She angled her head and looked directly at Meg. "Now, how about you, hon? You're still very pale."

"Too many nightmares," Meg said immediately, making a face. "You know what's strange? I keep dreaming about Eddie Como. He's the man lurking over me. I know that's not right. I know it was Ron Viggio, but somehow . . . We spent so long focused on Eddie, it's like my subconscious can't make the change."

"He's a symbol," Jillian said softly.

"Exactly."

Now they all made a face and looked away. Eddie was still a tough subject. They had spent too long hating him. Viggio seemed almost like an abstraction, whereas Eddie remained tangibly real. Poor Eddie Como, railroaded for crimes he didn't commit, framed by a psychopath and then sacrificed at a courthouse just to lure a certain state detective onto the case.

Tawnya had finally dropped her lawsuit. Because Eddie's semen was definitely found at the four rape scenes, her lawyer explained that he could no longer make the case for police negligence or corruption. Plus, the police had found the editing software that Ron Viggio had used to make the computer image file of Eddie threatening Jillian with violence, further evidence that Eddie had been deliberately framed by a madman. In the end, Eddie really hadn't done anything worse than be in the wrong place at the wrong time. Just like them, he had been a victim.

Two months ago, Jillian, Carol and Meg had gone together and put flowers on Eddie's grave. It was as much as they could do for now. After that visit, on her own, Jillian had written another check for Eddie, Jr.'s, college fund.

"At least there won't be a trial this time," Meg said now.

"Thank God," Carol echoed.

Jillian was more philosophical. "It would've been too hard for D'Amato to argue the case. Viggio's lawyer would simply keep saying Eddie, Eddie, Eddie, and the whole thing would've grown too confusing. A plea bargain was probably better all the way around."

"Cool, composed, Jillian," Carol said, but smiled.

Jillian's look was more somber. "He killed my sister, Carol. I would've liked to see him on trial. I would've liked to hear twelve jurors find him guilty. And maybe it would've helped us make a better transition, refocus our anger where it belongs."

"He's never getting out of jail," Meg spoke up.

"Yes, but if only he could've died like David Price."

No one argued that. As part of Viggio's plea bargain, he had to make a full allocation of his and Price's scheme. The details had been chilling. How Viggio had grown increasingly convinced that he needed to come up with the perfect way to commit rape. How he had approached David Price while they were both being held in ACI's Intake and worked with David to devise the perfect plan. Viggio had already heard about Korporate Klean from his last time behind bars. One of the big jokes among inmates was that when you finally get out, the only job you could get would be cleaning up after a bunch of "jerk offs" – everyone knew Korporate Klean had the contract for the sperm bank.

From there, things fell into place. Viggio spotted Eddie in the waiting room and realized they were a close physical match. He struck up a conversation with the guy, found out he worked for the Rhode Island Blood Center and needed some extra money because his girlfriend was pregnant. He started shadowing Eddie at the college blood drives and realized this was the perfect opportunity. He could attack socially conscious college coeds, and it would simply further implicate Eddie in the eyes of the police. He'd written the details to David Price, who had recommended using latex ties. That would make the frame airtight. David had also kindly suggested Meg as the first victim. A suitable "trial run," he'd called her.

Even if Viggio did screw up, they figured Meg wouldn't go to the police. She wouldn't want to have to admit her association with David Price, whose name Viggio made sure to mention during the rape. That the trauma of the attack induced amnesia wasn't part of the plan, but hardly hurt them.

Viggio scoped out the other victims in advance. Carol was a last-minute substitute but felt safe to him: he'd spent enough time in her neighborhood to figure out her husband's car was never in the driveway. Trish met his criteria of a young coed living alone. Jillian's intrusion had startled him, but it had proved irrelevant to his plan.

By this point in the allocution, Viggio's voice was cocky. In theory, he'd suffered three complications – Meg's memory loss, Carol's substitution and Jillian's unexpected arrival, and none of them had stopped him. He was invincible. Then the women had gone on TV, and not even that mattered. The police did the sensible thing. They arrested Eddie Como, and phase two of the plan went into effect.

David's involvement hadn't been free, of course. He saw Eddie's frame-up as the perfect opportunity to get out of prison. Viggio had instructions to hire an assassin, kill the assassin, then immediately strike again, leaving Eddie's sperm at the scene. The new rape would stir the public into a panicked frenzy. And David could step to the plate with his offer to save the day. A hop, skip and jump later, and David would finally be out of prison.

Viggio, of course, had had his reservations. But once he figured out he could kill David Price the same way he'd killed the hired gun, he hadn't minded anymore. He'd followed David's instructions and inserted the wooden lock pick and Alka-Seltzer tablets into David's favorite pair of clothes, which were then dutifully retrieved by David's lawyer from David's storage area. Then Viggio had kidnapped Meg to increase police pressure to release David. Finally he'd secured a getaway vehicle, to be left at David's former home.

Of course, what David didn't know was that Viggio had taken the liberty of booby-trapping the getaway car with a bomb. For Viggio, David getting out of prison equaled David winding up dead, which equaled Viggio attacking, torturing and killing young women forever. It was the perfect plan.

Until the police pulled up in his driveway, and Detective Waters tackled him in a neighbor's salvage yard. Viggio wasn't going anyplace anymore.

And the three women . . . The three women were doing their best to heal.

Now Meg turned to Jillian. "Your turn," she said. "Carol is getting a fresh start with Dan, I'm getting a fresh look at my sordid past. Now what's new with you?"

"Not much."

Carol and Meg exchanged looks.

"I would never call Sergeant Griffin 'not much,' " Carol drawled.

Jillian promptly blushed.

"Uh huh," Carol said. "So that's the way it is."

"You have a dirty mind!"

"Damn right. Come on, Dan and I are seeing a sex therapist who has literally banned us from having sex for the next six months. I have to live through someone."

Both Jillian and Meg looked at her curiously. "Does that work?" Meg asked.

Carol's turn to blush. "Actually . . . well, yes. It . . . it takes the pressure off. Sometimes, before, when he would touch me, I would freeze up. I was already thinking, then he's going to want to touch here or touch there and I just couldn't handle that level of intrusion. I wasn't ready. Now – now I know a kiss will be just a kiss. I can focus on that. On him kissing me. And when I do that, all the other things go away. I'm not in the bedroom anymore. It's not dark, the TV's not on. I'm just a woman kissing her husband of over ten years. It's . . . nice. Honestly, we're dating again."

"I'm going to cry," Meg said thickly, and rubbed her eyes. "You're getting to fall in love all over again, and I can't even figure out if I'm ever going to have a normal relationship. Look at me! I'm almost twenty-one, my sister is really my daughter, and the total sum of my sex life boils down to one pedophile whom I thought I loved, and one rapist who was a present from the pedophile. Now that's *sick!*"

"Molly is your sister," Jillian said evenly. "You've said yourself it's better to keep it that way."

"If I'm her mother, then she must have a father. I don't want her to *ever* ask about her father."

"Then remove that from the equation. Molly is your little sister, you love her, your parents love her and she is very happy."

"Molly is very happy."

"The rest . . . Meg, you were only thirteen when David first approached you. That's much too young to know better. And you certainly can't blame yourself for being

435

raped. So that means you've made only one mistake, as a thirteen-year-old girl. You're nearly twenty-one now. You're strong, you're resilient, you're smart. You're going to be all right."

Meg sniffled a little. "What if I meet the right guy, freeze up, and he goes away?"

"Then he's not the right guy," Carol said firmly.

But Meg was looking at Jillian. "I wasn't raped," Jillian told her.

"You were assaulted."

"I . . . I have moments."

"You think about your sister," Meg said quietly.

"I do."

"Poor guilt-ridden Jillian."

She didn't deny it. "Griffin told me something earlier, during his investigation. And it was one of the hardest, saddest, truest things I ever needed to hear: Trisha loves me."

"She does," Carol said immediately.

"She does," Meg seconded.

Jillian smiled at them. "I lost sight of that. I don't know why. But I'm remembering now. I'm . . . enjoying . . . my memories of Trish, and that feels good. And Griffin understands that Trish is a part of me, just as I understand that Cindy is a part of him. Sometimes we just talk about them. It feels right."

"He's a lucky man," Carol said seriously.

"I'm a lucky woman. Well, and Libby isn't doing so badly either. Have you seen how much she flirts with him? I swear, she hasn't taken this much care with her appearance since she discovered the UPS man was single."

"Ooh, competition!" Meg teased.

"He definitely has a soft spot for her. Next thing you know, she's going to add the word *stud* to her picture book."

Carol and Meg chortled. Jillian rolled her eyes, but she was smiling, too. She felt lucky these days. Sometimes she found herself humming at work for no good reason. Clients seemed less annoying, the days were brighter, the evenings more beautiful. When the weather was nice, she had picnic lunches with Libby and Toppi in the park. And sometimes she left work early, sometimes she came in late, and one day she brought in four giant pots of yellow mums simply because she'd seen them at the florist and thought they were beautiful. Her employees looked at her curiously a lot, but no one complained.

"Speaking of family," Jillian said.

"We should return to the fold," Carol agreed.

"Think they're done with the kitchen?" Meg asked. "We could pick up some pizzas."

Food would be good, they all agreed. They climbed up from the floor and headed downstairs. In the kitchen, Jillian spotted Griffin first. He had Molly perched on his shoulders, running a duster along the top of the kitchen cabinets.

"I'm a dust bunny!" she cried.

"Well look at you," said Meg and held out her arms for her little sister.

Griffin swooped the giggling girl down onto the ground. He was wearing jeans and a T-shirt today, with dust on his left cheek and cobwebs in his hair. Griffin looked good in jeans and a T-shirt. Libby had actually blushed when he'd pulled into their driveway and assisted her into the van.

Right now, his twinkling blue eyes were on Jillian. She felt his gaze as a warmth in her chest. Tonight, they were having Mike Waters over for dinner. Toppi had taken quite a bit of interest in the lanky detective's recovery. She'd bought a new outfit for tonight. You never knew.

Now Griffin opened his arms and wagged a brow in a look that could only be called a leer. She, of course, pretended to look coolly away. In response, he thundered across the kitchen and playfully swept her into his embrace.

Molly shrieked, Meg and Carol smiled. Libby pretended to chastise.

Jillian simply slipped her arms around Griffin's narrow waist. She leaned into the warmth of his broad chest, felt the strength of his arms around her shoulders. He didn't step back.

"Pizza!" Molly yelled, and they all prepared for dinner.